M
Dorsey

Dorsey, Tim.

Gator a-go-go.

TIM DORSEY

Gator A-GO-GO

WM
WILLIAM MORROW
An Imprint of HarperCollinsPublishers

GATOR A-GO-GO. Copyright © 2010 by Tim Dorsey. All rights reserved. Printed in the United States of America. No part of this book may be used or reproduced in any manner whatsoever without written permission except in the case of brief quotations embodied in critical articles and reviews. For information address HarperCollins Publishers, 10 East 53rd Street, New York, NY 10022.

HarperCollins books may be purchased for educational, business, or sales promotional use. For information please write: Special Markets Department, HarperCollins Publishers, 10 East 53rd Street, New York, NY 10022.

Library of Congress Cataloging-in-Publication Data
Dorsey, Tim.
    Gator a-go-go / Tim Dorsey. — 1st ed.
        p. cm.
    ISBN 978-0-06-143271-2
    1. Storms, Serge (Fictitious character)—Fiction. 2. Florida—Fiction.
I. Title.
PS3554.O719G37   2009
813'.54—dc22   2009016053

10 11 12 13 14 OV/RRD 10 9 8 7 6 5 4

For Kelly

Life is short. It's also pretty wide.
—**SPANISH PROVERB**

Gator
A-GO-GO

PROLOGUE

*T*hey threw the midget over the balcony, and I was off on the spring break vacation of a lifetime . . .

"Serge, hit pause. I don't want to miss anything."

"What's taking so long?"

"I'm getting dinner."

"Coleman, you've already seen my documentary five times."

"No, I haven't. Just hit pause."

Sigh.

PAUSE

Coleman waddled into the living room cradling a plastic bowl the size of a small satellite dish. Five beer cans in their plastic rings dangled from a special tactical hook on his belt.

"What's that?" asked Serge.

Coleman plopped next to him on the couch. "Dinner."

"A half gallon of beer and two pounds of barbecue Fritos?"

Coleman pointed at the frozen TV screen. "Hey, I've seen this already."

"Told you."

Coleman crammed his mouth and licked his fingers for valuable Frito-Lay Incorporated dust. "I don't want to watch it again."

"I do."

Crunch, crunch. "Can't we watch something else?"

"What about the bonus material?"

"Your documentary has bonus material?"

"Bonus material is the key to life."

"Hit it." *Crunch, crunch.*

Serge pressed buttons on the remote, navigating on-screen options.

MAIN MENU

BONUS MATERIAL

THEATRICAL TRAILER

[Guitar riff: Alice Cooper, "School's Out"]

Serge's voice from the TV:

"It's a documentary epic you won't want to miss, featuring a cast of thousands, including many you've come to know and love. Coleman . . ."

"How long have I been out?"

"Johnny Vegas . . ."

"Baby, it's just a little head wound."

"City and Country . . ."

"Ditch us again and we'll cut your nuts off."

"The G-Unit . . ."

"Hey, stud-muffin."

"The performers and crew of *Girls Gone Haywire* . . ."

"More nipple!"

"Plus some of Florida's trademark jerks . . ."

"Please don't kill us!"

"The state's finest law enforcement officers . . ."

"Two mutilated bodies, Home Depot supplies, and a bunch of old View-Masters. Not again . . ."

"Students from the nation's most elite universities . . ."

"I'm going to throw up again."

"More jerks . . ."

"Dear God, don't kill us!"

"It's spring break madness at its maddest!"

"I hate you."

"Filled with mystery! . . ."

"*What's going on?*"

"Suspense! . . ."

"*I still don't know what's going on.*"

"Romance! . . ."

"*You're crazy if you think you're putting that thing in me . . .*"

"Special effects! . . ."

"*I am so stoned.*"

"Vocabulary! . . ."

"*Doppelgänger.*"

"Souvenirs! . . ."

"*Help me unbolt this street sign.*"

"And a breathtaking assortment of exotic locations, including Fort Lauderdale . . ."

"*I'll call the police if you don't leave!*"

"Daytona Beach . . ."

"*Get the hell out of my store!*"

"Panama City . . ."

"*I'm calling the police!*"

"The footage is shocking! The implications yet to be gauged! And whenever shit's going down, Serge always knows the score! . . ."

"*Forty-two.*"

"They came to take over the Sunshine State, but they've just fucked with the wrong Florida buff! . . . Not yet rated."

The screen faded to black.

Coleman cracked a beer. "That looks freakin' cool! Let's watch it."

"Thought you didn't want to see it again."

"I don't remember any of that stuff." *Crunch, crunch.* "Probably thinking of another movie."

Serge's thumb pressed the remote.

BACK TO MAIN MENU
RESUME PLAY FROM PREVIOUS POINT

". . . It all started quietly enough in early March, when innocence still flowered, and nobody could have imagined the chain of events rushing toward them from just around the corner . . ."

"This is Jessica Pierce, reporting live from Panama City Beach, where spring break migration has reached full boil. Authorities anticipate the student population ballooning to three hundred thousand by nightfall, with no signs of slowing. Meanwhile, as you can see behind me, the main cruising strip is at its regular afternoon standstill as more and more youth arrive for the annual rites of passage . . ."

A convertible rolled behind her. *"Show us your tits!"*

"Well!" Jessica said with a nervous chuckle. "They seem to be having lots of fun, and we're thrilled to welcome their return to our fair city. Back to you, Katie . . ." A warm smile. "Are we off?"

The cameraman nodded.

Jessica tossed him her microphone and stormed away. "Assholes."

Sports cars and pickups inched along, kids hanging out windows, yelling, hoisting open containers. Stereos cranked. Bumper stickers and window pennants. Ohio State, Syracuse, Rutgers, West Virginia, Seton Hall, Villanova, Wisconsin Badgers. Sidewalks even more crowded than the streets, students rolling luggage and coolers. Bleached bellies, beach bar hand stamps, T-shirts and backpacks, Penn State, Boston College, Tennessee Vols, parading past tiki huts, moped rentals, MTV broadcast trucks, cut-rate liquor, tattoos for less, a row of pricey new hotels and La Vela, the largest nightclub in the contiguous United States.

Wedged between the upscale towers was an occasional old-growth budget motel, like the Alligator Arms. The Alligator described itself in brochures as "student friendly," which meant mildew. It was the first to sell out each year.

A rented Hertz crawled through traffic and turned into the Alligator's parking lot. Four men slammed car doors. Moved quickly toward the motel. Out of place in linen jackets. And age.

Sophomores in bikinis frolicked by. "Hey, pops!" Giggles.

Didn't even register. Stride increased.

On the fifth floor, two students galloped down the outside landing as fast as they could, pushing a luggage cart. Two others rode inside with crossed legs and heads tucked low. A spring break bobsled. The cart's front corner clipped a balcony rail and wiped out. The students uprighted it and switched positions.

Elevator doors opened. Four men stepped out, then stepped back as a brass cart zipped by. Brisk footsteps down the landing. Music pounded from each passing door. They reached number 543. More loud tunes. Vintage Doors.

Knock-knock.

"*. . . Woke up this morning, and I got myself a beer . . .*"

No answer.

Harder knocking.

"*. . . Said I woke up this morning . . .*" The stereo was turned down. "You guys hear something?"

A fist. *Bam, bam, bam.*

"Someone's knocking."

"So get it."

A shirtless young man in swim trunks opened the door. "Yeah, Grandad?" He chugged from a plastic souvenir mug. Background laughter.

"Are you Andy McKenna?"

"No, who are you?"

"Is Andy McKenna here?"

"There's no Andy. Get lost." He started closing the door.

An arm in a linen sleeve went up and braced it open. The student's upper body indicated he pumped his share of iron. Clearly an edge on the slim, older man in the eggshell-white jacket. The youth strained to close the door. A cement wall would have budged more. He realized he was dealing with something not of his experience.

"May we come in?"

The student answered by walking backward.

Four men entered. The door closed behind them.

The student bumped into the TV. "Who are you?"

"My friends call me Guillermo. You can, too."

"What do you want?"

"For your pal over there to put the phone down."

A receiver bounced on the floor. Hearts thumped. Students became statues. Guillermo's associates searched the one-bedroom suite and checked the balcony. "All clear."

"W-w-what's going on?"

"You need to relax more," said Guillermo. "You're on vacation."

"I'm really sorry about the 'Grandad.'"

"Already forgotten about it. Now just stay right where you are, and we'll be leaving soon."

"I swear there's no Andy here—"

"Shhhhh." Guillermo circled the room to his left, so a wall was behind the students instead of the balcony. He counted five. "Is this everyone staying in the room?"

"Yeah."

"Raul, turn up the stereo."

"... *Got myself a beer!* ..."

Guillermo snapped his fingers in rhythm. "Good beat. You like this song?"

"I ... guess so. But what's—"

A silencer-equipped pistol flew out from Guillermo's jacket with such facility that the first student didn't have time to be surprised. *Pfft-pfft-pfft.* Tight forehead pattern. The shooting arm swung without intermission. *Pfft-pfft. Pfft-pfft* ...

A freshman dropped where he stood. Targets moving now, Guillermo in a calm pirouette. *Pfft, pfft, pfft. Pfft-pfft* ...

A crash through the coffee table.

Pfft-pfft-pfft ...

Backward over a couch.

The last student reached the door and grabbed the handle. *Pfft-pfft-pfft.* He slithered down the blood-streaked wood with a rising number of exploding back wounds as Guillermo made certain.

Pfft, pfft, pfft, pfft, click, click, click.

Empty.

Guillermo high-stepped over bodies, ejecting an ammo clip and turning off the stereo.

Quiet. Just a light haze with that burnt gunpowder smell.

A toilet flushed.

Guillermo's head snapped toward the sound. "Who didn't check the bathroom?"

Three linen jackets shrugged.

The door opened. "What the hell was all that noise?" An unusually short person came out wearing a motorcycle helmet. He saw the room and froze—"Holy shit!"—backing up, slowly at first, before turning in full sprint toward the balcony. He reached the railing and looked down at the distant patio. Cornered.

Four men arrived at a casual pace. Each grabbed a diminutive limb.

"Please! No!"

They began swinging the tiny captive back and forth to build momentum.

"On three," said Guillermo.

"One."

"I'm begging you!"

"Two."

"But I'm just the midget!"

"Three . . ."

Part One

PANAMA CITY BEACH

CHAPTER ONE

FIFTEEN YEARS AGO

Small children shrieked and chased one another around a swing set. One with an autograph-covered plaster cast on his left arm hung upside down from the monkey bars as he had been told so many times not to.

Boynton Beach, closer to West Palm than Miami.

A cork ball rattled inside a referee's whistle. An adult waved.

Children hopped off playground equipment and, after a period of mild disorganization, formed a single line behind the jungle gym. They followed their teacher back inside a cheerful classroom at Kinder Kollege.

Nap time.

Foam mats unrolled beneath walls of finger paintings with gold and silver stars.

Tires squealed. The teacher went to the window.

Five sedans and a windowless van skidded to the curb outside the chain-link fence. No fewer than twenty people jumped out, dressed in black and white. Dark sunglasses. Running.

As the team raced for the school's entrance, it shed members at intervals, creating a grid of sentries across the lawn. The teacher was straining for a sideways view from the window when the classroom's door flew open. Five strangers moved quickly. The teacher moved just as fast, blocking their path. They met in front of the alphabet.

"You can't come in here!"

The first agent flashed a badge with his right hand and looked at a photograph in his other. "Which one's Billy Sheets?"

A tiny boy sat up in the back of the room. The agent checked his hand again. He hopped over tot-filled mats and seized the boy under the arms.

The teacher ran after him. "I demand to know what's going on!"

From behind: "It's okay, Jennifer."

She turned to see the principal in the doorway with a look of grave concern, but also a nod to let the visitors proceed.

Moments later, the teacher, principal and all the children were at the windows. Car doors slammed shut in a drum roll. Vehicles sped off, Billy in the middle sedan, growing smaller, staring back at classmates with his hands against the rear glass.

And a look on his face: This is new.

PRESENT DAY, EARLY MARCH

Southwest Florida.

A white '73 Dodge Challenger sped south over the Caloosahatchee River.

It came off the Edison Bridge into Fort Myers.

The driver's head was out the window.

"Can you smell it?" said Serge, hair flapping in the wind.

"Smell what?" asked Coleman.

"You know what time of year this is?"

"Fall?"

"Spring!"

"I always get those confused."

Serge's head came back inside. "I love everything about spring! Reeks of hope, new lease on another year, blooming possibilities, lush beds of violet wildflowers along the interstate, nature's annual migration: whooping cranes, manatees, Canadians."

Coleman cracked a beer. "I'm into spring, too."

"Who would have guessed?"

"Definitely! *High Times* named West Florida the 'shroom capital of the country. Each spring they sprout like crazy in cow poo."

"I still don't comprehend the allure," said Serge. "You boil them into a tea, drink a giant tumbler, then turn green with cramps before running into the bathroom and sticking your finger down your throat."

"Because you can't let that poison build up in your body. I thought you were smart."

"I'm overrated." They continued west on MLK. "So what's the point of these toadstool ceremonies?"

"To party!"

"But isn't all that throwing up unpleasant?"

"Some things are worth vomiting for."

"I think I've seen that crocheted on a pillow."

Early-afternoon clouds parted. Patches of sunshine swept up the street.

"Excellent," said Serge. "Afraid the game was going to get rained out."

"Game?"

"Spring training is the best!"

Coleman looked at the running camcorder in the middle of the dashboard. "Your documentary?"

"Haven't found the hook yet. Because the hook is key. Otherwise it'll incorrectly look like I'm filming aimlessly."

A distant siren from behind.

"Shit!" Coleman stuffed a joint in his mouth. "The Man!"

Woo-woo-woo-woo-woo! . . .

Serge checked the rearview. "Just a fire engine." He hit his blinker and eased to the side of the road.

Traffic blew by.

Serge's face reddened, cursing under his breath.

"What's the matter?"

"Look at all these jackasses not pulling over for an emergency vehicle," said Serge. "When the fuck did this deterioration start?"

Coleman twisted around in his seat. "We're the only car stopped."

"Another sign our civilization will soon be covered with dust."

Coleman popped another beer. "What's wrong with people?"

More cars sailed by as the siren grew louder.

"These are the first responders," said Serge. "Our state's finest, putting their lives on the line for the rest of us every single day, and what thanks do they get? A highway of dickheads who don't want to miss the next traffic light."

"It just isn't correct."

"Not stopping for these heroes represents an inexcusable affront to the entire community. You might as well walk down the street throwing handfuls of shit at everyone you see."

"That really happened," said Coleman. "I saw this TV thing about a guy in Miami—"

"Get a grip," Serge told himself. "A heart attack will solve nothing."

"Wait," said Coleman, looking out the back window. "Another car's stopping. He's pulling up behind us."

"Thank God I'm not alone," said Serge. "Maybe all isn't lost."

Honk-honk! . . . Honnnnnkkkkkkk!

"Serge, why is he honking at you?"

"Because he didn't stop for the fire engine. He just got boxed in behind me from all the other rule-breakers flying by in the next lane."

Honnnnnkkkkkk! Honnnnnkkkkk!

Serge reached under the seat for his .45 automatic. "No, it'll only increase work for first responders." He slid it back under.

Honnnnnnnnnkkkkkk!

Coleman stuck both arms out the passenger window, shooting double birds. "Eat my asshole!"

He came back inside and smiled.

Serge looked across the front seat. "That was Gandhi, right?"

The honking was now nonstop, just leaning on the horn, thanks to Coleman.

Serge closed his eyes and took slow, deep breaths. ". . . two . . . three . . . four . . ."

"Here comes the fire engine," said Coleman. The siren whizzed by, dropping in Doppler pitch. "And there it goes."

Serge opened his eyes and took his foot off the brake. "Finally. Our lives can diverge, and he's free to go his own separate way toward an anti-future."

"He's not going his separate way," said Coleman, kneeling backward in his seat. "Still right behind us."

"Because he hasn't found a gap yet in the next lane to pull around."

"Then why is he still honking?"

"Involuntary genetic reflex, like getting a mullet."

"He's still there."

"I'll speed up and open a gap."

"Still there."

"Then I'll slow down and force him to pass."

"Still there. Still honking."

Serge took another deep breath. "Okay, I'll turn down this next side street."

"I'm amazed," said Coleman.

"I know," said Serge. "As the saying goes, the difference between genius and stupidity is genius has its limits."

"Not him," said Coleman. "You."

"What about me?"

"I've never seen you go this far to avoid an idiot."

Serge hit his turn signal. "I've completely rededicated myself to a life of nonviolence."

"But you still have that gun."

"No need to *obsess*."

The Challenger swung around a corner.

"He's turning, too," said Coleman. "Still following."

Serge's head sagged in exasperation. "And I've got a full to-do list."

"He just threw something out the window."

"Litter," said Serge. "A beer can, no less."

The Challenger pulled to the side of the road behind an aluminum scrap yard. A low-riding Toyota parked behind. The driver got out. Barrel gut, stained tank top. He walked to the Challenger and banged hard on the driver's window.

Serge stared straight ahead. "Haven't we been here before?"

Coleman grinned and waved across Serge at the other driver. "I can't count that high."

Bam! Bam! Bam!—Right up to the Underwriters Laboratories shatter point. "Get the hell out of the car! I am so going to fuck you up!"

Serge rolled his window down a crack. "What seems to be the problem?"

"Did you tell me to eat your asshole?"

"Not me." Serge turned. "What about you, Coleman?"

"Might have mentioned it in passing. But I don't want him to actually do it, if that's what he's asking."

Serge returned to the window slit. "Apparently it was figurative. He'd rather you not eat his asshole. Are we done now?"

The Challenger was a beaut, Serge's dream car ever since *Vanishing Point* and *Death Proof*. Recently restored, new rings and valves. Snow-white paint job, tangerine racing detail. And now shivers up Serge's neck, as a car key scraped the length of the driver's side.

Serge grabbed the door handle with his left hand and reached under the seat with his right. "Coleman, I won't be long."

SOUTH OF MIAMI

Ringing on a triangle bell.

"Dinnertime!"

Four men, twenty-nine to thirty-five years old, filed in from the back porch where they'd been smoking. Chairs filled around the long cedar dinner table of Cuban-American cuisine in steaming bowls and casserole dishes. Beans, rice, mashed potatoes, yams, plantains. In the middle was a large paella, a slab of roast beef and a ceramic pitcher of milk.

The woman said grace. They made the sign of the cross. Serving bowls passed clockwise.

It was a three-bedroom Spanish stucco ranch house with an orange tile roof and black burglar bars. One of those homes that seemed smaller inside because its owner was from the culture that respected too much contents. Sofas, quilts, pillows, family pictures, magazine racks, display cabinets of china. It used to be an upper-middle-class neighborhood, just off Old Dixie Highway between Palmetto Bay and Cutler. Now it was lower. The home stood out with its regularly maintained yard, because of the men at the table.

The woman stood in a red-and-white checkered apron, slicing meat with an electric carving knife. She offered a generous piece balanced on the tip. "Raul?"

He raised his plate. "Thanks, Madre."

She was slightly plump at sixty, hair always up in a tall, dark bun with streaks of gray. Her name was Juanita, but they all called her Madre. They weren't related.

The men ate with manners and strong appetites. Cuban loaves at one end, Wonderbread in its original sack at the other. Bottle of sangria. Idle conversation, weather, sports, relatives' diseases. Against the wall, eighty bank-wrapped packs of hundred-dollar bills on a dessert cart.

The woman rested back in her chair, sipping wine. She looked to her left. "Guillermo, will you be able to take care of our situation today?"

He washed down a bite with milk. "Yes, Madre. No problem."

"Good." She paused and nodded. "Very good."

Behind her on the kitchen counter, stacks of tightly bound kilo bricks and a yellow raincoat.

"What about civilians?" asked Miguel.

Juanita shrugged. "If that's what it takes to be certain." She stood and dug two large wooden spoons into the paella. "Pedro, you're getting too thin."

He placed a hand on his stomach. "Stuffed."

She turned with the spoons. "Miguel?"

He pushed his plate back. "Can't eat another bite."

The rest set napkins on the table.

Juanita reached into her apron and handed Guillermo a folded sheet of stationery. "Here's the list of names he gave me."

"Glad *he's* not working for us." Guillermo stuck the list in his pocket. "Didn't hold out very long."

"They never do," said Juanita.

Everyone turned toward the head chair at the opposite end of the table.

Juanita stood again. "Is he secure?"

"Won't be running off anywhere soon."

"Funny," said the woman. "Didn't touch his food."

A round of laughter.

Juanita walked along the back of the table. Her shoes made a crinkling sound on the plastic tarp under the last chair. She looked down at the tied-up man, a black hood over his quivering head.

Guillermo came over from the other side and yanked off the hood.

The man stared up at them with pleading eyes, gag in his mouth.

Juanita simply held out her arms. Two others at the table quickly got up, grabbed the yellow raincoat and slipped it on her. She smiled and patted their involuntary guest on the head, then turned her back.

When she faced him again, the man's eyes went to what was in her hands.

Juanita leaned forward, placed the electric carving knife to his neck and pressed the power switch.

CHAPTER TWO

hud, thud, thud.

Coleman turned around in his passenger seat. "We got another that likes to bang."

"Note to self," Serge said into a digital recorder. "Soundproof trunk."

The Challenger pulled into a strip mall.

"What are you doing?"

"My new business. Spring-training tickets and trunk insulation aren't free." Serge got out, popped the rear hood and motioned with a pistol. "Would you mind rolling a little to your left? You're on top of something I need . . . Thanks."

He closed the trunk.

Thud, thud, thud.

They started at the far end of the shopping center. Dry cleaners. Bells jingled. Serge approached the counter.

"Can I help you?"

"No, but I can help *you*!" said Serge. "Hate to cold-call like this, but spring training left me no choice."

"I'm sorry," said the clerk. "We don't allow solicitors."

"Then we're brothers in the struggle!" Serge held up his hand for a high five that never came. The clerk looked curiously at Coleman, swaying and drinking from a paper bag.

Serge slapped the counter. "Pay attention! Opportunity knocks! Sometimes it plays a tambourine or makes shadow puppets, but mostly it knocks. Are you ready? Bet you can't wait! Knock-knock! Hi, I'm

Opportunity!" Serge placed a pile of large, thick-stock white cards on the counter. He flipped up the top one, covered with Magic Marker handwriting.

No Soliciting.

The clerk scratched his head. "You're soliciting to sell 'No Soliciting' signs?"

"I know! Can't believe it hasn't been thought of before: The perfect mix of product and presentation. We came in here creating a problem *and* providing the solution. Just look at my friend here . . ." —Coleman burped and fell back against the door frame—". . . Do you need this kind of nonsense all day long?"

"I—"

Serge pounded the counter again. "Hell no! You have important stains to get out and can't waste time with every bozo who wanders in from the street with bottles of the latest stain-removal craze, but they're really just giving all their money to a doomsday cult with their fancy suicide machines and little or no interest in the laundry arts. I'm sure they've already been in here a thousand times."

"Not really—"

"Five dollars," said Serge. "I'll even throw in 'No Public Restrooms.' That's actually more critical. Ever seen a restroom after Coleman's done his fandango?" Serge whistled. "Not a pretty picture."

"I don't think—"

"There's a guy in our trunk," said Coleman.

"Maybe I need to amp the presentation." Serge leaned comfortably against the counter and stared at the ceiling. "I love dry cleaners. Could hang out for hours . . ."

Coleman raised his hand. "Can I use your bathroom?"

". . . Always wondered," said Serge, idly tapping his fingers. "What the fuck's Martinizing?"

"If you don't leave I'm calling the police."

Next stop, dentist office. Same story. Accounting firm, ice cream parlor, nope, nope.

Computer repair, walk-in clinic. "Howdy! Pay no attention to the man behind the beer . . ."

The owner of the dog-grooming service pointed at an already-posted No Soliciting sign.

"My point exactly," said Serge. "Did it stop *us*?"

"Out!"

They reached a drugstore. Serge pulled a handwritten list from his wallet and headed toward the back.

"Wait up," said Coleman. "Aren't you going to sell your signs?"

"Not yet. Have to pick up a few things. Let's see . . ." He began grabbing items off shelves. ". . . Nylon rope, pliers, razor blades, duct tape—naturally—nine-volt batteries, broom, saw . . ."

"One of your projects?"

Serge turned up the next aisle. "If this baby doesn't win me a grant . . . Kwik Dry superglue, wire cutters, tape measure, kite string . . ."

He finally arrived at the counter and tried to pay with some signs, but the cashier said they only took dollars and credit cards.

"But America was founded on a barter economy." Serge reached for his wallet. "That's the whole problem with stores. It's all about money."

Serge walked across the parking lot and opened the Challenger's trunk. A head popped up. He smacked it with a tire iron. "Not your turn."

Coleman peed on the side of the building. The front side. He straggled over. "We didn't sell any signs . . . What are you doing now?"

"The free market was built on artificial demand."

Serge rummaged through the trunk and removed a larger sign on a wooden stake. He hammered it into the ground next to the road.

They drove away. Downtown came into view.

"Fort Myers, City of Palms!" Serge raised a camera. *Click, click.* "And there's the new baseball stadium!"

"Serge, do we really have to watch a stupid baseball game?"

"It is not stupid."

"Nothing happens. Dudes stand in a field a long time, then every once in a while someone runs a little bit, then they stand around again."

"They serve beer."

"I love baseball."

A few miles back, passing motorists stared curiously at a sign in front of a strip mall.

Clean Public Restrooms (Solicitors Eat For Free).

"We're here!" said Serge, screeching into the parking lot. "Spring training home of the Red Sox!"

"Thought the Tampa Bay Rays were your favorite team."

"They are," said Serge. "Boston was my team before Florida had any, but now we do. And that's why we drove down here today. They're playing the Rays! Anyone who doesn't root for his home team deserves to be spat upon and have his head shaved like those French chicks who screwed Nazis during the Resistance."

"Are there Nazis at spring training?"

"Yes, but they keep a low profile in the bleachers and are now too old to goose-step and start their shit again." Serge grabbed a baseball glove from the glove compartment. "I'm getting a ton of foul balls!"

"How can you be so sure?"

"You haven't seen me in action."

19 DEGREES FAHRENHEIT

City plows had pushed the previous day's snowfall into dirty banks. People bundled in thick coats walked quickly along Lansdowne Street, heads ducked low in the icy wind. They were made even colder by a structure towering up the south side of the road that blocked the sun. At its top, thirty-seven feet above street level, sat a cantilevered balcony. More foot traffic came around the corner, scurrying past the back side of the Green Monster, the fabled left-field wall at Fenway Park, home of the Boston Red Sox.

One of the pedestrians blew into freezing hands as he reached Brookline Avenue and made a sharp right turn, climbing through the gray, wet crust. He grabbed a door handle and jumped inside. Rambunctious chatter and cheering. Waitresses rushed by with teetering trays.

Overhead TVs everywhere, all the same channel.

The man rubbed his arms and climbed onto one of the few vacant stools. A finger went up for the bartender. "Sam Adams."

The televisions showed a news correspondent in bright natural light, surrounded by palm trees and dozens of screaming, waving people with baseball caps and ghostly non-tans fighting their way into the camera frame.

"*This is Jill Montgomery down in sunny Fort Myers, Florida, where the temperature is a fabulous seventy-eight degrees, and the faithful of Red Sox Nation have begun their annual migration to the spring training home of their beloved team. Let's talk to one of them right now . . .*" She motioned for a bald man in a Josh Beckett jersey. "*Sir, where are you from?*"

"*Red Sox going all the way! Wooooooooo!*"

"*And where are you from?*"

"*Yankees suck!*"

Beer arrived. The man on the next stool looked out the windows at dreariness, then up at the TV. "I'm jealous."

"Tell me about it."

"Well, if you can't be there in person . . ."—he glanced around the pub's crowded interior—". . . Cask'n Flagon is the next best."

"Won't argue with that."

The man extended a hand. "Carl Lemanski."

They shook. "Patrick McKenna."

Eyes back to the TV. "Lucky sons of bitches."

"*. . . But a down note this morning as emergency personnel hospitalized an eighty-one-year-old fan from Quincy bludgeoned in a local economy motel. Under arrest are two unemployed construction workers who were on a weeklong crack binge in the next room . . . Now, back to the game!*"

"I'm a supervisor at the water department," said Carl.

"Day off?"

"No." He signaled for another beer. "So what are you into, Pat?"

"Hard to explain."

"Try me."

"Fancy title is 'commercial location specialist.'"

"Never heard of it. What do you do for that?"

"Count parking spaces."

"Spaces?"

"Or at least ones with cars in them."

"Seriously, what do you do?"

"Seriously."

"*. . . Varitek doubles to the right, bringing home Pedroia! . . .*"

"That's really a job?"

"Boring stuff."

"I'd like to hear."

"You would?"

In most circumstances, Patrick was economical about himself. But more beer came and the Sox took the lead.

"Niche specialty, skyrocketing demand."

"From who?"

"Chain stores and mall developers," said Patrick. "Always expanding into new markets. But pick the wrong location, it's an expensive mistake. And at least one person's job."

"That's where you come in?"

"Scout the competition. If a rival chain's already got a store in the target locale, we count customers' cars in the parking lot. Various hours, weekdays, weekends, Christmas rush. Then crunch raw numbers into usable data that determines whether the location can support a second store. Or a whole shopping center."

". . . *Youkilis takes strike two, looking not happy with the call . . .*"

"But doesn't that take a lot of time?"

"Back in the day, it took a *hell* of a lot of time," said Patrick. "We actually had to drive to the sites, stand on ladders and count manually with binoculars."

"Every car?"

Patrick shook his head. "Estimates with geometric sampling equations, but statistically reliable."

"I had no idea this was going on."

"It isn't anymore. Today, computers do it all."

"Computers count cars?"

"No, satellites."

"You just lost me."

"Like the proliferation of the Internet. In the beginning, when they first made orbital photography available to the private sector, resolution was too low. Plus you'd be lucky to find a picture a month of your site—not enough to extrapolate consumer behavior. But now . . ." He made an offhand gesture toward the pub's ceiling. ". . . So many whizzing around up there I'm amazed they don't crash into one another, and not just government ones anymore. If you buy from all the services—which we do—you can get several shots a day."

"Must cost a fortune."

"It does. But our customers pay even more because it's nothing compared to the price of an empty store," said Patrick. "And photo resolution's gotten so good we just started a new service: analyzing makes and years of cars so we can sell reports on shopper demographics, including income level."

"You can tell all that from a satellite photo?"

"Up to seventy percent accuracy, but we're shooting for ninety by year's end."

"Wow. Sounds really interesting."

"More so than actually doing it."

". . . Jim, there's some kind of disturbance in the right-field stands over a foul ball. Let's see that on slow-motion replay . . . Holy cow! . . ."

The water supervisor looked up at the TV. "Is that guy out of his fucking mind?"

"And here come the security guards," said Patrick.

". . . We'll take a short break in the seventh, Sox up five to three . . ."

The TVs switched to a local news update. ". . . Authorities are still seeking the public's help in the disappearance of an eighteen-year-old Boston freshman last seen Saturday night leaving her Cambridge dorm . . ."

Carl formed a disgusted look. "Been following this story?"

"Horrible."

"They act like there's hope, but frig it. She's already dead." He drained his mug. "What's happening to the country? It's a constant backbeat of abducted kids and college students . . ."

"Or wives who go missing," said Patrick, "and the husbands appear on camera like they're okay with it."

". . . Meanwhile, city officials are responding at this hour to a major water line break near the Charles . . ."

"Shit." Carl jumped up and grabbed his coat. "You didn't see me."

CHAPTER THREE

A ’73 Challenger sped away from City of Palms Park and made a hard left. Three baseballs rolled across the dashboard.

"What an excellent game!" said Serge.

Coleman unscrewed his flask. "What was the score?"

"Three."

"I thought scores had two numbers, one for each team."

"I don't keep track of teams, just foul balls. My best game yet! And that was only seven innings. Imagine if I was allowed to stay for the rest, let alone back end of the doubleheader."

"Those security guards were really mad."

"Because of envy."

"What about?"

"First, my foul ball collection. Second, I can outrun security. They *really* hate that. But it's their own fault, not willing to leap from heights."

"Maybe it was that last ball you got, diving over four rows into those people. It was raining popcorn."

"It's a *baseball* game. That's what separates the sport from all others and makes it my favorite!"

"How so?"

"The entire stadium's in play. Anyone who sits in the stands knows and assumes the risk: One second you're munching a hot dog and hearing the magnificent crack of a Louisville Slugger, the next you're hit with a frozen-rope line drive. Or me diving to catch it. Either way, you end up on a stretcher, covered in mustard. No better way to spend an afternoon."

The Challenger slowed and circled a budget motel in the heart of downtown, walking-distance from the stadium. Litter, vacancy, lengths of fallen-down roof gutters stacked behind overgrown shrubs, rusty fence surrounding a drained swimming pool with a busted TV at the bottom. An unhinged sign dangled sideways by the office, saying they spoke French.

"We staying here?" asked Coleman.

"No." Serge leaned over the steering wheel. "Another of my spring traditions."

"What's that?"

"Tourist protection. We've been getting a bad rap lately, because we deserve it. And I mean to fix that. Keep your eyes peeled for anyone wearing a Red Sox cap."

"Why?"

"Because fans come down here for spring training, see magnificent tropical surroundings and think they can stay in just any ol' budget motel. They don't realize that wearing those baseball caps at certain accommodations is like stumbling through Central American guerilla strongholds with 'Kidnap me' signs on their backs."

"But we stay at these kinds of motels."

"Right," said Serge. "We're part of the problem."

"I forgot about that."

Serge rounded the back of the motel. "Oh my God! Shit's on!"

BOSTON

The fifth-floor corner office had views of both the Hancock and the Prudential. Two computers running. Plus a small personal TV, which was against the rules.

Patrick McKenna had the biggest accounts. He decided to put in a couple hours on his day off, studying satellite photos from the Midwest. As the computer panned an image, his firm's proprietary optical-recognition software tabulated parking lot occupancy and entered data on a spreadsheet. Large numbers for a Wednesday afternoon. Patrick closed the image and opened another, this one

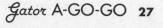

darker: Thursday, sunset. Numbers rang up again like a telethon tote board.

First impressions of Patrick McKenna were uniform: not impressed. Mainly it was his five-foot-six stature, but it was more. People told him he looked like Michael J. Fox with darker hair. Patrick had just turned forty-two, maintained his weight and was one of the few people at the company who placed his *R*s in the correct parts of words. He disliked neckties, loud personalities and nonessential conversation. In fact, Patrick would have kept to himself entirely, except he was driven to support his family. He consciously forced himself to look others in the eye. He was a loner disguised as a people person.

As Patrick moved his mouse over the next satellite image, he wasn't watching the computer. Because the Florida Marlins had the bases loaded on his personal TV.

A knock on the door.

Patrick hit the television's remote. The channel changed to the second game of a Red Sox doubleheader.

His boss came in. He looked at the small TV, then Patrick. "Watching the Sox on company time?"

Patrick grinned sheepishly.

"Got the game on in my office, too," said the supervisor. "One of these days I'm going to have to get to Fort Myers for spring training. Numbers?"

Patrick swiveled his chair toward the computer. "Solid. As long as they continue holding, but I'm sure they will."

"Good. They've been calling." The boss walked back to the doorway. "Think you'll finish by tomorrow?"

"Today."

"I'll let them know." The door closed.

Patrick tapped his keyboard through time: Friday morning, noon, evening, then three more Saturday images and four on Sunday. Sure enough, the numbers remained strong.

A spreadsheet filled. Patrick saved the file and attached it to an e-mail. He pressed the send button. "Western Indiana, hello, Big Mart!"

Then he opened another file. This time the computer superimposed a template with overhead images of vehicles, like World War II silhouette cards used to identify enemy and Allied aircraft. Except this program contained a database with more than ten thousand permutations of automotive make, model and year. Patrick had personally spearheaded the software's development. The corner office followed. His company was DPX Technologies Inc. The initials didn't stand for anything, but a consulting agency said *its* computer determined the letters were the combination that potential customers responded most favorably to, especially the X.

Aerial shapes on the computer flickered rapidly. With each positive match, a tiny car in the parking lot stopped flashing and turned red. Patrick watched the hits climb until they stopped at a record 81 percent recognition. "Yes!" He opened the next day's image . . .

The Red Sox reached the seventh-inning stretch; local news filled the gap: *"Authorities received a break this morning in the case of a missing Boston freshman and released this security video from inside a local department store, where she can be seen leaving at three P.M. with two shopping bags . . ."*

"Shoot!" said Patrick, remembering his neglected Marlins game. He grabbed the remote to change the channel. He stopped and turned up the volume instead.

". . . A second surveillance camera picks her up outside as she loads the bags in the trunk of her Hyundai Sonata, which was found by police with the key still in the driver's door. Unfortunately, the vehicle was at the edge of camera range, and the location of her abductor is just out of view. All we can see is the assailant's arm . . ."

Patrick sat intently through the rest of the report. When the Sox came back, he shuffled feet on the floor, wheeling his chair across the office to a second computer. He opened files from another client.

Ten minutes later, the door to a fifth-floor corner office opened. Patrick emerged into cubicle land. "We got a VCR machine around here?"

FORT MYERS

The Challenger sat clandestinely in the back of a budget motel parking lot.

"See that old guy with the cane and baseball cap?" asked Serge.

"Yeah," said Coleman. "He's talking to that dirtbag. So what?"

"This is how it always starts." Serge shook his head. "They exploit the open friendliness of our fine visitors, who don't realize Florida is still the Wild West."

"What if he's a nice dirtbag?" asked Coleman. "Most of my friends are."

"You're right," said Serge. "Dirtbags are people, too. We'll sit here and see what develops so I don't jump to conclusions and barge in waving a gun like at that bridal shower."

They sat.

Coleman turned an empty can upside down. "I'm out of beer."

"Not now." Serge leaned over the steering wheel. "Something's happening."

"What is it?"

"The old dude's inviting that dirtbag into his room. This is the takedown. Roll!"

Serge ran across the parking lot and pressed himself against a wall.

Coleman came up behind. "Anything happening yet?"

"Don't know." Serge crept forward and placed an ear to the door.

"What do you hear?"

"Too quiet," said Serge. "That's a bad sign. We're going in!"

Serge pulled a chrome .45 automatic from under his tropical shirt, took a step back and kicked the door open.

"Freeze, motherfucker. The nightmare is over. Serge is on the case!"

Two stunned men looked up from a small table, where they had been drinking soda and playing cards.

"I-I-I just got paid," said the dirtbag, removing his wallet with a shaking hand. "You can have it all!"

The old man in the Red Sox cap removed a wristwatch. "It's gold. Just don't hurt us!"

"Hurt you?" said Serge. "I'm here to *protect* you."

Speechless.

"What's the matter?" asked Serge. "You don't look so good."

He noticed their eyes on his gun.

"Oh, *that*." He tucked it back in his pants. "Sorry for the mis-understanding. Think I've got the wrong room. Was looking for the one where someone had a huge knife at his throat. Enjoy your card game."

Serge closed the door and headed back to the Challenger. "Shit!"

"What is it?" asked Coleman.

"Not sure, but I'm guessing I just made things worse image-wise." Serge climbed in the car and sagged. "If only there was some way I could make it up, so he'll forget all about the gun and go back to thinking Florida is fairyland."

Serge stared at the center of the steering wheel in concentration. An index finger suddenly rose. "Got it!" He grabbed a baseball off the dashboard. "I'll give him an authentic souvenir—this one was hit by David Ortiz, I think. Fuck it; I'll just say it was. He'll be so tickled to see me!"

"But I don't think—"

Serge was already out of the car, running across the lot. Without breaking stride, he kicked the door in again and thrust the treasure over his head. "Have I got a surprise for you!"

Silence.

The ball bounced on the terrazzo floor, rolling through scattered playing cards and spilled soda cans.

Serge whipped the gun from under his shirt. "Don't make any sudden moves. Now slowly, take the knife away from his throat."

CHAPTER FOUR

BOSTON

*P*atrick's face was practically against the computer screen when the knock came.

His boss walked in. "Usually when people want to see me, they come to *my* office."

Patrick waved him over without looking up. "Check this out."

"What am I supposed to be seeing?"

"Know the missing freshman?"

"Of course. Been all over the news."

Patrick spun his chair toward the TV.

"Where'd you get a VCR?"

"Barney had one." Patrick hit play. "They've been running the surveillance tape every half hour."

"I saw that thing. Chilling."

"They actually recorded her being grabbed."

"Can't imagine what her parents are going through. What's it got to do with us?"

Patrick switched the grainy, black-and-white footage to slo-mo. "Okay, this is it. She walks around to the driver's door and gets out her keys . . ."

"Patrick, is everything all right?"

". . . Keep watching. Here's where the passenger door on the next car opens, and the guy grabs her and pulls her out of view." He stopped the tape.

The boss waited a moment. "So?"

"Police caught a break. Or half of one. The edge of the surveillance camera's perspective is right next to her vehicle. The only thing we see of the abductor is his arm. If the camera had been turned just a few degrees to the left . . ."

"That's what everyone's talking about," said the boss. "Again, what's it got to do with us?"

Patrick spun back to the computer and pulled up an image. "Remember the Kitchen and Linen account?"

"Yeah, it's late."

"I knew the shopping center on TV looked familiar." He pushed his chair out to create room.

The boss leaned closer. "Don't tell me a satellite got the kidnapping."

"No. Odds would be astronomical." Patrick tapped a spot on the screen. "But right here. The satellite pass was an hour before the time stamp on that surveillance video."

"And?"

"Here's her Sonata. Our software confirmed it. The vehicle next to hers is an '05 Ford Ranger." Patrick zoomed the image back and pointed at the top of the screen. "Shopping center's right by this entrance ramp to the turnpike. That would be the logical getaway. Toll booth probably has a picture of the license plate."

"What are you, Columbo now?"

"I know it's a long shot. He could have left a different way. And the Ford might not even have anything to do with it. Maybe it was just in the same parking space and left before the kidnapper arrived." He picked up the phone. "Still, if I was her parents, I'd want the police to know."

FORT MYERS

Six A.M.

A '73 Dodge Challenger with a keyed driver's door took an underpass to the east side of I-75.

Bulldozers and mounds of burned trees lay on one side of the road; a golf course was already in business on the other.

No traffic at this hour. The Challenger rolled through woods with For Sale signs offering five hundred acres and up. Another bulldozed clearing. Then a dense thicket of identical houses and screened-in pools around a man-made pond. A fountain that sprayed during daylight was still.

Developer world.

Serge turned off the highway and wound through residential streets that weren't on the map yet. Only one completed house for every dozen lots. In between, fire hydrants, concrete footers and new streetlights waiting to be wired into the power grid.

Someone was awake in one of the homes, reading a book upstairs. Others had cars in driveways. Serge studied each passing residence. Nothing he liked. The Challenger drove on. More isolated homesteads. More checkmarks in the negative column.

The Challenger reached the back of the future subdivision and rounded a broad cul-de-sac with surveyors' stakes. Serge parked and studied the last house three lots up. No cars or other signs of life, but the porch light was on, which meant electricity, essential to his science project. A rolled-up garden hose hung from its cradle by the back fence. The mailbox: THOMPSON.

Owner-occupied. Excellent.

Just one last thing. Serge got out of the car without closing the door and tiptoed to the mailbox. He opened it. Full.

Serge ran back, started the car and whipped up the driveway. "Coleman!" Shaking his pal's shoulder with a hand holding a pistol. "We're here!"

Snoring.

"Wake up!" Serge jabbed him in the cheek with the gun.

A groggy Coleman startled. Another jab with the pistol. A loud groan. Coleman's eye blinked and stared into the barrel of a huge gun. He grabbed his heart. "Thank God! I was having a nightmare I was out of dope."

Thuds from the trunk.

Coleman found some potato chips in his pocket. "I wish they'd stop all that racket."

"It will soon be peaceful in the jungle." Serge aimed a rectangular plastic box at the house.

"What's that?"

"Garage door opener." Serge turned a knob.

"I didn't know garage openers had dials. Or were that big."

"Mine's the only one." More intricate twisting. "I bought a regular opener, extracted the gizzards and made a trip to my beloved RadioShack. Then I rebuilt the components inside a blank electronics box. All other openers have a button you temporarily press, so I soldered the power circuit to this on-off toggle switch, allowing continuous transmission. Also, openers only broadcast on a single, fixed frequency, which I bypassed with a variable gang capacitor attached to this dial, permitting me to tune it like a radio across the entire garage bandwidth."

"Variable gang?"

"Long explanation." The dial rotated farther. "But a childhood of building crystal radios put me in the kill zone."

Crunch, crunch. "The door isn't opening." *Crunch.*

"What are you eating?"

"Potato chip pieces and lint."

More careful tuning. "If my guess is correct . . ."

A quiet mechanical grinding in the night.

"It's opening," said Coleman. "It works."

Serge grabbed his drugstore shopping bags and a broom. "Justice is afoot."

The trunk lid popped open. Whining from two bound and gagged hostages.

"My manners," said Serge, reaching over them for a small toolbox. "Forgot the formal introduction . . . Tourist-robbing motel dirtbag, meet not-pulling-over-for-fire-truck horn-honking car-keyer, and vice versa . . . Eeny, meeny, miney, mo—which social goiter has to go?"

"What are you doing?" asked Coleman.

"Choosing."

"Why not do both?"

"Want to save one for dessert. It's like when fortune shined on me as a little kid and I found myself with two Reese's peanut butter cups. I'd always hide one for later to make the magic last, but they always melted in my underwear."

"That still happens to me."

". . . My . . . mother . . . said . . . to . . . pick . . . the . . . very . . . best . . .

motherfucker . . . and . . . you . . . are . . . it! . . . Coleman, give me a hand with the dirtbag."

After a forced gunpoint march, the would-be robber was flung down on cold cement. Serge flicked the toggle on his plastic box. The garage door lurched and cranked back down behind them.

"Coleman, hit that light switch on the wall."

The hostage squinted in sudden brightness. Then puzzlement at the ensuing flurry of activity.

Serge dragged a ladder to the center of the garage, then climbed up with pliers and metal snippers. He stretched a tape measure along the lifting chain of the garage opener's motor. Bending and cutting. Twisted links of broken chain bounced on the floor. He grabbed kite string in his teeth and flicked open a pocket knife . . .

Ten minutes later, Serge folded the ladder against a wall. He placed the broom on a workbench, sawed off the business end and carved a lengthwise groove down the shaft.

"Coleman, kill that light."

In darkness, Serge raised the door again. He walked to the garage's threshold, reached up and tore weather stripping off the bottom edge, then generously applied a ribbon of superglue. The truncated broom went in place, reinforced with duct tape. He knelt on the ground, unscrewing the back of his custom transmitter.

Coleman felt inside his other pocket and pulled out something round and tan. He tasted it. "What are you doing now?"

"Removing the nine-volt battery so I can wire my alternate power source." He stood with the resulting configuration, left the garage and placed the automatic opener in the driveway. "I need your help. Grab that rope."

Coleman threw a pebble over his shoulder. "What do you want me to do?"

"After I finish these knots, pull as hard as you can . . ."

CHAPTER FIVE

BOSTON

*P*atrick McKenna arrived for work, punctual as always.
He got off the elevator. All the cubicle people stood and began clapping.

"What the heck?" Patrick went in his office and sat down at the computer.

A colleague opened the door and ran in. "Turn on the TV!"

"What's happening?"

"Just turn it on!"

He hit the remote.

"*. . . It was an emotional homecoming after FBI agents raided a remote farmhouse in Essex County and rescued a college freshman who'd been held hostage for more than a week. The big break came when a local satellite imaging company . . .*"

A commotion back in the doorway. His boss rushed in, followed by three TV crews jockeying for position. Patrick jumped up.

The boss threw an arm around his shoulders. "Here's your hero!"

Blinding camera lights. Patrick shielded his eyes. "Get them out of here!"

"Smile," his boss whispered sideways. "It's great publicity for the firm."

"I don't want publicity."

A thrusted microphone. "How does it feel to be a hero?"

Shafts of light hit the empty street.

"Sun's rising," said Serge. "We have to work fast." He threw another rope to Coleman. "Pull!"

Moments later, they were done. Serge stood proudly before another enigmatic scene.

Their guest lay on his back, lashed into precise position with a spiderweb of thick rope stretching his limbs to the aching point and knotted around open wall studs and various heavy objects. His body was inside the garage, head resting on the ground outside, just over the threshold, staring up at the edge of the open automatic door.

Serge chugged a coffee thermos, then grinned gleefully and rubbed his palms together. "This is usually the part where I get a thousand questions! But I pride myself on being the perfect host and anticipate them all. Let's get to it!"

Serge held a plastic box to the captive's face. "Dig! RadioShack! I rigged my own universal garage door opener, conveniently tuned to this house's frequency." He reached up and carefully ran a finger along ultra-sharp metal. "Also sawed a horizontal groove in the broomstick attached to the bottom of the door. Now that's patience! No need to thank me. Then I took the liberty of applying Kwik Dry superglue the entire length of the notch and inserting a bunch of razor blades I got at the drugstore."

Coleman picked his nose. "Wondered what you were going to do with those."

Serge squatted next to the head. "By your eyes I can tell you've guessed it. That's right: Serge's Garage-Door Guillotine! Patent pending."

Fierce wiggling and gag-muffled screams.

"Better conserve energy because there's a lot of work ahead if you want to make it out of here." Serge looked back at the growing dawn light. "You'll have at least an hour to free yourself." Serge smiled again and tapped the man's terrified cheeks. "Just joking. I wouldn't put you through that kind of inconvenience. I made sure you can't get loose . . . Although I could be bluffing. You've probably noticed I'm a different kind of cat. Maybe I made one of the knots a *slip*knot. Ain't this a fun riot! Ha, ha, ha, ha, ha. More coffee for everyone!"

"But, Serge," said Coleman, "garage doors come down pretty slow. It'll just cut him a little. Don't take this the wrong way, but I'm not very impressed by your guillotine."

"That's the whole beauty." Serge walked to the middle of the garage and pointed up at the motor mounted to the ceiling. "This is a newer model I wasn't familiar with, so it took a bit of extra analysis, but I finally cracked the code. The special chain here is key, with sprocket holes that go around the main gear." He kept pointing above as he walked forward. "And here's the end of the chain, which reaches the gear when the door gets near the bottom. Notice how I've removed a section of metal links and tied the other two ends together with kite string. Then I used my pocket knife to slice partially through the twine." Serge spread his arms upward like a preacher. "And there you have it!"

Coleman fired a jay. "Have what?"

"When activated by my remote control, the chain lowers the door halfway, until it reaches the string, which snaps because the load's too heavy, and the door free-falls under its own weight."

"Is that enough to chop his head off?"

"Of course not. What is it with you always asking about chopping heads off?"

He shrugged. "Never seen it done."

"Razor blades aren't that long, but more than enough to do a number on major blood vessels, like the jugular and carotid, just to name a couple." Then, looking down: "Will you stop trying to scream? That's so impolite when someone's attempting to have a conversation."

Serge dragged garbage cans and a lawn mower into the driveway— "Blocking views from the street, in case you were curious."

"When do we get to watch?" asked Coleman.

"We won't be here."

"Knew you were going to say that." Coleman sighed and took a hit. "I always wait bored while you do your hobbies, but then you don't let me see the good stuff."

"Coleman, it's going to get ridiculously bloody." He shivered at the image. "Not something a normal person would enjoy."

"But how will it happen if we're not here?"

"The crowning cherry!" Serge held up a shiny, square plate with a lacquered surface encasing loops of embedded metal strips. "My alternative power source."

"What is it?"

"Solar cell. I've decided to go green." Serge laid it in the driveway. A wire extended from the side and into his modified garage opener. "When the sun rises high enough, it'll activate my transmitter." Serge reached toward the box.

"Can I?" asked Coleman.

Serge stepped back. "Be my guest."

Coleman threw the toggle switch to "On."

Serge stood over his guest a final time. "My advice? Pray for rain."

SOUTH OF MIAMI

The early-afternoon sun gave everything a harsh yellow haze. All across Metro-Dade, long lines spilled from convenience stores and bodegas, people handing pink-and-white cards across counters. Lottery machines clattered and spit out tickets at a blistering rate.

"Those are my grandchildren's birthdays . . ."

"I just feel extra lucky . . ."

A royal poinciana struggled to rise from a tight alley between two pastel green apartment buildings in West Perrine. The rest of the landscaping was accidental. Weeds; abandoned tires; a smattering of old-growth palms, some dead, leaving withered, topless trunks. Spanish store signs and billboards for menthol. Children played in broken glass, throwing rocks at lizards.

A late-model Infiniti sat across the street with the motor running.

"How long are we going to wait?" asked Miguel.

Guillermo's eyes stayed to his binoculars. "As long as it takes."

Raul leaned forward in the front passenger seat and twisted a knob.

Guillermo lowered the binoculars. "What do you think you're doing?"

"Listening to the radio."

". . . With no winners for the last five weeks, Florida's Lotto jackpot now stands at forty-two million dollars, and merchants are reporting huge backups—"

Guillermo clicked it off. "We're working."

The sun drew down.

"Maybe they're not even home," said Pedro.

"They're home all right," said Guillermo.

"How do you know?"

"Here they come now."

The Infiniti's passengers looked up at the second-floor balcony, where a door had just opened. Three men filed out. Colombian. They trotted down a concrete staircase by the poinciana and piled into the boxlike frame of a vintage Grand Marquis with gray spray-paint splotches over body work.

Guillermo threw the Inifiniti in gear and followed.

Raul unzipped a small duffel bag, handing out Mac-10s with extended ammo clips. "When do we move?"

"Not until I say." Guillermo made a right behind the Marquis. "Let's see where they're going."

"But we could pull alongside right now."

"And a cop comes around the corner," said Guillermo. "I personally want to get away."

The Marquis reached South Dixie Highway and turned left.

"Brake lights," said Miguel. "They're pulling into that parking lot."

The Infiniti slowly circled the gas pumps of an independent convenience store with water-filled potholes and a lunch window for Cuban sandwiches. Four steel pylons had recently been installed at the entrance after a smash-and-grab where a stolen Taurus ended up in the Slim Jims. The Marquis's passengers went inside.

Guillermo parked facing the quickest exit back to South Dixie. He opened the driver's door. "Don't do anything until I give the signal."

"But they're all in there."

"And armed," said Guillermo. "Wait until they're in the checkout line. Otherwise we'll be chasing them all across the store, shooting at one another over the top of the chips aisle like last time."

The crew tucked Macs under shirts and slipped to the edge of the building. They peeked around the outdoor self-serve freezer of ten-pound ice bags.

"Look at that fuckin' lottery line," said Raul.

"They're all up front," said Guillermo. He pulled a wad of dark knit cloth from his pocket, and the others followed his lead. "Try to keep your spread tight."

Customers forked money across the counter and pocketed tickets of government-misled hope, just as they had every minute since the owner unlocked the doors.

The Marquis's passengers looked down at their own penciled-in computer cards. One sipped a can of iced tea. Another idly looked outside. Four ski masks ran past the windows.

"Shit."

He reached under his shirt for a Tec-9. The others didn't need to see the threat, just reflexively went for their own weapons upon noticing their colleague's reaction.

The doors flew open.

Then all hell.

Ammo sprayed. Beer coolers and windows shattered. Screaming, running, diving over the counter, two-liter soda bottles exploding.

Miguel took a slug in the shoulder, but nothing like the Colombians. A textbook case of overkill. They toppled backward, their own guns still on automatic, raking the ceiling.

Stampede time. Guillermo and the others whipped off masks and blended with a river of hysterical bystanders gushing out the door. After the exodus, an empty store revealed the math. Three seriously dead Colombians and four crying, bleeding innocents, lying in shock or dragging themselves across the waxed floor.

Sirens.

The Infiniti sailed over a curb and down South Dixie.

CHAPTER SIX

A bong bubbled.

Coleman looked up from the couch. "Hey, I'm on TV."

On the screen, a bong bubbled.

"Serge, when did you shoot that?"

"Couple minutes ago." He loaded a fresh tape in his camcorder.

Coleman watched as the TV scene panned around their one-bedroom apartment. Souvenirs, ammunition, row of ten bulging garbage bags against the wall.

A cloud of pot smoke drifted toward the ceiling. "You filmed the inside of our crib?"

"The big opening of my documentary." Serge switched the camera to manual focus and aimed it at the television. "I finally found my hook."

"Why are you filming the TV? It's only playing what you just filmed."

"This is bonus material. The 'making of' documentary of the documentary. You need that if you expect decent distribution in Bangkok."

"What's your documentary about?"

"Everything."

"Everything?"

The camera rolled as Serge walked into the kitchen and grabbed a mug of coffee with his free hand. He filmed the cup coming toward the lens. "If you're going to do something, shoot for the best. People have made documentaries about the Civil War, baseball, ocean life, Danny Bonaduce, but as yet nobody's attempted to document absolutely everything. My director's cut box set is slated to top out at seven hundred volumes."

"Will it include Danny Bonaduce?"

"Volume three hundred and twenty-four."

"But how can you do a film on *everything*?"

"Spare batteries."

"That's it?"

"I'm also thinking of getting at least three more cameras that run continuously." He held up the current unit. "This will be angle one, pointing forward with the viewfinder. Then I'll have two waist-mounted cameras on a special belt, and finally a fourth in a sling on my back, aimed behind me, in case something important happens after I leave."

Serge drained his coffee and turned off the camera. "My documentary on everything is complete."

"Thought there were seven hundred volumes."

"Flexibility is critical during production." Serge ejected the tape from his camera. "The key to filmmaking is knowing what to leave out. That way you make the audience think, filling in gaps themselves and arguing about it on the way home."

Coleman scraped out his bong and strolled over to the row of garbage bags.

"Been meaning to ask," said Serge.

"The bags? I'm letting them age."

"Silly question."

"It's all timing." Coleman bent down and read adhesive labels he'd stuck on each: drugstore addresses and dates. "This one's ready."

Serge watched, puzzled, as Coleman carried it into the kitchen and dumped the contents on the table. "Let's see what we've got . . ." He pawed through refuse. "Here's something promising . . . here's another . . . and another . . ."

"Prescription bags?"

"Three weeks old," said Coleman. "Between the pharmacy counter and the front door, a lot of people just rip their sacks open, pocket the bottle of pills and toss the rest in the trash can outside the door. Then I make my rounds."

"I'm guessing there's a point, but I've been wrong before."

Coleman held up one of the small paper bags. "See? Got all the information: patient's name, medicine, day prescribed and, most crucial of all, any refills."

Serge sat back at the table with amused attention.

"Of all people, I thought you'd figure it out by now," said Coleman. "When was the last time they asked for ID picking up a prescription?"

"Never, but—"

"I calculate the pill quantity and dosage directions off the bag, then call a day or two before the person would normally order a refill."

"What if the real customer's already called? You'll get caught."

"Let me see your cell."

Serge handed it over. Coleman dialed. He read the side of the bag, pressed a sequence of numbers and hung up.

Serge took the phone back. "What just happened?"

"Big chain stores now use automated phone refill systems. If the customer already called, you'd get a robot's voice saying it's too soon to refill. No harm, no foul."

"I'm amazed at the level of thought," said Serge. "And yet you still put your shoes on the wrong feet."

Coleman looked down. "There's a difference?"

Serge logged on to his laptop.

"Whatcha doin'?"

"Planning my next documentary. But not too hasty: This one must be stunningly insightful and redirect the flow of culture as we know it."

"Why?"

"My Documentary on Everything set the bar prohibitively high. Reviewers unfairly hold that against you."

Coleman pulled up a chair. He took off his shoes and switched them. "The pain's gone."

"It definitely has to be about Florida." Serge surfed various history sites. "Just haven't zeroed in on the specific topic."

"Why does it have to be about Florida?"

"To set the record straight. Remember the highest-grossing movie ever filmed here?"

"You told me. *Deep Throat.*"

"Bingo. And the state's bestselling documentary?"

Coleman shrugged.

"*Girls Gone Wild: Spring Break.*"

"Oh, yeah!" said Coleman. "Great plot!"

"Plot?"

"Get chicks drunk and have them make out with each other."

"That's your idea of a plot?"

"The best there is," said Coleman. "Unless, of course, they can convince *three*—"

"That's exploitative!" Serge tapped his way around the Internet. "I cannot idly stand by and allow that gooey stain to sully my home state's fabric."

"There's a sequel," said Coleman. "They have this hot tub—"

"Enough!" *Tap, tap, tap.* "Now I absolutely must make this film. But what subject? Calusa shell mounds? The eight 'lost' Florida parishes when the Panhandle used to extend to Louisiana? Tampa's Great Blizzard of 1899? Mosquito control through the ages? . . ."

Time flew. Coleman passed out at the table with his cheek on a wicker place mat.

". . . Sports? Rail infrastructure? Osceola's heartbreak? Our chief export behind citrus: fucking up national elections? . . ."

Coleman raised his head and looked around. "Am I here?"

"Why can't I find the hook?" *Tap, tap, tap . . .*

Coleman drank from the open beer he discovered in his hand. "Just remembered. What about the horn-honker in your trunk? He's been in there a day now."

"That's why I hung gerbil-pellet and water dispensers from the spare tire." *Tap, tap, tap . . .*

"What are you doing?"

"Checking my in-box."

"Wow, you really won the Irish lottery?"

"Coleman—"

"We're rich!" He jumped up and broke into a Riverdance jig. "We're rich! We're rich! We're-rich-we're-rich-we're-rich! . . ."

"Coleman—"

He plopped back down and wedged his head between Serge and the laptop. "How much did we win?"

"Nothing."

"No, really?"

"I'm serious."

"Nothing?" Coleman sat back in his chair. "Then why do the Irish buy the tickets?"

Serge scrolled down the screen, deleting more spam. He stopped. "What's this?"

"What?"

Serge opened the next junk e-mail: *Online Pharmacy Spring Break Blowout! Quality meds without prescription!*

"Coleman, it's a sign from God!" Serge got up and pulled a suitcase from the closet. "That's two references this afternoon, which can be no coincidence. I've just got my new documentary."

"What's the subject?"

"Serge and Coleman do spring break!"

UNIVERSITY OF MICHIGAN

Friday afternoon, last class of the week.

Gray sky. Gusting wind.

Students in bulky coats and parkas dragged luggage down snow-covered dormitory steps. Others with wool scarves up to their eyes pumped gas.

Madison, Wisconsin. Ice scraped off windshields. Portable stereos went in trunks.

Columbus, Ohio. Car heaters warmed. Traffic stacked up at red lights heading out of town.

The same scene across the northern tier of the country. Milwaukee, Chicago, East Lansing, Hartford. Everyone in the starting gate. Heading south, expressways, truss bridges, railroad yards, brick chimneys, leafless trees, frozen riverbanks.

Rear window paint:

FLORIDA OR BUST.

In Durham, three University of New Hampshire students loaded final bags into a station wagon with wood paneling.

"Hope you didn't forget to make reservations like last time," said the driver.

"No," said another student, slamming the rear hatch. "Taken care of. Alligator Arms."

"Sounds like a dump."

"It's cheap."

The driver checked his watch. "Where is he? We have to get moving."

"He doesn't realize he's going yet."

"What?"

"You know the guy. He'd never come on his own. And even if he did agree in advance, he'd back out at the last minute like he does for everything else."

"Nobody told me about this." The driver looked at his wrist again as a snowflake landed on the Timex. "It's going to blow our schedule. Weather's turning."

"But he's our friend. All that studying can't be healthy. We owe it to him to show him some fun."

"When do we break the good news?"

"When we find him."

"You mean you don't know where he is?"

"Sure I do. Somewhere studying."

"This is already a disaster," said the driver.

"It won't kill us to do a good deed. I'm actually starting to worry about him."

"You overthink shit."

"Don't tell me you haven't noticed. The more I'm around him, the more I get this vibe."

"What kind of vibe?"

"Like he's trying to hide something."

CHAPTER SEVEN

FLORIDA

A 1973 Dodge Challenger raced up the gulf coast on U.S. 19. Coleman's window was down, his head outside like a cocker spaniel. "Are the chicks from the videos going to be there?"

"By the thousand."

"Cool!"

"Coleman, this is a serious documentary. We're not interested in drunk babes flashing tits."

"Serge, a space creature has taken control of your vocal cords."

"Spring break is one of the most profound social influences Florida has given the rest of the nation. Because of our state, kids not only come here, but now flock to Mexico, the Lesser Antilles, even Colorado ski slopes. And it all started in a single swimming pool in 1935."

Coleman hung farther out the window. "Show me your tits!"

"Dude, get a grip. There's nobody around."

"Spring break! Wooooooo! I'm Gertrude Schwartz! . . ."

Serge pulled him back inside by his belt. "Coleman, that's seriously ripped, even for you."

Saliva began stringing from Coleman's mouth, pooling on his stomach.

Serge passed a Kleenex from his door organizer. "Thought you had that problem mastered."

Coleman placed the tissue on his chest like a bib and handed Serge a dark-orange safety bottle.

Serge read the label: GERTRUDE SCHWARTZ. Then the contents.

"Coleman, this is one of the most powerful narcotics known to man. How'd you get it? You're not a woman."

"*Dfjoiakl*—said I was her son—*msdffkdsflsd . . .*"

An hour later, Coleman's head lolled on its neck swivel. "Serge, someone messed with that highway sign. Says we're going north."

"We *are* going north."

"Who drives north for spring break?"

"People who want to travel back in time."

"I thought we were heading to a beach."

"We are. But time travel is the structure of my award-hoarding documentary," said Serge. "Florida's always had a love-hate relationship with spring break. First a community wants the money and rolls out the red carpet. Then they get rich and weary of hotel damage— 'Yo, students: Thanks for the cash, now scram!'—deploying police harassment. So another city with a lesser economy says, 'Hey, kids, why put up with that crap? We'll treat you right.' Then *that* place prospers and asks, 'Why do we have to put up with this crap? Get 'em out of here!' And so on."

"How many times has it happened?"

"The history of spring break in Florida can be divided into three distinct epochs: Panama City Beach, the current party mecca; Daytona Beach, which ruled the late eighties and nineties; and Fort Lauderdale, where it all began."

"So we're going to . . . ?"

"Panama City. I'm working my way back through time."

"I thought this was about Florida."

"What are you talking about? It *is* Florida. The Panhandle."

Coleman tapped an ash out the window. "Then why's it called Panama?"

"A rare relevant question. The city's original developer, George West, bestowed the name because if you draw a line from Chicago to the Panama Canal, it runs through there."

"That's fucked-up . . . Serge, I see fish with nipples."

"Weeki Wachee, home of the famous mermaid shows and one of the first roadside attractions in the state."

"Real mermaids?"

"I wish. They just wear costumes and breathe from special tubes hidden in underwater rocks. Tourists watch from below-ground grandstands through giant windows . . . And from the only-in-Florida file, a classic newspaper photo three decades ago of mermaids on strike in full uniform, picketing along the side of the highway."

A billboard went by: SWIMMING OUR TAILS OFF SINCE 1947.

"You aren't stopping," said Coleman. "You always stop."

"Not this place." Serge shot photos out the window without slowing. "My mug shot's probably posted in their ticket booths on the no-fly list. And just because I dove in the pool during one of the shows in a selfless attempt to save the attraction. Who knew they had big capture nets?"

"How were you trying to save it?"

"By spicing up their act as the Creature from the Black Lagoon—1954, filmed in Florida—which is why I dragged that mermaid to the bottom, but then I forgot which rock had the breathing tubes."

"What happened?"

"Reached the surface just in time, but no thank-you, only another 'We're calling the police.' That's usually a good time for lunch. On the bright side, a disgruntled mermaid with Broadway aspirations chased me across the parking lot and asked for a lift. Hit it off right away. And the sex!"

"You had mermaid sex?"

"Around the clock. Name was Crystal, like the river. Barely left the motel room for a week, but finally had to slow down when I started walking bowlegged. Then we broke up."

"Why'd you break up with a mermaid?"

"Other way around. You know how women are? Mermaids are even worse. Started getting pissed that I always insisted she wear the costume to bed. Accused me of really being in love with it instead of her. I said, 'Is that a problem?' When chicks decide they're leaving you, they really fly. At least I got to keep the suit."

"Did you try it on?"

"Of course. How often do you get the chance? Except those things are pretty binding, and I had to cut a long slit in the tail to go shopping, but it turned out the stores didn't want my business anyway."

Onward. North.

Flea markets, RV parks, drive-through liquor barn, civil war reenactment, sign beside a house selling Peg-Boards, direct-to-you outlets of preformed pools tipped up toward traffic. Sun umbrellas shaded roadside squatters hawking fresh produce, Tupelo honey, jumbo shrimp, salted mullet . . . Into Citrus County. Homosassa city limits. Serge jumped the curb and dashed into a visitors' center.

Coleman ran after him. "Serge? Serge, where are you? . . ." Peeking through doors. "Serge? . . . There you are." He looked around. "What is this place?"

A digital camera flashed nonstop. "The Florida Room at Homosassa Springs Wildlife State Park. Exhibit honoring my favorite artist, Winslow Homer." Sprinting around the room, flash, flash, flash. "Painted these watercolors of local nature during vacation in 1904. And look! Here's a page of the guest register he signed at the Homosassa Lodge!" Flash. "I could stay here forever! Back to the car!"

Farther north, Crystal River, swim-with-the-manatees country. Tour boats and dive specials and viewing platforms. Red-white-and-blue manatee statue in front of city hall.

"Coleman, did you know that hundreds of years ago, manatees were thought to be mermaids?"

"By who?"

"Pirates at sea too long."

Bang, bang, bang.

Coleman turned around. "I think the guy in the trunk wants something."

"Gerbil dispensers are probably empty."

MIAMI

People in smartly pressed suits came and went through a high-security gate.

Inside the utilitarian government building, an anthill of movement and efficient activity. Phones rang, reports filed.

CNN was on. A repeat of the breaking story on the missing college student found alive in Massachusetts.

A case agent named Ramirez looked up at the TV.

Patrick McKenna's face filled the screen.

"... I don't feel like a hero ..."

Agent Ramirez closed his eyes. "Oh, no."

NORTH FLORIDA

A '73 Challenger entered Levy County.

The tiny hamlet of Inglis. REDUCED SPEED AHEAD. Serge tried to time a stoplight but lost.

He punched the steering wheel. "Life drains from my body at red lights!"

Coleman popped a can. "I use them to drink beer. Green lights, too."

"Come on! Come on! ..." He began unscrewing a thermos. "Hold the phone. I can't believe it!"

"What?"

Serge pointed up next to the traffic light, where a green-and-white sign marked the cross street.

Coleman squinted. "Follow That Dream Parkway?"

"It's a sign."

"Yeah, metal. See them all over the roads."

"No, I mean a religious one. God wanted that light to turn red, like a burning bush. From now on, I'll never question the apparitions of the red lights."

"What are you going to do?"

Serge hit the left blinker as the light turned green. "Follow that dream!"

The Challenger skidded around the corner. "There's the chamber of commerce. They'll have answers." He pulled into the parking lot.

"Serge, it's closed."

"What the hell? The economy doesn't stop on Sunday."

Coleman burped. "Back there, I saw a—"

"Not now." Serge grabbed his camera. "Maybe I can find answers through the office window with my zoom lens."

"But, Serge—"

He was out of the car. He came back.

"Answers?"

"Only more questions." He stuck a key in the ignition.

"Serge, what was that brown sign we passed racing around the corner?"

"Coleman, I'm trying to think!" He stopped and turned. "Did you say *brown*?"

"Yep. Big one."

"Brown means information, which means God left another message on my machine."

Serge threw the Challenger in reverse and squealed backward a hundred yards. He stared at the sign, then at Coleman.

"Why are you looking at me like that?"

"He speaks through you."

"Cool." Coleman switched to his flask. "What's this dream parkway jazz about anyway?"

"The sign reveals all."

Serge got out and stood fervently before the sun-faded paint. At the top, a rust-streaked logo of an old-style movie camera. Below: Elvis spent July and August of 1961 in this area filming his ninth major motion picture *Follow That Dream* . . . The main set was located 5.8 miles ahead at the bridge that crosses Bird Creek.

Serge dashed back to the car. Coleman dove in after it began moving.

They sped west through Crackertown.

The odometer ticked under Serge's watchful eye. ". . . Based on the novel *Pioneer, Go Home!* by Richard Powell . . ."

Coleman pointed at the running camcorder on the dashboard. "I thought this documentary was about spring break."

"It is," said Serge. "In the movie, Elvis plays Toby Kwimper, whose family drives to Florida and homesteads on the side of the highway. Presley was such a force of nature, he created his own spring break. Plus another righteous Florida footnote: One of the film hands from Ocala brought his eleven-year-old nephew to the set, and he was bitten by the Elvis bug, dedicating his life to rock 'n' roll. That child? Tom Petty!"

The odometer reached 5.7.

"Is that the bridge?"

"Elvis lives!"

The Challenger skidded to a stop on the tiny span. Serge got out with his camcorder, filming the surrounding marsh. "Coleman, there's much to do. We must get down on that bank and fashion a bivouac like the Kwimpers' from available natural materials. Then I'll buy a guitar and rehearse the theme song while you round up extras from the day-labor office. Nothing in the universe can make me waver until this mission is complete."

"What about the guy in the trunk?"

"Or we can do that."

CHAPTER EIGHT

A British Airways jumbo jet cleared the Dolphin Expressway and touched down at Miami International. The control tower had to-the-horizon visibility for minimum landing separation. Minutes later, another transatlantic from Berlin. And Rome. And Madrid. Then the domestics, Minneapolis, Phoenix, Nashville.

The cadence of swooping turbines rattled the inside of a tiny bar on the back of an ill-stocked package store with Honduran cigars and a bulletproof Plexiglas cage for night sales that was so thick it was like looking at the cashier through an aquarium.

Only four customers in the late afternoon. Guillermo and his boys. The bar sat just north of the airport on the side of Okeechobee Boulevard. The interior was dark, choked with cigarette smoke from insufficient ventilation, which consisted of an open back door on a windless day. Out the door: roosters and roaming dogs pulling wet clothes from laundry lines. Beyond that, an unassuming drainage canal that began a hundred miles away near Clewiston, cutting south through a million sugarcane acres, then the Everglades, past western quarries and jumping the turnpike for a perfect, man-made straight diagonal shot through Hialeah, eventually assuming natural bends when it became the Miami River before dumping into Biscayne Bay.

The connectivity of that waterway could stand as a spiritual metaphor for the irreversible series of events Guillermo and his colleagues were about to set in motion, but that would just be shitty writing. Before coming to the lounge, they'd fished the bullet from Miguel's shoulder with tweezers and tequila. Not a bad job of swabbing the wound. Now Miguel wanted more tequila, and Guillermo wanted quiet as the TV over the bar went *Live at Five* from the so-called Lottery Massacre in West Perrine. When the report finished, Guillermo asked the bartender to change the channel. There it was again. And the next channel. Guillermo exhaled with relief. He'd been worrying that they had jumped the gun and removed ski masks too soon in their rush out the door. Another channel, CNN taking the south Florida firefight to the nation. But still no surveillance footage of the assailants, because the low-grade convenience store couldn't afford real security cameras and went instead with decoy boxes and blinking red lights.

"We lucked out," said Guillermo.

"Tequila," said Miguel.

BIRD CREEK

Serge stood in the middle of the bridge with coils of white rope. He threw one end over the west side and the other over the east.

"What are you doing?" asked Coleman.

"Making a guitar."

Serge walked twenty yards and tied monofilament fishing line to the bridge's railing. Then he went forty yards the other way and tied another.

"Guitar?" Coleman looked around. "Where?"

"The *bridge* is the guitar." Serge tested a hitch knot. "Elvis deserves only the biggest."

"But how can a bridge be a guitar?"

"Just a matter of proportion. The tones of an instrument's strings are determined by their thickness." Serge pointed. "That braided, inch-thick nylon would be the E string"—he turned—"and the fishing line is—let me think. Treble scale. 'Every good boy deserves fudge'— probably G."

Serge ran to the end of the bridge and down the bank.

A horn-honker lay in the mud, gagged, hands behind his back.

Serge grabbed two discarded crab traps and splashed out into the shallow creek. He stacked them beneath the bridge.

Ten minutes later, the hostage stood on top of them.

"That rope gives you balance," said Serge, clamping a D-ring.

"Which is important because you definitely don't want to fall off those crab traps."

Coleman stood knee deep with a Pabst. "No noose?"

"Been there, done that." Serge crouched and stretched fishing line. He looked up at his captive. "Remember: The traps are everything. If you can stay balanced on them long enough, someone's bound to find you. If not, they'll still find you, but you won't like it."

Coleman crumpled his empty can and pointed. "What are those for?"

Serge knotted lines through crab trap wires. "Refreshment."

The hostage stared in front of his face at a pair of gerbil dispensers hanging from the underside of the bridge and inserted through his mouth gag.

"Well, time to run." Serge stood and smiled. "Gotta follow that dream!"

MIAMI

Transcontinental flights continued thundering over a bar next to Okeechobee Boulevard.

Miguel got deeper into the tequila.

TV still on CNN.

The bartender started changing the channel to Marlins spring training.

"Stop!" shouted Guillermo. "Keep it on this."

The bartender withdrew his arm and went back to his own drink.

Guillermo leaned for a better look at the screen, now into the next segment from the cable channel's Boston affiliate.

"...I don't feel like a hero..."

Below the interviewee's face: HERO PATRICK MCKENNA.

"So that's what he goes by now."

"Who?" asked Raul.

"You're too young to remember," said Guillermo. "Son of a bitch looks exactly the same."

"What are you talking about?"

"Quiet." He flipped open his cell and dialed. "...Madre?... It's me, Guillermo . . . No, there aren't any complications from our business meeting . . . You're not going to believe this. Sitting down? . . . Because I just found an old friend."

HIGHWAY 98

A '73 Challenger blazed north on the desolate stretch with scarce traffic lights. Otter Creek, Chiefland, Fanning Springs, Perry, through forested hunting country—Woody's Famous Cajun Boiled Peanuts—and west into the Panhandle.

Coleman burnt his fingertips on the nub of a joint. "Are we there yet?"

"Almost. Just have to make one more stop at a police station."

"Police station?" The roach went out the window. "Are you nuts?"

"Don't worry—it's not open anymore." Serge crossed his fingers. "If it's there at all."

Another reduced-speed zone in Carrabelle. Serge scanned the side of the road. "There it is!" He parked at the curb and handed Coleman his video camera. "Film this."

"A phone booth?"

"Not just any phone booth. The world's smallest police station. I'm getting inside—shoot me through the glass . . . *Help! Help! I'm innocent! It was the one-armed man! . . .* That's enough."

Through Apalachicola and Port St. Joe, past a roadside display with replaceable numbers:

ONLY 89 DAYS LEFT TILL HURRICANE SEASON.

A series of bone-rattling roars over the car.

Coleman looked at the ceiling. "What the hell was that?"

"The sign we're almost there." Serge pointed through the windshield at a cluster of tiny specks disappearing out over the gulf. "Fighter jets from Tyndall Air Force Base."

They caught the first whiff of spring break in Mexico Beach. Students in front of a convenience store, cracking open Budweiser twenty-four-packs and draining melted cooler water on the ground.

"Regular unleaded is going back up *again*? This seriously cramps my lifestyle," said Serge. "Remember when gas was four dollars a gallon?"

"No."

"They made a windfall, then deliberately pulled back before we mustered sufficient motivation to wean ourselves off the black heroin. I predicted at the time they'd ratchet it back up again and here we are. Ever see those oil assholes testify before Congress?"

"Is that where, like, on TV nothing's moving?"

"I'd love to get my hands on just one of them for some private testimony."

Finally, they were there. Stuck in traffic. Kids on the sidewalk moving faster than cars. Small planes flew over the beach, pulling banners for drink specials and the Geico cavemen.

Coleman grunted as he struggled to open Gertrude's prescription bottle again.

"Having problems?"

He passed the vial to Serge. "It's childproof."

"Here you go."

"Thanks." Coleman popped a tablet in his mouth like a peanut. "Which one's our hotel?"

"Right up there. The Alligator Arms."

BIRD CREEK

A dozen police cars parked every which way on a tiny bridge in Levy County.

A corporal looked over the side. "Isn't this where they shot that Elvis movie?"

The detectives arrived.

"Where'd you find him?" asked the lead investigator.

The corporal pointed. "Top half above the navel washed up in those reeds . . ." He turned. "Tide took the rest downstream."

"What's with *those* people?"

They looked toward a Buick with Mississippi plates and a damaged grille, where another officer consoled a retired couple on vacation.

"Pretty shaken up," said the corporal. "Claim the rope just came out of nowhere."

"Rope?" said the detective.

"Wrapped across the front of their car, and they pulled it to the end of the bridge until it finally snapped and the Buick spun out."

"Is it connected to the homicide?"

"Our forensic guy's still working on it."

"Where is he?"

"Under the bridge."

The detective examined a frayed piece of fishing line tied to the railing. "What the hell are we dealing with?"

The forensic tech climbed up the bank in rubber boots. "Think I got it solved."

They waited.

Boots squished across the bridge. "Rope was wrapped around his stomach and held in place with a D-clamp so it wouldn't slip."

"You saying *rope* cut him in half? How's that strong enough?"

"More than enough," said the tech. "Human body's some of the most fragile material on the planet. This was like wrapping a string around a banana and pulling the ends. Banana slices right in two."

"That's disgusting," said the detective.

The corporal looked back at the Buick. "But what's with those people saying the rope came out of nowhere?"

"That was the trigger," said the tech.

"Trigger?" asked the detective.

The tech nodded. "This is where it gets . . . fancy." He swept an arm behind him. "Whoever's responsible wired the bridge like a giant guitar."

The corporal nodded. "Death by Elvis."

"This isn't for your amusement," said the detective.

"Sorry."

The tech pointed down. "Killer looped the rope in a complete circle over the bridge's railings and down to the victim, with the extra coils I mentioned around his stomach. But he left enough slack so the part across the top of the bridge just lay unobtrusively on the ground where a driver wouldn't notice it or give a second thought. That's how it came out of nowhere."

"How *did* it come out of nowhere?"

"This is a pretty remote road," said the tech. "Dead end. Almost no traffic, but a car passes by every now and again. That's where the

fishing lines come in, tied to the crab traps the victim was forced to stand on under the bridge."

"That's weird."

"Gets weirder. The assailant was thorough, didn't know which direction the next car would come from, so, twenty yards on each side of the big rope, he stretched clear, hundred-pound-test monofilament lines across the bridge at radiator level, invisible to motorists."

"Starting to sound like the roadrunner and coyote show."

"Fitting analogy," said the tech. "The thick nylon rope would remain flat on the road as long as the victim stayed on top of the traps. Then a car comes along, hits the fishing line he doesn't see, jerking the traps out from under the deceased, dropping him in the water, pulling the rope tight around his waist, which suddenly jerks the rest of the rope up off the roadway—again, to radiator level—just as the car reaches it and . . . two halves of a banana."

"Holy Jesus," said the detective.

"What are those things in your hand?" asked the corporal.

The tech looked down at gerbil dispensers. "Haven't figured that part yet."

The detective stared across the marsh. "What kind of monster is out there?"

CHAPTER NINE

PANAMA CITY BEACH

*J*he lobby of the Alligator Arms was jammed and loud. Galvanized-steel parade barricades separated lines of students at the check-in.

Coleman dragged luggage and huffed. "What's with the barricades?"

"A hint," said Serge.

"About what?"

"If you ever want to be treated like shit by the hospitality industry, check into a spring break hotel. That's why I booked four nights."

"We're staying that long?"

"No, the reservation is for four. But we're only staying three."

"Why?"

Serge nodded toward a sign: Checkout 8 a.m.

"Eight?" said Coleman. "I never heard of such a thing."

"Welcome to Give-Us-Your-Money Town. Population: You suck."

They eventually reached the desk. "Reservation, Storms, Serge." He winked at Coleman. "Eight a.m.? Is that sign correct?"

The receptionist relished firing another routine bow shot. "Look, I got two hundred rooms and it's the only way we can turn them around in time."

"Really?" said Serge. "I've stayed in five-hundred-room Marriotts, and they seem to manage. But you must know better, because the pay at a dump like this can only attract the best and brightest." A grin.

Glare in return. "Fill out this form. And we need a twenty-dollar deposit for the phone."

"But you have my credit card."

"We need cash."

"Can I get a receipt for the deposit?"

"Don't have any."

"What a shock." Serge scribbled a false address, then tapped the desk with his pen. "I don't remember my license plate. Sheraton lets me slide with just the make and model. Is it okay?"

"No."

"That was a test." Serge leaned over and scribbled. "I know my plate number."

"Test?"

"Quality check to ensure no leaks in your exquisite business model: Making us feel like family . . . the Gambino family." Another grin.

The receptionist's face turned bright red. "Your keys!" Slapped on the counter.

Serge grabbed them and raised his video camera. "I'm shooting a documentary. May I capture the recreational rudeness that is the high-water mark of your existence?"

"No! Turn that off!"

"More! . . ." Serge beckoned with his free hand. "Give me more!"

"Turn that thing off right now!"

Serge raised a clenched fist. "Now with feeling!"

"I said turn that goddamn thing off!"

"Excellent!" Serge lowered the camera and gave her another iridescent grin. "You take the 'service' out of 'customer service.'"

They hit their fifth-floor unit.

Coleman dropped bags. "It's huge."

"I got the one-bedroom suite. You snore . . . Here, take this."

"Another video camera?"

"I picked up a second for you to film the 'making of' documentary. Can you handle that responsibility?"

"Which way does it point?"

Unloading routine: Serge with his usual electronic gadgets, souvenirs and weapons. Coleman's paraphernalia: an endless assortment of clips, glass tubes, circular metal screens and hypodermic needles.

Serge stared at the last items. "Coleman, please tell me you're not riding the white pony."

"Heck no. That's dangerous." He pulled something else from his bag.

"Oven mitts?"

"Needles and oven mitts are the cornerstones of commercial-grade partying."

Serge darted one way with a small zippered bag, and Coleman went another for the TV. He pointed the remote and channel-hopped, stopping on a beach backdrop.

"Hey, Serge, look! It's that cool new show *Ocean Cops*." Coleman got an odd sensation. He looked at the television, then off the balcony. "I think they're filming here . . . Yeah, they're definitely filming here. Just said on the screen, 'Spring Break Special, Panama City Beach.'"

Serge hung a tri-fold toiletry bag in the bathroom. "What's happening?"

"Some unconscious guy on a raft is drifting out to sea."

"Sure it's not you?"

Coleman looked down at the front of himself. "Pretty sure." He wandered onto the balcony for a joint break. He raced back in. "Serge! Come quick! There's so much tits and ass you can't see the sand!"

"It's spring break." Serge organized dental-care products and plugged in his rechargeable razor.

"Something's going on," said Coleman. "They're throwing this little guy around."

"How little?"

"Pretty little."

"Is he wearing a crash helmet?"

"Yeah."

"That's the midget."

"Midget?"

"High-society tradition that started in Australia."

"Why do they throw midgets?"

"Sometimes for distance, sometimes style points, like when they're

covered with Velcro and stick to walls." Serge joined him on the balcony. "Or greased up for bowling lanes."

Coleman leaned over the railing. "Looks like they're just tossing him around the sand."

"Because the legislature intervened."

"*Legislature?* Are you just making up words now to fuck with me?"

"In 1989, we became the first state in the union to ban midget tossing." Serge uncapped a water bottle. "Bunch of people thought, it's about time. Finally, Florida's forward-thinking . . ."

"Serge, cops are moving in with riot shields."

". . . But those of us who live here know the truth. It wasn't legal foresight; they were simply forced to extinguish another wildfire weirdness outbreak."

"What does it have to do with him being out on the beach?"

"Because of that law, he can't work anymore except on the sly . . ."

"Ooooooh, the little dude just bounced off a shield."

". . . So he's forced to strike out on his own in public venues like street musicians."

"You don't mean—"

"That's right." Serge nodded solemnly. "The Wildcat Midget."

Down on the shore, a TV correspondent worked quickly with a brush. "How's my hair?"

Thumbs-up from the cameraman. He gave a silent countdown with his fingers.

"Good afternoon. This is Meg Chambers, reporting live from spring break in Panama City Beach. Homelessness is a difficult life, particularly for dwarfs, who are often driven into the midget-tossing trade for spare change and leftover pizza. As you can see behind me, local police are continuing their crackdown on the controversial sport, which has drawn mixed reactions from the midget-advocate community . . ." The camera swung left, where a tiny person in a helmet was handcuffed, to loud jeers from students. "It looks like they've again arrested local favorite Huggy 'Crash' Munchausen . . . Let's see if I can get a word . . ." She stepped forward as police led him by. "Crash, anything to say to our viewers?"

"It's a victimless crime. Why not legalize and tax it?" Police hustled him into a squad car.

The reporter turned back to the camera. "Victimless crime? You be the judge! . . . This is Meg Chambers reporting for Eyewitness Close-Up Action News Seven."

The cameraman signaled they were clear.

She threw the microphone down in the sand. "I got a master's for this shit?"

The correspondent stormed past Serge and Coleman.

BOSTON

A United 737 from Miami landed in a light dusting of New England snow at Logan International.

Two case agents walked purposefully through the terminal.

"We're all FBI," said Ramirez. "Do we not talk to each other anymore?"

"How were they supposed to know who he was?" said his partner.

"What an unbelievable cluster-fuck," said Ramirez.

A local junior agent met them at baggage claim. He went to shake hands but saw that wasn't happening. "Awfully sorry. Just want you to know everything's under control now."

"Everything *was* under control."

Their unmarked sedan sped south to Dorchester and pulled up in front of an older, two-story brick house surrounded by field agents, TV crews and satellite trucks. A sniper stood on the roof behind a chimney.

Ramirez took a deep breath and massaged his forehead. "Is this what goes for 'under control' up here?"

Sedan doors opened. An armored van screeched up. G-men sprinted across a brown lawn as TV lights came on. A correspondent broadcast live to lead the six o'clock.

". . . Tom, we have yet to learn exactly what's happening, but something major has developed at the home of hero Patrick McKenna, now swarming with FBI . . ."

Moments later, the front door flew open. A ring of agents circled a man in a Kevlar vest and rushed him toward the curb.

". . . Tom, I think it's our hero now, but I can't be sure because of the coat over his head . . . Let me see if we can get a closer look . . ."

The feds ran for a dozen government vehicles lining the street, assembling a protective convoy. They shoved Patrick in the van, and a shielding agent jumped on top of him.

"Mr. McKenna, how does it feel to be a hero? . . ."

The motorcade took off.

CHAPTER TEN

PANAMA CITY BEACH

Coleman trudged through sand, toting a plastic convenience store bag. "We missed the midget riot."

"There'll be others." Serge's eyes stayed on the viewfinder as he filmed continuously, the only person on the beach with a cup of coffee.

They reached the advertising. Twenty-foot inflatable suntan lotion bottles and promotional booths for energy drinks. Army recruiters had set up an obstacle course, where drunk students fell from rope ladders. Closer to shore, navigation became tricky with the growing concentration of bodies on blankets.

"*Hey, watch it, asshole!*"

A Frisbee glanced off Coleman's head. "Ow."

"One of nature's awesome mating spectacles." Serge stopped and panned. "This shames any salmon run."

"I hear a loudspeaker." Coleman turned in a circle. "Where's it coming from?"

"Over there." He gazed several hundred yards up the beach at a massive stage with scaffolds and amps. "A free concert from MTV."

"You mean the channel that doesn't play music?"

"That's the one," said Serge. "MTV has become the pork and beans of television."

"What do you mean?"

"You buy a can of pork and beans, getting all excited about upcoming pork, and then you open the can and go, 'What the fuck?' So you poke around and the only thing you find is a single, nasty-

ass slime cube from a liposuction clinic. I wouldn't even mind that if they'd just be straight and call it what it is on the label."

"Who would buy 'nasty-ass slime cube and beans'?"

"Me," said Serge. "Just to taste truth."

Coleman peeked back and forth, then furtively popped a can of Schlitz inside his convenience store bag. Another suspicious glance. He raised the bag to his mouth and chugged.

"What are you doing?" asked Serge.

"Not getting arrested."

"Coleman, look around."

He did. "Serge, everyone's drinking openly. How can that be possible?"

"It's not only possible, it's encouraged."

"Don't tease me."

"That's the core history of spring break I was telling you about." Serge filmed a beer-bong contest. "When I mentioned that communities alternately welcome and reject students, their chief tool is the alcohol-on-the-beach policy: either look the other way or crack down like Tiananmen Square. And right now, Panama City Beach is the most party-friendly town in Florida, maybe the whole United States."

Coleman stopped and placed a reverent hand over his heart. "I'm never, ever leaving this place."

"We've barely scratched the surface."

"There's more?"

"You have no idea."

Coleman discarded the plastic bag and carried the six-pack by his side. "Wait up."

Serge approached a group of students tanning beneath a giant Georgia Bulldogs flag.

"Howdy!" Serge drained the foam coffee cup and aimed his camcorder.

Coleman: "Check out the chicks' butts! . . . Ooooh, don't feel good . . ."

An engineering major stood. "You guys from *Girls Gone Haywire*?"

"No," said Serge. "I'm from the Florida Betterment Coalition of One, and my friend"—he gestured at Coleman, on all fours, burying his puke in the sand—"is working on his thesis."

"What's his freakin' problem?"

"A special case I've been studying for years," said Serge. "Coleman's the only human afraid of vacuum cleaners."

The student gave him a condescending up-and-down appraisal. "What the hell do you want?"

"Just a few questions for my documentary on the zeitgeist of today's top scholars. Number one: pork and beans. Your thoughts?"

"Get lost!"

"I'm already lost. In my love of history! Did you know Colgate University started spring break in 1935?"

"Want to move along or be hurt?"

"That's an easy one. Come on, Coleman . . . *Coleman?*"

Serge wandered the beach. "Coleman! . . . Where are you? . . ."

He came across a group of Yale premeds standing in a circle, looking down. Conversation in the back row:

"Amazing . . ."

"Some kind of genius . . ."

"Probably has a chair at MIT . . ."

Serge tapped a shoulder. "What's going on?"

"This guy's teaching us thermodynamics of maintaining proper beer temperature."

Serge cupped his hands around his mouth. "Coleman!"

"Is that you, Serge?"

"Excuse me," said Serge. "Mind if I slip through?"

He reached the inner circle. Coleman was on his hands and knees again, sand flying out between his legs as he rapidly dug a hole like a Labrador retriever. ". . . It's best to start below the mean high-tide mark, then excavate until you reach the water table . . ."

"But what about our coolers?"

"Sun's too hot out here," said Coleman. "Wet sand is a better insulator. Someone hand me a sixer . . ."

A student complied. Coleman crammed it in the hole. "If you plan on power-partying into the late afternoon, insulation technique is absolutely critical."

"Thanks, mister. Any other advice?"

Coleman scratched his crotch in thought. "Well, you got any events back up north where they allow coolers but not alcohol?"

"Yeah," said a sophomore. "We try to hide the booze in plastic soft drink bottles, except they always catch us."

"That never works." Coleman stood. "What you want to do is get a clear liquor—vodka, gin—pour it into a strong Ziplock bag, then freeze the sack inside a block of ice."

Serge filmed as Coleman was rewarded with a hearty round of back slaps and all the beer he could carry.

"I'm never leaving this town."

DINNERTIME

A triangle bell rang.

Men came inside the stucco house south of Palmetto Bay.

A full-course meal awaited on the cedar table. Place settings precise as usual, except this time each also had a one-way plane ticket to Boston under the fork.

After saying grace and passing bowls, Juanita poured sangria for Guillermo. "You're a good boy."

"Thank you, Madre."

"So Randall Sheets now calls himself Patrick McKenna?"

Guillermo mixed beans and rice on his plate. "Yes, Madre."

Juanita smiled. "It only took fifteen years." She reached into her apron and handed him a single-page computer printout. "From our private investigator. Those are the addresses of his home and business, plus vehicle information."

They ate faster than normal because of flight departure.

At the front door, Guillermo gave Juanita a kiss on the cheek. "I'll call as soon as we know something."

She waved as the car pulled out of the driveway. "Be safe."

NEW ENGLAND

A highway sign with a pilgrim's hat went by. The Mass Pike.

The government convoy remained in tight formation.

"Get off me!" yelled Patrick McKenna.

"It's okay," said the case supervisor. "You can release him now."

The shielding agent got up.

Patrick pushed himself off the van's floor and pulled the coat from his head. "Was that really necessary?"

"Was it necessary for you to go on TV in front of the whole world?" asked a Boston agent.

"Why are you talking to him?" said Ramirez. "It's not his job to know *your* job."

"You Miami hotshots fucked this whole thing up."

"Mother—"

Everyone blew. A loud, overlapping, profanity-laced exchange.

"Hey," said Patrick. "Guys."

Nonstop yelling.

Then, uncharacteristically: "Everyone! Shut up!"

They all stopped and looked at their star witness.

"Sorry," said Patrick. "But what about my son?"

"You have a son?" asked a Boston accent.

Ramirez shook his head. "Typical you didn't know." The Florida agent placed a reassuring hand on Patrick's shoulder. "We're taking care of him." Then, with an edge of sarcasm, "Someone had to."

"This isn't going anywhere," said the ranking Boston agent. "Let's start over from right now. Status on the son?"

"My people should have arrived at the college the same time we got to Dorchester," said Ramirez. He opened an encrypted cell phone. "I'll check in—probably already have the son and are on their way back to meet us now . . ."

CHAPTER ELEVEN

PANAMA CITY BEACH

$\mathcal{S}$erge tilted the viewfinder as he walked. Hair-care products went by on both sides. He turned the corner and headed up the toothpaste aisle.

"Serge," said Coleman, "what are we doing here?"

"My eye-opening documentary must be the final word on spring break." He zoomed in on an endcap display of paper towels. "The footage is more compelling than I'd hoped."

"Wal-Mart is part of spring break?"

"Not until 2006." Serge entered the pet section, filming bird seed. "That's when Drake University sophomore Skyler Bartell decided to spend his entire spring break in a twenty-four-hour Iowa Wal-Mart."

"That's odd."

"No odder than what we've already seen here." He panned across litter boxes for all income levels. "From March nineteen to twenty-one, Skyler spent forty-one straight hours in the store before detection. I mean to break that record. Wild horses can't drag me out of here before I succeed and am written up in medical journals."

"Where did he sleep?"

"On toilets."

Coleman wandered through electronics. "I don't want to sleep on toilets."

"You do it all the time." Serge checked his wristwatch, then shook it and held it to his ear.

"What's the matter?" asked Coleman.

"Thought my watch had stopped. Could have sworn we'd been here more than three minutes."

"Seems like hours."

"I've just made an important discovery of the galactic bent-space continuum. Time slows down in Wal-Marts."

Coleman followed his buddy back toward the front of the store. "Serge, where are you going?"

"Leaving."

"Thought you were staying for at least forty-one hours."

"I may have already." They approached automatic doors. "Back through the wormhole to check regular clocks."

FIFTEEN HUNDRED MILES NORTH

The southern border of New Hampshire is guarded by a string of sales-tax-free state liquor stores, militarily positioned like pillboxes. Their parking lots are full of Massachusetts plates, half customers, half Massachusetts alcohol agents who follow residents back over the commonwealth line for citations. Except they can't, because New Hampshire agents block them in until customers make a clean get-away. Such is the delicate fabric of the republic, no more evident than in a state with the motto "Live Free or Die" stamped on its license plates, which comedians note are manufactured in prison.

New Hampshire's trademark is the Old Man of the Mountain, an uncanny, eons-old geological rock formation high up the side of Franconia Notch. Its profile is ubiquitous: postage stamps, the state quarter, a thousand highway signs, flags, welcome centers, the capitol rotunda, history books, maps, pot holders, paperweights, snow globes and every tourist brochure ever printed. Residents proudly identify with the Old Man in a fierce emotional bond, much like Parisians and the Eiffel Tower or Texans and the Alamo. On May 3, 2003, the face slid off the mountain and disintegrated.

Somewhere between the liquor stores and the collapsed head is Durham, home of the University of New Hampshire, where a team of FBI agents raced down dormitory steps.

It began to snow.

A phone rang.

An agent flipped it open on the run. "Oswalt here . . . No, still at the college . . . Not yet . . . Of course we checked the dorm . . . It's spring break. Everyone's either gone home or to Florida . . . I realize that . . . I know that . . . We did try his cell phone . . . Three times, no answer . . . You sure he wasn't going back to Dorchester for the week? . . . I didn't mean it that way . . . We're headed to the student paper where he works . . . Right, I'll call as soon as we learn something."

The phone went back in a jacket.

PANAMA CITY BEACH

Heavy foot traffic on the strip.

Everyone over thirty was ignored or insulted. There were always exceptions.

Young women's heads universally turned as a suave Latin hulk strolled down the sidewalk. Tanned six-pack abs; long, sexy dark hair. Easily a movie double for Antonio Banderas.

Two blondes wore long, wet Indiana State T-shirts over bikinis, giggling at suggestive boys in passing pickups. Then they saw *him*.

"*Rrrrrrrrrrrow!*"—double-taking as he went by.

"But he's old enough to be your father."

"So fucking what?"

"Good point."

Two pairs of bare feet made a U-turn on the sidewalk.

Johnny Vegas continued along the strip to more female rubber-necking. He'd just had his fortieth birthday, and he wasn't playing around anymore.

The reaction of the opposite sex had been the same Johnny's entire life. His trust fund didn't hurt either. Almost as much attention from the same gender: "That son of a bitch must have more tail falling off his truck than we'll ever see. It's not fair."

It wasn't.

Despite appearances to the contrary, Johnny Vegas held a deep secret that would have shocked the populace. He'd never been able to close the deal. Not once.

Oh, sure, with the least flirtatious glance from those smoldering dark eyes, he could form a rock-concert line of willing partners. But it was always something. Always Florida. Some kind of typical Sunshine State strangeness invariably erupted at the worst possible moment. Hurricanes, brushfires, wayward alligators, overboard passengers, meth freaks, bodies under hotel beds, Cuban exile unrest. The odds were off the charts. Then again, there are a lot of guys in the world, and someone's chips had to be resting on the unluckiest roulette square.

That would be Johnny Vegas, the Accidental Virgin.

His body clock ticked deafeningly between his ears. How long could he count on his drop-dead looks? Time to go fishing with dynamite.

Johnny had seen the *Girls Gone Haywire* spring break videos. What the hell was wrong with the world? Here he was, the ultimate bachelor. Then he pops in a DVD, and all these hometown-values girls are stripping for dorks with video cameras. What a colossal corruption of youth and moral decay. Johnny had to get there as fast as possible.

It wasn't five minutes since he'd parked his Ferrari when the wolf whistles began.

"Hey, handsome."

Johnny turned around on the sidewalk. Indiana State blondes. Good Lord, *two*, and he'd just gotten into town. No need for some dishonest ruse; Johnny would take the high road.

"I work for *Girls Gone Haywire*."

"Let's party."

The roommates made the choice for him. "I think I'll get some more sun on the beach. Behave yourself, Carrie." Wink.

She took him by the arm.

"My name's Johnny," he said as they continued up the sidewalk.

"Johnny, where's your hotel?"

CHAPTER TWELVE

PANAMA CITY BEACH

*S*erge and Coleman wove up the sidewalk against the college tide. Standard mix of rolling luggage and coolers. Serge held his running camcorder at chest level. People handed out coupons for nightclub drink specials; the Coors girls waved; an airplane dragged a banner for faster Internet service; church youth flapped posters at traffic, offering free pancakes and a road map to salvation.

The pair stepped into a beachwear shack to adopt the proper spirit and came out in new T-shirts reflecting their respective outlooks.

Coleman's: ALCOHOL, TOBACCO AND FIREARMS SHOULD BE A CONVENIENCE STORE, NOT A GOVERNMENT AGENCY.

Serge's: THERE ARE 10 TYPES OF PEOPLE IN THE WORLD: THOSE WHO UNDERSTAND BINARY, AND THOSE WHO DON'T.

The documentary continued.

Coleman drew a steady stream of insults. Frat boys noticed something on Serge's ear, snickered and made sideways wisecracks to their buddies. Until Serge returned the look. They noticed something unfamiliar in his eyes and wanted to keep it that way.

"Serge," said Coleman, "what's that funny thing on your ear?"

"A Bluetooth."

"I never figured you for the Bluetooth type."

"That's why it's not a real Bluetooth. I *hate* Bluetooth types, walking around all self-important like they have to be plugged in every second of the day. Can't tell you how many times I'm in a public place having a pleasant conversation like a normal human being, and one of these fuck-heads walks right between us talking at the top of his lungs."

"If it's not a real Bluetooth, then what is it?"

"A piece of plastic garbage I found on the street that I rigged with paper clips. Got the idea from the smash-hit HBO series *Flight of the Conchords*. Except that guy had a real Bluetooth, just no receiver. I decided to take it the rest of the way and go completely anti-Bluetooth."

"Don't those paper clips hurt?"

"Yes. A lot."

"Why wear it?"

"Because, like Bluetooth people, I'm also constantly walking around talking to myself, but just because I don't have that stupid crap on my ear, people give me a wide berth and jump to the mistaken conclusion that I'm simply another jabbering street loon. Yet ever since I attached this thing to my head, completely new attitude, no matter what I'm saying: 'I'll destroy that motherfucker for ten generations!'"

"People dig that?"

"No, they still recoil—but in admiration. Now they think I'm a killer in the boardroom." He nodded and smiled to himself. "Yes, sir, total respect."

Beach babes passed the other way, pointing and laughing.

Coleman tugged Serge's shirt as they reached a makeshift liquor stand. "Hold up—"

"No! Told you we can't stop. The documentary is practically filming itself." He stepped in front of a sloshed brunette from Rutgers. "Excuse me, miss . . ."—raising the viewfinder to his right eye—". . . mind if I ask you a few questions?"

She began pulling up her shirt.

"No, not your tits." Serge reached and yanked it back down. "I want your soul."

"Fuck off, weirdo."

"Is that like your generation's catchphrase?" asked Serge. "Because I've been getting it a lot lately."

She brushed past him. "Blow me."

"That's a close second." Serge turned off the camera.

Another tug on his shirt.

"Coleman, we don't have time to stop for liquor."

"Not booze. Look!"

Serge followed his pal's gaze up toward the sky. Two massive steel towers rose like a giant V. Between them, even higher, distant screams from a tiny flying ball. The sphere had open-air seating for two students, who were held in place by a triple-reinforced roller-coaster harness. A pair of super bungee cords ran from the tops of the towers to the sides of the ball.

Moments earlier, the ball had been sitting at street level. Underneath, a large metal latch held it to the base platform. The ride's operator worked controls that turned gears on the tips of the towers, stretching the elastic cords to the max. Then he hit the button, releasing the latch and firing the catapult.

The kids went vertical, zero to 120 miles per hour in under three seconds. They pulled six Gs before the ball reached its apex high above the city and the cords stretched the other way, jerking them back down. The bungees stretched almost to the ground, launching them again, this time slightly less high. Then down again. Up again, tumbling randomly, students shrieking all the way. Down, up, down, each time dissipating energy, now slowly arcing over at the peaks.

In less than two minutes, it was over. The ball sagged motionless thirty feet from the ground, and the operator reversed his controls. The towers let out line, lowering the kids the rest of the way. They climbed from the ball, dizzy and sick. "That ruled!"

The students left through a safety gate and past a sign—THE ROCKET LAUNCH—where Serge waited impatiently, waving cash. "Ooooooh! Me, me, me! I'm next!"

The operator led Serge and Coleman onto the platform and pointed at a pair of plastic bowls. "Empty your pockets and take off anything loose. Sunglasses, hats, that thing on your ear."

Serge's wallet, cell phone and keys went in one bowl. Coleman filled the other with a bottle cap, M&Ms and twigs.

The operator looked at Serge's left hand. "You can't take the camcorder."

"It's all right," said Serge. "I'm filming the most shocking documentary ever made."

"No, I mean there's no way you'll be able to hang on to it. You're going to snap pretty hard the first way up."

"But I'm recapturing state pride."

The operator pointed at the restraint bar. "We got a tiny camera mounted toward the seats. You can buy a souvenir DVD afterward if you want."

"What a deal!"

The pair climbed into the ball, and the operator strapped them in. Then he left the platform, positioning himself behind the control panel. Gears stretched cords again.

Serge grabbed handles on the front of the massive, padded harness pressed against his chest. "Coleman, what an excellent idea! I've seen these all over Florida—here, Kissimmee, Daytona Beach—but I was always in too much of a rush."

"Knew you couldn't resist." Coleman wiggled against the restraint to reach a hip pocket. "Always talking about going into space."

"This is like the Gemini missions. They were the best! Capsules held two astronauts, just like us." Serge bobbed enthusiastically in his seat and stared at the heavens. "Also, Gemini was the fastest manned flights off the pad, using converted Titan intercontinental ballistic missiles. Until the ride's over, call me Wally Schirra." He turned his head sideways toward the unseen operator. "Can you give us a countdown?"

"You want a countdown?"

"And call me Wally."

"Wally?"

"Thanks. Means the world."

"Whatever . . ."

Elastic cords finished stretching.

"*Ten . . . nine . . .*"

Coleman finally achieved success with his hip pocket.

"Coleman!" said Serge. "You were supposed to put everything in the plastic bowl!"

"*. . . six . . . five . . .*"

"There's no way he was getting my flask. Plus I wanted a swig for the ride." He unscrewed the top.

Serge faced forward and gripped the handles harder. "Houston, we have a problem."

Gator A-GO-GO   **81**

"... *two ... one ... liftoff!*"

The latch released.

The pair went screaming into the sky.

In mere seconds they reached the top, hundreds of feet above the strip. Then a hard yank from the cords.

"My flask!" Coleman watched it quickly sail high into the blue yonder until it disappeared.

The guys bounced up and down for another ninety seconds, until the operator reeled them in.

The harnesses unlocked. Serge jumped from the ball and snatched his wallet from a plastic bowl. "I absolutely must have the DVD."

NEW HAMPSHIRE

Agents rushed into the office of the student paper. A morgue. One lone kid in sweats, staying behind to wrap up a three-part series on the education budget.

A badge. "Seen Andy McKenna?"

The student shrugged.

"Know where he might be?"

"Try the dorm?"

Agents ran into the cafeteria. Only two students, both female. Then rounds of all the popular study areas and TV lounges, giving themselves a full self-guided tour of the evacuated campus.

"Let's check the dorm again."

They met the agent they'd left behind in the room in case the sophomore returned.

"I take it he hasn't come back."

"You mean you didn't find him?"

"Great."

"Sir ..." The agent gestured at the trashed interior. Papers, CDs, candy wrappers everywhere. Underwear and pizza boxes on the floor. "Looks like someone ransacked."

"It's a college student's room," said Oswalt. "They all look like this. Mine was worse."

"I got a weird feeling something's not kosher."

"How's that?"

"Can't quite put my finger on it. The room just seems light, like stuff's missing."

"Anything more specific?"

"Not really."

Another agent: "Maybe ring his cell again?"

Oswalt flipped open his phone, hit buttons and placed it to his ear.

A faint, muffled musical tone came from somewhere in the room.

The agents listened and walked silently, trying to home in on the source. Four of them ended up in a circle, staring at the floor. One reached down and lifted a pizza box. The tone got louder.

"At least we found his phone."

"I'm not laughing," said Oswalt. "Let's go . . ."

They stepped into the hall. A solitary student walked by with a watering can and containers of fish and bird food.

"Excuse me." The badge again. "What's your name?"

"Jason Lavine."

"You know Andy McKenna?"

He nodded.

"Know where he is?"

He shook his head.

"Any chance he left campus?"

"No . . . Definitely not."

"How are you so positive?"

The student pointed into the room with a canister of pellets. "He's got an aquarium."

"So?"

"I make a fortune staying behind during spring break, feeding pets. And watering plants—but those are just the girls' rooms."

"How does that mean he couldn't have left?"

The student looked through the open door at guppies. "He didn't pay me."

Oswalt sighed.

"Can I go now?"

The agent answered with an offhand wave.

The team trotted down the dorm's front steps again.

Snowing harder.

Oswalt put his hands in his pockets and stared across the barren commons. "Where can he be?"

MEANWHILE . . .

Johnny Vegas accelerated his pace up the sidewalk toward his hotel.

"In some kind of a rush?" joked Carrie, clutching his arm harder. A couple of times she reached back and squeezed his ass. He attributed it to the fact she was already halfway in the bag. His kind of girl.

They reached the edge of a parking lot. "Here we are!"

Carrie got on her tiptoes and whispered something in his ear.

Johnny coughed and pounded his chest. "Holy God!" he thought. "She wants to do *that*." He closed his eyes and mentally pumped a fist in the air: "Yes! I've finally done it! Nothing can go wrong now!"

He opened his eyes and began leading her toward the lobby doors.

Suddenly, Johnny felt his arm released. He looked left.

No Carrie.

He looked down. There she was. Lying unconscious on the pavement with a nasty forehead gash. Next to a dented flask.

CHAPTER THIRTEEN

PANAMA CITY BEACH

*R*ood Lear reached a net worth of twenty million by his thirtieth birthday. Which was two years ago. Total now closer to forty. Mansion in the Hollywood Hills, Park Avenue penthouse, private jet on call.

Despite the staggering wealth, Rood still went to work every day.

Rood's company, Bottom Shelf Productions, had booked the top floor of one of the strip's finest hotels under his lawyer's name.

Noon.

The floor's largest suite was brightly lit, even with curtains closed. Wires and cables ran everywhere, held firmly to the carpet with black electrical tape. Large white umbrellas in the corners filled facial shadows from camera lights.

Rood looked at least seven years younger, because he was so short and had to shave only every three days. He surveyed the suite's bedroom and bit his lower lip. Something wasn't up to Rood's high standards. He found the answer. "Give 'em liquor."

"I think they've already had more than enough," said his executive assistant.

"I say they haven't."

"Sir"—the assistant held a pair of well-worn laminated cards— "I don't think these drivers' licenses are legit. See the edges? Someone slit them with razor blades and resealed 'em on an ironing board."

"You work for CSI now?"

"I've seen this trick a hundred times. And we just paid a million in fines."

"They gave us the IDs, and we accepted them in good faith," said Rood. "If they're fake, *we're* the victims."

The assistant turned toward the bed, where a pair of topless, tipsy seventeen-year-olds swatted each other with pillows.

"Harold!" said Rood. "Are you going to give them more liquor or look for another job?"

The assistant walked out the door and slammed it behind him.

"Stop filming!" Rood stomped across the room. "Guess I have to do everything!"

He went to work at the wet bar, ice clanging in a sterling cocktail shaker. Then he approached the bed with two tumblers of his personal recipe: Hawaiian Punch, 7 Up and grain alcohol. "You girls look thirsty."

Giggles. A feather floated by.

"Bottoms up!"

The first took a big sip. "What's in this? I don't taste anything."

"Exactly." Rood walked back behind the cameras. "Jeremy, start filming." Then louder: "Pillow fight!"

Swatting began again.

One of the girls' knees slipped, and she spilled off the bed.

"You all right?"

The teen stifled more giggling and nodded extra hard.

"Okay, back on the mattress."

The girl started getting up but fell down again, pulling a sheet with her.

"Jeremy," said Rood. "Give her a hand."

The cameraman helped her the rest of the way.

He returned. "I think they're ready."

"I think you're right. Roll camera." Rood raised his voice toward the bed: "Make out with each other. And I want to see lots of tongue on nipples!"

"Forget it!"

"That's gross!"

Rood went over to the wet bar.

BOSTON

A buzzer sounded. A belt jerked to life in baggage claim.

Anxious travelers ringed the carousel and bunched near the front where luggage came out, trying to see through the hanging rubber strips as if it would accelerate the process.

People snagged suitcases and tote bags. Some placed them back on the belt when the name tag was wrong. Others were easily identified from a rainbow of ribbons their owners had tied to the handles.

Guillermo saw an orange ribbon and snatched a Samsonite. His colleagues grabbed their own luggage, which came by at random intervals.

Finally, they had retrieved everything. And they stayed there.

A taxi stopped outside at the curb. A man with red hair and freckles emerged. One of the few people bringing baggage *into* baggage claim. He took a spot on the opposite side of the carousel from the Florida visitors. Two grandparents rolled bags away; he stepped forward and set a black suitcase at his feet. Guillermo knew the man was there, but neither looked. After sufficient time to allay suspicion, the man studied the name tag on the black suitcase and pretended it wasn't his. He placed it on the belt.

Guillermo watched it make the turn and nonchalantly grabbed a handle on the way by. They headed for the rental counter.

Thirty minutes later, a Hertz Town Car cruised south on I-93. Raul rode shotgun, opening the black suitcase in his lap. He reached into the protective foam lining and passed out automatic weapons. "What was the deal back there with the Irish guy?"

"Raul," Guillermo said patiently, "what is it about not checking machine guns through in your luggage that you don't understand?"

They took the Dorchester exit at sunset and reached a bedroom neighborhood in the dark. Large oaks and maples. TV sets flickering through curtains. The Town Car slowed as it approached the appointed address. Guillermo parked a house short on the opposite side of the street.

Miguel leaned forward from the backseat. "Is that the place?"

Guillermo checked his notes, looked up and nodded. Everything appeared normal. That is, except for the fiercely bright spotlight in the middle of the front yard.

The gang watched as a last, straggling TV correspondent wrapped up a taped spot for the eleven o'clock report. The yard went dark. Guillermo opened his door.

"Excuse me? Ma'am?"

The woman turned.

Guillermo jogged toward the station's truck as a cameraman removed his battery belt. "Do you have a second?"

"What is it?"

"Is that the home of hero Patrick McKenna?"

"You know him?"

"Went to school together. Amazing what he did!"

"You went to school with him?" She looked over her shoulder. "Gus, get the camera. We might have something."

"No!" Guillermo's palms went out. "I mean, no, my wife will kill me. I was supposed to go to this boring dinner party but told her I was working late."

She sagged. "Forget it, Gus."

Guillermo looked toward the house. With the camera off, it became obvious there wasn't a light on in the place, not even the porch. He turned back toward the woman. "Anyone home?"

She shook her head and opened the van's passenger door.

"Expect him back?" asked Guillermo.

"Not any time soon." She climbed inside.

"Why do you say that?"

"Because he moved out."

"Moved? When?"

"This morning. It was crazy."

"How was it crazy?"

"If you can tell me anything at all about him, I won't use your name," said the reporter.

"I'll try," said Guillermo. "But what happened this morning?"

"All the stations were set up on the lawn, waiting for him to show, and suddenly these cars came flying up, and a bunch of government guys rushed him out with a coat over his head. You wouldn't have any idea what that was about, would you?"

Guillermo shrugged. "Last time I saw him, we were in the chess club . . . These guys say they were government?"

"No, but you could just tell. All business, not even a 'no comment.' Then, fifteen minutes later, two giant moving vans pulled up, except they didn't have any markings on the side. And they had like twenty guys. Cleaned the place out in less than an hour."

"Thanks."

The TV van pulled away.

PANAMA CITY BEACH

A camcorder scanned the west end of the strip. Nightclubs, hotels, swimsuit shops, condos. The lens passed something and backed up. It stopped on a neon sign.

The camera fell to Serge's side and dangled by its shoulder strap. "I don't believe it." He broke into a trot, then a run.

A half mile later, Serge grabbed a hitching post and panted beneath colorful curved glass tubing: HAMMERHEAD RANCH BAR & GRILLE.

He went inside.

Everything was dark wood with heavy layers of varnish to preempt wear and tear from the beach crowd. Sunlight streamed through open veranda doors. Strands of beer pennants hung from rafters. Walls and ceiling covered with old license plates, old photos, old fishing equipment—all bought from a restaurant supply company to give new businesses artificial age. The T-shirt shop took up a quarter of the floor space.

The joint was empty, too early yet for the student shift. Chairs still on tables from mop duty. Singular movement behind the bar: A Latin man in a polo shirt inventoried liquor stock with a clipboard. He jotted a number.

"Tommy?" Serge yelled across the dining room. "Tommy Diaz? Is that really you?"

The man looked up from his paperwork. "Who wants to know?"

"Tommy, it's me, Serge!"

"Serge?" Tommy set the clipboard against the cash register. "You're still alive?"

"Rumor has it."

"What the hell are you doing up here?"

"Just about to ask you the same thing."

"We've gone legit," said Tommy.

"No way!"

"Way," said Tommy. "You wouldn't believe how packed this place gets. We're making it hand over fist. And I thought there was a lot of money in cocaine."

"What about the old motel—" Serge caught himself. "Don't tell me you sold out. That's our heritage!"

"No, it's still there, dumpy as ever."

"Whew!"

Early birds in Iowa State Hawkeye jerseys arrived and grabbed stools. Tommy checked his watch. "Where are those bartenders?"

Serge grabbed his own stool and looked up at a stuffed hammerhead shark painted psychedelic Day-Glo and wearing sunglasses. "Tommy . . ." He winced at the shark and waved an arm around the interior. "It's so . . . *yuck*."

Tommy checked student IDs and stuck frosty mugs under draft spigots. "Got to stay up with the times. Our motel in Tampa Bay has become something of a landmark, everyone pulling over to take snapshots of that row of sharks, but it ain't makin' shit. So we decided to franchise the name recognition."

Serge frowned. "Feels like I'm in Cheers."

"If you're between gigs, we could always use a bouncer . . ." He looked back at the swinging "staff only" doors to the kitchen that weren't swinging. ". . . and bartenders who show up on time!"

"Personnel problems?" asked Serge.

Tommy poured off foam before setting the students' mugs on cardboard coasters. He strolled over and leaned against the other side of the bar from Serge. "That's the only rub. You hire the hottest babes available, dress them accordingly and cash just avalanches. But then you have to put up with their lifestyle."

Swinging doors creaked.

One of the Hawkeyes looked up from his beer. "Holy God!"

Tommy turned and tapped his wrist. "Late again. We got customers."

"Bite me."

Students' jaws unhinged. Before them, visions from Victoria's Secret. Both statuesque six-footers in stretch-to-fit black tank tops and matching skimpy silk shorts. Perfect bookends: one a classic blond farm girl from Alabama, the other a gorgeous Brooklyn import who gave Halle Berry a run.

"Serge," said Tommy. "What are you drinking? On the house."

"Bottled water."

"Haven't changed." Tommy faced the just-arrived employees. "Call me crazy, but can I ask you to work? Man wants a water."

The blonde sneered, then placed a coaster in front of Serge and twisted off the plastic cap. Something made her pause. She stared into his ice-blue eyes. Serge stared back.

Mutual traces of faint recognition, but they couldn't quite piece it together because of geographical displacement.

Then, suddenly, the woman's arm sprang out and stuck a finger in Serge's face. "You!"

Serge's brain caught up. "Hey, long time! How's it been going?"

"Motherfucker!" She turned to her colleague. "Guess who just slimed into our bar?"

"Who?"

"Serge!"

"Motherfucker!" A hand flew into a purse and whipped out a .25-caliber automatic.

CHAPTER FOURTEEN

DORCHESTER

*G*uillermo sat in a Town Car across from an empty house, staring at his cell. "This is one phone call I'm not looking forward to." He took a full breath and hit a number on speed dial. "Hello, Madre? It's me. I'm afraid we're too late. Looks like the feds pulled him back in this morning."

"You did your best," said a maternal voice on the other end.

"But we didn't succeed."

"Maybe I have some good news."

"What is it?"

"Randall had a son."

"That's right," said Guillermo. "What was he? Four, five at the time?"

"That would make him about twenty now."

"But how's that good news?"

"Billy Sheets is now Andrew McKenna. Got something to write with?"

Guillermo to the rest of the car: "Give me a pen." One appeared. "Ready."

"University of New Hampshire . . ."

He scribbled the rest of the data, including dorm and room number. "But how'd you get all this?"

"Our investigator. He's good," said Juanita. "Once we had Randall's new name, it was a simple public records search. And a few diplomatic phone calls for nonpublic records."

"People just give our private eye confidential info over the phone?"

"He lies to them."

Guillermo paused to choose words. "Madre, I don't want to disappoint you again. If the feds already scooped up Sheets, I'm sure they also went to the school."

"You may be right," said Juanita. "But who knows with college students? They don't keep routines like other people. We might get lucky."

Guillermo opened a map in his lap and hit the dome light. "Madre, we're leaving now—shouldn't take more than ninety minutes."

"You're a good boy, Guillermo."

He was still on the phone as the Lincoln went in gear and proceeded slowly down the tree-lined street. "If we do find him, you want us to, uh"—he considered the unsecure line—"invite him for an interview?"

"No, our government friends would never agree to an exchange."

"Then what?"

She didn't answer, which was the answer itself.

"I'll personally handle it," said Guillermo. "And, Madre, I've always learned from you, so may I ask a question?"

"Please."

"If it's the father we're after, what purpose would *that* serve?"

"The best purpose of all."

"Which is?"

"Revenge."

PANAMA CITY BEACH

Tommy Diaz jumped into action. He grabbed his bartender's wrist and pushed it down, sending a bullet through the wooden floor. "Not in my bar!"

She gritted her teeth. "Get your fucking hands off me."

"Agree first," said Tommy. "Not in the bar."

"You're hurting me!"

"Give me the gun and I'll let go."

Still gritting, then a slight nod. Tommy released her.

She joined her friend, staring daggers across the counter.

Tommy wandered over. "Serge, looks like you're winning another popularity contest. Some history here?"

The blonde pointed again. "That shit-eating bastard left us stranded on the side of the road!"

"What? . . . I . . . Huh? . . ." Serge tapped his own chest. "Me? . . ."

"It was the middle of the damn state," said the other. "Hot as fuck!"

The Hawkeyes leaned as a group, digging the babes' dirty talk.

"Huge misunderstanding," said Serge. "I thought *you* were tired of being around *me*."

"Bullshit! You peeled out of the parking lot . . ."

". . . And you looked back as we chased your car down the street. I was combing dust out of my hair for hours!"

"Ouch," said Tommy.

"That was *years* ago," said Serge. "Life's too short. You should focus on all the laughs we had."

"I can't believe I actually sucked your dick," said the blonde.

Hawkeyes adjusted their bulging pants.

Serge squinted at a blue butterfly. "See you got a tattoo."

"Don't try and change the subject!"

Then a crash next to Serge as a stool went over. Coleman pulled himself up from the floor. "Yo, Serge. Sorry I'm late . . ."

"Who's that boob?" asked the blonde.

Serge put an arm around his buddy's shoulders. "Coleman, this is a special day! I'd like you to meet a couple of dear old friends, City and Country."

"What happened to Lenny?" asked Country.

"Still living with his mother. Probably grounded again . . . Coleman's the original: Lenny, beta version, initial glitches intact."

"We're still going to kill you," said City, glancing at her boss. "Just not in the bar."

Tommy saw this could go one of two ways, and he couldn't afford to lose his best meal tickets. Plus he'd grown fond of Serge.

"Let's make peace."

He gave them the afternoon off, placed a few calls and tended bar himself until reinforcements arrived.

The foursome grabbed a corner booth, and Tommy set them up with sweating metal ice buckets of Rolling Rock.

Electric tension around the table. The women steamed with

crossed arms, cats ready to claw eyes out. Then alcohol began oiling conversation. Two hours in, empty green bottles scattered everywhere. The women switched to Jack Daniel's.

Coleman awoke and lifted his face off the table. Serge brought him up to speed, making an extremely long story *USA Today*–short.

City and Country. From the blue-collar side of the usual town-gown friction at any university. Both ingenues back then, which was a decade, sweet as pie before the highway life as fugitives. Bogus murder case. Never should have gone into that student bar. Trash talk about them being trash. The ringleader was a sorority president from a prominent donor family. Then, in the restroom, the coked-out sister fell on the knife she'd been using to cut rails in one of the stalls. Country tried first aid but lost the patient and her future. Only one thing to do when you're outside the local power structure, uneducated and panicking with blood on your hands and fingerprints on the knife:

Florida road trip!

Before entering that fateful saloon, they barely drank, didn't smoke, *definitely* didn't do drugs and had no legal scrapes of any sort. Since then, shit. Anything went. Anything. A ten-year mountain of petty and not-so-petty crimes. Never caught. Whatever it took to get by. Prison didn't turn them out any tougher.

With almost anyone else, the lifestyle ushered a downward spiral. In rare cases like City and Country, it sharpened survival skills to a fine, glinting edge and, all things considered, allowed them a half-decent existence in the gray margin of society.

"Some story," said Coleman.

"Sucks," said Country, expertly rolling a joint on the table.

"Jesus!" Serge glanced around. "Trying to get us pinched?"

"Fuck it."

"Cool," said Coleman.

Country lit the number and passed it under the table to City.

She passed it back. "On three . . ."

They did shots.

The Hawkeyes were turned around on their stools with backs against the bar.

In love.

So was Country; her altered blood chemistry drooped eyelids and formed a coy smile at memories of old times with Serge. She got up, whiskey hips swaying, and, without intention, couldn't have caused more drooling on her way to the jukebox.

Her right hand braced against the domed glass; her left pressed buttons, mechanically flipping miniature album covers. Flipping stopped.

B-19.

The bar echoed with the slow, immediately recognizable forty-year-old cadence of a cowbell. Charlie Watts joined on drums. A single guitar chord.

Country sauntered to the middle of the floor, giving Serge a bedroom smile and making a naughty "come hither" motion with an index finger.

Serge could dance, but it wasn't a smooth prospect. He had only one speed: open throttle. Duck-walking, backflips, jumping jacks, sliding across the floor for imaginary home plates. Country told him to just stand still.

"... I met a gin-soaked barroom queen ..."

She did all the work. Her back to him, slithering up and down against his chest, running hands through her wild, curling hair.

Over in the corner booth, Coleman raised his eyebrows toward City and nodded toward the dance floor.

"Are you retarded?"

Coleman strained to think.

She hit her joint.

He reached for it.

"No."

Back on the dance floor, Country continued grinding into Serge, shifting tempo perfectly with the music. The chorus came around again and she flung her head side to side, that blond mane whipping back and forth in front of her face.

"Honnnnnnnnky-tonk women ..."

At the bar, six Hawkeyes with outstretched arms pointed cell phone cameras.

CHAPTER FIFTEEN

NEW HAMPSHIRE

now fluttered.

Big, thick flakes clumped before they hit ground. Accumulation reached three inches on the steps of the Dimond Library. Inside, toasty and empty.

Only four students. Three on the main floor and another in archives.

Andy McKenna sat at a microfilm machine, researching an article for the student paper on plans to attach a full-scale plastic replica of the Old Man of the Mountain at the top of Franconia Notch.

His iPod earphones: *"More than a feeling . . ."*

He didn't hear the door open behind him.

Several pairs of feet moved quietly across the carpet. Andy's eyes stayed on the screen as he advanced the reel.

Feet moved closer. Fifteen yards, ten, five . . . the back of Andy's head growing larger . . . four, three . . .

At the last second, Andy caught a reflection in the microfilm's screen, but it was too late.

A thick forearm wrapped around his neck. Andy grabbed it with his hands, thrashing left and right, earbuds flying, feet kicking the ground.

No use.

A voice from over his shoulder: "Just accept it and this will go a lot easier."

"Let go of me!"

The arm released.

Laughter. The three amigos: Joey, Doogie and Spooge.

Andy jumped up and grabbed his chest. "That wasn't funny. You nearly scared me to death!"

More laughing.

"What's this about?" asked Andy.

"A kidnapping. It's futile to resist."

"Leave me alone." He sat again. "Got work to do."

A hand reached down to the wall and unplugged the microfilm viewer. Andy's head fell back with a deep sigh.

"Come on," said Joey. "We have to get going before the snow's too deep."

"Going? I'm not going anywhere."

Joey was the one with big forearms, thanks to the rowing team. "Guys?"

They snatched Andy under his arms.

"Okay, okay!" He jerked free. "Where are we going? If, that is, I agree."

"Agreeing's not part of it," said Spooge.

"Florida," said Doogie.

"Florida? I can't go to Florida!"

"You don't have a choice . . ."

". . . Andy, it's spring break!"

". . . It'll be wicked excellent!"

"Send me a postcard." Andy reached for the electrical plug. He was blocked. Another sigh.

"Besides, you have to go."

"Why?"

"We used your credit card to reserve the room. You have to show picture ID at check-in."

"Dang it!"

"Relax, we'll pay it all back. You were the only one with a card, at least not over the limit."

"This already sounds like a disaster."

"We're looking out for you. All this work isn't healthy."

"I can't just *leave*. I've got too much to do."

"That's why this is a kidnapping. We knew you'd never come on your own."

"But I'll have to pack. It'll make you late."

A smiling face. Joey raised a gym bag and backpack. "All taken care of."

"You broke into my room?"

"You'll thank us someday."

"But I don't have my cell phone."

"It's spring break."

"What about my fish?"

"We'll call Jason from the road."

"My dad will be worried."

"We'll call him, too."

"I don't know . . ."

"Andy, be spontaneous for once."

Outside, three sedans parked in a fire zone. Agents bounded up library steps.

"This is crazy," said Andy. "I should have my head examined."

"Now you're talking!"

An elevator opened on the ground floor. Agents rushed inside. The doors closed as the next elevator opened and four students got out.

"This is going to be wicked excellent!"

PANAMA CITY BEACH

Coleman was down for the count, leaving Serge on solo night patrol. He reached a bend in the sidewalk and focused his camcorder on three cheerful youths waving homemade posters.

"Oooooooh," Serge said with delight, lowering his camera. "Free pancakes!"

He walked over.

"Howdy! I'm Serge!"

"Hi, Serge. Want a free pancake breakfast?"

"But it's night."

"That's when all the kids eat breakfast. Soaks up alcohol."

"What's the catch?"

"There is no catch."

"There's *always* a catch."

"Why don't you come inside with us?"

Serge followed and was soon seated in a church activities room. On the table in front of him: the largest pile of pancakes the volunteer group had ever seen anyone assemble.

Three sparkling kids pulled out chairs and joined him. They didn't have pancakes.

Serge, chewing: "Great breakfast. *Deeeeeeeelicious!*"

"It's Serge, right?"

He nodded and stuck a fork in his mouth.

"Serge, have you ever heard of the one true living God?"

"Of course," said Serge. "He's like a household name."

"Are you saved?"

"That's a long story."

They handed him inspirational pamphlets.

Serge smiled. "Knew there was a catch."

"No catch. It's the path to redemption."

"Fair enough," said Serge, setting his fork on the plate. He leaned back and folded his arms. "You gave me a great meal, I can at least listen. But if this turns into a time-share thing, I can't guarantee your safety."

"It's not."

"Then give me your best shot."

The trio took turns effervescently sharing the marvelous change in their lives. A pastor circulated through the room, hands clasped behind his back. He smiled at the youths around Serge's table doing the Lord's work. The kids finished their pitch.

"Impressive," said Serge. "Sounds like you got quite a program there. Unfortunately, no sale. I already have my own program."

"You belong to a religion?"

Serge returned to his food. "Absolutely."

"Which denomination?"

"My own."

"What do you mean your own?"

"So far I'm the only member. But it cuts printing costs for the monthly bulletin."

"Your religion can't have just one member."

"Why not?"

"It's . . . you just can't."

"Every religion started with only one person." Pouring syrup. "Even yours."

"No, it didn't—"

One of the others nudged his friend and whispered, "Actually, it did." He turned to Serge. "So what *is* your religion?"

"Well," said Serge, digging in his fork again, "it's an awful lot like yours, except with massive confusion."

"Confusion?"

"I question everything. And I'm still totally baffled. Which only makes my faith stronger—God's so incredible, he's beyond comprehension!"

"You're devoutly baffled?"

"All questions, all the time! And as the lack of answers mounts, the infiniteness of the Almighty swells in my soul. People who claim to know his every last thought in order to bully others are just shortchanging his omnipotence. Like politicians who say, 'Pay no attention to our performance on the economy. Look! Over there! Gay people are trying to get married!' "

"But homosexuality is a sin against God. Says so in the Bible."

"That's what I thought, too," said Serge. "But it just didn't jibe. So I took another look at Genesis   "

"You know Genesis?"

"And Nehemiah, Ezra, Proverbs, Lamentations—one of my favorites, hilarious subtext, but I can't read it on airplanes, where people get upset with laughing fits. The whole book's a classic."

"You read the whole Bible?"

"Couple times. And you know how in Genesis, Lot's the only good guy in the twin cities, Sodom and Gomorrah. These two male angels come to stay with him. Apparently they're lookers. Think Matt Damon and Ben Affleck in *Dogma*. And these people from his street bang on Lot's door, wanting him to let the houseguests out so they can have gay sex. Now Lot's always been an accommodating neighbor, but this ain't no potluck dinner. They argue back and forth, going nowhere. So, finally, in an attempt to show that sex with girls is much more fun and convert them to heterosexuality, Lot offers to turn over his two underage, virgin daughters for gang rape."

"It doesn't say that!"

"Let me see your Bible." Serge executed a perfect sword drill, finding chapter nineteen in seconds. He turned the book around, slid it back across the table and tapped verse eight.

Three youths crowded over the page. "It *does* say that. But how can it be?"

"Because God blessed us with curiosity. Read it with an open mind and you realize it's actually a brilliant satire on homophobia. Think as an individual: The Lord doesn't want a train pulled on little kids. It's like reading Swift's *Modest Proposal* and thinking he really wants to eat babies. What the Bible's trying to say is we're all his children. But if you take Lot's story literally, well, nice family values, eh? But that's just my interpretation, which I'm now questioning. I could be way off."

The youths got up and went over to their pastor.

"I think we've been wrong about gay people . . ."

". . . They're fellow children of God."

At the next table, a homeless midget in a crash helmet spread whipped butter.

The youths returned.

Serge smiled. "Looked like your preacher was telling you to stay on message."

"Do you realize the only path to righteous glory—"

Serge took another bite. "Let's talk about evolution . . ."

CHAPTER SIXTEEN

NEW HAMPSHIRE

A Hertz Town Car crossed the Durham city line. Snow melted to ice. The car parked at a dorm.

Four Latin men ran up steps. Guillermo led the way down a hall. He stopped in front of a door and checked the number against his scrap of paper. Then he motioned for Raul, the lock-pick specialist.

He eased the door open, and they went inside.

Empty.

The gang fanned out, carefully combing the room for any clue to track Andy. Day planner, travel receipts, phone numbers, anything.

Failure.

Finesse gave way to destructive ransacking. When they were done, the room was neater.

"Guillermo," said Miguel, "I don't understand it. We usually at least find something. It's like he has no routine at all."

"It's college."

They left the room and closed the door. Halfway down the hall, Guillermo called a huddle.

"Any ideas?"

"Stake out the dorm from across the street?" said Miguel.

"Campuses have too much security," said Guillermo.

"Then what are we going to do?"

"Let me think . . ."

Pedro nodded up the hall. "Who's that?"

They looked back, where someone was entering the room they'd just left.

"It can't be this easy," said Miguel.

Guillermo led the way back. "We'll soon find out."

Flakes of fish food were tapped into an aquarium and spread out across the water's surface. Guppies darted. A door opened.

Jason turned around. "Who are you?"

Guillermo walked toward him. "Andy McKenna?"

Jason shook his head.

The rest of the men came inside and closed the door behind them. The butt of a Mac-10 submachine gun protruded from one of their jackets.

Jason's breathing became rapid. His eyes swung back and forth.

Guillermo smiled and stepped forward. "Is this your room?"

"No," said Jason, backing up. "Just feeding fish."

"Can I see some ID?"

"What for?"

"ID, please."

The calmness of Guillermo's tone was unnerving. Jason pulled a driver's license from his wallet and presented it with an unsteady hand.

Guillermo read it and stuck it in his own wallet. "Know where we might find Andy?"

"What's going on?"

"We're close family friends. His mother's sick."

"His mother's dead," said Jason.

"Then it's worse than we thought."

They stared a moment, Guillermo's smile broadening. Jason felt faint and almost knocked over the aquarium.

"Someone get him a chair."

Raul brought one over and Jason fell into it.

Guillermo pulled up his own and sat in front of him. "Where did he go?"

"S-s-spring break. Panama City Beach. Bunch of guys."

"You're doing great," said Guillermo, patting an arm that flinched at the touch. "When did they leave?"

"I don't know. I mean, they called me from the road. I think it was a last-minute thing."

"Where are they staying?"

Jason's mouth opened, but no sound.

"I know they told you the hotel."

Jason nodded.

"It's very important we reach him. What hotel?"

Jason still had trouble getting his mouth to work.

Guillermo leaned. "Whisper it."

Jason did.

Guillermo stood. "Now, that wasn't so hard." He noticed a clip on Jason's belt. "Give me your phone."

"Why?"

"Give me your phone."

Jason handed it over, still shaking. "What are you going to do to me?"

"Do to you?" said Guillermo, flipping open the cell. "We don't have to do anything to you."

Jason's expression said he didn't understand.

Guillermo wrote something on a paper scrap. "You're a college student?"

Jason nodded.

"Well then, you must be pretty smart." Guillermo gave the phone back. "So you probably figured out that when we want to find some-one, we don't stop, no matter how long or far." He patted his wallet, which now contained Jason's license. "And if you make us want to find you again, it'll go differently."

Jason's chest heaved.

"It's smart to forget we were ever here."

The men left.

Jason slowly rose on unsteady legs, then jackknifed over and threw up in the aquarium.

Guppy heaven.

PANAMA CITY BEACH

Three youths crowded around Serge in a church activities hall. A fourth came over. "I got your coffee."

"Thanks." Serge blew on it and took a sip. "The thing about evo-lution is needless bickering among groups who should be enjoying life together. I've noticed some people making a creationist end run with the Trojan horse called intelligent design. Except they accidentally stumbled onto something without realizing it. What you need to be marketing is self-organization."

"What's that?"

"Evolution only makes my faith stronger. Except the problem with evolution—and this is where I totally understand your objection—is emphasis on the godless randomness of natural selectivity. Like those Galápagos turtles with the longest necks were the only ones who could reach higher leaves and survive when low-hanging food was gone, so now they all have long necks. That's true, but there's more. Much more."

The youths leaned with rapt attention.

"Many evolutionary scientists subscribe to an additional component of their theory. Anyone?"

"Self-organization?"

"Shazam! Anti-religious types would have you believe that the universe follows the ol' axiom 'Given an infinite amount of monkeys, typewriters and time, one of them will eventually write *Hamlet*.'" Serge swept an arm in the air. "Look around you. That can't be right. It's more like one of the monkeys is Shakespeare in a chimp suit. All life aggressively yearns to organize itself and become more complex, springing forth from every corner of the planet. You think we started with a bunch of prehistoric ooze, and some of it just happened to turn into Bella Abzug?"

They shook their heads.

"There were some dead ends along the way, hence natural selectivity. But for my money, the rest is God in a Darwin costume. So if you can wrap your brain around self-organization, then evolution *is* intelligent design. The Lord is even greater! . . . But I'm not sure."

They got up for another pastoral visit.

"I think we've been wrong about evolution."

"What on earth's going on over there?"

"He has a lot of good points. I've never felt my faith so strong."

"You're supposed to convert him, not the other way around."

They returned.

Serge smiled again. "Warned you about going off the reservation?"

"Eternal life is only possible through belief—"

"Glad you brought that up," said Serge. "Let's talk about eternal life . . ."

The pancake feast hit its peak hour as students felt that empty beer rumble in their tummies. The pastor stood at the entrance, welcoming waves of newcomers.

"Now everyone close your eyes," said Serge. "This is what I want you to imagine . . ."

More and more students came pouring in. The pastor was smiling and shaking hands when suddenly, hysterical shrieking erupted from the far side of the hall. Everyone turned.

Serge frantically raced around the table, grabbing shoulders of uncontrollably sobbing youths. "Guys! It's all okay! Forget everything I said!"

The pastor ran over. "What did you do to them?"

One of the tearful kids looked up. "He said many people believe in God only because of the selfish reward of eternal life . . ."

Another blew his nose. "So in order for our faith to be pure, we have to *stop* believing in God."

"What!"

"Only temporarily—just long enough to imagine eternal darkness . . ."

". . . Then, once we could handle that, we were free to return and believe selflessly."

". . . My belief's never been stronger."

Serge grinned awkwardly. "Harmless experiment. I hear they do it all the time in college philosophy classes."

The pastor shot him a steely glare.

"Give me one more chance," said Serge. "I promise you won't be sorry."

CHAPTER SEVENTEEN

UNIVERSITY OF FLORIDA

ars poured out of Gainesville in all directions, past the football stadium and brick dorms.

In one of the rooms:

"Who goes north for spring break?" asked Melvin Davenport.

"We do," said his roommate, Cody. "It's Panama City Beach! MTV's there!"

"And?"

"Everybody's going to be fucking!"

"I can see why the women love you."

"Don't be a jerk. We graduate next year and we've never been to spring break. This could be our last chance."

"I don't know." Melvin sat at his desk, proofing a term paper. "You're talking about leaving right now, and we haven't done any planning. Did you even make reservations?"

"That's the whole point of spring break. You don't plan—you just *go!*"

"Why don't *you* just go?"

"Because I need your truck."

"Figured."

Cody snatched the term paper.

"Hey!"

"You'll thank me later."

NEW HAMPSHIRE

Snow seriously started coming down.

A Hertz Town Car headed south from campus. It avoided the

interstate in favor of a looping, scenic night route through empty countryside. Last homes and streetlights miles behind. Nothing but high beams and black ice on a two-laner through white-blanketed woods.

"I don't get it," said Raul. "Why'd you let the kid back there live? We never leave a witness unless there's a good reason."

"There's a good reason," said Guillermo. "I need him alive for disinformation." He punched numbers on a cell and placed it to his head. "Panama City Beach . . . Holiday Isles . . . Yes, I'd like you to connect me for a modest charge . . ." He let off the gas as the road took a series of hairpin twists down a small mountain. "Front desk? I'd like the room of Sam Jones, please . . . You don't have a Sam Jones? Well, I think Sam's his middle name. Probably registered under his first . . . No, I don't know it. You have any Joneses at all? . . . Four? What first names are they under? . . . I understand you can't give out that information, but this is an emergency . . . Okay, connect me to the room on the top of your list . . ."

"What are you doing?" asked Miguel.

"Shhhhh!" said Guillermo. "It's ringing . . . Hello? Is Mr. Jones there?"

"Speaking."

"Sam Jones?"

"No, you got the wrong Jones."

"Are you sure?"

"Who are you?"

"Mr. Jones, this is room service. Someone at the pool just charged two hundred dollars of champagne on your account. As a courtesy to our guests, we always like to verify when it's an amount that high."

"I didn't order any champagne! I'm not paying that!"

"You're not Sam Jones?"

"No, Kyle. Listen, you have to—"

"Already taken care of, Mr. Jones. We'll get hotel security right on it. Sorry for the inconvenience." Guillermo hung up and dialed again, this time for the dorm they'd just left.

Raul looked confused. "I don't understand—"

"Quiet!" Guillermo raised his deep voice an octave. "Hello? Is this Jason? . . . Jason Lavine? . . . This is Kyle Jones . . . I realize you don't know me. I'm from Boston College—just hooked up with your friends at a rest stop . . . Guess they saw 'Florida or Bust' on our windows. Anyway, I was asked to give you a call. They're switching hotels and wanted you to know in case you need to reach them. Something about feeding fish . . . Because we got a killer block of rooms super-cheap at a better place, but some of our guys dropped out, so your friends are taking up the slack . . . Holiday Isles in Panama City . . . Right, it's in my name, Kyle Jones . . . Uh, sure, it's going to be wicked excellent." He hung up.

High beams sliced through the New Hampshire night. Two glowing dots appeared in the distance. Headlights hit a small deer on the center line. It darted into trees. The Lincoln approached a bridge over a tiny creek. Guillermo carefully applied brakes on the slick surface.

"What's that business about switching hotels?" asked Pedro.

"Buying time with our government friends." Guillermo opened his phone again.

Raul lowered his electric window on the passenger side and braced himself against the abrupt arctic blast.

"Madre?" said Guillermo. "Good news . . . No, we don't have him. But our friends don't either . . ."

The Lincoln stopped in the middle of the bridge.

". . . Because I know exactly where he's headed . . . Thank you, Madre . . ."

As previously instructed, Raul began collecting automatic weapons from the other occupants and flinging them over the side of the bridge.

". . . On our way to the airport right now . . . Looks like we're going to spring break . . ."

A Mac-10 sailed into the darkness.

". . . No, they won't get there before us. At least not at the correct hotel . . . Because I made a couple phone calls . . ." Guillermo turned toward an odd sound from Raul's open window. ". . . I'll let you know as soon as we get there. Good night, Madre." He hung up. "Raul, did you check—"

"Check what?" The final gun was flung.

Crack.

Guillermo reached for the glove compartment. "Don't tell me."

Car doors opened. The gang shivered at the bridge's railing. Guillermo swept a flashlight beam thirty feet down into the chasm below, where three Mac-10s sat motionless. The fourth slowly spun to a stop on the iced-over creek.

"Guillermo, how was I supposed to know?"

"Just get back in the car."

PANAMA CITY BEACH

Four people stood on the side of the road waving signs for free pancakes. Three kids wore T-shirts with the Jesus fish. Serge flapped the fourth sign. They'd given him a shirt, too. He'd drawn feet on his fish with a Magic Marker but hadn't changed the name inside to Darwin.

A line of sporty cars came to a standstill at a red light. People hung out windows, waving drinks. "Look at the loser freaks!"

"Hey, Jesus Crispies, eat me!"

The light turned green. The cars drove off.

Serge turned with raised eyebrows. "You get that a lot?"

"All the time."

"What do you do about it?"

"Nothing."

"Nothing?"

"It's okay. We turn the other cheek."

"Good for you," said Serge.

They resumed poster waving.

Another red light. More insults.

And so on.

An hour later, a student dangled out the passenger window of a Mustang, vigorously shaking a beer. "Yo, Christian faggots!" He popped the top, spraying them with suds. "Ooops . . . please forgive me!" The car filled with cackles.

Before the passenger knew what was going on, Serge had both hands through the open window, seizing hair. The youth's face repeatedly smashed the dashboard in rhythm with Serge's instructions: *"Treat . . . others . . . as you . . . would have them . . . treat you!"*

He released his grip, and the unconscious student flopped back in his seat, blood streaming down his frat shirt. The others in the Mustang normally would have jumped from the vehicle at the welcome opportunity to whup butt, but the intensity of Serge's onslaught made them screech off instead.

Serge rejoined the stunned roadside gang. He pointed at the ground. "Dropped your posters."

"But I thought you believed that turning the other cheek was a good thing?"

"My complete quote was, 'Good *for you*.' It's just like the Bible: One must consider the overall context. Remember when Jesus went on that money-changers-in-the-temple lights-out cage match? I really like that part . . ."

Sudden yelling from behind: "Inside! Now!"

They'd never seen their pastor so angry. The foursome headed for the activities room.

"No!" The preacher pointed at Serge. "Not you!"

The remaining trio demurely ducked inside for an unprecedented tongue-lashing. "I couldn't believe what I just witnessed in the street!"

A tentative hand went up.

"What is it?" snapped the pastor.

"But nobody's ever defended us like that before."

"Violence is wrong! It's against everything we stand for!"

"You don't know what it's like out there. They say all this stuff."

"Turn the other cheek!"

"What about money changers in the temple?"

"Did Serge tell you that?"

The boy lowered his head. "Maybe . . ."

The pastor took a deep breath. "From now on, you are to go nowhere near that man!"

"But . . ."

"But *what*?"

"We . . . kind of like him. And he knows the Bible inside out."

"The devil can quote scripture with the best. He's trying to make you nonbelievers."

"Just the opposite. He said that unlike politicians and TV preachers, we're magnificent ambassadors for our religion because our faith is so pure and beautiful, and we should never stop nurturing it."

"I saw his T-shirt!" said the pastor. "He drew feet on the Jesus fish!"

"But he didn't change the name to Darwin."

"So?"

"That's the magnetic appeal of his theology: He respects all religions, then mixes and matches for himself."

"No!" yelled the pastor. "No mixing and matching!"

"Why not?"

"It's against the rules."

"But we already have. Even you."

"What do you mean?"

"He said that if Jesus and the apostles didn't mix and match, our own religion never would have gotten off the ground."

The pastor turned purple. "I've heard more than enough! My decision is final! Stay away from him! Am I understood?"

INTERSTATE 95

A station wagon with a University of New Hampshire parking decal crossed the Virginia line.

Each new state called for another beer. It was the law.

The driver crumpled a State of Maryland speeding ticket and threw it on the floor.

"What are you doing?" asked Doogie.

"When am I ever coming back to Maryland?" said Spooge.

"On the return trip, hopefully."

"So someone else will be behind the wheel."

Their drive had been touch-and-go for a while. The increased snowfall back on campus was the leading edge of an approaching blizzard that would soon hammer most of the northern seaboard. Visibility had almost stopped them in southern Connecticut, but the New England quartet pressed on and outran the system's front by Delaware.

Now, clear sailing.

Andy held a borrowed cell phone.

A phone rang in Dorchester. And rang.

Andy closed it again. "Still no answer. He's going to be worried if he tries to reach me."

"Leave a message on his machine," said Joey. "You're an adult. It's not like you have to ask permission."

"He doesn't have a machine. It's one of those answering features from the phone company."

"What's the difference?"

Andy shrugged and dialed again, letting it ring through to an automated message.

Beep.

"Hey, Dad. It's me, Andy . . ."

"You're his only child," said Doogie. "Calling him 'Dad' kinda clues him in—"

"Shut up! . . . Dad, I know this sounds nuts, but some friends and I are driving down to Florida for spring break. We'll be staying in Panama City Beach at—" Andy called to the front seat, "What's the name of that hotel again?"

"Alligator Arms."

"Dad, we're staying at—" Andy stopped at the sound of a robotic voice on the other end: *Mail . . . box . . . full . . .* From all the reporters calling nonstop for hero interviews.

Andy hung up.

Spooge glanced over his shoulder. "Why didn't you tell him the hotel?"

"No more recording time. He's going to be worried."

"*You* worry too much. If it's so important, why not try his cell?"

"Don't remember the number."

"You don't remember your own dad's number?"

"Don't need to. It's stored in my cell—I just hit his name. But *someone* wouldn't let me go back to my room."

"You'll thank us."

Doogie turned on the radio. Weather report.

"We lucked out. They're snowed in at Logan . . ."

At Logan: Agent Ramirez stared up at a screen of flight info, all delayed. He was on the phone. "We're snowed in. I'll call when I know more." He hung up and dialed again.

All around, people made pillows from rolled-up clothes and settled in uncomfortably.

". . . So keep looking," Ramirez told Oswalt, who breathed heavy as he backtracked across campus in the dark. ". . . Then start from the beginning and check every place again . . . No, I don't care how long it takes." He hung up.

Next to him, Patrick McKenna closed his own phone.

Ramirez turned. "Any luck?"

"Still no answer in his room."

"Try his cell again?"

Patrick hit numbers. The phone was on speaker mode. Someone answered. *"Agent Oswalt here . . ."*

Patrick turned. "You want to talk to him?"

Ramirez rolled his eyes. "You sure he was staying at school over the break?"

"Positive. Said he had a ton of work and needed quiet." Patrick held up his phone. "I know my son. He would have called if anything changed."

". . . Hello? Anyone there? . . . Is that you, Ramirez?"

Ramirez snatched the phone and clapped it shut. "Maybe he tried you at home."

"No, he just calls my mobile number."

"Worth a shot." Ramirez handed the phone back.

Patrick dialed again. A disconnected phone in Dorchester rang through to the answering service. He worked a retrieval menu and entered his PIN, then listened.

Ramirez saw the expression. "What is it?"

Patrick closed the phone and scratched his head. "Says he's going to Florida."

"Florida?"

Patrick nodded. "Spring break. That's not like him."

"Where?"

"Panama City Beach."

"Did he say which hotel?"

"About to, but the mailbox filled up."

Ramirez walked over to the terminal's windows. "This is a nightmare." He dialed Oswalt again and stared out at snow swirling over runway lights.

CHAPTER EIGHTEEN

THE NEXT MORNING

*B*right sunshine.

A camcorder panned toward a tall wooden wall on the beach, where the U.S. Army had set up their obstacle course. The wall had thick, knotted ropes running down the side.

The filmmaker turned off his camera and approached a recruiter. Three church youth waited in the background.

"Howdy! I'm Serge! Do you have any coffee?"

"Uh, no."

"It's okay, I brought my own. Essential for war." He unhitched a canteen from his waist and chugged. He looked around. "Where's the line?"

"Line?"

"For the obstacle course. I love obstacle courses! They're just like life! Perfect metaphors for both obstacles and courses . . . Ooooooh! Are those trophies over there for the obstacle course? I'd give anything to win a trophy!"

"Don't you think you're a little old?"

Serge did stretching exercises. "Maybe in earth years." He touched his toes. "That's why I use the outer planets, where I'm still an infant."

"I mean the obstacle course is meant for people who still meet age requirements for service."

Serge twisted side to side. "There's nobody here. The spectacle of my record-shattering technique is bound to fix that and draw an overflow crowd, boosting enlistment. What's the harm?"

The recruiter shrugged. "Then I guess you're next."

"And I want a trophy." Serge went over to the starting line, crouching and digging his toes into the beach. "You going to time me?"

The recruiter raised a stopwatch.

"Ready when you are," said Serge.

"On your mark . . . Get set . . . Go!"

Serge blasted out of his sprinter's stance with blazing speed, sand flying behind him. He raced past the tires, metal tubes, wooden ramps, water jump, monkey bars and finally the rope wall.

Recruiters stared in disbelief as Serge launched himself into the air and dove across the finish line. He collapsed, catching his breath. "What's my time?"

"You didn't do any of the obstacles. You ran around all of them."

"Exactly," said Serge. "They're *obstacles*."

"But you missed every one."

"Perfect score," said Serge.

"But you're supposed to *do* the obstacles."

"That's stupid." Serge stood and brushed off his arms. "By definition, obstacles are things you avoid. Can't believe nobody thought of that yet."

They just stared.

Serge retrieved his canteen from a table. "Which one's my trophy?"

"You didn't do any of the obstacles."

"We already went over that," said Serge. "I think that's the problem. You're enlisted. I'm obviously officer material . . ."

Farther up the beach, a large group of students circled some kind of attraction. In the middle, Coleman sat on the sand with a tangelo and syringe. He stuck the needle in the fruit and drew back the plunger.

"The key is to extract an identical cubic centimeter volume as the agent you intend to introduce. That's the most common mistake: Excess alcohol dribbles down your shirt, the authorities smell it and you're history." He squirted juice in the sand, then filled the syringe from a bottle of vodka and injected the tangelo. They heard yelling up the beach behind them.

"*Let go of me!*"

"What's all that noise about?" asked Coleman, removing the hypodermic.

One of the students stood and shielded his eyes against the sun. "Looks like those army guys are throwing some dude out in the water."

"Here's another trick," said Coleman. "One of the most important turbo-partying tools that everyone overlooks. Only ninety-nine cents." He reached in his pocket and dramatically held aloft a serrated orange plastic device.

Students took a closer look. "Isn't that a kid's citrus sipper from those roadside souvenir stands?"

Coleman carefully twisted the cutting edge into the tangelo. "Most people try to suck the doctored fruit through an unsecured aperture. Mistake number two. Big mess and more heat from the Man." Coleman stuck the sipper in his mouth and squeezed the tangelo to a flat peel. "Ahhhh! That was refreshing. And not a single valuable drop lost."

Murmurs rippled through the crowd.

"*. . . Amazing . . .*"

Behind the last row of onlookers, a trophy-less Serge walked by, filming.

"Coleman?" Another direction: "Coleman? Where'd you go?" Shuffling down the shore. "Coleman?"

BOSTON

Bedlam at the airport.

The blizzard was over. At twenty-six inches. Plows worked the runways.

Travelers pitched heated battles with ticket agents. Their win-loss record: zero to infinity. Others stared up in defeat at overhead departure screens. Status columns flashed.

All flights delayed.

Unless they were canceled.

The low-pressure front finally passed, but planes that had already taxied from the terminal were stacked twenty deep at de-icing machines by the foot of each runway.

At every gate, rows of vinyl chairs connected in single racks. All taken. A stress farm. Babies wailed, complainers complained, others phoned relatives to whine in different time zones. Candy bars, laptops, handheld video games. Some tried catching winks on the floor.

In a remote corner of the airside, a rare patch of empty seats, where agents formed an alert perimeter around Patrick McKenna, sitting with a floppy hat pulled down over his face. The sign at the gate's departure desk: ANCHORAGE.

Ramirez paced with a cell phone to his head. University administration in Durham. On hold.

Another agent walked over. "Any luck?"

"Campus security turned up something," said Ramirez. "Found one kid at the dorm feeding pets."

"Didn't Oswalt already talk to that guy?"

"Something new—" He returned his attention to the phone. "Yes, Sergeant, I'm still here . . . Under sedation? What's he doing in the infirmary? . . . I see. Did he say anything before— . . . One second . . ." Ramirez flipped open a notebook and clicked a pen. "Fire away . . ."

Other agents strained for a glimpse as Ramirez scribbled in unrecognizable shorthand. "Thanks, Sergeant. I owe you."

The rest were waiting: "Get the name of the hotel?"

"And the room. Holiday Isles, registered to one Kyle Jones." He stuck the notebook in his pocket. "We're splitting up. Johnson, Malone, Polaski: You take McKenna. The rest of us are going to Florida. Hatfield, check with the airlines." He opened his phone again.

"Who are you calling now?"

"We're not going anywhere soon with this snow. I'm getting some local people to that hotel before Madre's crew can beat us there."

Travelers grumbled. A plow went by the windows. Agent Hatfield finally returned, waving three electronic tickets. "Last seats, Atlanta."

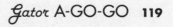

"Atlanta?" said Ramirez.

"Everyone's rebooking. It's the closest I could get without waiting till tomorrow."

"Aren't any of the bureau's own planes available?" asked another agent.

"They *all* are," said Ramirez. "Stuck in snow." He looked at the Georgia tickets. "At least we're out of here in six hours."

"Gate's at the other end of the terminal," said Hatfield.

The agents began walking.

At the other end of the terminal:

"Atlanta?" said Guillermo.

"Closest they had," said Pedro, waving tickets. "Everyone's trying to get out."

"Which is our gate?"

"That one."

They took seats, facing dim windows.

Guillermo was back on his cell. "Yes, I'm trying to reach Andy McKenna, room five forty-three . . . He hasn't checked in yet? . . . But five forty-three is his room number, right? . . . Thanks for your help." *Click*.

"Do we even know what the kid looks like?" asked Raul.

"Saw him once with his dad." Guillermo stuck the phone in his jacket. "Back in the day."

"Fifteen years ago?"

"Right, we have no idea what he looks like. That's why I just made that phone call. Ensure we have the right room."

"But if we don't know what he looks like, how can we be sure we get the right one?"

Guillermo gave him the same look he'd gotten just before they'd gone in that convenience store.

"Oh."

A row away, three agents settled into seats with newspapers and magazines.

"So Madre's people already visited the campus?" asked Hatfield.

Ramirez nodded. "That kid who feeds the pets was pretty shaken. Means they're close."

"How close?"

Behind them, Raul offered an open foil bag to Guillermo. "Chex Mix?"

A TV hung from a bracket between the gates.

The G-men and Guillermo's crew looked up.

"And for those of you snowed in back in Boston, we bring you another day of Red Sox spring training from sunny Florida . . ."

CHAPTER NINETEEN

PANAMA CITY BEACH

*B*ehind one of the beach motels, another massive event at a swimming pool. Hundreds of plastic beer cups. Students rimmed the patio ten deep.

A loudspeaker: "*. . . our next contestant. Please give it up for Coleman!*"

Thunderous applause.

Coleman wobbled to the end of the diving board with a pilot's scarf around his neck. He licked an index finger and raised it to gauge crosswind. Then he bounced twice and sprang into the air.

Enormous belly flop.

A row of judges marked scorecards for style, splash height and stomach redness.

Four blocks away, on the other side of the road from the beach, a pastor walked out of a church activity hall. He reached the edge of the street and rubbed his chin. "Where'd they go?"

He returned to the building. Leaning against the outside wall: four free-pancake signs.

"Holy . . ."

Serge stopped behind the Holiday Inn SunSpree to empty sand from his sneakers.

Church kids took seats around him on the ground. "What else do you have?"

"Well," said Serge, putting his left shoe back on. "There's Casey Kasem's *American Top Forty*. You know where the oldest lyrics ever to be heard on his show came from?"

Heads shook.

"Book of Ecclesiastes." He stood. "Adapted for the Byrds' mega-hit 'Turn! Turn! Turn!'"

"Cool."

Serge moved west up the beach, and his flock followed.

Heading the other direction, farther toward the waterline, a growing procession followed Coleman. ". . . This is the Boardwalk Beach Resort, headquarters of MTV . . . And that's La Vela, largest nightclub in the entire United States. Afternoon special: all the beer you can drink, twenty bucks, but the catch is, unless you pay extra for a jumbo plastic mug and rights to the VIP filling station"—he held a thumb and finger slightly apart—"you get these tiny cups and have to wait forever . . ."

They approached the club's entrance. Beefy guards checking drivers' licenses from twenty states. One of the kids quickly produced a wallet to pay Coleman's cover.

Pounding music greeted them on the massive party patio. The students got in a seemingly endless beer line. Another wallet came out, buying Coleman a giant mug and VIP-line status. All around: hooting and hollering. In the middle of the pool stood a concrete dance-contest island connected to the patio by a small bridge. A driving beat boomed from a 360-degree sound system as a parade of young women strutted onto the island and jiggled their rears.

Coleman found an empty table in back where the previous occupants had left empty cigarette packs and a pile of giveaway sample condoms. Students quickly cleared the surface to make space for Coleman's beer mug. It was promptly empty. He began getting up.

A student's hand on his shoulder. "Sir, we got it . . ."

"I'm never leaving this town."

For the next three hours, proxy students made perpetual trips to keep Coleman's mug full.

At the four-hour mark, Coleman and his new friends were all in the pool, lining the edge of the dance island, surrounded by hundreds of other tightly packed students holding identical orange plastic cups. As many more kids hung over balconies wrapped around the patio.

"Woooo! . . ."

"Shake it, mama! . . ."

A new contest on the island. One girl lay on her back with a balloon in her mouth. Another climbed on top, trying to pop it with her tits.

"How do they possibly think of this clever shit?"

Music started again for the next competition. An emcee whipped the crowd into a sexual froth with double entendre. Then he looked at a list in his hand and introduced the first contestant, a drop-dead biology major from the Tar Heel State, who began a grind that would shame most pole dancers.

"Coleman!" said one of the students. "What an excellent place! Thanks, dude!"

Another stunning series of the hottest coeds pranced around the island with skimpy swimsuits and contortionist moves. Illinois, Ball State, Duke. The audience roared.

"Coleman! You rock! . . . Coleman?" The youth turned to a friend. "Where'd Coleman go?"

The second student looked around. "I don't know. He was just here."

A junior from Nebraska finished her butt wiggle, and the emcee came back out. "Let's give a huge hand for Missy! . . . And now our final contestant . . ." He checked his list, and his voice became a question. ". . . *Coleman?*"

His followers erupted as Coleman strutted out. He interlaced his fingers behind his head and began thrusting his sunburnt belly.

Students banged cups on the edge of the island. *"Shake it, Coleman! . . ."*

Coleman hit the concrete stage and rocked back and forth on his stomach like John Belushi.

Everyone came unglued.

"The dude parties without a net! . . ."

SIX BLOCKS AWAY

An FBI team from Tallahassee swarmed a room at the Holiday Isles Resort.

An agent came through the door and handed front-desk phone records to his supervisor.

The guest sat on a bed. "I'm telling you, I don't have any idea what's going on."

"Your real name's Kyle Jones?" asked the agent in charge.

He nodded.

"And you say you only got one phone call? From room service?"

Another nod.

"Just stay seated."

Other agents pulled luggage apart, opened every drawer. His cell phone was checked for recent activity.

An hour later, the lead agent pulled out his own phone, dialing a number that rang in Logan Airport.

"Agent Ramirez? This is Baxter from Tallahassee. The guy you asked us to check out is clean." He flipped a notepad. "Kyle Jones, real estate broker from Oshkosh. Not even here for spring break. Said he has no idea who McKenna is or how they got his name."

"Something's not right," said Ramirez.

"I agree," said Baxter. "He's forty-three and never went to Boston College. And that business about charging champagne to his room? The hotel has no record, refunded or otherwise."

"What about the call from room service?"

"Never happened. The hotel has record of just one incoming to his room. We traced it to a prepaid disposable."

"Hold him till I get there."

"When will that be?"

"Don't know. With the drive from Atlanta, probably tomorrow morning."

"But I said he came up clean."

"Just hold him," said Ramirez. "He might be lying and working with the people on the other end of that phone, which means he was waiting in that room to ambush our guy. If not, someone's using him as a red herring. Either way I want to know the connection."

"Anything else?"

"Do a full background workup, the whole nine yards, like he's applying for Secret Service."

"You got it." Baxter closed the phone.

"Excuse me," said Kyle. "Can I go get dinner now?"

"No."

Serge had his favorite light for documentary filming.

Three church youths stood in the background as their mentor interviewed a Michigan State Spartan. The student smiled big. "I'm really going to be on CNN?"

"Haven't gotten all the bids yet," said Serge. "Please stick to the questions. You're from a prestigious university, so what on earth can you be thinking?"

The youth contemplated his answer when a fellow Spartan whispered in his ear.

"He's doing *what*?"

"Hurry up," said the second student. "It's about to start."

"Sorry," the interviewee told Serge. "I gotta run."

"What's happening?" asked Serge.

The student hopped up. "Man, if you're doing a documentary on spring break, you definitely don't want to miss this . . ."

Serge and his disciples followed the Michigan students, who were soon joined by rivers of other spring breakers streaming in from all directions.

They funneled through the back deck of a jumbo-capacity beach bar that was quickly packed beyond fire-marshal code. The chant had already begun.

"*. . . Cole-man! . . . Cole-man! . . . Cole-man! . . .*"

Serge pushed his way forward.

On the stage for the nightly band, Coleman lay on his back with a clear tube in his mouth. Three assistants continued pouring a staggering amount of Budweiser into the beer bong.

"*. . . Cole-man! . . . Cole-man! . . . Cole-man! . . .*"

"Incredible," said Serge.

"You know him?" asked one of the church youth.

"Unfortunately." He turned for the door.

"Where are you going?"

"Back to my motel room."

"Can we come with you?"

"Knock yourself out."

CHAPTER TWENTY

THAT EVENING

𝒮 top-and-go traffic on the strip. A high-mileage pickup with a Florida Gators bumper sticker rolled into town.

"Look at all the babes!" said Cody.

"We need to find a hotel room," said Melvin Davenport.

"Which one do you like?"

"We just need to find something. All the signs I'm seeing say 'No Vacancy.'"

"I ignore those."

"This one," said Melvin.

He pulled into the parking lot. Then pulled out.

"How about that one?" said Cody.

In and out again.

"Knew we should have gotten reservations," said Melvin.

"That's just the first two," said Cody. "Here's another . . ."

Ten motels later: "This isn't good."

"You worry too much," said Cody. "Something will probably open up later tonight."

"Who checks out at night?"

"Whoa!" said Cody. "Check that ass!"

"I'd rather check into a hotel."

They passed the Alligator Arms.

ALLIGATOR ARMS

Room 534.

Three kids sat on the floor around Serge.

"Never heard of that."

"It's true," said Serge. "Major first-century schism between Paul and Peter. The apostles were divided. Should the new Messiah be just for the Jews, or should the gospel also be preached to Gentiles? Arguably the most critical turning point affecting life as we know it today."

"How do you know all this stuff?"

"It's history. How can you not be fascinated?"

"Serge?"

"Yeah?"

"What's the matter?"

"What do you mean?"

"That look on your face."

"Sorry. My mind drifted into negative country. Got cheated out of a trophy today."

"When?"

"At the army obstacle course. Remember? You were there."

"Oh, you mean when they threw you in the ocean instead?"

"I guess that's second place. And I wanted it so bad. I've never won a trophy for anything my whole life. Been eating at me ever since Little League, and this morning it was so close I could taste it—"

They heard a violent slam against the outside of the motel room door. Then loud talking. Something shattered on the ground. Another crash against the door.

The students jumped. "What the heck's that?"

Serge stood. "It's how Coleman always enters a room."

"You mean the guy from the stage?"

The door flew open and banged against the wall.

Coleman stumbled in, followed by a dozen students from across the eastern United States.

Serge stared bug-eyed at Coleman's arms, overflowing with trophies. "Where'd you get all those?"

"What a great day!" Coleman walked past Serge and began lining gold statues atop the TV cabinet. "This one's for the belly flop, this is for dirty dancing, here's the chugging contest, goldfish eating—but they were only those little crackers because of animal rights people—and this is for the fat-guy sunburn, and . . . I don't remember this one. I was pretty fucked up. They just handed it to me. And I got this big mother with these three chicks . . ."

Serge walked away and plopped down next to the church youth. One of them raised a hand. "So what happened to the schism?"

"Paul prevailed and sent a bunch of junk mail to the Galatians."

"Wow."

Other side of the room: Coleman and a dozen helpers spread rolling papers across the coffee table. They picked apart buds from a half O-Z.

Coleman sprinkled liberally along Job 1.5s. "It's called the Seventh Son of the Seventh Son."

"Why's that?"

He licked a gummed seal. "You smoke forty-nine joints, then tear open the roaches and use the contents to roll seven more joints. Then you smoke those and use the last seven roaches to twist up one kick-ass doobie with such concentrated resin it'll blow your eyeballs out."

"Wow."

Someone tugged Serge's sleeve on the other side of the room. "Are you okay?"

"I can't believe he has a bigger congregation."

Coleman: ". . . Works every time. We should try it tonight."

"Sounds like an urban myth," said one of the students. "Where'd you hear about it?"

"On a Keys radio station," said Coleman. "I would have doubted, too. But you have to know the Keys—anything's possible. Then me and my friends tried it ourselves and pay dirt!"

"How'd you do it?"

"Know how police stake out certain bars at closing time for DUIs?" They nodded.

"Coleman," Serge yelled from across the room, "that stupid story's on the Internet."

"If it wasn't true before, it is now. Me and my friends did it, remember?"

"Sadly."

"Never mind him." Coleman turned back to his ring of acolytes. "My gang was tying one on at this funky Key West dive on Simonton.

Almost closing time, and Johnny Law is parked across the street as usual. So my wingman, Bonzo, staggers into the parking lot, falling down, dropping his keys, getting up, tripping over the curb, crashing into garbage cans—while the rest of us leave the bar and drive away until the parking lot's empty except for one last car."

"Bonzo's?"

"Correcto-mundo. And as soon as Bonzo starts the engine and moves an inch, blue lights everywhere. Cop gives him the Breathalyzer and he blows a zero. Then a field sobriety test. Walks a straight line, touches his nose, says the alphabet backward and forward."

"Doesn't make sense."

"That's what the cop thought. He says, 'You were falling-down drunk a minute ago and now you're sober as a judge. What's going on?'"

"Bonzo says, 'All my friends drove away without getting DUIs. Tonight I was the designated decoy.'"

INTERSTATE 95

A station wagon with New Hampshire plates blew through early-evening traffic.

Continuous snowbanks began showing small breaks until the breaks became larger than the frozen stretches. Another state line went under the headlights. Beers popped.

A crumpled speeding ticket hit the floor. "Let Virginia try to find me."

The car stopped.

Slamming doors awoke Andy McKenna in the backseat. He looked around the nightscape. Cars pulling in, tractor-trailers idling, picnic tables, square building in the middle.

He yawned and rubbed his eyes. "Where are we?"

"Welcome center."

"Florida?"

"North Carolina."

Other student vehicles arrived. Vermont. Rhode Island. Football stickers. Greek letters.

The rest of the station wagon's occupants returned from restrooms and vending machines. Doritos, coffee. They switched drivers and pulled back onto the highway. Radio low.

"... *Good, good, good! Good vibrations!* ..."

The signs began. Every few minutes. SOUTH OF THE BORDER, 112 MILES ... 105 MILES ... 98 ...

"Aren't we going to find a motel?" asked Andy.

"Absolutely not," said Joey.

"It's spring break," said Doogie.

"And?"

"You have to drive straight through all the way or it doesn't count."

SOUTH OF THE BORDER, 53 MILES ... KEEP YELLING, KIDS. THEY'LL STOP.

"When do you think we'll get there?"

"Three A.M., maybe four," said Spooge, the just-relieved driver snuggling against a backseat door with a bunched-up beach towel.

Andy opened a borrowed phone. "I'm going to try my dad again."

"You've called a dozen times now."

"I'll eventually catch him." He dialed. *Ring, ring* ... Andy noticed the numeric display. "Shoot, I must be tired. Accidentally dialed my own cell number." *Ring* ...

"Gimme that." Spooge snatched the phone away.

"Agent Oswalt here ..."

The phone folded shut.

"What'd you do that for?" asked Andy.

"We're on spring break. Chill out."

A thousand miles north, Agent Oswalt looked at the unfamiliar number of the disconnected call. He hit call.

"New rule," said Spooge, reaching for a switch on the commandeered cell. "All phones off."

Click.

South Carolina line.

SOUTH OF THE BORDER, 1 MILE.

Andy stared out the window at a giant, lighted sombrero marking the historic kitschy rest stop. "I got Mexican jumping beans there when I was a kid."

"What did you say?"

"Just talking to myself."

He lay back and closed his eyes. Snoring . . .

A wild cheer went up in the station wagon.

Andy shook his groggy head. "What is it?"

The driver pointed at a passing sign:

WELCOME TO FLORIDA.

"How long was I asleep?"

"Two states." A traffic citation ripped in half. "I just need to stay out of Georgia for seven years."

They still had a good ways down to the gulf coast. But finally, twenty-nine hours after leaving their New England tundra, the students arrived in the hot, sticky Panama City night.

"There's our hotel."

The pasty foursome stared up at a flickering neon sign of a smiling alligator standing on its hind legs. It was one of those older, animated jobs from the sixties. Every other second, the gator pumped its reptilian claws up and down like a go-go dancer.

The station wagon pulled into the parking lot. Students rolled baggage toward the office, past a newspaper box with a photo of Andy's father on the front page.

Next to the box, two students in orange-and-blue T-shirts sat sullenly on the curb, chins in hands.

Andy stopped rolling luggage. "You guys okay?"

"We didn't make reservations," said Melvin Davenport.

"That's crazy," said Spooge. "The whole city's sold out. You do realize you're not going to find anything."

Melvin gave Cody a look.

"I got an idea," said Spooge. "It's a budget motel, but it's still beach priced."

"We *could* use the extra scratch," said Doogie. "You guys have money?"

"And sleeping bags," said Cody.

"But then we're up to six," said Andy. "It's over the room limit."

"That's practically empty compared to our other trips," said Doogie.

"Room limits are just suggestions," said Spooge.

"I'll go check in," said Joey. "You two wait here so they don't see you."

The others walked the rest of the way across the lot and pushed open the lobby door of the Alligator Arms.

ALLIGATOR ARMS, ROOM 534

Loud knocking on the door.

Serge opened up. "Welcome to hell."

Two women entered with duffel bag straps over shoulders. Country began coughing. "What's all that smoke?"

City fanned the air in front of her face, staring at the dozen students toking up around Coleman. "Who are all these people?"

"Coleman likes to bring home strays." Serge reached for Country's bag. "Let me help you. Any trouble with the landlord?"

"Doesn't know yet."

"Smart thinking." Serge threw the duffel in a corner. "Skipping out on rent always prevents those sentimental farewells."

"It sucks."

From across the room: "City! Country!" yelled Coleman. "Welcome to Party Central!"

The students were agog at the sight—"They're gorgeous!" "I'm in heaven!"—and even more stunned when the women took seats on the couch next to them and grabbed joints.

"Coleman," asked one of the students, "you actually know them?"

"We go way back. Very close friends." He turned to the sofa. "Aren't we?"

"Shut the fuck up."

Serge waved for Country to come over. She handed the number to City and met him by the kitchenette. "What is it?"

"Let me give you the grand tour." He led her inside the suite's bedroom and locked the door.

Soon, the rest of the unit was silent, everyone listening to ecstatic female shrieking through the wall.

"... *Fuck me harder!* ..."

Students gulped.

The bedroom door opened and a bare-chested Serge stuck his head out, wearing a Gatorland baseball cap. "Coleman, my souvenirs . . ."

"Got you covered." Coleman grabbed an antique cigar box from a dresser drawer, walked over and handed it to Serge.

"Thanks."

The door closed. Listening resumed.

"*. . . Oh God, oh God . . . I'm almost there . . . Fuck me faster! . . . Don't stop! . . .*"

"*. . . And this swizzle stick is from Alabama Jack's. That's Card Sound Road in Key Largo for those playing along at home . . .*"

Twenty minutes later, Serge emerged with a towel around his neck and a cigar box. Behind him, Country stumbled out of the room and bounced off a wall, looking like she'd just finished a triathlon.

The couple went out on the balcony. City joined them and closed the sliding glass door. They gazed out across the calm, moonlit Gulf of Mexico.

"What a great view," said Country.

"Incredible," said City, turning to Serge. "But don't *ever* leave us stranded like that again."

"I told you it was just a big misunderstanding."

The sliding door opened. "Excuse me," said Coleman. He stuck the end of a Heineken bottle in the door frame. The cap popped, followed by foam. A student behind him made a check mark on a sheet of hotel stationery. Coleman closed the door.

City looked through the glass. "What kind of stupidity now?"

"Who knows?" said Serge. "We're in uncharted damage-deposit territory."

The trio went back inside. Coleman wedged the end of another Heineken under the TV and gave the green barrel a quick smack with his fist. A cap flew. A student made a check mark.

Serge turned to someone in a Rutgers T-shirt. "What's going on?"

"Nobody had a bottle opener, so Coleman's showing us one hundred and one ways to open bottles with *his* bottle opener."

"What's *his*?"

"The room's the bottle opener." He read the checklist. "So far he's shown us the flange method, pneumatic, heat exchange, friction damper . . . and he also got into a wine bottle with only a safety pin."

"The guy's amazing," said another student. "How does he do it?"

"Easy," said Serge. "He's been on spring break since 1977."

City rummaged through the mini fridge. "Country, screwdrivers?"

"I'm in."

"Serge?"

"Coffee."

The three huddled and watched the proceedings from the relative safety of the kitchenette. Coleman stood on a chair and raised a bottle toward the smoke detector.

City opened cabinets fully stocked with spotless plates and cups. "Impressed." She closed them. "When you offered your place, I pictured a dump."

"Got the one-bedroom suite. It has everything, which reminds me . . ." Serge opened a closet door and grabbed an electric cord. "I heard a comic say this is what separates us from animals, but I beg to differ."

"You're going to do housework?" asked Country.

"Observe." Serge plugged in the vacuum cleaner.

A beer bottle shattered on the floor, and Coleman ran and hid in the bathroom.

CHAPTER TWENTY-ONE

PANAMA CITY BEACH

$\mathcal{T}$radition continued.

Bars closed in the wee hours.

Ten minutes later, the night people appeared. Silhouettes on the beach against the edge of the surf. They stumbled through the sand, individually and in bunches of five or six, trying to find the way back to their hotels. Some made several passes in both directions. A freshman carrying a pizza box tried climbing over the locked back gate of the Alligator Arms.

Serge used low-light mode to film the spectacle from his balcony, then went back to bed.

Country opened her eyes. "Where'd you go?"

"The documentary continues."

"What's that yelling?"

"Kids on other balconies. After last call, the ones who make it back to their hotels resume partying where they're most likely to take dangerous falls."

Down on the pool patio, a night security guard in a smartly pressed uniform made rounds. His shoulder patches featured gallant eagles that projected the intimidating authority of someone who has cheap shoulder patches. He walked across the patio, helped a student up off the ground and peeled pizza from his chest. Then he returned to his post, stationary, back against the fence on the far side of the pool.

Staring upward.

At hotels in other cities, night watchmen patrol for muggings and car break-ins. In spring break towns, they're on balcony duty. Some of the cheaper, off-beach joints along the Panhandle had seen enough and didn't need the liability headaches. Balconies overlooking the pool were caged in with burglar bars or chicken wire.

These options weren't available to the higher-priced waterfront properties, where that kind of low-rent eyesore would run off a profitable slice of their rest-of-the-year clientele. Hence the guard right now behind the Alligator Arms. Tonight he had his hands full, eyes on five different balconies spread across the back of the hotel. Kegs and coolers and shouting.

He continued round-robin surveillance, scanning two seconds on each balcony. The guard saw something three floors up and dashed around the pool. He clicked on his flashlight. "Hey! . . ."

A kid sat backward on the balcony railing, swaying with a plastic cup. The beam hit the side of his face. "What the hell?" He looked down.

"Are you crazy?" yelled the guard. "Get off that."

"Sorry."

The guard went back to his post, taking deep breaths to lower heart rate. It was the same all night, every night, like monitoring a kindergarten class issued razor blades, racing to head off the next brainless crisis almost before the last had ended.

Inside Serge's one-bedroom suite, a crash.

Country raised her head. "What was that?"

"Don't know . . ." Serge listened. More bad noises, things banging. He threw the sheets off his legs. "But I have a good idea."

He went out to the living room. "Coleman?"

No Coleman.

He turned the corner. "Oh my God! Coleman! No! Don't do it!"

Coleman was on the balcony. He'd climbed atop a plastic chair, braced his left arm against the side wall and put an unsteady foot on top of the railing.

Serge ran forward. "Whatever it is, we can talk about it! This isn't the answer."

Coleman got his other foot on top of the bar, and without hesitation: "*Wheeeeeeeeeeee!* . . ." —voice trailing off as he disappeared.

Serge sprinted for the balcony.

Down below, the security guard assisted another student who'd

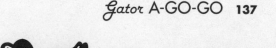

taken a nasty spill over the locked gate. His back was to the pool when he heard the explosion of Coleman's cannonball.

"Oh my God!" He ran toward the edge of the water, kicking off shoes, but Coleman cheerfully bobbed to the surface and dog-paddled toward the stairs at the shallow end. The guard switched from rescue to enforcement mode. He grabbed Coleman roughly as he staggered up the steps.

The watchman had the disadvantage of not seeing which balcony Coleman came from. "What room are you in?"

"Uh, five forty-three."

"You're in big trouble!"

Serge watched it unfolding from the balcony and filled in the coming attractions. "Damn it, Coleman!" He raced for the front door.

Country came out of the bedroom. "What's going on?"

"Just stay here."

He sailed down flights of stairs and onto the pool deck. The unamused guard led Coleman by the arm.

Serge went for the respect approach. "Is there a problem, *officer*?"

"You know this man?"

"We've met."

"Better get some bail together."

"I don't understand."

"It's a misdemeanor. I'm calling the police."

"Is that really necessary?" said Serge. "I'll take him into my personal custody. You have my word it won't happen again."

"And you're out of the room, too!"

"Wait. Stop walking," said Serge. "We can discuss this. How much for your trouble?" He opened his wallet. "I have three hundred."

"You trying to bribe me?"

"It's only a bribe if you're a real cop," said Serge. "You just got eagle patches . . . Four hundred?"

"That's it. Conversation over." The guard stepped forward.

Serge blocked his path.

"Get out of my way."

"Let go of my friend."

"Just wait till the police get here." He tried to push by. Mistake.

Serge seized the guard's wrist and yanked it off Coleman's arm.

"You need to calm down. My very strong advice is to forget any of this ever happened."

The guard was in his mid-twenties, average weight and height. Not much to bring to a fight, but he'd gotten cocky handling confrontation at the hotel since all the kids were hammered. Now he felt the latent energy in Serge's sobering grip, and self-preservation made the correct decision to keep his powder dry.

He pulled away from Serge and backed across the patio, snatching the walkie-talkie off his belt.

"Crap." It was Serge's turn to grab Coleman's arm. "Time to leave."

ATLANTA

Muzak tinkled through a hollow terminal at Hartsfield. Just the janitors. Mop buckets and ropes across restrooms. CLOSED.

The last flight from Boston taxied to the terminal, hours late. Bleary travelers stumbled through the echoing airside. Unusually alert was a team of federal agents who were met at baggage claim by a local counterpart with a company car.

They watched hanging rubber flaps for luggage to appear.

Next to them at the belt, a man in a pulled-down baseball cap checked the name tag on a suitcase, pretended it wasn't his and set it on the conveyor. It traveled thirty feet until Guillermo grabbed the handle and headed for a rental counter.

PANAMA CITY BEACH

The gals were wide awake when Serge hit the door.

"We saw you guys from the balcony," said Country.

"What the hell did that idiot do now?" said City.

"No time." Serge threw his suitcase on the sofa bed. "Collect your shit. We have to get out of here."

"I'm not going anywhere," said City. "Except back to bed."

Serge looked in her eyes. Didn't have to raise his voice. "The cops are coming."

"Shit."

He'd never seen women move so fast. In under two minutes, they'd

packed essentials. Everything else would be memory. Serge opened the door.

The first patrol car was already in the parking lot as a backup arrived. The sound of elevator doors opening. Serge saw officers step out fifteen rooms down. He jumped back, crashing into the women.

"What's going on?" asked Country.

"They're already here," said Serge. "Not fair. Four-minute response time is the minimum."

The usually cool women looked at each other in panic, then at Serge. "What do we do?"

"Say good-bye to your luggage. There's only one exit strategy." He looked across the room.

"Jump off the balcony?" said City. "Fuck that!"

"They're going to be banging on the door any second," said Serge. "If Coleman can make it . . . Coleman, you think you can make it again?"

"Eyes closed."

Bang! Bang! Bang! Bang! "Police! Open up!"

The gang looked oddly at one another.

More door banging.

Except it wasn't their door.

Thuds and voices muted by distance.

"Don't make us knock it in!"

Serge slowly turned the knob and peeked outside. Two cops continued beating on the door nine rooms up, the security guard and hotel manager behind them in the wings.

City was right over his shoulder. "What is it?"

"Unbelievable. They got the wrong room."

"How's that possible?" asked Coleman. "I told the guard where I was staying."

"What'd you say?"

"Five forty-three."

"Coleman, we're in five thirty-four." Serge wiped his forehead with relief. "Sometimes it's better to be stupid than good." He peeked again. The cops had gone inside the other room. "This is our break. Now!"

Three people ran onto the landing with suitcases.

"Where's Coleman?"

Serge looked back inside just as fleshy feet left the balcony railing again. "*Wheeeeeeeeee!* . . ."

He groaned in agony. "Why is God doing this to me?"

"What happened to Coleman?" asked Country.

Serge raced for the elevators. "Didn't get the memo on the updated exit strategy."

Meanwhile, in room five forty-three:

The guard scratched his head.

An officer repeated the question: "You absolutely sure none of them is the guy you pulled from the pool?"

"This guy I'd definitely remember."

"We weren't even awake," said Andy McKenna, pointing at the sleeping-bag-covered floor. "We haven't done anything."

"Jesus," said the manager. "How many people are staying in this room?"

"Uh, six or seven. I think."

"They might be telling the truth," said the guard. "I didn't see which balcony."

"Bullshit," said the manager. "They're hiding him like the others . . . All you guys. You're out of my hotel!"

"Don't want any trouble," said Andy. "We'll be gone first thing in the morning."

"No! Now!"

One of the officers radioed their status to dispatch. He clipped the microphone back on his shoulder and turned to the manager: "Without a positive ID from your guard, we really can't do anything."

"That's okay," said the manager. "I got it from here. Appreciate your assistance."

The officers tipped their caps and left.

Down at ground level, four pairs of eyes peered from bushes. Three dry people, one not. Fishing Coleman out of the pool had critically delayed their escape. By the time they reached the parking lot, officers were getting off the elevators. The eyes followed blue uniforms across the pavement.

Patrol car doors slammed. One cruiser drove off; a dome light came on in the other.

"Why isn't he leaving?" asked Coleman.

"Crap." Serge swatted a mosquito. "He's filling out the report."

They all gazed at the Challenger, tantalizingly close, next to the police car.

A light rumbling sound.

"Get down!" said Serge. "Someone's coming!"

A half dozen deflated students rolled luggage from elevators, the manager right behind to make sure. "I've got all your names and license numbers! Don't ever come back!" He returned to his office.

The light went off in the patrol car. It drove away.

Students surrounded a pair of vehicles in the dark lot and loaded suitcases. "What are we going to do now?"

Four nonstudents broke from the bushes and rushed for the Challenger.

"They kick you out, too?" asked Andy.

"What?" said Serge, sticking a key in the trunk.

"Kick you out." He pointed at the fifth floor. "We just got tossed for something we didn't even do. What'd they get you for?"

"Get us for?"

"Why else would anyone check out at this ungodly hour, unless—"

"Oh, right," said Serge. "Kicked out. Assholes! We should Molotov the office! What do you say? It's looks really cool at night."

Another student put his hands up passively. "All the same, we don't need any more problems right now."

"Just joshin'," said Serge. He smiled. Then he didn't. "Wait. Your voice . . . Do I know you?"

"Doubt it." He grabbed a door handle.

"Damn it!" City yelled from the backseat. "Will you fucking get in already?"

"Hold that thought." He looked back across the Challenger's roof. His eyes suddenly lit. "Melvin! You're Melvin Davenport!"

The student released the door handle. "How do you know my name?"

"Melvin! . . ." —thumping his own chest—". . . It's me, Serge!"

Melvin squinted. "Serge?"

"We played catch when you were a kid. Don't you remember?"

"No, I remember. It's just—"

"Almost didn't recognize you either." Serge looked the kid over. "Wow, you really squirted. What? Six-one, two? But barely a buck thirty. Don't fret; you'll fill out soon enough. How's Jim?"

"Dad's fine."

"And your mom?"

"Seriously pissed at you."

"Still?"

"Probably strangle me just for talking to you like this."

"Hoo, they really don't forget." Serge shrugged. "But that's the whole point of college: Doing everything that would give your mother ten heart attacks. Speaking of which, I was only half-kidding about the Molotov. You in?"

"I'll pass."

"Good idea—it's like *forever* getting that gasoline smell off your hands."

"What the hell's taking so long?" yelled City.

"Relax! Doesn't Country have a joint or something?" Serge turned back around. "Sorry. Chicks." He gestured up the empty street as pot smoke curled out the Challenger's back window. "So where you heading?"

"No clue," said Melvin. "Still hasn't sunk in that we're out on the street."

A grin spread across Serge's face. "Got the perfect idea. Swear you won't regret it."

CHAPTER TWENTY-TWO

INTERSTATE 75

A Hertz Town Car sped south through the starry Georgia night.

An exit for Robins Air Force Base went by. Raul opened a suitcase and passed out guns again.

"Keep those things down," said Guillermo, letting off the gas and watching the speedometer drop to the posted 70 limit.

"What's the matter?" asked Raul.

Guillermo glanced in the rearview. "We got cops."

A Crown Vic with blackwall tires blew by in the left lane. Behind the wheel: "I just hope we're not too late," said Agent Ramirez.

One hundred and fifty miles southwest, a '73 Challenger sped through empty farmland. It picked up I-10 in Tallahassee and headed east out of the Panhandle.

"Breaker, breaker . . ."

"Is that you, Serge?"

Serge brought the walkie-talkie to his mouth again and looked in the Challenger's side mirror. "Coleman, you're supposed to say, 'That's a big ten-four, Captain Florida.'"

"'Captain Florida'?" Coleman said into his own walkie-talkie from the backseat of a New Hampshire station wagon.

"That's my handle," said Serge.

"What's mine?"

"How about 'Lord of the Binge'?"

"Has a nice ring."

The Challenger sped down open highway, followed by the station wagon and a Dodge pickup with Gator bumper stickers. They passed Live Oak, fifteen miles before the interchange with I-75, where a Crown Vic took the westbound ramp onto I-10.

"Breaker, Lord of the Binge . . ."

"That's a big ten-seven."

"Looks like we got us a convoy!"

The three-vehicle motorcade continued east, seeing no other cars for miles. Then:

"Breaker, breaker," said Serge. "Smokey, eleven o'clock."

Everyone cut back their speed as a Crown Vic driven by Agent Ramirez flew in the opposite direction.

"We're clear," said Serge. They sped on, approaching the I-75 cloverleaf, where a Hertz Town Car passed them going the other way toward Panama City Beach.

SUNRISE

"This is Maria Sanchez with Daybreak Eyewitness Action News Seven. I'm standing here on the crystal white sands of Panama City Beach as the sun peeks over the horizon and a number of college guests appreciating our wonderful community are up extra early to take in a morning stroll . . . Here comes one of them now . . . Sir, can you tell us what you've enjoyed most about your visit?"

"I don't know where my hotel is. And I'm really drunk . . ."

Nearby, a packed Pontiac with Ohio plates arrived on the famous strip.

Ritual beers popped. *"Spring break!"*

Like so many others, the students had just completed another marathon drive that began in the snow the previous morning. They crossed the Florida line two hours before dawn and hit city limits at first light. Another impulse trip. "Who needs reservations?"

Budget motels lined the opposite side of the road from the beach. They stopped. Nothing available. Then the next. Full. The next. Sorry. And so on, until they reached the end of the strip. "We should have made reservations."

The Pontiac turned around and headed back, this time trying

the more expensive hotels on the gulf side. Same story, again and again. Looked like they'd have to head inland and find something north of town. They passed the Alligator Arms. Red neon under the sign: NO VACANCY.

A passenger in the front seat turned around. "Did you see that?"

"What?" asked the driver.

"The 'No' on the 'No Vacancy' sign just went off."

"Maybe it burnt out."

"Can't hurt to try."

They parked out of view from the office, so the rest of the students could hide.

The manager looked up from his newspaper as the door opened. One of the kids pointed behind. "Saw the 'no' go out on the vacancy sign. Is that for real?"

The manager nodded and came to the counter. "One room left. Some other kids decided to depart early."

"How much?"

"How many staying in the room?"

"Just us two."

"That means at least five."

"No, really."

"Hundred and seventy a night."

"What!"

"You're not going to find another place for fifty miles."

The students pulled back from the counter and talked it over. Then nods.

"Okay, we'll take it. Let me go out to the car and get some more money from the other three guys."

The sun rose over the hotel roof as five Ohio students rolled luggage from their car.

Next to a newspaper box, someone sat on the curb with his chin in his hands.

"What's the matter?" asked one of the students.

"No place to stay."

"Why don't you stay with us?"

"Really?"

"Wait a second," said a second youth. "Why are you inviting a complete stranger to stay with us?"

"Because he's the midget."

They took the elevator several floors up and headed down the landing toward room 543.

SOMEWHERE IN NORTH FLORIDA

Another beautiful morning.

The '73 Challenger barreled east on I-10 as a rising sun burnt off dew. Close behind, a woody station wagon and a Dodge pickup. They reached a junction in Jacksonville and headed south on 95.

The occupants of the various vehicles had been redistributed, at Serge's insistence, "to resurrect the lost art of conversation."

Serge sat behind the wheel of the Challenger. Melvin and Country had the backseat. Andy rode shotgun.

In the middle car, half the New Hampshire students and Coleman: "Brownies are the best!"

"I think smoking works better."

"Much academic debate," said Coleman. "But for my money, ingesting ensures a more complete absorption of the tetrahydrocannabinol psychoactive component. Only trade-off is a forty-five-minute delay to kick in. I'll show you when we get to Daytona."

Melvin's roommate, Cody, drove the trailing pickup, with City and Joey filling out the rest of the tight front seat. Joey yawned and stretched out his arm in a furtive gambit to put it around City's shoulders.

"I'll break it."

The arm came back.

Serge reached over and playfully punched Andy in the shoulder. "Ain't this the bee's knees? You could have been stuck in the Panhandle, but now we get to travel back through spring break history! Look at that magnificent sky! This calls for coffee!" He grabbed a bottom-weighted travel mug off the dash. His other hand reached for his walkie-talkie. "Breaker, breaker. We got the big twenty-four lookin' green all the way on the flip side."

"*What?*"

"It's a great fucking day!" He stretched an arm to Andy. "Coffee?"

"No, thanks."

"Good, 'cause I want it all!" He sucked the mug dry, then turned his camcorder on and held it out the window. "There's just something magical about setting out on the road at night and watching the sky gradually lighten until the sun arrives. Reminds me of childhood. We'd take trips to Cypress Gardens, Busch Gardens, Miami Seaquarium. For some reason, my folks found it essential to make good time and leave in pitch blackness. Our car was loaded the previous night, except for the cheap Styrofoam cooler. They started making ice days ahead and hoarded it in the freezer. Money wasn't flying around like it is today, and people couldn't justify buying bags of the stuff at 7-Eleven, which actually opened at seven and closed at eleven. Do we have any more coffee in here? Fuck it, I'll just go: Mom made piles of bologna sandwiches ahead of time and stored them in Tupperware. America forgets its heritage, but back then Tupperware parties were hugely important tribal events, like Bar Mitzvahs for Gentiles. I want that on my tombstone: 'There's nothing's more goy than Tupperware.' Did I already ask about coffee? We owned an old Rambler, and I had the backseat to myself. Nobody thought about seat belts then, let alone child safety seats, and I sat on the floor behind Dad with my GI Joes and Tinkertoys. I once made a gallows from Tinkertoys and hung a GI Joe deserter, and my parents took me to a doctor. And on the other side of the drive-train hump, behind my mom's seat, was the Styrofoam cooler of Total Joy. The back of the Rambler seemed so big then, and I was constantly moving around, as you probably guessed from my personality. Down on the floor, up on the seats doing somersaults. After a few trips, Dad wasn't even distracted anymore by everything going on in the rearview mirror: little legs whipping by, flying GI Joes who'd stepped on land mines. But best of all—climbing up and lying on the ledge by the back window! Melvin? You can lie up on the ledge if you want. I can't understate the experience."

"Don't think I should."

"Why not? Coleman does it all the time."

"No, thanks."

"Anyway, childhood's over." Serge reached under his seat. "Now vacation means a whole new adult routine." He popped the ammo clip from a chrome .45 and checked the chamber.

"What's the gun for?" asked Andy.

"What do you think?" Serge replaced the magazine. "Florida."

CHAPTER TWENTY-THREE

PANAMA CITY BEACH

*A*nother stop-and-go morning on the strip. Agent Ramirez slapped the steering wheel of a Crown Vic, caught between overloaded Jeeps of hollering, mug-hoisting students. Holiday Isles was in sight, but who knew how long?

The government sedan crept past the Alligator Arms, where a Hertz Town Car pulled into a parking space. Four men headed toward the elevator.

Ramirez's Crown Vic only rolled another hundred yards in the next ten minutes.

"Hell with this." He put two wheels up on the curb and honked kids out of the way. The sedan sped up the valet lane at Holiday Isles. Agents jumped out and ran for the entrance.

Hotel employees in blazers: "Hey! You can't park there!"

Badges.

"Please park there."

They raced to a room on the ninth floor. Three local uniforms on the balcony guarded the door. Even more crowded inside. Ten agents compared notes.

A real estate broker fidgeted in a chair. "How much longer is this going to take? I'm paying a fortune for this room!"

Ramirez entered. "You Kyle Jones?"

"Yeah. And I demand to know—"

"You don't demand anything."

Jones muttered under his breath.

"I didn't catch that," said Ramirez.

"Nothing. But I've already answered a million questions. I have no idea what's going on."

"Shut it." He turned. "Baxter?"

"You must be Ramirez."

Shook hands.

"Thanks for sitting on this for me."

"Gets stranger the more we look at it." He gave Ramirez a print-out. "That's the background check you requested. Spotless, except for mortgage-fraud lawsuits."

"So he isn't working with them after all?"

"That's how it smells."

"It stinks," said Ramirez. "He showed up on *someone's* radar."

"Can't figure the connection except the one phone call. And that's a dead end."

Ramirez stared toward the balcony. "There's got to be something."

INTERSTATE 95

The southbound '73 Challenger blew past all three St. Augustine exits. Signs for five-hundred-year-old stuff and adult video stores.

"Melvin," said Serge, "how's it going back there?"

"Fine."

Serge checked his mirror and smiled. Melvin bashfully looked at Country, who returned a confident gaze. She'd been working on a bottle of vodka and poured generously through the open tab of a half-empty can of Sprite. Then she covered the hole with a thumb and shook. "Want some?"

"No, thanks."

Country shrugged and drank it herself.

"Melvin," said Serge, "what do you think of your traveling companion back there?"

"She's okay."

"Come on," Serge chided. "I've seen the way you been looking at her."

He blushed so brightly you could almost read a map by it.

"Serge," said Country, "I think your friend's kind of cute."

"Hear that, Melvin? She thinks you're cute."

More blushing.

"Have a girlfriend?" asked Country.

"No."

"*Ever* had one?"

"Well, in grade school."

"Serge," said Country. "He's adorable."

"Why don't you ask her out?" said Serge.

"Who?" said Melvin. "Me?"

"Anyone else back there named Melvin?"

"I couldn't. I mean she, I . . . What if she says no?"

"You'll never find out unless you ask."

Melvin couldn't get his mouth to work. Country poured more vodka.

Finally: "Would you consider, you know, maybe—"

"Sure." She handed him a soda can. "You need to drink that."

This time Melvin accepted. "How'd you get the name Country?"

"'Cause I'm from Alabama."

"So tell me something about yourself." He took a sip.

"I'm Serge's girl."

Melvin spit out the drink and made a panicked retreat to the farthest corner of the car. "Serge, I didn't know! I swear!"

"Relax." Serge checked his blind spot to pull around a slow-moving horse trailer with tails flapping out the side. "Me and Country got an open thing. Ask her when she wants to go out."

Silence.

"Melvin?"

"Uh, when do you want to go out?"

Country tilted her head. "This is a kind of date right now."

"What kind?"

She just smiled.

"Andy," Serge said sideways across the front seat, "ever been to Florida before?"

"Nope. This is my first time."

"Then you're in for a real treat!"

Andy McKenna leaned his head against the passenger window, faintly recognizing old billboards for citrus and marmalade stands. His mind drifted back to a childhood in Boynton Beach and that day fifteen years ago when the men in dark suits whisked him from kindergarten . . .

. . . Staring out the rear window of their car, watching teachers run down school steps, pointing and gossiping. The school disappeared. Someone gave him a lollipop.

"Who are you guys?"

"Billy, we're friends of your father."

"Where is he?"

"Taking you to him right now."

Then unstoppable crying, no matter how many lollipops.

The cars whipped into the parking lot of a run-down motel off Southern Boulevard near the West Palm airport.

Crying dovetailed to sniffles as the convoy stopped, and the child pressed himself against the glass. Lots more men, same suits. They stood along a row of rooms and in various spots across the lot. Billy's head swiveled back and forth. No Dad.

Then a burst of action. Five men ran to the car. One grabbed a door handle but didn't open it. Others stuck hands inside jackets.

Someone gave the signal.

Out of the car. Nothing gentle. One of the men grabbed Billy under the arms. The rest surrounded them, sprinting for a middle room. Billy thought they were going to crash into the door, but at the last second it opened from inside. More men. This time he saw guns.

The door slammed behind him. In front, an agent opened another door, the one to the bathroom. Someone came out.

"Daddy!"

Billy hit the ground running for the tearful hug. His father rubbed his sandy hair and squeezed him tighter than ever before. *"You okay, son?"*

"Daddy, I'm scared."

"That's all over now. You're with me."

"Are we staying in this hotel?"

"No, we have to be leaving soon." He held the boy out by the shoulders and tried to calm him with a false smile. *"Guess what? We're going on a vacation!"*

"Where?"

"You'll get to see snow!"

Gator A-GO-GO   **153**

"Snow? I've never seen snow before!" Billy realized something and looked around. *"Where's Mom?"*

"Already there waiting for us."

Five hours of motel room life. An uneventful evening in eventful circumstance. They watched TV and ate McDonald's the agents brought in. *"Son, I know this won't make any sense to you now, but it's very, very important. From now on, your name is Andy."*

"Andy?"

"Andy McKenna."

"I don't understand."

The father pulled the boy to his chest again. He saw one of the agents give him a look.

"Son, it's time to go . . ."

At the end of a long day, a Boeing 737 touched down in Detroit. "Andy" had a window seat.

"Wow, snow!"

A hand shook Andy's arm and he jumped. "What?"

Serge gave his passenger a double take. "Didn't mean to startle, but you were zoning. Like it was something distressful."

"Just tired."

PANAMA CITY BEACH

"Think!" yelled Agent Ramirez.

"Told you, I have no idea," said the real estate man named Kyle.

A breathless field agent ran into the room. "Think we got something."

"What?" asked Ramirez.

"Call from the hospital in New Hampshire. Oswalt talked to the kid again."

"What kid?"

"Pet feeder."

"I remember." Ramirez nodded. "Madre's boys paid him a visit. Surprised he's still alive."

"Still a basket case, but coming around. He remembered something. You know how he gave us the name of this hotel and Kyle's name?"

"Yeah?"

"The hotel info was a call he got from the road."

"Right, from Andy."

"Not from Andy. Kyle Jones of Boston College . . ."

"Who doesn't exist?" said Ramirez.

"The kid back at campus never heard of this Jones before, just got a call out of the blue from a guy who said he'd met his friends at a rest stop. Upon further questioning, turns out he never spoke to anyone known personally."

"But I thought he spoke directly to Andy about feeding fish."

"That was the first call."

"First?"

"Second was from our mystery man who said they switched hotels to this one."

"Don't tell me there's another hotel."

"Alligator Arms."

Memory flash. "Son of a bitch!" Ramirez ran onto the balcony and stared up the strip. An older, unsleek building stood in the distance. Out front, a neon alligator smiled at him.

A walkie-talkie squawked. A local sergeant guarding the room grabbed it. ". . . Ten-four, Alligator Arms." He looked at Ramirez. "Sorry, something's come up." Then to other officers: "Need to roll pronto."

They sprinted for the elevators. A growing chorus of sirens approached in the distance.

"Wait!" Ramirez ran after them. "Did you say Alligator Arms?"

CHAPTER TWENTY-FOUR

DAYTONA BEACH

*A*ndy." Serge shook his shoulder again. "How can you be tired? You're a kid."

"I've been up all night." He leaned back against the door. "Let me sleep."

"You can sleep tomorrow, or the next day," said Serge. "That's when I plan to. But not now—I've got a super-special adventure planned. Anything can happen."

"Like what?"

"Daytona! It's crazy! Twenty miles of beach you can drive on, right where they used to hold the old races and land-speed record attempts. Want to go for our own attempt?"

"Not really."

"Maybe you're right, because the speed limit on the sand is now ten miles an hour. But we could always shoot for eleven and set the modern record."

"Why are we going to Daytona, anyway? We could have just hit another Panhandle town."

"Time travel!" Serge stuck his camcorder back out the window. "You've already had the Panama City experience. Daytona was the previous hot spot. A few students had been going there for years, but it seriously took off in 1985. That's when the birthplace of spring break, Fort Lauderdale, drove kids out of town with draconian laws, and they migrated north. The next year, MTV held its first spring break jamboree in Daytona, and visitor estimates hit four hundred thousand. Then the place got cash-fat and gave students another heave. Today it's back down to barely a trickle, which means plenty of driving room on the beach. I'm *definitely* going for eleven!"

"But how are we supposed to have fun if the city doesn't want us?"

"Wear biker shirts."

"Biker?"

"Town shakers now woo two-wheelers because they spend more insanely than students. If you check the chamber of commerce home page on the Internet, there are two huge motorcycle fests but not a single word about spring break. For that, you have to go to a local-merchant site angling for the wholesome crowd with something called 'Spring Family Beach Break,' which is like radiation to college students. And since the kids aren't coming in effective numbers anymore, there's no money or reason to update the old beach arcades and boardwalk, inadvertently preserving them in their original historic state, like a mini Coney Island, not to mention the venerable band shell, Florida's version of the Hollywood Bowl. I'm getting a diamond-hard boner just thinking about it. That was probably too much information."

The sun rose high as the convoy grew closer to its destination. Palm Coast, Flagler Beach, Ormond Beach. It was quiet in the Challenger. Too quiet.

Serge glanced in the rearview. "Melvin, you haven't been saying much lately."

Melvin stared straight ahead, blinking and breathing rapidly.

"Melvin? You all right? . . . Melvin? . . ."

Then something else. Something out of place.

Serge leaned for a different angle in the mirror. "Where'd Country go? . . . Country? . . ."

Her head popped up into view. "I'm still here." She disappeared again.

"Melvin, you sly dog!" said Serge, smiling in the mirror. "I didn't know you were into road-trip tradition."

PANAMA CITY

A mass of students from the beach moved into the parking lot of the Alligator Arms. Beer, music, rumors, emergency vehicles and flashing lights. Everyone looking up at crime tape across an open door on the fifth floor.

Traffic cops waved a motorcade of government sedans through the entrance. Agent Ramirez ran for the elevator. A small plane flew over the roof of the motel with an advertising banner for coconut rum.

Ramirez raced down the fifth-floor landing as coroners wheeled another sheet-covered stretcher the other way. Police met him outside the room.

Only one question on his tongue: "IDs?"

A sergeant checked scribbled notes, rattling off five names gathered from out-of-state drivers' licenses.

"No Andy McKenna?"

The sergeant shook his head. "But that name sounds familiar." He called to a corporal. "Ray, where did I hear the name Andy McKenna?"

"That's who the room was registered to. Or was."

"Then where is he?" said Ramirez.

"Got kicked out yesterday."

"What for?"

"We went back and looked at last night's incident reports. Someone almost killed himself diving into the pool from the balcony," said the corporal. "It's a bit of a problem around here. Especially with the more educated types."

Ramirez felt himself slipping through the looking glass. Another stretcher rolled out the door. He raised the crime tape and ducked inside.

Walls a splatter fest. Local cops among themselves: ". . . Never seen anything like it . . ."

Ramirez had. Miami. The good ol' days. "Only one person could be behind this."

"Who?" asked his top assistant.

"Guillermo."

"Guillermo?"

"Madre's lead boy. Calm, calculating, complete psychopath. No conscience whatsoever." He quickly called a huddle with his team. "McKenna's still out there. As soon as the victims' names hit TV, Guillermo's crew will know they missed the target and come back. Call every hotel in the city, see which one he switched to. Question all other guests staying here and canvass the staff. Get out an APB on Andy, but for law enforcement eyes only. No press or it's up for grabs. Go!"

They dispersed.

Ramirez walked onto the balcony and dialed his phone. ". . . Need you to track a credit card for me . . . Andrew McKenna, address either Dorchester or Durham . . . And this is important. Except for you and the chain of command, nobody is to see it but me . . ." He didn't say why, didn't have to. An informant in the house.

"Thanks . . ." Ramirez hung up and looked down over the railing at an extra-tiny chalk outline on the patio.

Part Two

DAYTONA BEACH

CHAPTER TWENTY-FIVE

DAYTONA BEACH

*T*he Challenger drove slowly down route A1A. Serge scanned motels.

No vacancy.

"It's just like the Panhandle," said Melvin. "We're not going to find a place to stay."

"Something will open up."

"*Breaker, breaker,*" said Coleman. "*Why do they call it Daytona, anyway?*"

Serge keyed his own walkie-talkie. "Lord of the Binge, keep that childhood wonderment torch burning! Most people sell children short, saying how cutely they notice the little things, when they're actually noticing *big* things. Adults can live someplace three decades, and you ask, 'How'd your town get its name?' and they say, 'I dunno.' Then they shit on the children."

"*So how* did *it get its name?*"

"From Matthias Day, who established the city, 1870. Came *this close* to calling it Daytown or Daytonia."

"*Where do you find all this junk?*"

"Same as Panama City: the books of preeminent historian and local treasure Allen Morris, clerk of the House, 1966 to 1986, papers now preserved at Florida State."

Serge let off the gas, slowing further as they approached a single-story mom-and-pop motel. "This looks promising."

"But the sign," said Melvin. "'No Vacancy,' like all the others."

Serge pointed at a dozen students in the parking lot, cursing and throwing luggage in trunks. *"Can't believe we got kicked out."*

The Challenger turned up the drive as the others sped off.

In the office window, someone flipped No Vacancy to Vacancy.

"Where's my credit card?" said Andy.

"I gave it back to you," said Joey.

"No, you didn't."

"Thought I did."

"You lost it? Great."

"No problem," said Serge. "I'll cover it—pay me when you can." He got out of the car and came back with sets of keys for two adjoining efficiencies at the Dunes. City and Country took number 25, and the students made another crack deployment in 24. Minutes later, the room was ready for mayhem.

Serge replaced batteries in his digital camera and headed for the door. "I'm going on photo safari."

Coleman pulled out oven mitts. "I'll hold down the fort."

In camera mode, Serge always made absurd time on foot, starting with a dozen shots of the blue-red-and-yellow brick sunburst mosaic in the intersection of Atlantic Avenue and International Speedway Boulevard. Then, rapid succession: Tailgaters Sports Bar and Grill, Bubba's, *two* catapult rides like Panama City, Mardi Gras arcade, historic arched entrance for beach driving, the pier, *under* the pier, aerials from the gondolas, the Space Needle, back to earth again, surfers, traffic signs in the sand:

Do Not Block Vehicle Lanes.

He accelerated down the boardwalk through an aroma of carnival food—corn dogs, elephant ears, cotton candy—and the casino-like clatter from inside the dark, open-air game rooms: pinball, Skee-Ball, foosball, fortune-telling machines . . .

Back at the Dunes. Students gathered 'round Coleman, whipping brown batter in a mixing bowl. "Rule number one: Keep baking supplies in your luggage at all times—and an electric pepper mill." He left the stirrer sticking straight up in the bowl and opened the top of the grinder. "This is critical." Coleman pulled a plastic bag from his pocket and dumped a half ounce of killer red-bud in the cylinder. Then he replaced the top, held it over the mixing bowl and hit the power switch. Mechanical whirring began as a fine, sweetly pungent dust fluttered down into the batter. "For maximum release and consistent dosage, the particles must be of weaponized fineness."

"I still can't believe this is better than bong hits."

"Believe it," said Coleman, stirring again. "Slow-cooking effect and batter medium retains ninety-nine percent potency. Just remember it's got a delayed kick-in, but well worth the wait. Almost like tripping." He held out a hand. "Baking tin . . ."

A student slapped it in his paw. Coleman emptied the bowl's contents into the pan and slid it inside the efficiency's preheated oven . . .

A half mile away, Serge reeled off another burst of roadside photos—swimsuit shacks, pizza shacks, head shops, NASCAR restaurants—until he'd come full circle back to the motel parking lot. He climbed in the Challenger and pulled a map from the sun visor. Across its folded top:

The Loop.

"I've wanted to do the Loop my entire life! And now the moment's here!"

He peeled out and sped north.

An oven timer dinged inside room 24 of the Dunes. Coleman removed the tin with oven mitts and set it on the counter. A student reached.

Coleman grabbed the wrist. "Have to let it cool. Got anything you need to do?"

"Hit a pawnshop. We're almost out of money."

"Let's rock." Coleman threw mitts on the counter. "It'll be ready when we get back . . ."

. . . Serge sped north on A1A, camcorder running on the dash, up along Ormond Beach's inspired seaside, west through Mound Grove, taking Walter Boardman Road to Old Dixie Highway and south again, down into unblemished old-growth Florida. Nothing but oak-canopy two-lane and marshland overlooks. Serge held the camera next to his face for narration: "The Loop isn't particularly known, even among Florida residents, but the pristine twenty-

two-mile route is nationally famous among the motorcycle community . . ."

A column of two dozen Harleys thundered past, Serge videotaping, honking and waving.

His camera captured the bikers as they swerved back in front of him and reconstituted standard safety formation, staggered left-right on the sides of the lane to avoid potential traction loss from car-fluid drip down the center. ". . . But now subdivisions and golf courses threaten the works, and back-road enthusiasts from all over rush to catch her while she lasts . . ."

FIFTEEN YEARS AGO

Luxury cars filled the driveway of a modest Spanish stucco house south of Miami.

No food on the long cedar table in the dining room. There had been a cake, for Guillermo's twentieth birthday, but its empty platter of crumbs now leaned in the kitchen sink.

Festivities over. Down to business.

In place of the cake was paperwork running the length of the table in evenly spaced piles.

Another family meeting.

Juanita was there, along with her two older brothers, who were running things. Guillermo and a few other young men knew to keep their mouths shut and learn.

"What about these prospects?" asked Hector, the eldest.

"All solid, very experienced," said Luis, next in line, who oversaw the clan's data collection.

Hector bent over and placed palms flat on the table, scanning reports. "Any openings?"

"Maybe," said Luis. "A couple have typical issues, though not severe enough to gain a foothold. But this one"—he tapped a page in the middle—"very promising."

"Gambling?"

"Into our Hialeah friends for thirty large after doubling down on *Monday Night Football*."

Hector handed the pages to Guillermo. "You know what to do."

Guillermo nodded respectfully, picked up a briefcase by the door and left with the other silent young men.

THE PRESENT

Four Harleys roared south into Daytona Beach.

They throttled down and parked at the curb. Each rider had a petite female passenger dressed entirely in leather hanging on from behind.

The women hopped off and removed black, Prussian-style helmets, revealing four heads of snow-white hair. All in their nineties. A club of sorts. Edith, Eunice, Edna and Ethel. The media had dubbed them the E-Team a while back when their investment klatch outperformed most mutual funds and made national headlines as a feel-good story patronizing old people. The women never took to the name and definitely not the cutesy "granny" references of TV hosts. So they turned those last remarks on their head for their own self-imposed nickname.

The G-Unit.

Edith tucked a helmet under her arm and stepped onto the sidewalk. "Thanks for the ride, Killer."

"Yeah," said Edna. "The Loop was even more beautiful than you described."

Killer politely tipped his helmet visor. "Anytime, ladies."

Eunice waved. "Keep the wind at your back!"

Harleys rumbled away.

The women walked up the sidewalk. "Bike Week's over," said Ethel. "Shit."

"What do we do now?" asked Edna.

"How about spring break? We're in Daytona Beach. And it's spring."

"I heard kids don't come to Daytona anymore. They go to Panama City."

"Some still do."

"I haven't seen any."

"What's it matter? We'll do shots without 'em."

"But I want to look at ripped chests."

"There's some kids now."

"Where?"

"Coming toward us."

The women veered for the right side of the sidewalk to make room for Coleman and his followers.

Andy jumped.

"What's the matter?"

He turned around. "Someone goosed me."

The guys crossed the street and pushed open the door to Lucky's Pawn.

Ting-a-ling.

The manager smiled. "Buyin' or sellin'?"

"Selling."

Class rings came off fingers.

The manager laughed. "Should be a betting man." He thoughtfully examined each, announcing price as he set one down and picked up another.

"Can't you go any higher? The Dunes are gouging us because we didn't have reservations."

"Market's glutted in every spring break town. Even the old ones." He pulled three velvet display trays from under the counter. "I keep the best in these. Beat-up ones go there . . ."—he pointed back at two brimming metal pails near the waste basket—". . . for melting."

More haggling that didn't work.

The students reluctantly accepted crisp twenties that the manager counted out in their hands. "And I'll need your drivers' licenses."

"What for?"

"Have to file all sales with the police department within twenty-four hours."

"Who steals class rings?"

"Nobody. But they'll pull my permit if I don't."

Students reached for wallets. "That's a lot of paperwork."

"Used to be, but now it's all computers. I file instantly so there's no misunderstanding."

Back at the Dunes, Serge unlocked room 24. "Coleman! I finally did it! I finally rode the Loop! . . . Coleman? . . ." He walked to the balcony and back. "Where'd everyone go?" He sniffed the air. "What smells so good?"

Serge traced the scent to the kitchenette. "Oooooh! Brownies! My favorite!"

CHAPTER TWENTY-SIX

PANAMA CITY BEACH

*T*he shore was packed again by noon. Bikinis, boom boxes. Frisbees and footballs flew along the waterline behind the army obstacle course. Guys dug holes to keep beer cool.

A ten-man camera team zigzagged through the giant quilt of beach blankets, all wearing identical red T-shirts: GIRLS GONE HAYWIRE.

Everywhere they went, young women reached for their chests.

Rood Lear led the way. "This is even better than last year." He turned to his newly promoted chief assistant. "Sisco, we getting all this?"

"Need more cameras."

"And I thought five would be plenty."

On the other side of the hotels, a series of SUVs and minivans pulled off the road. Middle-aged women jumped out with posters and rushed the beach.

The film crew continued south, bikini tops coming off everywhere.

Then jackpot. An entire sorority stood up in a row.

"Perfect," said Rood. "Have them take 'em off in sequence like the Rockettes . . ."

Sisco gave the instructions. "Roll film. On three . . . One, two . . ."

Angry shouting in the background.

"Where's that coming from?" said Rood. "It's wrecking our take."

Yelling grew louder as cameras panned a row of bare chests. The chief assistant pointed toward a break between hotels.

"Oh, no," said Rood. "Not them again."

The older women ran down to the blankets and stood behind the sorority, waving signs over their heads:

MOTHERS AGAINST GIRLS GONE HAYWIRE.

"Exploiters!"

"Go home!"

"What if they were your daughters?"

The cameras turned off.

"I think we need to move along," said Rood.

Behind every hotel, it just got worse and worse. Yelling moms ruining all the shots. For miles up the sand, picketers relentlessly dogged the crew.

"They just don't give up," said Sisco.

"It's so unjust," said Rood. "What did I ever do to them?"

"Maybe this is a good time to audition for in-room sessions."

"Not a bad idea."

The crew began checking IDs and handing out waivers on clipboards.

Same song, different verse.

"You'll ruin your life!"

"Don't sign it!"

"They're just using you!"

Clipboards came back unautographed.

An hour later, protesters stood in a resort hotel parking lot, cheering as the custom GGH motor coach drove away in surrender and out of Panama City.

DAYTONA BEACH

Coleman reached in his pocket for the room key.

"Still think we should have held out," said Spooge. "Twenty bucks for a five-hundred-dollar ring."

"You saw those pails."

"This will soon make it all better," said Coleman, opening the door. "It's brownie time!"

They went inside.

"Hey, Serge."

Serge sat on the couch, reviewing video footage. "Where'd you guys go?"

"Pawned class rings." Coleman went into the kitchenette and froze. "Holy shit! Half the brownies are gone!" He looked toward the sofa. "Serge, please tell me you didn't eat all those brownies."

"Sorry. I was hungry." He set the camera down and picked up a book of vintage Daytona postcards. "And they smelled so good."

"Serge!"

"What's the big deal? If it means that much, I'll buy some fresh ones from a bakery."

"That's not what I'm saying. Those were laced with ferocious weed."

"You mean marijuana?"

Coleman ran over. "Serge, you just ate the most pot brownies I ever heard of in my entire life."

"I don't feel anything."

"How long ago did you eat them?"

"Maybe twenty minutes? Why?"

"There's a delayed effect."

Serge went back to his postcard book. "I'm probably impervious. My metabolism and all."

"An elephant can't eat that much and not be affected."

Serge wasn't convinced. He held a magnifying glass over Model Ts driving on the sand. "So when is it allegedly supposed to kick in?"

"Believe me, you'll know."

FIFTEEN YEARS AGO

The day moved into a warm, blustery afternoon. A tattered orange wind sock snapped on a flagpole. It swiveled east to south.

A Cessna cleared a chain-link fence at the end of the runway and made a wobbly landing in the sudden crosswind. The pilot taxied to safety. Other single-engine planes were covered with tarps, secured to mooring posts on a concrete storage slab behind the hangar.

It was another of the many small landing strips west of the turnpike that characterized south Florida, this one slightly nicer than most because it catered to Coral Gables.

Inside the hangar, a second pilot stood on a small ladder, working under the hood.

A BMW turned through the open gate on the far side of the airstrip and sped across the runway. Four men in tropical shirts got out.

The pilot finished replacing a manifold and wiped oily hands on a rag. He climbed down from the ladder and stopped when he noticed visitors standing in a line.

The tallest stepped forward. "Cash Cutlass?"

"Who are you?"

"Want to rent a plane," said Guillermo. "And a pilot."

"Sorry, fellas, I'm not for hire."

"You are," said Guillermo. "Just don't know it yet."

"If you're looking for sightseeing, I can recommend—"

"We're not tourists. We need a shipment delivered."

"*Oh*," said the pilot. "Then I'm definitely not for hire."

"Heard you like football," said Guillermo.

"What?"

"Too bad about Monday night. Seemed like a lock."

The pilot went white and stumbled backward. "Listen, I told Ramon I was good for it. Just need a few more days."

Guillermo smiled.

"I swear." The pilot kept retreating. He placed a hand on the tail rudder. "I'll sell the plane if I have to."

Guillermo took another step.

"This isn't necessary," said the pilot. "You don't have to do this."

Guillermo set something on the ground next to the plane. Then he went back and rejoined the others.

The pilot looked down. "What's the briefcase for?"

"You."

"Me?"

"Found it outside the hangar," said Guillermo. "Must have misplaced it."

"It's not mine."

Guillermo just smiled again. He turned and led the others back to their car.

"Hey!" the pilot called after them. "I'm telling you it's not mine."

The BMW drove off.

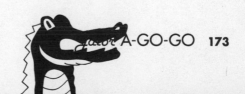

It was empty and still. The wind sock drooped. Cash stared at the briefcase for a good ten minutes. Then he knelt and flipped latches.

The pilot thumbed packets of hundred-dollar bills. Heart racing. Not from fear. Junkie anticipation. He finished tabulating and placed the last pack back in the briefcase. Enough to cover his losses, and some more to play with. He dialed his cell.

"Ramon? Me, Cash. Give me a nickel on the Dolphins . . . Hold on . . . I can explain . . . Will you stop yelling? . . . Just stop shouting one second . . . I got it all . . . What's it matter to you? . . . Let's just say it fell out of the sky, even cover this weekend's Miami parlay, which you won't be seeing after Marino picks apart the Jets . . . I'm at the hangar . . . Right, it's all with me . . . I'll be waiting."

And that's how Cash Cutlass found himself in the delivery business.

The whole proposition had become tricky with the government's beefed-up shore patrols and AWACS surveillance flights. So it turned into an island-hopping exercise. Aruba, the Caymans, Dominican Republic, and finally the Bahamas, where small fishing boats brought product ashore on South Bimini, because it had a dusty airstrip and Cash's waiting Cessna. But even with the island shell game, dueling the DEA was still an incredible risk.

Perfect for a gambler.

THE PRESENT

Agent Ramirez hadn't slept. Good thing Waffle House served breakfast twenty-four hours. He sat in a back booth on the Panama City strip. Table covered with worthless anonymous tips.

He strained to see some type of commotion on the other side of the street.

A waitress refilled his coffee.

"Excuse me, miss. Do you know what's going on out there?"

"Mothers Against Girls Gone Haywire just ran the film crew out of town. They're celebrating."

She left. Starched shirts came through doors.

Ramirez looked up. "Tell me it's good news."

"It is." An agent unfolded a fax. "Got a hit from that APB."

Ramirez grabbed his coat. "Credit card?"

He shook his head. "But might as well be."

"So he's where?"

"We don't know."

"How's that good news?"

"We're close. A pawnshop—"

"Pawnshop?"

"Required by law to get photo ID from everyone who makes a sale, then submit lists to police. That's how we found him. McKenna pawned his class ring."

Ramirez threw money on the table. "How far? This end of the strip or the other?"

The agents glanced at each other.

"Well?"

"A little farther than that."

CHAPTER TWENTY-SEVEN

DAYTONA BEACH

The balcony of room 24 at the Dunes was jammed with students. Just like many other balconies at all the other hotels. The reason was down on the shore.

Wild yelling.

It came from the direction of the beach driving lanes. Slow traffic in the sand: Mustang, Cougar, Nova, Hornet, Fairlane, GTX, Dart and, of course, a perfectly restored 1969 Dodge Charger Daytona, cruising between 10 mph signs. Muscle cars all. Almost all.

The exception was in the middle.

"Woooooo!" yelled Serge. "I'm doing eleven! I'm doing eleven! I've set the modern record!"—no car, running up the beach, steering with an invisible wheel.

Lifeguards intercepted him.

"Sir, are you feeling okay?"

"Where's the presentation stand? Matthias Day. Allen Morris. The Loop. Shit on the children. Are you getting all this? Are you from the Answer Tunnel? What happened to Space Food Sticks? Bosco, Tang, Trix are for kids, Genesis, sodomy, Elvis, *viva Viagra*! Kill those limp-dick motherfuckers! At the current rate, our economy will eventually be based entirely on phone minutes. Nothing else except the care and feeding of minute providers and users. Vocabulary Mash-Up Party Volume Seven: ennui, insouciant, de rigueur, cross the Rubicon! What the hell did Coleman do to my brain?"

Students pointed from balconies. "He's on the move again."

"What are the lifeguards doing now?"

"Same thing we are. Watching."

Down on the beach, lifeguards stood with hands on hips as Serge ran in wild figure eights in the sand.

"Can't catch me!" yelled Serge, whizzing by. "Try to catch me! Can't catch me! . . ." He ran up to the guards. "Okay, you win." He placed an index finger under his right eye and pulled the skin down. "Psych!" Then off in another figure eight. "Can't catch me! . . ."

FIFTEEN YEARS AGO

Another meeting in the Spanish stucco house. Another spread of paperwork across the cedar table.

"They all look too solid," said Hector. "I don't see any weaknesses."

"Because there are none," said Luis. "Every last man an upstanding citizen."

"Thought you said we had something very promising."

"We do—"

"I don't understand," interrupted Guillermo. "Cash Cutlass has a perfect delivery record. Why do we need to switch pilots?"

The brothers bristled at the silence-rule violation. Juanita intervened because Guillermo was her favorite.

"It's been six months," she explained.

Guillermo's face said he still didn't get it.

"There's an expression in the stock market," Juanita continued. " 'Everybody who makes money always sells just a little bit too soon.' In our business, if you want to *stay* in business, you sever relationships while everything's still smooth and no chance for the feds to turn someone. Six months, no exceptions. The principle has served the family well."

Guillermo began to nod.

"Can we?" Luis snapped at his sister.

A glare in return.

"You were saying?" asked Hector.

"This one." Luis passed a stapled packet to his brother.

"If not a weakness, then what?"

Luis told him.

"Interesting." Hector rubbed a finger over an eyebrow. "Moral dilemma. I like it."

"Just has to be played differently."

Hector handed the pages across the table. "Guillermo, you're chatty today. Think you can talk him into it?"

THE PRESENT

Perry, Florida. Between everything and nowhere.

The town of six-thousand-and-falling sits inland, at the state's armpit, as the Panhandle swings down into the peninsula. It's a long drive from any direction, Tallahassee, Tampa, Ocala, Jacksonville.

Maps show other small towns in surrounding counties, but they're not really there. The region's main industry is lapsed cellular reception.

Most people's experience of Perry is waiting at traffic lights on the way to somewhere else, not seeing a soul, an evacuated dead zone giving little reason to stop.

The perfect place to hide out.

Guillermo and his crew had taken a strategically convoluted route out of Panama City Beach. Up to Blountstown, down through Port St. Joe and across Ochlockonee Bay to a prearranged drop spot in Panacea, where a Miami associate had been dispatched to swap their rental for an Oldsmobile Delta 88, which continued east and was now the only car in the parking lot of the Thunderbird Motel.

Rooms had dark wood paneling and anti-skid daisy stickers in the shower.

They had been instructed not to set a toe outside until getting an all-clear from the home office. Standard procedure, like the other times: Stock up on cigarettes, decline maid service, order pizza. The guys sat on dingy, coarse bedspreads, playing cards and passing a bottle of Boone's Farm. Miguel slapped the side of the room's original color TV, whose color was now raw sienna.

Guillermo hushed the others for a crucial phone call.

". . . Madre, it's me. Good news. We concluded our business meeting. It's finally over."

"No, it isn't," said the voice on the other end.

"What do you mean?"

"Guillermo, I'm very disappointed in you."

"I don't understand."

Juanita stood in her south Florida living room, watching CNN with the sound off. "They just released the names. None of them is our friend."

"That's not possible. I was thorough."

"Sure you had the right room?"

"Definitely. Got the number from a kid back at his dorm."

"And you just took his word for it?"

"No, I did like you taught—double-checked by calling the front desk from the airport, then confirmed again when we got into town."

"What a mess," said Juanita. "It's all over the news."

"It isn't the first time our work has been on TV."

"Guillermo, Guillermo . . ."—he could picture her shaking her head over the phone—". . . We always must take into account public relations. You brought me heat without a fire."

"I'm so sorry, Madre. I promise I'll make it up to you."

"I haven't any doubt," said Juanita. "No matter what I say to you about business, you will always be my favorite."

"Madre, I just need a little time to find out where he is."

"I know."

"Thank you for understanding."

"No, I mean I know where he is."

CHAPTER TWENTY-EIGHT

DAYTONA BEACH

*W*e should take up surfing," said Edna.

"But we don't know how," said Edith.

"That's why it's called 'taking it up.' " She looked down a hundred feet at a handful of surfers in black wet suits trying to milk meager East Coast waves breaking off the Daytona Beach Pier. "It looks easy."

The G-Unit continued out over the Atlantic Ocean in a pair of ski-lift-style gondolas that chugged slowly over the length of the pier and headed back to shore.

"Doesn't this thing go any faster?" said Eunice.

"It's a gondola," said Ethel.

"This ride bites."

As the cable cranked down to the docking station, a sudden, distant scream.

"What was that?" said Eunice.

"Up there." Ethel pointed. "Those kids."

"Now *that's* a ride!"

Moments later, the G-Unit members each had twenty-five dollars in hand.

The ride's operator collected money and pointed at a stack of plastic bowls. "Put all your personal possessions in those."

"Why?"

"You don't want anything flying off."

Ethel and Edna went first.

"*Wheeeeeeeee!* . . ."

The remaining gals shielded their eyes, squinting up into the bright sky as an open-air ball sailed up until it was a tiny dot. It reached the ends of its bungee cords and jerked back down. Then up again, down, bouncing over and over with decreasing range until it ran out of steam.

The ride's operator stepped onto the platform and raised the padded safety bars. The women climbed down.

"How was it?"

"Mind-fucker!" said Ethel.

The others' turn on the Rocket Launch. The operator locked the safety bars over Eunice and Edith. "Sure you put everything in the plastic bowls?"

They nodded.

He went back to his control station. "Ready?"

"Hurry up before we croak."

The catapult released.

"Wheeeeeeeeee! . . ."

At the top of the arc, Eunice covered her mouth and looked up at a jettisoned piece of space debris heading for orbit.

"What was that?" asked Edith.

"My dentures."

Edith looked at the safety bar and into the tiny camera filming them. "I'm definitely buying this video."

Down below, Coleman led the students across the beach. ". . . I once bought a modified Frisbee from a head shop that had a secret pot chamber in the middle. It was called Catch a Buzz . . ."

One of the kids looked up at faint screams. "Hey, check out those old ladies."

They continued through the sand. A rescue team from *Ocean Cops* ran by with paramedic bags. They knelt and rendered aid to an unconscious young coed from Vanderbilt with a bloody forehead wound where dentures were embedded.

Johnny Vegas sat in the background, tears trickling down his cheek.

FIFTEEN YEARS AGO

"What do you mean a preexisting condition!"

Randall Sheets caught himself and lowered his voice on the phone.

"It was not preexisting. She was in perfect health when we bought the policy . . . What? She already had it and we just didn't know? That's garbage! . . . But I don't have the money and she's going to die without treatment . . . Could you repeat that? . . . It's classified as uncovered hospice care instead of corrective medicine? . . . Now you're just making up reasons . . . Look, don't think I won't sue . . . Why can't you talk to me anymore? . . . What company directive? . . . Because I mentioned litigation I can only talk to your attorneys from now on? . . . Wait! Don't hang up!"

Click.

Randall slowly closed the phone.

"Honey . . ." The voice came from down the hall. Randall entered the master bedroom, his weak wife propped up on pillows. "Who were you talking to?"

"Nobody important."

"Insurance people again?"

Randall pulled up a chair. "I'll take care of it."

"Aren't you supposed to be somewhere?"

He lightly grabbed her hand. "I'm supposed to be here."

"I'll be fine. You should go to work." She smiled. "It's not like we need the money or anything."

"But—"

"Go ahead." She grabbed a remote control. "One of my shows is coming on."

Randall drove across town with a head full of thoughts.

An hour later, a Cessna came into view. It cleared the fence of another private strip, this one in southern Palm Beach County. The landing was more than shaky, skipping twice before the wheels stayed down for good. No cross draft.

The propeller slowed to a jerky stop. Randall removed headphones and turned to the dermatologist in the passenger seat. "Not bad for a first landing. Same time next week?"

They climbed down from the four-seater with cursive lettering on the side:

Tradewinds Flight School.

The student hopped in a Corvette and sped off. Randall headed the other way for his own car. Next to it, four men with arms crossed leaned against the front of a BMW.

"Randall Sheets?"

"How can I help you fellas?"

"We need to hire a plane."

"You want flying lessons?"

Guillermo shook his head.

"Then what?" asked Randall.

"We'll get to that later." Guillermo bent down and released a handle.

"What's the briefcase for?"

"You."

Randall hadn't been in trouble a day in his life, the proverbial community pillar, as far removed from criminal circles as one gets. But he'd also been a pilot in Florida during the eighties, and he'd seen this movie before—what temptation had done to other pilots he'd known.

"I think you should leave."

"How's your wife?"

Randall's expression changed. "What about my wife?"

"If we're going to be friends—"

"We'll never be friends! Leave! Now!"

"Have we offended you in some way?"

Randall reached in his pocket, "I'm calling the police."

"That won't be necessary." Guillermo opened the BMW's driver-side door. "We're late for an appointment."

The others piled back in.

"You forgot your briefcase," said Randall.

"No, I didn't." Guillermo started the car. "Give my best to Sarah."

They drove off.

Randall stood motionless and stared down at the brown leather case for what seemed like an eternity. Brain racing. He finally crouched, set it on its side and slowly raised the lid. Breathing shallowed. Then he heard something, like a far-off explosion.

Randall looked up through yellow aviator glasses at the clear southeastern sky: a tiny fireball smaller than a dime a thousand feet above the horizon toward Bimini. At a range of thirty miles, the sound of the blast still carried, but nothing like what the boats below in the Atlantic heard as twisted metal fluttered into the ocean from a Cessna registered to Cash Cutlass.

Coleman and followers continued along the Daytona shore.

"What's going on over there?" A student pointed up the beach. "Looks like a concert or a fight. There's a big crowd."

And getting bigger. Word spread about something happening at the historic band shell. People running over from the hotels, the water, the bars.

Coleman's gang arrived at the back of the audience. Someone in a necktie took notes. A press ID hung from his neck. Davis.

"Why are you taking notes?"

"I'm a reviewer for the *News-Journal*"—not taking eyes off his steno pad.

"What's the deal onstage?" asked a student. "Is that some DJ warming up for a band?"

The reviewer shook his head and kept writing. "Incredible monologuist, like Eric Bogosian or Spalding Gray. He's been going nonstop for over an hour. I don't know how anyone can jump rapidly between so many topics and keep it all straight, let alone memorize an act this disjointed and long."

"I didn't know they had monologuists on the beach," said a student.

"Neither did I." The reviewer flipped a page. "Nothing about it in our events calendar—going to complain to the city about not getting us a press release. Luckily, I was down here covering something else."

Coleman felt a tug on his arm. "Melvin, what's the matter?"

"Holy cow! Look who it is."

"Serge!"

"You know that guy?" asked the reviewer.

"My best friend," said Coleman.

"What's his secret?"

"Special diet."

They looked back up at the band shell. Serge cartwheeled toward the front of the stage, doubled over and laughed until his sides ached.

"Ooo-gah-chaka! Ting-tang-walla-walla-bing-bang! Su-sussudio!" He stood upright. "Sorry, got the giggles. Just thinking about Florida's first family. That's right, the Hulk Hogans. They're everything our state stands for: weird, dangerous, crazy, childish, attention addicts, but above all, a freakin' hoot! Victimized by a car-crash *victim*! Hurts too much to laugh! They nearly killed the guy and tried to squeeze a reality show from his morphine-drip bottle! News flash: They already have a reality show, and all of us are in it, too. It's called the Sunshine State. Watch any national news. It's the *local* news: Passenger boards plane at Tampa International with three gunshot wounds and asks flight attendant for Band-Aids, youth sodomizes grandmother's Yorkshire terrier named Duchess, man arrested for selling beach sand on eBay, body found in orange grove, body found half-eaten by gator, body found in line at Disney, 'The lone clue was a sawed-off thigh bone,' 'Wesley Snipes's tax attorney claims the truth will shock and surprise the public.' And who can forget those future brain surgeon teen girls who beat the snot out of a classmate, videotaped it and posted it on the Internet? Then Dr. Phil invites one of the *attackers* on his show, and everyone gets bent in pretzels. I say, No! No! No! Those Rhodes scholar predators are exactly the global TV face we want to put on our state. How else are we going to stop this viral, doomsday overdevelopment? The Hogans and that chick posse deserve citizens of the year. They're helping get the word out that the quality of people down here is so fucking bad, you don't want to come near us." He doubled over again with giggles. "Whoa, just noticed my feet. Aren't feet insane? All day long: left, right, left, right. How *do* they do it? I suddenly want five pizzas and a loud stereo. Look, there's an osprey. It's got a fish in its claws. Every time I see an osprey flying with a fish, I always think: Fish lives entire life in the sea, then at the end, he's looking down at everything from hundreds of feet up, thinking, 'Oh, *now* I get it.'" More giggling. "Actually, he's thinking, 'Hey, watch the talons, man.' Back to the headlines! Trapped retiree dials 911 with big toe; hurricane reporters in Key West jeered and hit with Super Soakers; frozen iguanas rain from trees during cold snap, injuring five; more families opting to live in storage units; man attempts to avoid DUI by abandoning car and jumping on horse in pasture; armed bandits invade home demanding nothing but an egg beater. Let's sing! Everybody, after me: *Biscayne Bay, where the Cuban gentlemen sleep all day . . . Free-credit-report-dot-com . . .* Don't you love those ads? Here's mine: *Florida-crime-report-dot-com, don't let winos pork your mom. F-L-A, that spells flaw, tourists goin' home in a box, doo-dah.* Is it me, or do colors seriously rock today? I'm looking in your direction, Mr. Green." Another giggle fit. Serge felt something and looked down at a growing bulge in his pants. "Yowza. Who out there owns a stereo, wants to fuck and eat five pizzas? But you say, 'Serge, what can *I* do about development?' Give money to every street-corner lunatic you see with a cardboard sign and pipe cleaners in his hair. It's like those minimum-wage roadside people in gorilla suits, waving you off the road for tax preparation. Except in reverse: The cardboard-sign brigade drives would-be residents *away*. But again, I know what you're thinking: 'Serge, if we promote "crazy," then what kind of place is left for us to live in?' And that's exactly the litmus test for any true Floridian. It may be crazy, but it's *our* crazy, it's *fun* crazy, and in Florida, *being* crazy is the only way to stay sane. That circus-geek colony in Gibsonton is now the most normal place we got. The whole state's an asylum, and I love every last freak show, even the schizos at the bus station who yell at me, 'Motherfucker, we know the planetary council sent you to implant transmitters!' And I smile and go, 'Say no more. You had me at "motherfucker."' . . . Speaking of transmitters, I'm picking up ten channels in my noodle: Rooftop bandits steal copper from strip mall air-conditioners, DNA proves restaurant's grouper is Asian catfish, Patriot missile found in Ybor City junkyard, missing children, missing wives, drag queen bingo night, boot camp deaths, baby formula thefts, loggerhead die-offs, red tide outbreaks, 'Anglo flight,' Solarcaine beats sunburn pain . . . Why am I so hungry? Could eat a horse, don't cry over spilled milk, all that and a bag of chips, Jimmy crack corn, Jack Sprat could eat no fat, proof's in the pudding, plum tired, bought a lemon, selling like hotcakes, bun in the oven, on the gravy train, my meal ticket, since sliced bread, we're toast, you're dead meat, stick a fork in it . . . *Coleman! . . . Where are you? . . . How . . . do . . . I . . . turn . . . this . . . shit . . . off! . . .*"

CHAPTER TWENTY-NINE

PERRY, FLORIDA

*B*lastoff.

Guillermo had the gang packed and loading the car in record time. Peaceful in the parking lot—silence so complete that when it was broken by the occasional car, the vehicle could be heard coming and going a half mile in both directions. Then stillness. Nothing but a lone pedestrian with a bag of pennies and a spatula, who suddenly disappeared into bushes as a career move.

The last door slammed, and the Oldsmobile Delta 88 sped away from the Thunderbird Motel.

"How did Madre find out?" asked Miguel.

"One of our informants. Been following the APB in state police computers. He pawned his class ring."

"Never been to Daytona," said Raul. "Hear you can drive on the beach. That's fucked up."

"We're not on vacation." The AC had been leaking freon since the Panhandle. Guillermo rolled down his window and held a flapping map against the steering wheel. No direct shot across the peninsula for where they were heading. Country roads, a spur at Bucell Junction, up through Foley and Fenholloway. Water towers, boarded-up feed stores, ancient granite courthouses from when there was population. Then across a wide, rolling expanse of Florida where the economy is state prisons and renting inner tubes out the backs of trucks to people rafting the Ichetucknee.

A couple hours later, they reached the Daytona coast and cruised

down A1A. Guillermo found a parking space in front of the old Sta-mie's Swimwear shop with a vintage fiberglass bathing beauty diving off the porch roof.

"Bathing suits?" said Pedro.

Guillermo ignored him, looking one block up at a logo with three dangling balls from the crest of Italy's Medici family.

Lucky's Pawn.

They got out and trotted up the sidewalk.

Bells jingled.

The short-sleeved owner leaned with hands atop a glass case. "Afternoon."

Guillermo sported another warm smile. "You must be Lucky."

"No, he got killed. Lookin' for anything particular?"

"Actually I am. Class rings."

The owner laughed. "You look a bit old for regret."

"Why do you say that?"

The owner pulled a display tray from under the counter. "Wouldn't believe how many of these I sell back to the same kids after they return to their senses and wrangle some cash."

"I kinda do the same thing. Except there's more money contacting the parents—once the yelling stops after they find out what their children did."

Another laugh. "Have to remember that."

Bells jingled. Hungover students entered with a set of hubcaps and a car jack. The owner shook his head. They left.

Then back to Guillermo. "Where were we?"

"Rings. My best harvests are spring break destinations." Guillermo bent over the tray. "Let's see what you got here . . ." He pulled one out of its velvet slot.

"You're looking at a real corker there."

Bells again. A student walked up with something cupped in his hands.

"Don't need hash pipes," said the owner. "Try High Seas up the block."

Guillermo turned the ring around. UNH on one side, 2012 on the other. "Guy still doesn't graduate for a couple years. This must have just come in."

"It did," said the owner.

"Remember him?"

"Sure. Nice boy. But the reason it stuck with me was the rest of his gang, especially this older, drunk guy. Nearly broke the display case."

"Got a loupe?"

The owner handed him a round magnifier. Guillermo brought the ring to his eye and checked the engraving inside the band. A. Mc-KENNA.

Bells again. A student in a full leg cast hobbled inside.

"What am I going to do with crutches?" said the owner. "I can *sell* you some . . ." pointing at a pile in the corner.

Guillermo handed the magnifier back but kept the ring. "I'll take it."

The owner rang him up.

"Hear them talking about anything?" Guillermo said with feigned idleness.

"They never *stopped* talking. Like what?"

"Coincidentally, I went to the same school." He stuck the ring in his pocket. "That's how it caught my eye. Be kind of nostalgic to catch up with the new class."

"Dang. What was it?"

"What was what?"

"One of them mentioned where they were staying. I remember 'cause they wanted more for their rings since they were paying top dollar without reservations. And I know the place well, know them all. Easy name, too . . ." He stared off at a shelf of clarinets. "What the heck was it? . . ."

The kids with hubcaps returned. "Sir, can't you give us anything at all for these? They're about to kick us out of the Dunes."

"The Dunes!" said the owner. "That's it. I'm positive."

THE DUNES

A day in full swing. Blender going, Led Zeppelin. Coleman continued slicing up limes with bandages on three fingers.

"*. . . I'm gonna send you . . . back to schoolin'! . . .*"

Serge staggered into the room. "Coffee . . ."

"Hey, Serge. How do you feel?"

No answer until he'd drained the dregs of an old pot. "That shit's insane. No wonder you don't have any ambition . . . What are the kids doing over there?"

Coleman looked up at a crowd around the television. "News from Panama City. Think they found some bodies."

Serge walked up behind the students. "What's going on?"

"*Shhhhh!*"

On TV, a female correspondent stood in a parking lot, intentionally framed with the Alligator Arms sign over her shoulder. "*. . . Police are releasing few details about the massacre in this unassuming motel. All we currently know is that authorities removed five bodies from room 543, the apparent victims of multiple gunshots . . .*"

Behind her, students waved and held up beer cans. "*Woooooo!*" "*Party hearty!*" "*I see dead people!*"

"*. . . One source who spoke on the condition of anonymity said the entire room had been sprayed heavily with automatic weapon fire. We'll report more as soon as we know it. But for now, it looks like a real spring break buzz-kill . . .*"

The report ended, and the students came alive with chatter.

"That was our room!"

"Happened just after we left!"

"Can you imagine if they hadn't kicked us out?"

"What kind of madman would do such a thing?"

"Not a madman," said Serge. "Professional job."

"Why do you say that?"

"Standard protocol for a Miami hit."

"If it's Miami, then why up there?"

"Probably some connection to a smuggling operation," said Serge. "The whole state's one big northern pipeline."

"All those kids were in on it?"

Serge shook his head and walked back to the coffeemaker. "That's why I said standard protocol. Most likely after just one target. They like to be thorough."

"But it was all students. How could any of them be involved in something that major?"

"Guessing they weren't." Serge dumped scoops of Folgers in the filter. "Smells like a case of mistaken identity. Shooters were probably after someone else who was supposed to be staying in that room."

The students were practically dizzy, running the fatal near miss through their heads. They changed channels to a special Daytona Beach edition of *Ocean Cops*.

Serge came back with a fresh cup. Something wasn't right. He looked around. "What happened to your class rings?"

"We pawned them."

"You what!"

"Pawned them . . . Hey, Coleman, come quick! You're on again!"

"When did you do this silliness?" demanded Serge.

"Recently."

Coleman arrived with a triple-strength piña colada. "Where am I?"

"Right there." On TV, rescuers on Jet Skis chased an unconscious person floating out to sea in an inflatable swim ring with a seahorse head.

Spooge high-fived Coleman. "You take no prisoners!"

"You can't pawn your class rings!" said Serge. "That's heritage, some of the best souvenirs of all!"

"I know," said Andy. "But what's done is done."

"Not as long as I'm alive," said Serge.

"What do you mean?"

"I can't let you do this." Serge checked the contents of his wallet. "We're going to get them back right now. I'll spot you, though I doubt I'll see any of it again. But that's how I roll."

They went downstairs and drove out of the parking lot.

A Delta 88 pulled in.

CHAPTER THIRTY

LUCKY'S PAWNSHOP

Jing-a-ling.

A pack of students entered.

The owner looked up from his racing form. "Back so soon?"

"I want to buy their class rings," said Serge.

"No problem." The owner hoisted a metal pail onto the counter. "They should be somewhere near the top. But you understand there'll have to be a modest surcharge. I got rent."

"Of course." Serge turned to the students. "Go get 'em."

The kids dug through rings from all years and states. The owner set two velvet display trays beside the bucket. "Some also might be here."

"I found mine!" A ring slipped on a finger.

"Me, too . . ."

"There it is . . ."

Soon, all hands had jewelry again. Except one.

Andy McKenna scanned velvet slots.

"What's the matter?" asked Serge.

"Can't find mine."

"Oh, just remembered," said the owner. "What school do you go to?"

"New Hampshire."

"That's right. Guy bought it."

"When?" asked Serge.

"Just before you came in."

Serge placed a consoling hand on Andy's shoulder. "Very sorry."

"I'll live."

"You might still get it back," said the owner.

"How's that?" asked Serge.

The owner turned to Andy. "Your name was engraved inside the band, right?"

Andy nodded.

"Man said he was an investor. Selling rings back to parents of kids who, well, spring break happens."

"I wouldn't get your hopes up," said Serge.

"Who knows?" said the owner. "Guy went to the same college."

"UNH?" asked Andy.

"Real nice gent." The owner put a pail back against the wall. "Told him where you were staying."

"Why?"

"He asked."

"That's weird," said Serge.

"Got the feeling it was a school pride thing," said the owner. "Told me he wanted to catch up with the new class, maybe even give it back to you for free."

"But how'd you know where we were staying?"

"You told me, remember? No reservations." The owner slid velvet trays under the counter. "Man, these rings sure are getting popular."

"Why do you say that?" asked Serge.

"A second guy was in here. Showed me a badge."

"Cop?"

"Latin name, Ramirez or something."

"What did he want?"

"Same as the other guy. I told him you kids were staying at the Algiers."

"We're at the Dunes," said Andy.

"Whoops," said the owner. "Well, I guess he'll be coming back. At least I told the first guy the right place."

FIFTEEN YEARS AGO

Another family meeting.

Prospect reports covered the cedar table in a stucco house south of Miami.

Guillermo thought—but didn't say out loud—"Has it really been six months already?"

"This one," said Luis. "Likes to sample product . . . Everything in Bimini on track?"

"Like glass," said Hector. "Wiring explosives into the fake shipment as we speak."

Sixty miles away, Sarah Sheets puttered around the house. Her husband checked the mailbox. More medical bills. So what? He sat at the kitchen table and made out checks.

Sarah packed sandwiches. "Can't believe the insurance company just reversed their decision."

"Guess when I mentioned suing . . ." Randall licked a postage stamp. "Lawyers must cost more than doctors these days."

She gave him a lunch box and a kiss at the front door. "When do you think you'll be home?"

"Late. Got a full schedule of students today."

"Again?"

"Told you not to worry. Everything eventually works out."

Randall drove across southern Palm Beach County, out past the turnpike and through the gate of an empty airfield. He pulled a tarp off his Cessna. Preflight checklist. Everything in order. He looked up at a clear sky and a deflated wind sock. Perfect day to fly.

Randall climbed inside, put on his headset and radioed the flight plan to Bimini.

A propeller churned to life. The plane taxied a short distance and rotated in place at the end of the strip. One last survey of instruments. He pushed a lever forward. The prop increased to a high whine. The Cessna started down the runway. It quickly gathered speed, approaching takeoff velocity.

Randall was monitoring an oil pressure gauge and didn't notice the tight formation of sedans race through the gate. He looked up at a dust trail speeding toward the runway at a ninety-degree angle.

"God!"

The first cars screeched to a stop, blocking takeoff. Randall jerked the throttle back, almost breaking the lever.

"Please, please, please . . ."

The Cessna began to skid, bleeding off speed. But not fast enough. Cars filled his vision.

"Come on! Come on! . . ."

Fifty miles an hour, forty-five, forty . . . The plane fishtailed. Agents scattered.

Thirty, twenty-five, twenty . . . The aircraft spun sideways and slammed into a pair of Crown Vics. A prop blade snapped and landed a hundred yards away in a field.

Grogginess. Randall pushed himself up from the controls and removed a headset that had shifted around and covered his eyes. He looked out to see the plane surrounded, dark sunglasses, guns drawn. The next sequence happened in a blink from academy training.

His pilot door flew open. No fewer than six hands grabbed Randall and threw him facedown on the tarmac. Arms twisted behind his back. Cuffs. Then he was yanked roughly to his feet before another hand pushed his head down, shoving him into the back of an undamaged car. What was left of the convoy sped off.

THE PRESENT

A Delta 88 sat below one of the strip's many half-burnt-out neon signs. A camel on a sand dune. When it came on at night, the camel winked.

Guillermo winked at the plump receptionist in a hairnet. "Hoping you can help me."

"Sorry, we're sold out."

Like many mom-and-pops, the Dunes hadn't been updated since the fifties. Original wooden mail slots behind the desk and real metal keys on numbered plastic fobs.

"I don't need a room," said Guillermo.

"Then how can I help you?"

He reached in his pocket. "Found this ring in the parking lot. You have an 'A. McKenna' staying here?"

She checked paper files. "Yes, we do."

"Great. What room?"

"Can't give that out."

"Understand." He looked over her shoulder at numbered mail slots. "Just want to make certain he gets this back."

"I'll make sure he gets it."

"Don't want it to get stolen or anything."

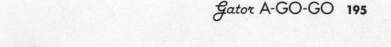

"It's okay. Everyone who works here is family."

"I have a business like that, too."

He handed over the ring. She was on the short side and dragged a footstool, then climbed two steps and reached for slot 24. "Want me to leave a note with it?"

She turned back around. The door to the empty office was closing.

CHAPTER THIRTY-ONE

THE DUNES

Serge's entourage arrived back in the parking lot and headed for the stairs.

The office door opened behind them. "Excuse me," said a woman in a hairnet. "Aren't you the guys in room twenty-four?"

"Yeah."

"Someone left you a message. Well, not really a message. Think it was just a ring."

Serge looked at the woman, then up at their room. Could have sworn he left those curtains open. "Guys, wait here a minute." He followed the receptionist inside.

She walked back behind the front desk. "Real nice guy. I think he wanted to give it back himself, but we don't disclose room numbers. Security, you know."

Serge looked up at a ring sitting in a wooden slot marked "24."

"Ma'am," said Serge, "was he standing right where I am when you put that in the slot?"

"I guess so." She dragged over a footstool again, grabbed the ring and climbed back down. "Here you go—"

The glass door to the empty office was closing.

Serge bolted for the Challenger. "Back in the cars! Back in the cars!"

"What's going on?"

"Just hurry!"

The vehicles raced a half mile, and Serge whipped up a circular drive to the valets.

"Staying with us?"

"Only dinner." He took the ticket. "Hear your food's great."

Serge hustled the gang into the lobby of one of the strip's newest luxury resorts.

"Where are we going?"

"Just keep up."

They ran out the back doors on the ocean side.

Minutes later, a row of kids sat mutely along a stone ledge, legs dangling over the side.

Serge paced feverishly in front of the seventy-year-old coquina band shell.

"I pray I'm wrong, but I seriously doubt it . . ."

Serge's voice echoed back at them from the concave dome. He spun and paced the other way. "That shooting in Panama City Beach? Now I'm a hundred percent it *was* mistaken identity."

Melvin raised his hand. "Why do you think that?"

"Because they were really after you."

"Us?"

"Well, *one* of you."

Murmurs shot down the row, students glancing at one another.

Another hand. "Why would someone want to kill one of us?"

"Who knows? Anyone witness a murder lately?"

Heads shook.

"Maybe a second case of mistaken identity," said Serge. "But unlike those poor kids in the Panhandle, this case follows you around."

"Why?"

"They've got one of your names." Pacing resumed. "I'd bet my life on it. Could simply be an identical name they confused with the target they're really after."

"It was Andy's ring," said Joey. "Must be his name."

"Or not," said Serge. "You booked Panama City with his credit card. Maybe they just think it's someone staying with him." He turned. "Andy, anything in the family closet?"

Andy heard guilty thoughts blaring out his ears. "Uh, nope."

"What about the rest of you?" Serge slowly walked down the row of students, each wilting under his gaze. "We're all in this together now. If someone's got a secret, this is the time."

Heads shook again.

Serge hopped up and sat on the ledge, leaning with elbows on knees. "This is a tough one."

"So we're going to take off," said Andy. "Right?"

"Absolutely not. This is our big chance."

"Chance?"

"We have a rare window of advantage. They don't know where we are, but I know where they are."

"Where?"

"In your room. The guy got the number from the mail slot in the office when he dropped off the ring. And I'm positive we left the curtains open."

"Oh my God! They're *here*?" said Spooge. "In our room!"

A group freak-out. "We should definitely split! . . ."

"I'm calling my parents! . . ."

"No!" snapped Serge. "Stop pissing yourselves. If one of you really is the target, the first thing they'll do is watch relatives' houses and tap their phones."

"But they're not cops. How do they get inside to tap?"

"They can do it across the street in a car. Parabolic receivers pick up portable phones and now even hardwired landlines. Back in the eighties, Miami had a counter-surveillance store on every block." Serge hopped down from the ledge. "Until I find out what we're dealing with, nobody makes any outside contact."

"What about the police?"

"*Especially* the police," said Serge. "Coleman and I do a lot of pawning, and I have a pretty good idea how they found that ring."

"How?"

"You don't want to know."

"If you want us to trust you . . . ," said Spooge.

"Okay," said Serge, and he told them.

"Dear Jesus," said Doogie. "The police are in on it?"

"Only takes one," said Serge.

"Where do we go in the meantime?"

"I'll get you registered into this place." Serge headed back toward the resort. "Then I have some business."

The Challenger sat behind a liquor store three blocks up A1A from the Dunes.

Serge whistled merrily up the sidewalk, climbed stairs and walked along a second-story landing. Eyes peeked from a curtain slit as he passed room 24. He stuck a key in the next door.

City and Country were kicking back with a bong and HBO.

"There you are!"

"We thought you ditched us again!"

Serge went straight for the door to the adjoining room and quietly locked it. He pressed his right ear to the wood.

"What the hell are you doing?"

"We have a problem," said Serge.

Country blew City a shotgun. "*You're* the one with a problem."

"This isn't a joke. I need a favor."

"What's happening?"

He told them, play by play. ". . . They're in twenty-four right now, but they don't know we have the adjoining room. I can't do this without you."

"Bullshit on that," said City.

"Double bullshit," said Country. "We got enough trouble as it is."

"But these kids are sheep," said Serge. "They don't stand a chance."

The pair stared and stewed. Finally, City snatched the bong and lighter. "You bastard."

"That means you'll help?"

FIFTEEN YEARS AGO

Randall Sheets saw his future disintegrating.

"Turn the other way," said Agent Ramirez, sitting with him in the back of a speeding sedan.

The agent twisted a tiny key; cuffs popped loose.

Randall rubbed his wrists. "What's going to happen to me?"

"Better than if we didn't show up."

Waves of panic were so strong, Randall felt himself drowning. Then it came from nowhere, an eruption of sobs and babbling. "I'm so sorry! I didn't know what to do. My wife. The bills. These guys. The briefcase. I'm so sorry! . . ."

Ramirez gave him a handkerchief. "We know about your wife."

Randall blew his nose. "You do?"

Ramirez continued facing forward. "So did they. You got played. It's how they operate. You never had a choice."

"I didn't. What would you have done?"

"Same thing. But that's behind you."

"It is?"

"You're going to testify before the grand jury."

"Not a chance. They'll kill me for sure."

"There's a duffel bag waiting for you in Bimini," said Ramirez.

"You know about that, too?"

"Weighs the same as the others with coke."

"Not coke?"

"Bomb."

"Doesn't make sense. I've got a perfect delivery record, making them a fortune."

"They change pilots every six months. And not by mutual agreement. That's why we had to take you in now."

Randall's face fell in his hands. "How long have you known?"

"Two days. Finally got an informant, someone on their inside. Been trying to get a pilot for years but, well, you're the first."

"Oh my God!" Randall just remembered. "My family!"

"All taken care of. Picked up your wife and son an hour ago."

That's what mattered most to Randall, the next less so: "How much prison am I looking at?"

"None. You testify, we put you in the witness program."

"Where?"

"Won't be as warm as here."

"How long do I have to stay?"

"You don't understand." Ramirez gazed out the window as a DC-10 touched down at West Palm International. "These people never forget."

THE PRESENT, MIDNIGHT

Pop.

Country uncapped a wine bottle in the backseat. "Nobody's left the room for hours. Maybe they're not there."

"They're still there, all right." Serge leaned toward the windshield of the Challenger, strategically parked face-out in an alley with a full view of the Dunes. "They don't want to open the door and give away their ambush position in case the kids are on their way back."

"So why are we waiting over here?"

"Everyone eventually gets hungry."

Another hour.

"Now *I'm* hungry," said City, stubbing out a roach.

"Me, too," said Country.

"So is someone else." Serge looked up at the second floor, where a man had quickly slipped out the door of room 24, then pretended he hadn't. He leaned nonchalantly against the landing's rail, scanning the parking lot and street. All clear. Cowboy boots trotted down stairs.

The Challenger rolled out of the alley without headlights.

Boots clacked across the street and up the opposite sidewalk.

"You were right," said Country. "He's heading for Taco Bell."

"I'd kill for a taco right now," said City.

Serge pulled along the curb. "You're going to get your wish."

Pedro's arms were weighed down with bags of *grande* meals when he finally came out the restaurant's side door.

A distressed female voice: "What are we going to do?"

"I don't know," said City. "We might have to ask a stranger."

"But that's dangerous."

"Excuse me." Pedro politely bowed his head. "Couldn't help but overhear. Are you in some kind of trouble?"

"Flat tire," said Country, reaching in one of his bags for a taco.

"But the lug nuts are too tight." City reached in another bag. "We're not strong enough."

Pedro puffed out his chest. "You beautiful ladies shouldn't have to change a tire. Especially at night."

"You'll help us?" said Country.

"You'd really do something that nice?" said City.

"Of course Pedro will help you. Where's your car?"

"Right around the corner. Just follow us."

He did.

They turned the corner.

Pedro dropped his tacos. "Who's that guy?"

"Oh," said Country. "You mean the one with the gun?"

CHAPTER THIRTY-TWO

FIFTEEN YEARS AGO

*B*elle Glade sits near the middle of the state, on the southeast shore of Lake Okeechobee. The horizon low and flat. Cane fields forever. Plumes of dark smoke rose in various directions, some from intentional burns of harvested fields, others out the stacks of sugar-processing plants. Below the town was a prison camp. A yellow crop duster swooped, the one that terrorists with rashes on their hands had tried to hire. To the north, an uninviting, single-row motel with a leaking tar roof on the side of Route 715. Scraggly bushes, termite damage, a cracked office window fixed with masking tape.

The motel was almost always closed, except when the government needed it. Because it owned it.

Currently, no vacancy. Lights on in all eight rooms, but the front sign remained dark. Agents in T-shirts and jeans stood watch outside, pretending to work on a carburetor. They didn't blend in. People of their sort never put up in the glades unless there's a bad reason. All locals avoided them, except sheriff's deputies, who knew something was up during their first stay but couldn't get to the bottom of it despite hours of questioning in the parking lot. Almost blew the safe house. So feds began bringing tackle boxes and towing bass boats. Near every deputy fished that lake.

In the middle room, Randall Sheets rocked nervously on the edge of a bed. They'd just reeled him back from Detroit for his big day of testimony. A digital clock said five A.M. Ramirez sat facing him. "It'll all be over in a few hours."

"Can't come soon enough."

"Just remember what we talked about. The prosecutor will guide you through everything. Keep your answers direct and tell the truth. We'll put them away."

"I don't see how my testimony can do that. I think the guys I was dealing with were at the bottom."

"We have another witness. Management insulates themselves by staying away while the lower rungs get their hands dirty. Between the two of you . . ."—he interlaced his fingers—". . . we connect the whole operation."

"Will . . . *they* be there?"

"Not in the grand jury. Not even their defense attorneys. You have nothing to worry about."

Three spaced knocks on the door.

An agent standing next to Ramirez—the one with the machine gun—went over and checked out the window. He opened the door.

Six more agents entered. "We're ready."

Everyone put on dark windbreakers with hoods. Ramirez handed one to Randall.

"What's this for?"

"Just put it on."

"Wait," said Randall, looking around a room of identically dressed people. "Snipers?"

"Just an abundance of caution. Put it on."

A string of headlights filled the dark parking lot. Engines running. Vehicles in a perfect line, facing the exit.

Room number 4 opened, and windbreakers ran for the convoy.

Pop, pop, pop. Sparks on the pavement. Pinging against fenders.

"Where's Randall?" yelled Ramirez. "Get him down!"

Agents flattened the witness and formed a pile.

Pop, pop. Ping, ping.

"Where the hell's that coming from?"

"Over there!" An agent braced behind a Bronco and returned fire toward distant muzzle flashes. "The cane field!"

"Get him in the car!" Ramirez slapped the trunk. "Go!"

The front half of the motorcade sped east into the waning night. The rest of the team remained behind, raking sugarcane with overwhelming firepower.

The convoy reached Twenty Mile Bend, dashboard needles at the century mark. Randall wanted to see outside, but they were sitting on him again. The approaching dawn brightened over Southern Boulevard, where they were joined by helicopters for the final turnpike leg to the federal courthouse in Miami-Dade County. But back then it was just Dade.

They brought Randall through a secure garage gate in back. He entered the courtroom and took the stand next to a jury with less interesting mornings.

Randall Sheets was, as they say, the perfect witness. Steady, confident testimony. Even he was surprised by his grace under pressure.

Indictments came down.

Across south Florida, a series of predawn raids.

The front door of a Spanish stucco house opened. The SWAT team brought Hector, Luis, and Juanita out in handcuffs—"Call the lawyers!"

Same scene at five other locations, two dozen associates in all. Everyone was booked. And bonded out just as quickly by one of Florida's top law firms. TV crews waited in the street. *"Is it true you're kingpins?"*

An agent in the Miami FBI office picked up a phone and dialed.

A cell rang somewhere south of Miami. "Hello?" A hand quickly went over it, and the person walked outside. "Are you crazy calling me now? . . . No, I can't talk. They're circling the wagons. Everyone's under suspicion . . . What I'm saying is they know you've got an informant in the family . . . How can you say there's no way? *We've* got someone inside with you . . . I don't know who our guy is, sheriff, janitor, anyone. Point is that's how they must have found out . . . I understand you'd really like the name of our informant—I just need more time . . . Don't even joke about taking back immunity. I'll contact you as soon as I hear something. And never call me on this line again!" The phone slammed shut.

Another phone rang. Another person answered. ". . . Yes, I can talk . . . I see . . . You think you know who the informant in our family is? Very good, who? . . . You've only narrowed it to two people? That's not good . . . I realize it's a huge risk getting at the files right now. That's what we pay you for . . . No, time's already run out. Haven't you been watching the news? . . . Okay, what are the two names?"

THE PRESENT

Four A.M.

Serge's surveillance had synchronized his watch with the rounds of local police.

The latest squad car rolled toward him. And kept going. Serge jumped from a hedge on the side of A1A.

Pedro was already bound and gagged in his seat. Serge popped open a toolbox. He began loosening hex-head bolts with his largest socket. Some were stuck from the years, needing WD-40 and a hammer banging on the wrench handle.

Minutes later, all the right bolts lay on the ground. Serge's wristwatch said to dive in the bushes. Another cruiser drove by.

Quiet again. Serge dashed back.

Stifled screams under the gag. Serge untied it.

"Please! Dear God! Whatever you're thinking . . . I'll, I'll pay you. Cash, cocaine, anything!"

"The name," said Serge.

"What name?"

"Who you're after."

"They'll kill me."

Serge turned to walk away. "Suit yourself."

"Okay, okay. Andy McKenna."

"Andy? He's just a kid. What's he ever done to you?"

"Nothing. It's his dad . . ." And Pedro laid it all out from soup to nuts.

"How many of you are there?"

"Four."

"Good, very good," said Serge. "Now, who's behind it?"

Silence.

"Come onnnnnnnnnn . . ." Serge gave him a buddy jab in the arm. "You're doing great."

"Guillermo."

"Guillermo?"

"But he's just the crew leader for Madre."

"Wait . . . but . . . you don't actually mean *the* Madre."

Pedro nodded.

"I remember reading about her back when *Miami Vice* was still on the air." Serge blew a deep breath through pursed lips. "Thought for sure she'd be dead by now."

"Far from it," said Pedro.

"So history comes full circle." Serge stroked his uncharacteristic two-day stubble. "What impressed me is how you've been able to track him. Students on spring break are like stray cats. But I have a theory."

Pedro clammed up again. Then: "I'd rather you kill me."

"So it is what I think?"

"They keep me in the dark on that. You have to believe me."

"I do. Does this Guillermo have a cell number?"

Another nod.

Serge got out a scrap of paper and pen. "Ready when you are."

Pedro rattled off digits. Serge stuck the note in his pocket. "Most excellent. See how easy that was?"

"So you're going to let me go?"

"In a manner of speaking." Serge replaced the gag, then whistled in awe. "And how!"

Another cruiser rolled up the street.

When it was gone, Serge poked his head from the bushes and walked to a breaker box . . .

CHAPTER THIRTY-THREE

DAYTONA BEACH

*T*he 911 call came just after dawn from a commercial air-conditioning repairman. He'd been cleaning coils on the pebbled roof of a two-story motel just south of the band shell.

Soon, the roof swarmed with detectives and a forensic team, photographing Pedro from every angle. Or what used to be Pedro. Now he was more like Flat Stanley, his clothes a thin package of human jelly in a fly-swarmed stain.

They combed the rest of the roof. No sign of a trail from the maintenance doors—or anywhere else. It was like he just materialized out of the blue at the very spot they'd found him.

How the hell did he get there? And in that condition?

Nobody could figure it.

Until another 911 call. This time from the amusement boardwalk.

Luxury suite number 1563.

Two gentle knocks at the door, followed by two more. Students flinched.

"Who the hell can that be?"

"It's Serge's signal."

"What if it's someone *using* Serge's signal?"

Melvin checked the peephole and undid the chain.

They saw Serge and bent forward as one, anxiously awaiting any news.

He strolled into the room like nothing happened.

"Well?" asked Joey.

"Just boring investigative work. Tedious documents and records."

"That's it?"

"That's it."

"Can we leave the room?"

"No. You're okay for now, but I have some more chores until it's completely safe."

Speculation shot around the room.

"Andy," said Serge. "Could I have a word?"

"Sure."

They stepped into the bathroom. Serge placed a paper bag by the sink and combed his hair in the mirror. "Or should I say 'Billy'?"

Andy crashed into the tub, taking down the plastic curtain.

"I'm sorry." Serge helped him up. "Have a weakness for the dramatic."

The student grabbed a towel rod. "How much do you know?"

"Everything. Your father, the flights, yanked out of kindergarten . . ." Serge poured a cup of water from the faucet and handed it to him. "Why didn't you tell me at the band shell?"

"Because I'm not supposed to," said Andy. "That's the big rule they gave us. Any exposure, and the whole family must relocate and start over. Almost happened a couple times in third grade when there was another Billy. Then we *had* to move. Michigan to Massachusetts."

"What happened?"

Andy stared at the floor.

"Can't be that bad."

A tear fell. "My mom shot herself."

"Sorry," said Serge. "Didn't mean to pry."

"That's okay. Long time ago."

"Because of the witness program?"

Andy shook his head. "I was just a little kid. Dad told me she'd been very sick and was finally at peace. Went into remission before we left Florida, but it recurred. Because of how she'd . . . chosen to leave, local authorities had to run a mandatory investigation and officially rule the cause of death. Our witness liaisons thought it was too much attention, and off they shipped us again."

"You still should have mentioned something," said Serge. "Didn't that business back in your Panama City room make any lights go on?"

"I was absolutely certain it couldn't be the reason. We're talking over fifteen years ago."

"These people have been known to hold grudges."

"Okay, so now we figured it out." Andy braced an arm against a tiled wall and lowered himself onto the closed toilet lid. "Take me to the FBI."

"Afraid I can't do that."

"Why not?"

Serge gave him a penetrating look.

Andy got a different expression, backing up against the wall. "You're . . . not . . ."

"Relax. I ain't with nobody. It's something Pedro told me."

"Who's Pedro?"

"Better you not know. Especially now."

"What'd he say?"

"My suspicions were correct," said Serge. "They have someone on the inside. That's how they've been tracking you. And until I find out who, we can't contact the authorities."

"But what about my dad?"

"I can only solve so much. Right now you're my responsibility. Consider me a guardian angel."

"*You?*"

"Couldn't be in better hands." Serge reached for a white paper bag by the sink. "Here. Have a taco."

FIFTEEN YEARS AGO

A rented Taurus drove west from the Detroit airport.
Snowdrifts.

"I don't know if I can get used to the cold," said Randall.

"You will in time," said Ramirez. "And thanks to your testimony, we rounded them all up."

"I'm safe now?"

"As long as you stick to the program." Ramirez had opted for the rental instead of the obvious government sedan. He handed a thick brown envelope across the front seat. "That's your kit, everything you'll need. New Social Security cards, Michigan driver's licenses, birth certificates, credit cards with phony transaction histories, bank accounts. We made some deposits to get you started."

Randall looked at the documents in his lap. "But why Patrick McKenna?"

"Because it's a common name."

"Couldn't I have picked something?"

"Flash Gordon was taken."

Randall stared at him.

"Sorry," said Ramirez. "That was supposed to be a joke. Break the tension."

An exit sign.

Battle Creek.

They got off the interstate and wound through anonymous neighborhoods.

"Remember what we talked about," said Ramirez. "It's critical. Randall Sheets never existed. And Patrick McKenna always has. You need to set aside some quality time rehearsing with your family over the next weeks, calling each other by new names."

"I think we're smart enough to—"

"I'm serious. Can't tell you how many people we've had to move again because of slipups in the wrong place, and it usually happens at the beginning. After a while, it'll come naturally."

"I guess you're right."

"One more thing," said the agent. "The phone in the living room. Its wire runs through a little tan box. That's the encrypter. There's a switch on the side. Don't call me unless you absolutely have to, but if you *have* to, flip the switch for a secure line."

Patrick looked out the windows as they swung onto a sleepy, tree-lined street. "I just want to see my family."

The car pulled up to the curb. Patrick grabbed the door handle, then stopped and turned. "I never thanked you."

"Go on, they're waiting."

Patrick ran up the walkway and rang the doorbell.

Ramirez watched the tearful reunion on the front steps. He waited until the door closed, then drove back to the airport.

Police headquarters.

An evidence bag of hex-head bolts lay on the conference table. Detectives gathered around a TV set. Someone inserted a DVD that had been discovered by the employee who'd made the 911 call from the Daytona Beach boardwalk.

An early-morning glow had just broken over the Atlantic, but not the sun, giving the image a grainy, low-light effect.

On-screen: Pedro, secured in his seat, gagged, eyes of horror.

Offscreen: "...*Five ... four ... three ... two ... one ... liftoff!*"

The video camera on the safety bar showed Pedro suddenly accelerate skyward in the open-air ball of the Rocket Launch. The beach and boardwalk receded quickly, tiny buildings and cars like a child's train set.

Then the ball reached its zenith, and elastic cords jerked hard. The padded, U-shaped restraining bar over Pedro's chest—minus its bolts—flew off like the pilot's canopy of an F-16 Falcon during subsonic ejection.

Followed by Pedro.

The now-empty ball continued bouncing on its cords, camera still running.

A detective slowed the DVD to frame-by-frame. On one of its last bounces, the ball caught the background image of a miniature Pedro sailing out over motel row.

CHAPTER THIRTY-FOUR

FIFTEEN YEARS AGO

A late-model Mercedes raced west through Little Havana on Calle Ocho. The road became the Tamiami Trail. A half hour later, they left civilization behind and entered the Everglades.

Hector was driving, Luis riding shotgun. Guillermo sat in the backseat like an only child, arms around a big briefcase.

"No deviating from the plan," Hector said over his shoulder. "We can't be in the same place as the payment."

"Why not?" asked Guillermo. "You raised him like my brother. Don't we trust him anymore?"

"Yes, but he may be followed. He's on the inside now."

"I still don't understand how we got him there. He had a record, from when Madre first picked him up at the jail."

"Juvenile. Had it sealed."

Guillermo looked out the windows. "Where is he?"

"Nearby, but he won't know the final location until you call him."

Fifty miles into the 'glades. No shade from the withering swamp heat. People in wide-brimmed straw hats reclined on lawn chairs along the shoulder of the Tamiami, cane-pole fishing an alligator-filled canal. Vultures picked at unrecognizable remains, taking flight when the Mercedes blew by. Hector slowed as they passed one of the water district's drainage control dams. A quick look around. No other cars. He hit the gas for a dust-slinging left turn onto an unmarked dirt road.

"Where will you be?" asked Guillermo.

Hector jerked a thumb north. "Back on the trail. When we see his car leave and are sure he had no tails, we'll come back to pick you up."

"But why do we have to pay one of our own extra for the name?"

"You talk too much," said Luis.

"He's got to learn sometime," said his brother, looking over his shoulder again. "We're not paying *him*. The files on their confidential sources are sealed tighter than ever since that grand jury. He needs the money to bribe someone *else*."

"I still can't believe we have an informant in our family."

"It's the business we've chosen."

The Mercedes rolled to a stop in a small clearing. Dragonflies, sun-bleached beer cans, a single sneaker in weeds.

Guillermo opened his door, filling the car with a blast of scorched air and the buzz of insects.

"We'll be waiting for your call." Hector reached for the gear-shift.

The car's horn suddenly blared. Solid.

"What on earth—" Luis looked toward his brother.

The inside of the driver's windshield was splattered red, his brother facedown on the steering wheel. Luis spun toward the open back door. "Have you lost your fucking mind?"

A pair of nine-millimeter rounds entered Luis's forehead through the same hole.

Guillermo calmly placed the pistol back in his briefcase and walked around to the driver's side. A dust cloud appeared in the distance as another Mercedes came up the road from the direction of the Tamiami. He opened Hector's door and pulled him back by the hair. The horn stopped.

So did the second Mercedes.

Guillermo walked to the trailing vehicle and retrieved a gas can from the passenger seat.

"Remember to roll their windows down," said the driver. "Those other fools left too much evidence when the fire suffocated itself from lack of air."

Moments later, Guillermo climbed into the second car, which made a tight U in the clearing and drove back out the dirt road. Behind them, flames curled from open windows.

"The last people I would have expected," said Guillermo. "Why would they turn on the family?"

"One of them did."

"One?"

Juanita nodded. "Our informant couldn't figure out which."

"So you had me kill *both* your brothers?"

She smiled and patted his hand. "You're a good boy, Guillermo."

"Thank you, Madre."

THE PRESENT

A '73 Challenger raced up the strip.

Serge reached into a small drugstore shopping bag.

"Smelling salts?" asked Coleman.

"Explain later." Serge removed a greeting card from the same bag. "Right now I must depend on your particular talents. Nearest liquor store?"

"Three hundred yards. Left one block, then right, north side of the street."

He hit the gas.

"But, Serge, you don't drink."

The Challenger hung a hard left. "It's not for me. It's for one of Guillermo's goons."

"You're buying one of his goons a drink?"

A skidding right turn. "Several."

They dashed into the store. "Coleman, time's of essence. Your expertise again—liquor store layout. Where's the . . ."

Coleman quickly guided Serge to respective products on his mental list. They ran for the cash register with arms full of bottles.

Minutes later, the Challenger patched out of the parking lot.

"What's the big rush?" asked Coleman.

"Pedro just made the TV news."

"And?"

"So up to now we've had the advantage of them not knowing what we know. But as soon as Guillermo sees the news, he'll realize they've been made. We already might be too late."

"Too late for what?"

"Before they have a chance to clear out, I'd like to thin the herd a little more and improve our odds."

"How does all that liquor fit in?"

"It has to be a quick strike. I wanted to set up a series of levers, gears, bowling balls and axes on roller skates, but this is no time for fun. Had to think up something quick—that also *works* quick. Unfortunately, my plan leaves us trapped without escape from Guillermo's murderous retaliation."

"I usually prefer a way out of that."

"Most people do, which is why I added liquor to the Master Plan's cocktail. It simultaneously accomplishes both objectives: taking out the target and creating an escape clause."

"How does it do that?"

"Through a potent mix of French cuisine and *The Simpsons*."

FIFTEEN YEARS AGO

Twenty people with latex gloves walked extra slow, performing a grid search in the dirt and weeds around the charred carcass of a Mercedes.

Just another day in the Everglades.

"Looks like he picked up the shell casings."

"Obviously knows what he's doing. I'm guessing those windows weren't originally rolled down in this heat."

A cell phone rang.

"Ramirez here."

"What the hell's going on?"

"Calm down." The agent walked to the side of the clearing for privacy. "Is the encryption box switched on?"

"How can you tell me to calm down at a time like this?" Patrick McKenna paced in front of the TV set in his Battle Creek living room with snowflakes on windowsills. "Have you seen the news? Prosecutor says they have to drop all charges."

"The encryption box!"

"It's on! Jesus!" McKenna paced the other way, past a televised press conference in the Miami sunshine. "You told me it was a done deal. They'd all go away for a long time."

"Immunity's still intact." Ramirez paced behind a burnt-up car and wiped stinging sweat from his eyes. "This doesn't change anything with your family."

"One of the dead guys in the Everglades was your other witness, wasn't he?"

No answer.

"Oh, my God! What am I going to do?" Children across the street stuck the carrot nose in a snowman. ". . . They're going to find us, I just know it."

"Listen very carefully. Nobody's going to find anyone. You have my word."

"I'll bet your other witness had your word."

"It was completely different with him."

"Right, he's dead."

"No, I mean he wasn't only a witness. He was a top member of their organization."

"What'd you do, promise him the same sweet deal as me?"

"I had leverage. Caught him on his yacht, but that's all I can say except we offered him life without parole or work with us."

"I'm only a flight instructor. I wasn't made for this."

"Just hang in there."

CHAPTER THIRTY-FIVE

THE DUNES, ROOM 24

*R*aul peeked out the curtains for the hundredth time. "What could have happened to Pedro?"

Miguel joined him at the window. "And when are those kids ever going to come back?"

"They're not," said Guillermo.

"How do you know?"

Guillermo watched TV. Live aerial footage from a helicopter hovering over the roof of a nearby motel, where cops clustered around a sheet-covered body. "We just found Pedro."

Outside, Serge and Coleman ran up the concrete stairs and into room 25.

"Where the fuck have you been?" said Country.

"Booze run," said Coleman, lining bottles on the counter.

"You left us bored in here while you were out having fun?"

"It's not like that," said Serge. "I'm working."

"Doesn't look like you're working."

"Trust me." Serge uncapped bottles. "You won't be bored for long."

"I've heard that before."

"Now's not the time to argue. We still have a tiny advantage."

"What are you, playing fort again?"

"Guillermo knows the kids were in room 24 from the class ring in the mail slot . . ."—uncapping more bottles—". . . But like I told you before, he doesn't know we also have *this* room—not yet. And when he does . . ." Serge tossed his keys to City. "I parked the car in front of the convenience store at the end of this block. Wait for us there."

"Another place to wait? And this time in the heat? Fuck that!"

"Please." Serge pulled pliers from his pocket. "I'm thinking of your safety. And I'm taking a wild guess this will draw the cops."

"Come on, Country." City sneered at Serge as they headed for the door. "You owe us big-time."

"Will you hurry?" Serge opened the rest of the bottles.

Other side of the wall: "How does that mean the kids aren't coming back?" asked Miguel.

"I'll speak slowly for you." Guillermo grabbed his keys. "We've been identified. Apparently those kids aren't as harmless as we'd thought."

"Maybe they had help," said Raul.

"Gee, you think?"

Guillermo went to the curtains for his own parking lot assessment.

"What do we do now?" asked Miguel.

"Clear out," said Guillermo. "Who knows who's involved? Maybe Andy's not even here. We don't know what he looks like. The feds could be using young undercovers as bait."

"That class ring *was* kind of easy. You sure we can trust our inside guy?"

"Don't talk anymore." Guillermo grabbed the door handle. "I'll get the car. Miguel, you do a final walk-around of the hotel for anything out of place. Raul, wipe the room for prints and meet us."

Two men left and slammed the door. Raul grabbed a bath towel.

Room 25: Serge heard the door slam in the next room and peeked out the curtains. Guillermo and Raul trotted down the steps. They split up, Guillermo climbing into a Delta 88. Serge closed the curtains. "Excellent. We're not late after all. And if Pedro's count was correct, that leaves one."

Serge ran for the bathroom.

Coleman strolled at a less purposeful pace. He looked down and saw legs across the floor.

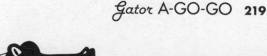

"Serge, what are you doing under the toilet?"

Serge adjusted pliers. "Killing the pressure feed. I need a dry tank and bowl."

"Is this the *Simpsons* part?"

A twist on the pipe valve. "Just flush that, will you?"

Coleman hit the lever.

Swoosh.

Serge crawled back out and ran into the kitchenette. He wet paper towels under the faucet.

"What are you doing now?" asked Coleman.

"Need a total seal." He crammed balls of wet paper down the drain. "Don't want to trust the sink trap. Grab some bottles."

Down in the parking lot, Guillermo kept checking his watch and glancing out the windshield at the second floor.

Miguel finished circling the motel and climbed in the passenger seat. "Nothing."

"What the hell's taking him so long?"

"Probably trying to do a good job."

"He couldn't find his own ass if he had three hands." Another look at his watch. "You better go check."

Miguel got out of the car and ran toward the stairs.

Room 25: Serge's right ear was against the adjoining door to the next unit.

"What's going on?" asked Coleman.

"Shhhhhh!" said Serge. "It's falling in place just like I planned. They're beginning to get sloppy."

Serge pulled the .45 from his waist and silently opened the connecting door. Guillermo's crew had failed to check the tandem door on their side, which was still unlocked from when Serge and the kids moved freely between the two rooms. He slowly turned the knob . . .

Outside, Miguel ran up the stairs and along the landing.

Serge crept quietly into room 24. Just ahead, Raul, with his back to him, rubbing the dresser with a towel. He never heard ginger footsteps from behind. The butt of the pistol came down.

Stars.

Serge grabbed Raul under the arms and dragged him into the

other room. He closed the adjoining side door as Miguel opened the front one.

"*Raul? Where are you? . . .*"

"Coleman," said Serge. "Hand me that bottle and my smelling salts. Here's what I need you to do . . ."

Guillermo watched from the parking lot. Miguel went in . . . then came out. He leaned over the second-floor railing and lifted upturned arms in a haven't-got-a-clue gesture.

"Unbelievable." Guillermo hopped out and ran up the stairs to 24.

In 25, Serge's ear was against the door again. Heavy footsteps. "Perfect. Lured them back into the room and away from the car, where they would have been able to intercept and retaliate."

"Escape clause?" asked Coleman.

"The exit window won't stay open long. We have to work fast." Serge waved smelling salts under Raul's nose. His woozy head snapped sideways. Another whiff of the salts, and he was back with the living. Raul felt something wet in his hair. He reached up with his hands.

"Don't touch it." Serge aimed his .45. "On your feet!"

"Who are you?"

"Pedro says, 'Hi.' Actually, he says, '*Ahhhhhhhhh!*' "

"You're so dead!"

"Someday," said Serge. "Save me a seat."

As previously instructed, Coleman walked behind their guest.

Raul glanced over his shoulder, then back at Serge. "What are you going to do to me?"

"Here's a critical fact you need to remember," said Serge. "No matter how much you panic, the closest source of water is the toilet."

"Why do I need to know where water is?"

Guillermo raced around number 24.

"Sure he didn't slip out without you seeing him?" asked Miguel.

"Positive. Never took my eyes off the room." Guillermo opened the sliding glass door and looked down off the balcony. He came back in with a puzzled look. "What could have happened to him?"

"It's like he vanished into thin air."

On the other side of the wall, Serge tapped his nose. That was Coleman's cue. He flicked a disposable lighter behind Raul and touched it to the Bacardi 151 in his hair.

Raul's hands shot up. "*Aaaaaauuuuhhh!* I'm on fire! I'm on fire!"

"The toilet!" yelled Serge, pointing toward the bathroom. "Don't forget the toilet!"

Raul ran by screaming.

"I love flambé," said Serge.

"But there isn't any water in the toilet," said Coleman. "You filled it with another bottle of one fifty-one."

"Did I do that?"

"*Ahhhhhhhhhhh!*" Raul came running out. "I'm more on fire! . . ."

Guillermo heard the hysterical screaming in Serge's room. But then, there was even louder yelling from spring breakers in the unit on the other side.

"Guillermo . . . ," said Miguel, picking up a towel dropped in front of the dresser.

"Quiet. I'm trying to think." Guillermo slowly rotated. He stopped and stared at the adjoining door.

"What is it?" asked Miguel.

"The next room. That's it."

Guillermo ran over and opened the first door but the second was locked. He put his shoulder into it. The door gave slightly, but the deadbolt held. He hit it again.

"Serge," said Coleman, watching Raul run in frantic circles, slapping the top of his head, "I think I hear someone trying to knock down that side door."

"Right on schedule. This is going to be tight timing." Serge grabbed Raul by the arm and pointed. "The sink! Water in the sink!"

Raul ran.

Coleman stepped up next to Serge and looked toward the kitchenette. "More one fifty-one?"

"That would be repetitive. One-ninety-proof grain alcohol."

A shoulder hit the side door again.

Coleman looked at the ceiling. "Why aren't the sprinklers going off?"

"He's not staying in one place long enough, and alcohol burns at a low temperature," said Serge. "But he still doesn't like it."

"*Ahhhhhhhhhhhhh!* More fire! . . ."

Another shoulder into the door. This time the frame began to fracture.

"The pool!" Serge pointed at the open sliding glass doors. "Water in the pool! You can make it!"

Raul dashed across the room and never broke stride as he dove off the balcony.

Serge and Coleman ran out and looked over the railing.

"Oooooh," said Coleman. "He didn't make it."

Guillermo had given up on his shoulder and pulled a .380 automatic, preparing to shoot his way through.

Suddenly, even louder shrieking from some kind of pandemonium outside.

"Guillermo!" Miguel shouted from the balcony. "Come quick! The patio! I think I found him!"

Guillermo ran to the railing. People splashed water from the pool onto a smoldering Raul.

"Serge," said Coleman. "The guy stopped trying to knock down the door."

"Shhhhh!" Serge counted under his breath. "Five, six, seven . . . They must be out on the balcony now, trying to figure where their pal fell from . . . Escape window just opened!"

They ran out the door and down the stairs. "I get the *Simpsons* part now," said Coleman. "Flaming Mo."

Guillermo leaned over the balcony, tracing Raul's flight trajectory up to the next room. "Miguel! Quick!" He ran back inside and unceremoniously shot the locks off the connecting door with excess ammunition.

They rushed inside. Empty but recently occupied.

Miguel fanned his nose. "Jesus, what is that smell?"

"Liquor."

Another urgent room sweep. They checked the bathroom, closet, under beds. Then a second round. Guillermo ran past the TV and hit the brakes. He looked back. "Fuck me."

"What is it?" asked Miguel.

They both looked on top of the television. A propped-up envelope. In big letters across the front: GUILLERMO.

He tore open the flap and pulled out a get-well card.

Howdy, Guillermo,

Ain't spring break a gas? All the history! Here's your first hint: Follow time backward. Bet you can't catch me . . . before I catch you.

Warmly in Florida,
Serge A. Storms

CHAPTER THIRTY-SIX

GUILLERMO

*B*ack in the nineties, Juanita was always taking in strays.
Young street boys looking for trouble.

She waited in a Mercedes outside the county jail.

Her extended family was growing in both size and loyalty. She should have been a psychiatrist.

Guillermo was barely eighteen when he finished a three-month stretch for petty larceny. He walked out the back of the jail with two plastic bags of personal junk and no direction.

Juanita rolled down her window. "You need a place to stay?"

"What do I have to do?"

"Whatever I tell you."

He got in.

To the cast of surrogate sons, she was the mother they never had. To Juanita, it was business.

Guillermo quickly became her most valuable asset. Grooming time.

One Saturday afternoon, he sat alone watching TV in a Spanish stucco house south of Miami. The Mercedes returned from jail.

Juanita came through the front door. "Guillermo, this is Ricky."

"Hey."

She set her purse on the table and removed a blood-pressure gauge. "Ricky, come here."

"What's that for?"

"Just put out your arm."

Juanita fastened Velcro and pumped a rubber bulb. She reached in

her purse again and handed Ricky a nine-millimeter automatic with a full clip and an empty chamber.

"Guillermo, stand up."

He did.

She turned to Ricky. "Shoot him."

"What?"

"You heard me. Shoot him."

"Is it loaded?"

"Shoot him."

"What the hell's going on?"

"A test."

Ricky aimed the gun with a trembling arm. Juanita checked the pressure gauge, needle spiking.

He dropped his arm. "I can't do it."

Juanita ripped the Velcro off. "Guillermo, come here." She refastened the inflatable sleeve around his left arm, then turned her back to them, removing and replacing the clip. "Ricky might have just saved your life."

Guillermo was confused.

She handed him the pistol. "Shoot him."

"A test?"

She nodded.

Ricky got it now and smiled. No way the gun was loaded.

Guillermo took aim. The gauge's needle hung steady at the low end. "One question, Madre."

"What is it?"

"Did he pass the test?"

"He didn't do what I asked."

Bang.

The smile disappeared. Ricky looked down incredulously at the broadening stain in the middle of his chest.

A crash to the floor.

Juanita checked the gauge again. No movement. "Interesting. You can take that off now."

Guillermo ripped it from his arm.

She stuck the gun back in her purse. "How do you feel?"

"Hungry."

"Good boy. I'll make you a sandwich."

Luxury suite number 1563.

Near panic.

Students pounding beers as usual. Except this time it was self-medicating.

"You don't know who this Serge character is?" said Spooge.

"Thought he was with you."

"He's not with us. I thought he was with you."

"Holy God. Maybe everything he's said is bullshit. Maybe *he's* the killer."

"But he left Panama City with us before that mess in our old room."

"That just means he's working with someone else. Remember, he's the one who started all this talk about assassination."

"Spooge is right. We never saw anyone in our room at the Dunes. He could have closed those curtains himself."

"We've got to get out of here!"

They all jumped up at once, stuffing what was left of their luggage.

Melvin walked out of the bathroom. "What's going on?"

"We just realized nobody knows who Serge is."

"I know Serge."

They stopped and stared at Melvin.

"You do?"

"Yeah."

"So you trust him?"

"It's really my father who knows Serge."

"But your dad will vouch for him, right?"

"My dad's scared shitless of him."

"Screw this. We're out of here!"

"Why?" asked Melvin.

Joey said, "We think he might be the killer."

"Serge?" said Melvin. "No way."

"How can you be sure?"

"Serge may be a lot of things, but I guarantee he's not the killer," said Melvin. "Bet my life on it."

The students half relaxed.

"Still feel better if we moved. I'm getting nervous staying in one spot so long."

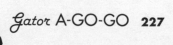

"I'm with Joey," said Spooge. "Even if Serge is legit, those bodies in Panama City were for real."

The other students picked up bags and headed for the door.

It flew open.

"Hey, everyone! I'm home!"

Serge strolled in with Coleman, City and Country. He headed for the coffee machine. "What's with all the packed bags? You going somewhere?"

"Uh, yeah," said Spooge. "I mean, we know you said to stay put, but we hadn't heard anything from you in so long . . ."

". . . That's right," continued Doogie. "Figured we'd use the time to pack and be ready when you said to split."

"Excellent thinking," said Serge. "In fact, we do need to roll."

"When?"

"Immediately. I've made contact with the assassins and baited them, so they could be kicking in the door any second and spraying the place with bullets. We leave right after my coffee's ready."

They began to unravel again.

"Look on the bright side." Serge poured water in the back of the machine. "We're going to a most righteous place. It'll be a blast!"

"Where?"

"Come on, use your brains. You can figure this out. Guillermo probably has."

"Who's Guillermo?"

"That will only upset you. Maybe you'll meet him, maybe you won't. But if you do, what good is it to die a thousand deaths in the meantime?"

"I feel faint." Cody grabbed a chair.

"Remember I told you it's all about history?" Serge switched the machine on. "We started in Panama City. Now we're in Daytona. What's the next logical progression? Anyone?"

They stared.

"The birthplace of spring break in America!" said Serge. "Guaranteed to be a killer!"

CHAPTER THIRTY-SEVEN

TAMPA BAY

*J*he single-floor Rod and Reel Motel hangs on as one of the great old Florida holdouts, resting on the shore of Anna Maria Island, just inside the southern lip of the bay. A small seawall and narrow ribbon of white-sand beach . . ."

Agent Mahoney didn't realize he was talking to himself, which meant off the meds.

". . . Behind the motel stands a short, weathered fishing pier—also called the Rod and Reel—and at the end sits a small, boxlike, two-story wooden building. Run-down, in the good way. Its top floor houses a casual seafood restaurant. The bottom sells live shrimp from large, aerated tanks giving off that unmistakably salty bait-shop funk. Inside is a cozy, rustic bar. The doors stay open. And through the great tidal surges at the mouth of Tampa Bay come some of the largest fish in the world. Without this knowledge, it seems improbable that from the tiny pier, just a few swimming yards from shore, on June 28, 1975, a then-record 1,386-pound hammerhead shark was landed. The jaws used to hang on a plaque in the bar, but now they're at a museum up the street . . ."

Mahoney sat on the wraparound deck behind the bar, the only person in a tweed coat and rumpled fedora.

He wasn't shark fishing.

Wasn't fishing at all, even though he had a pole and a line in the water. It was therapy. He was dangling for the natural approach because, like Serge, he found medication to be a thick glass wall between him and Florida. Mahoney removed his hat and relaxed on a splintered bench, casting his line again without design. ". . . And pelicans floated down by the pilings, hoping for toss-aways, as I absentmindedly bobbed my pole and scanned the wide, soothing view over water. Sunshine Skyway bridge in the distance, and Egmont Key in the middle of the mouth. The 1858 lighthouse still stood, but defensive fortifications from the Spanish-American War lay in ruins . . ."

Mahoney let a smile escape. Heart rate at a six-month low. His decade-long clinical obsession tracking Serge appeared to have gone latent. The detective was on indefinite sabbatical, with an open-ended reservation for room 3 of the Rod and Reel Motel.

Do Not Disturb.

". . . The sun tacked high at the hottest part of the day, and I retired to the bar. A trough of iced-down longnecks had my name. Nautical maps, oscillating fan, TV on a Weather Channel tornado report with overturned cars. Lacquered into the countertop were yellowed newspaper photos of anglers posing with catches . . ."

Mahoney chewed his toothpick and thumbed a morning paper. He reached the State section and read a lengthy wire report of the since-dubbed Spring Break Massacre in Panama City Beach. The toothpick went in the trash.

"So they threw the midget off the balcony," he said ruefully. "Isn't that how it always starts?"

A cell phone rang.

"Mahoney. Speak to me."

"Mahoney? This is Agent Ramirez with the bureau."

"To what do I owe the federal pleasure?"

"Just read your psychology article on profiling. Good stuff."

"You must have a very old pile of magazines."

"Found it on a computer search."

"Search for what?"

"Serge."

Mahoney winced.

"Hear what happened in Panama City?" asked Ramirez.

"Nasty business. Must have your hands full."

"Interviewed all the guests and staff—almost everyone came up clean."

"Almost?"

"One guy whose name wasn't in the registration book turned up on a number of surveillance tapes around the same time. Our database got a six-point facial recognition match."

"You're not looking for Serge," said Mahoney. "This isn't his signature. Innocent kids, and he likes to get complex."

"He was staying on the same floor at the same time. Then I saw his file . . ."—Ramirez whistled—". . . subject of interest in at least two dozen homicides."

"I'm telling you, it's the wrong tree to bark at."

"Still a coincidence we can't ignore."

"Anything from your credit card check?"

"What credit card check?"

"On the son of your protected witness."

Silence.

"Hello?" said Mahoney. "You still there?"

"How'd you know?"

"Did the math. Pro hit, spring break, your job specialty. Adds up to trouble."

"Card dead-ends at the Panama City motel. Hasn't been used since, but he did pawn his class ring in Daytona. Tracked down his motel there—another uncanny coincidence."

"Serge on security cameras?"

"And two more bodies."

"Kids?"

"No, pros. Weird murders."

"That's more like Serge."

"I need your help," said Ramirez. "Anything you got on him."

"You don't have that much storage space."

"Then just the latest. Here's my e-mail . . ."

Mahoney jotted it down.

"One more thing," said Ramirez. "Nobody else can know we talked or what you send me."

"Informant?"

"You're as good as I'd heard," said Ramirez. "Someone else was asking around at the pawnshop before I got there."

"Serge?"

"Don't know. But the APB that turned up the sale of the class ring was for law enforcement eyes only."

"That's a rodent smell, all right."

"Can I count on you?"

"Like blackjack."

Agent Mahoney strolled off the pier and returned to his room.

A vintage alligator briefcase sat on the dresser. Mahoney considered it for the longest time. Doubt. But he'd given Ramirez his word.

"I know I'm going to regret this . . ."

He flipped brass latches. Out came a laptop. He opened it and located a dedicated folder for Serge. The first item was a scanned Christmas message. The next two were digitized videos of commencement addresses—one at least a decade old from the University of South Florida, the other more recent. Mahoney involuntarily chuckled at the thought of the second. He'd practically fallen out of his chair when it first came in. Of all things, Serge delivering the graduation address at a kindergarten.

The agent attached them, plus lengthy data files, and sent the whole batch to Ramirez's e-mail.

Then another long look at the gator-skin case. He reached in a back pocket and removed the original copy of the Christmas message: a greeting card with a barefoot Santa lying against a palm tree on the beach. Inside was a folded sheet of paper with single-spaced typing. Mahoney sat on the edge of the bed, slipped on bifocals and began reading . . .

December 25

Dear friends and enemies,

> *Season's greetings! It's me, Serge! Don't you just hate these form letters people stuff in Christmas cards? Nothing screams "you're close to my heart" like a once-a-year Xerox. Plus, all the lame jazz that's going on in their lives. "Had a great time in Memphis." "Bobby lost his retainer down a storm drain." "I think the neighbors are dealing drugs." But this letter is different. You are special to me. I'm just forced to use a copy machine and gloves because of advancements in forensics. I love those TV shows!*

Has a whole year already flown by? Much to report! Let's get to it!

Number one: I ended a war.

You guessed correct, the War on Christmas! When I first heard about it, I said to Coleman, "That's just not right! We must enlist!" I rushed to the front lines, running downtown yelling "Merry Christmas" at everyone I saw. And they're all saying "Merry Christmas" back. Hmmm. That's odd: Nobody's stopping us from saying "Merry Christmas." Then I did some research, and it turns out the real war is against people saying "Happy holidays." The nerve: trying to be inclusive. So, everyone . . .

Merry Christmas! Happy Hannukah! Good times! Soul Train! Purple mountain majesties! The Pompatus of Love!

There. War over. And just before it became a quagmire.

Next: Decline of Florida Roundup.

—They tore down the Big Bamboo Lounge near Orlando. Where was everybody on that one?

—Remember the old "Big Daddy's" lounges around Florida with the logo of that bearded guy? They're now Flannery's or something.

—They closed 20,000 Leagues. And opened Buzz Lightyear. I offered to bring my own submarine. Okay, actually threatened, but they only wanted to discuss it in the security office. I've been doing a lot of running lately at theme parks.

—Here's a warm-and-fuzzy. Anyone who grew up down here knows this one, and everyone else won't have any idea what I'm talking about: that schoolyard rumor of the girl bitten by a rattlesnake on the Steeplechase at Pirate's World (now condos). I've started dropping it into all conversations with mixed results.

—In John Mellencamp's megahit "Pink Houses," the guy compliments his wife's beauty by saying her face could "stop a clock." Doesn't that mean she was butt ugly? Nothing to do with Florida. Just been bugging me.

Good news alert! I've decided to become a children's author! Instilling state pride in the youngest residents may be the only way to save the future. The book's almost finished. I've only completed the first page, but the rest just flows after that. It's called Shrimp Boat Surprise. Coleman asked what the title meant, and I said

Gator A-GO-GO   **233**

life is like sailing on one big, happy shrimp boat. He asked what the surprise was, and I said you grow up and learn that life bones you up the ass ten ways to Tuesday. He started reading and asked if a children's book should have the word "motherfucker" eight times on the first page. I say, absolutely. They're little kids, after all. If you want a lesson to stick, you have to hammer it home through repetition . . . In advance: Happy New Year! (Unlike 2008—ouch!)

DAYTONA BEACH

Serge and the gang pulled out of town as a custom motor coach rolled in.

Male motorists honked at the bus, as they always did wherever it went, because of the topless women painted on the side with strategically positioned CENSORED labels.

Someone near the front of the bus hung up a phone and walked to the back. He knocked on the RV's rear suite with circular bed.

Other side of the door: "Not now."

"Sir, it's important."

The door opened a crack. Camera lights. Seventeen-year-olds.

Rood stuck his head out. "Can't it wait?"

"Sir, we've been sued again by parents. Ten million dollars. This time they said she was *six*teen."

"So handle it like you always do."

"Sir, that was Charley. He quit. Remember?"

"Bastard!" Rood fumed at the thought of his former chief assistant walking out in Panama City. "After all I did for him."

"What do you want me to do?"

Rood looked back. "Guys, get the dildos." He stepped outside and closed the door. "Offer five hundred thousand, the cost of doing business."

"I don't think they'll take it. Pretty mad."

"Their lawyer will get them to take it."

"Their lawyer's booked them on TV."

"Everyone has a price," said Rood. "You make an appointment to see him and negotiate."

"But I'm not an attorney."

"Not as a lawyer. A potential client."

"I don't understand."

"He's only going to get a third of the five hundred K we're offering to settle for, which is why he won't take it." Rood lit a fat cigar. "So you say your company's staff attorney is a fuck-up and you want to hire him on retainer. Million a year."

"What does my company do?"

"I don't give a shit. Widgets, copper mines."

"But he won't have any work to do."

"He'll know that." Smoke rings drifted toward the ceiling. "It's a legal bribe."

The assistant coughed. "Isn't that unethical?"

"That's why it'll work."

"Won't he wonder that I walked in out of the blue?"

"Tell him you admire his lawsuit—that you hate my guts and am glad to see I'm getting what's due." Another big puff. "Say you hope he can wrap up a settlement in my case fast, a week tops, because your company needs him available right away or you'll have to go somewhere else. *Then* he'll be ready to accept my lowball five hundred K offer."

"He'll buy that?"

"No, he'll see right through it. But it'll give him plausible deniability . . . Put out your hand."

The assistant did.

Rood tapped an ash into it. "Can't fail."

"But you don't even know this guy."

"He's a lawyer."

"What about the girl?"

"Fuck her."

Squealing behind the suite's door.

Rood grabbed the knob. "Now if you'll excuse me."

Filming continued as the bus pulled into the parking lot of a luxury resort.

"Here." Rood handed the girls a presentation case. "Use the ben wa balls."

Suddenly, a screeching of cars all around the bus. Loud voices.

"Cut!" yelled Rood. He left the suite and headed toward the front of the coach. "What the hell's all that racket?"

"Sir," said his assistant. "They're here again."

"Who is?"

They leaned toward side windows. Middle-aged women in the parking lot, waving picket signs and yelling.

"How'd they find us so fast?"

"Don't know, sir."

"Son of a bitch." He turned to the driver. "Keep going."

The bus pulled away from the hotel and headed south.

CHAPTER THIRTY-EIGHT

NEW SMYRNA BEACH

*T*wenty minutes south of Daytona, the Challenger turned west on State Road 44. Serge parked beneath a neon outline of Florida.

"Another biker bar," said Coleman. "Cool!"

"Why are we stopping?" asked Andy.

"Because it's Gilly's Pub 44," said Serge. "I *love* Gilly's! 'Where everyone is treated like a local.'"

"But I mean, aren't we running for our lives?"

"Exactly." Serge opened the driver's-side door. "They'll never expect this."

Everyone grabbed stools. Coleman ordered four drinks.

"All right!" said Serge, looking at a TV on the wall. "A congressional hearing! Congressional hearings crack me up! Children argue better: *I know you are, but what am I?* . . ."

"What's this one about?"

"Eeewwww." Serge got a queasy feeling. "This one ain't so funny. They're questioning oil executives again, who continue bleeding my Florida travel budget. And if you know anything at all about Serge, you don't want to go there."

"Oh, *gasoline*," said Coleman. "So that's what everyone's been talking about?"

Serge turned slowly. "Did you just arrive on Earth?"

Coleman tossed back a shot. "No, I've been here almost my whole life."

"The part that kills me is their latest wave of commercials." Serge tipped back his bottled water. "The message now is that they're *against* oil. How stupid do they think we are? BP's new slogan: 'Beyond Petroleum.' The name of the damn company is British fucking Petroleum. They're not beyond petroleum; they're waist-deep in North Sea crude with the gas pump up our ass . . ."

"Serge, your head's turning that color again."

". . . Or the ones showing cute Alaskan wildlife, wheat fields and wind farms, with the voice-over from a woman who sounds like she's ready to fuck: 'Imagine an oil company that cares.' Holy Orwell, why not 'Marlboro: We're in the business of helping you quit smoking, so buy a carton today!' . . ."

Farther down the bar.

Four white-haired ladies in leather jackets watched TV. "I hate those oil company pricks."

"Why doesn't the government do something?" asked Edna.

"Are you listening to yourself?" said Edith. "The government?"

Back up the bar, Serge's ears perked. "Those voices . . ."

"The ones in your head?" asked Coleman.

"No, those are just the backup singers." He looked around. "Why does it sound so familiar?"

"Where are they coming from?"

Serge strained his neck. "Coleman! Over there! It's our old friends!"

He jumped off his stool, ran over and spread his arms. "The G-Unit!"

"Shit." Edith picked up her gin. "Another fan."

Edna slipped on chic sunglasses. "No autographs."

"I don't want an autograph." He hopped on the balls of his feet. "Don't you recognize me?"

"Not really."

"It's me! Serge! From that crazy cruise to Cancún. And a decade back on Triggerfish Lane."

"Dear God."

"Glad to see me? What are you drinking? I got it."

"Tanqueray."

Serge raised a finger for the bartender and opened his wallet. "What's with the leather getups?"

"We're bad to the bone," said Edith.

"So what have you been doing with yourselves these days?" asked Serge.

"Just ridin' the big slab," said Eunice.

"And hating this jackass," said Edith, nodding up toward the TV.

"That oil guy?" said Serge. "Don't get me started. Saying he's just a regular Joe with money concerns like the rest of us."

"Listen to that heartless fiction coming out of his mouth," said Edna. "When gas went back down under two dollars a gallon, I thought we'd seen the last of it, but these snakes were just lying in wait."

The TV switched to a correspondent standing outside the committee meeting room: *". . . Meanwhile, investors in the oil giant are elated with record profits, and CEO Riles 'Scooter' Highpockets III, who gave himself an eighty-million-dollar securities option this year, should receive a much more welcome reception when he appears at the company's annual stockholders' meeting at an Orlando resort tomorrow . . . Back to you, Blaine . . ."*

"How can he lie so completely and get away with it?" asked Eunice.

"Maybe he won't," Serge said with a grin.

"What do you mean?"

"How'd you like to have some fun?"

"We ain't never stopped havin' fun."

DAYTONA BEACH

Hotel business center.

Agent Ramirez tapped computer keys and opened his e-mail. An hour later, a cursor slid over "Serge Commencement #2."

The video opened with a post-event interview of the principal at police headquarters:

"Said he was a children's author?" asked a detective.

"That's right."

"And you didn't sense anything was wrong?"

"Claimed to be an alumnus, even knew the old playground layout," said the principal. "And that was years ago before it was replaced.

There's this advanced new safety padding under the teeter-totters in case someone plays a prank and jumps off—"

"I'm sure it's a fine playground. What about his commencement address?"

"That's why we started wondering. But whenever we thought, 'Where the heck is he going with this?' it snapped into place. By the time we finally caught on, he was already waving good-bye."

"This is most important of all," said the detective. "Any indication where he might have been going? Someplace we can pick up his trail?"

"When we ran outside to watch him drive away, I got the impression he was living out of his car."

The detective massaged his forehead. "How are the kids holding up?"

"Not too good," said the principal. "Most of them keep crying because he isn't their first-grade teacher next year."

The video became static, then flipping vertical lines, which soon cleared to reveal the view from a camera tripod in the back of a packed cafeteria. Drone of conversation. Hundreds of crowded parents taking snapshots from a sea of folding chairs. Up front, rows of cute tots in white caps and gowns. Serge pushed his way to the stage, where an active microphone picked up conversation.

The principal reviewed notes behind the podium. A tap on his shoulder. He looked up. "May I help you?"

"I'm the commencement speaker."

"We don't have a commencement speaker."

"They didn't tell you?"

"Who *are* you?"

"Serge A. Storms, bestselling children's author and legacy, Kinder Kollege class of '67." He extended a hand. "You must be the Principal Adams I read about in the paper. Great job you've done with the playground."

"Who's this guy with you?"

"My illustrator."

"They didn't tell me about a commencement speaker."

"Everything's okay now. I'm here."

Fast-forward . . .

Parents and children politely clapped as two men walked onto the stage. Coleman sat in a chair next to the podium, and Serge grabbed the mike: "Good morning!"

"*Good morning!*"

"This is Coleman, my illustrator." Serge opened his manuscript. "He'll be helping me today as I read from my upcoming blockbuster, *Shrimp Boat Surprise* . . . Prologue: Once upon a time there was a little girl named Story, bobbing along the sea in a big, happy shrimp boat . . ."

Coleman held up a crude drawing of a boat and a smiling stick figure with too many arms.

". . . Story had dreams of being a dancer. As she grew older, she never let those dreams die. And guess what? Those dreams came true! . . ."

Coleman held up a drawing of a larger stick figure doing a split on a catwalk.

Parents exchanged confused looks.

". . . And her dreams just kept getting bigger! . . ."

Coleman raised another sheet of paper. A stick figure swung around a fireman's pole.

Serge glanced up at growing murmurs. "Guess you're right. Still needs editing." Serge closed the notebook and began his trademark pacing across the stage.

"What a special day! I see you all can't wait to get out there in the workforce, make 401K contributions and drink lots of coffee. But I know what you're thinking: My legs are too short to drive. So you still have twelve more years and hopefully college. Use them wisely. Remember the bestselling book that said, 'Everything you need to know about life you learned in kindergarten'? Well, he lied. Everything you *really* need to know about life you learn in prison, but that won't be practical for a while. You don't want to go to prison yet, do you?"

Little heads swiveled side to side.

"Who's over there nodding 'yes'? That is *so* pre-K. You think this is a joke? Take a look at my illustrator . . ."

Coleman smiled and waved.

". . . The most important contribution you can make now is tak-

ing pride in your treasured home state. Because nobody else is. Study and cherish her history, even if you have to do it on your own time. I did. Don't know what they're teaching today, but when I was a kid, American history was the exact same every year: Christopher Columbus, Plymouth Rock, Pilgrims, Thomas Paine, John Hancock, Sons of Liberty, tea party. I'm thinking, 'Okay, we have to start somewhere— we'll get to Florida soon enough.' . . . Boston Massacre, Crispus Attucks, Paul Revere, the North Church, 'Redcoats are coming,' one if by land, two if by sea, three makes a crowd, and I'm sitting in a tiny desk, rolling my eyes at the ceiling. Hello! Did we order the wrong books? Were these supposed to go to Massachusetts? . . . Then things showed hope, moving south now: Washington crosses the Delaware, down through original colonies, Carolinas, Georgia. Finally! Here we go! Florida's next! Wait. What's this? No more pages in the book. School's out? Then I had to wait all summer, and the first day back the next grade: Christopher Columbus, Plymouth Rock . . . Know who the first modern Floridians were? Seminoles! Only unconquered group in the country! These are your peeps, the rugged stock you come from. Not genetically descended, but bound by geographical experience like a subtropical Ellis Island. Because who's really from Florida? Not the flamingos, or even the Seminoles for that matter. They arrived when the government began rounding up tribes, but the Seminoles said, 'Naw, we prefer waterfront,' and the white man chased them but got freaked out in the Everglades and let 'em have slot machines . . . I see you glancing over at the cupcakes and ice cream, so I'll limit my remaining remarks to distilled wisdom:

"Respect your parents. And respect them even more after you find out they were wrong about a bunch of stuff. Their love and hard work got you to the point where you could realize this.

"Don't make fun of people who are different. Unless they have more money and influence. Then you must.

"If someone isn't kind to animals, ignore anything they have to say.

"Your best teachers are sacrificing their comfort to ensure yours; show gratitude. Your worst are jealous of your future; rub it in.

"Don't talk to strangers, don't play with matches, don't eat the yellow snow, don't pull your uncle's finger.

"Skip down the street when you're happy. It's one of those carefree little things we lose as we get older. If you skip as an adult, people talk, but I don't mind.

"*Don't* follow the leader.

"Don't try to be different—that will make you different.

"Don't try to be popular. If you're already popular, you've peaked too soon.

"Always walk away from a fight. Then ambush.

"Read everything. Doubt everything. Appreciate everything.

"When you're feeling down, make a silly noise.

"Go fly a kite—seriously.

"Always say 'thank you,' don't forget to floss, put the lime in the coconut.

"Each new year of school, look for the kid nobody's talking to— and talk to him.

"Look forward to the wonderment of growing up, raising a family and driving by the gas station where the popular kids now work.

"Cherish freedom of religion: Protect it from religion.

"Remember that a smile is your umbrella. It's also your sixteen-in-one reversible ratchet set.

" 'I am rubber, you are glue' carries no weight in a knife fight.

"Hang on to your dreams with everything you've got. Because the best life is when your dreams come true. The second-best is when they don't but you never stop chasing them. So never let the authority jade your youthful enthusiasm. Stay excited about dinosaurs, keep looking up at the stars, become an archaeologist, classical pianist, police officer or veterinarian. And, above all else, question everything I've just said. Now get out there, class of 2020, and take back our state!"

CHAPTER THIRTY-NINE

ORLANDO

Serge flattened out the front of his jacket. "How do I look?"

"Hey, handsome," said Eunice.

Edna checked herself in the mirror. "Never thought I'd catch you in a tux."

"It's too binding for my lifestyle, but some things are worth sacrificing for."

The G-Unit had suspended the leather dress code for their most elegant social attire.

The adjoining door to the next suite opened. Students poked heads in. "What are we doing here?"

"The Master Plan has detours," said Serge. "Just don't leave that room."

"For how long?"

Serge pushed the door shut.

"*Ow.*"

"Okay," said Edith. "What am I supposed to do again?"

Serge walked across the suite of a swank resort on International Drive. Two sets of gloves sat on the dresser. A dainty white lace pair. And latex.

"Put the plastic on first, then the white ones will conceal them."

She slipped them on. "How's that look?"

"Perfect." Serge handed her a Ziplock bag containing a single dollar bill. "Now stick this in your pocket and don't open it until the last second. And when you do, make sure the dollar doesn't touch any part of your body but your hands. The inner gloves will protect them."

"It's just going to cause embarrassment, right?" said Edna. "I mean, he's not going to get hurt or anything."

"All my pranks are completely safe," said Serge. "Everyone ready?"

Elevators opened on the convention floor. A spiffy Serge stepped out with Edith on his arm, followed by the rest of the G-Unit.

A bustle of activity greeted them at the entrance of the largest conference hall. Reporters, TV cameras, hotel staff wheeling carts of water carafes. Enthusiastic applause roared out the doors.

Edith tugged Serge's arm. "You sure they're going to let us in?"

"Positive."

"But what if we get caught? None of us has any shares in the company."

"That's the beauty of stockholder meetings. Just dress appropriately. At this financial level, the last thing they want to do is insult investors with something bourgeois like asking for ID. And they *especially* don't want to demean my sweet grandmother who obviously controls a massive block of voting shares."

Just as Serge predicted, they strolled right in unquestioned.

Riles Highpockets was already up on the elevated dais. The hall remained extra dark except for the podium spotlight and a Jumbo Tron on each side of the stage, filled with his sweaty jowls.

Each time the tycoon bellowed another glowing financial number into the microphone, rolling ovations swept across a thousand padded folding chairs.

"What do we do now?" asked Edith.

Serge gestured toward the right of the stage. "That's the cable news people for the post-speech interview. We need to start working our way over. No chance he'll snub my charming grandmother's request in front of a national audience."

Another wave of wild applause. Riles reached his climactic conclusion. "*. . . And with the help of our government friends, next year will be even better!*"

A thundering standing O erupted as Riles made his way down stage steps toward the cable networks. Camera lights came out. A boom microphone dipped over the baron's head.

The interview had just begun when Serge stepped up. "Excuse

me, Mr. Highpockets, but my grandmother has wanted to meet you for years."

"Sir," said a TV correspondent. "We're in the middle of a segment."

Highpockets held up a hand. "It's okay. There's always time to respect our elders."

"You're a great man," said Edith. "America needs more like you. Could I possibly get your autograph on this dollar?"

Riles glanced toward the camera with a grin, thinking, my PR people couldn't have planned this any better. "Why it would be my pleasure."

He took the bill and a pen, scribbling a large signature. Then another practiced smile. "There you go."

Edith held open a plastic bag. "Just drop it in there. Wouldn't want it to smudge or anything before I get it framed."

The interview resumed.

Serge and the G-Unit watched from behind the news people.

"What happens now?" asked Edna.

Serge rubbed his palms. "Wait for the fun to begin."

Three minutes later, a handler interrupted and whispered in Riles's ear.

"Sorry," said Highpockets, "but they have me on a tight schedule." He gave a big wave to the crowd before being ushered out the side door to a waiting stretch.

The correspondent turned toward her camera. "Another busy day for one of the country's richest oilmen, who will now be flown by private jet helicopter to a drilling platform in the Gulf of Mexico, where he will personally thank his corporation's hardworking blue-collar employees . . ."

"What the hell?" said Serge.

"I didn't see any embarrassment," said Edna.

"Not enough time to take effect. Crap."

"All this for nothing?" said Edith.

"We might get lucky and see something later on TV." Serge took her by the arm and strolled out of the hall. "My guess is there'll be a camera crew on that helicopter for carefully choreographed photo ops of him mixing with the common man at the drilling platform. No way he's just doing it for the good and welfare."

Mahoney accidentally caught a fish.

He cranked it in, removed the hook and threw it back. "Be free. Have a long and productive life . . ."

A pelican waiting below caught it on the fly and gulped it down.

"Isn't that always the case . . ."

The agent stared off at a distant tanker making its way up the ship channel. A gut feeling had been nagging him ever since Serge's name came up. That business in Panama City just wasn't his guy. He threw a toothpick in the water.

"Something's not jake."

Mahoney cast his line again, set it in a rod holder and dialed his cell.

"Agent Ramirez here."

"It's Mahoney. What's the name of the kid?"

"That's confidential."

"One hand washes the other."

"What's this about?"

"If Serge is your man, there may be a connection. And nobody knows Serge like me."

"It violates about ten rules."

"Who got you those files? I scratch your back, you scratch mine."

"I guess you're right. Andrew McKenna."

"Consider us even."

Mahoney knew people, and he knew Ramirez was too by-the-book for his tastes. But Mahoney held markers from people all over the state. He dialed again. An old friend at the bureau.

". . . Should be under Andrew McKenna," said Mahoney.

"But the protection program files are confidential."

"Just bring me up to speed on background."

"I don't know."

"Who got you out of that scrape in Lantana?"

"I was innocent. You try to be nice and give a stripper a ride home, and she pays you back by smoking ten joints in the car when you're not there and leaving all the roaches in the ashtray."

"I'm waiting."

"Call you back . . ."

He did, giving Mahoney chapter and verse, right up until "his mother shot herself and we had to move them again out of Michigan."

"Shot herself?"

"That's what it says."

"One more thing: I need a trace on his credit card."

"I've already stuck my neck out."

"*My* neck was out for you at the other business in Boca."

"That's the thing about strippers: No good deed goes unpunished."

"So you'll do it?"

"I got your number."

"Thanks, Bugsy."

"It's Harold."

GILLY'S PUB 44

Edith sipped gin. Back in leather.

"Great to get out of those stuffy rags."

"Anything on TV yet about Highpockets?"

Edna shook her head.

"Serge," said Eunice. "Where'd you come up with that idea anyway?"

"Coleman gets the credit for this one. He's to drug knowledge what I am to Florida." Serge tipped back a bottle of water. "Plus it's from the sixties, which means I couldn't resist."

"What's the sixties got to do with it?" asked Ethel.

"Rumors circulated about radicals like Ken Kesey, the Jefferson Airplane and the Grateful Dead planning to mix LSD with DMSO, then spread it on doorknobs and stair railings at political conventions so the establishment would have a psycho-meltdown on network TV."

"What's DMSO?" asked Eunice.

"Dimethyl sulfoxide, from wood pulping," said Serge. "Powerful skin penetrant. Mix it with any other chemical, and it goes right to the bloodstream. If you put some on your arm and rub, say, a lime, you'll taste Key lime pie. Coleman scored the acid; I got the DMSO."

"And that's what you soaked the dollar bill in?"

"How was I supposed to know they'd whisk him away so fast?"

"That doesn't sound like a harmless prank," said Eunice.

"Not only is it harmless," said Serge, "it's totally fair."

"How's that fair?"

"Everything hinges on Riles's character." Serge took another calm pull of water. "If his inner soul's pure, he could actually come off looking more sympathetic than ever. If not . . ."

At the other end of the bar, Andy was tapped out. He searched his empty wallet. The bartender had seen it many times before and hovered with growing suspicion. As a last ditch, Andy tried the compartment behind his family photos, where he sometimes kept an emergency twenty for cab fare. "So there's my credit card . . . Here . . ."

The bartender relaxed with a smile and ran it through a magnetic slide.

"Look," said Edith. "Something's happening on TV!"

"Turn it up," Edna told the bartender.

He handed Andy his receipt and aimed a remote at the set.

"*. . . Breaking news at this hour concerning the shocking death of oil magnate Riles 'Scooter' Highpockets III in a bizarre drilling platform mishap . . .*"

"You promised just embarrassment," said Edna.

"Shhhhhhh!" said Edith.

"*. . . Our correspondent on Highpockets's personal helicopter noticed extremely unusual behavior on the flight out to the gulf, captured in this exclusive footage . . .*"

The image switched to a wild-eyed Riles grabbing the lens of the camera and pulling it to his nose. "*I'm rich! I'm so fucking rich. We can do anything we want and nobody can stop us! Everyone out there: Keep drivin', suckers! . . .*"

Back to the anchor desk. "*The erratic antics continued after landing on the platform, where Highpockets immediately ran to the massive drill. A warning to viewers: The following footage may be disturbing . . .*"

Riles looked down and spread his arms. "*Oil! Oil! I want to* [bleep] *it.*" He lunged. The TV abruptly cut back to the anchorwoman. "*We must stop the film here, but it was at this point that all witnesses agree*

Gator A-GO-GO **249**

Highpockets voluntarily took a running leap down into the drill shaft mechanism. The rig's crew briefly considered suspending operations out of respect and concerns of product contamination, but a petroleum engineer at the site assured them that the magnate's organic matter added octane and gas mileage . . . In a prepared statement just released by corporate headquarters in Houston, the board of directors extended its condolences to the victim's loved ones while lauding their CEO's actions on the platform. I quote: 'Riles was a dear friend to the entire Lunar Holdings family, and everyone is deeply touched by his ultimate sacrifice in the development of alternative biofuels. We are moving beyond petroleum to a greener America. Who would expect that from an oil company? Riles, that's who.' "

Part Three

FORT LAUDERDALE

CHAPTER FORTY

ROD AND REEL PIER

gent Mahoney bobbed a line in the water.

A phone rang.

"Mahoney here. Mumble to me."

"It's Harold. If you're still interested, I just got a hit on that credit card."

"Where!"

"Bar in New Smyrna. It's called . . ."

Mahoney knew the place inside out. "Thanks, Dutch."

He closed the phone. "Here, kid. Have a fishing pole."

"Gee, thanks, mister. And it's got a fish on it."

Mahoney cleared out of room 3 at the Rod and Reel Motel and sped east in a '68 Dodge Monaco.

PALM BEACH

The Atlantic was calm. A light chop sparkled from a late-morning sun and glistened off the windows of old-money mansions.

Unlike other parts of the state, the continental shelf drops like a cliff just a few miles out, where the big freighters and yachts cruise. Route A1A continued south, leaving the famous Worth Avenue shopping district and swinging out to the edge of the beach. A '73 Challenger rolled by security cameras at the entrance of the Trump compound, station wagon and pickup close behind.

Andy was up front with Serge. City and Country passed a bottle in the backseat. Coleman was there, too. Normally, it would have been tight quarters.

Serge looked in the rearview and raised his walkie-talkie. "Lord of the Binge, you okay?"

Coleman keyed his own walkie-talkie. "I like it here."

Andy visibly shook as he turned around and stared at Coleman lying up on the rear window ledge, then back at Serge and his walkie-talkie. "No offense, but I'm not sure I want to be riding with you guys anymore."

"Don't have a choice," said Serge, draining a travel mug of coffee.

"Is that a threat?"

"For your own safety." Serge set the cup back on the dash. "You know I'd never let anything happen to you."

"I get the feeling something will anyway."

"I was saving this, because I knew how spooked you were."

"Saving what?"

Serge took his hands off the wheel and clapped them together. "I have great news! This is going to make your whole day, sure to boost your spirits!"

"What is it?"

"Remember me mentioning the birthplace of spring break? I just found the original spot. I mean the exact, genuine GPS location, not like the Fountain of Youth, where they dug a hole in St. Augustine, planted a sign and took my fucking money without even letting me climb down the well, but I did anyway. More like fell—Coleman let go of my ankles. But what are you going to do?"

"I'd like to get out of the car now, please."

"We're going too fast."

They left Boynton and crossed the Broward line.

"I still think we should call the authorities," said Andy.

"Told you: There's a mole."

"But what can one guy do? If I call, they'll send a whole team like they did before . . ."

"And take you to a safe house?"

"Right."

"That's why I can't let you," said Serge. "I know this game. When there's a mole, the precise moment you're in greatest danger is during the hand-off. It's the last open shot they'll have. Besides, I got something better than a regular safe house."

"Which is?"

"Serge's Safe Fun House!"

Somewhere along the Atlantic coast, a cell phone rang.

"Agent Ramirez here."

"Received a hit on that credit card."

"Finally! Where? . . ."

The '73 Challenger continued down A1A, speeding past giant new condos and boutiques where history had been demolished.

"Serge," said Andy. "Why are you waving a gun out the window at those buildings and making shooting sounds with your mouth?"

"Does that bother you?"

They crossed Sunrise Boulevard. Recent construction gave way to the old Lauderdale strip. Andy looked out the window at a postcard view: endless sea, bent coconut palms, lifeguard shacks and the famous whitewashed balustrade along the sidewalk. "Where are we?"

"The cradle." He pulled into a convenience store parking lot, and students from the other vehicles gathered 'round

"Supply run," said Serge. "Stock up heavy. Gets expensive fast if you run out down where we're staying."

Coleman and the kids went for beer coolers. Serge spun racks of souvenirs. Melvin grabbed bags of chips.

Andy glanced around. "Pssst, Melvin. Can I ask you a favor?"

"Why are you whispering?"

"Don't want Serge to hear." Andy handed him his credit card and a disposable cell phone in a plastic blister pack. "Buy this for me."

"Why don't *you* buy it?"

"Serge doesn't want me making any calls."

"I don't think he wants anyone making calls."

"You're not worried?"

Melvin laughed. "You don't know Serge like I do. This is all just fake drama. That's what I was finally able to explain to the other guys. He's hilariously eccentric. I convinced them to sit back and go along with his imagination. Trust me, it'll be a riot."

"I don't think this is fake."

"Of course it is. Why? You know something we don't?"

Andy opened his mouth, thinking of all the things he wanted to say—canceling each one before it came out. "Can you buy the phone?"

"It's not my credit card."

"These people never check."

"I don't think Serge is going to let me."

"He likes you. Tell him it's about a girl."

Serge was at the checkout.

"Sorry," said the cashier. "We just have those magnets and key chains."

Serge leaned far over the counter and looked down. "Sure you don't have anything else back there? Bet you do if you look. Tequesta artifacts; Stranahan family mementos; Las Olas bricks; wood splinters from coastal forts, whence this city got its name."

"We have little thimbles."

"You should have bricks. I can get some if you want. Hot seller." He grabbed an item from a cardboard counter display. "Better than this cigarette lighter that looks like a penis. I can have you up to your neck in bricks by sundown. Just say the word."

"Sir," said the cashier. "Someone wants to buy something."

"Oh, sorry." He stepped aside. "Melvin, what are you doing with that phone? You know what we talked about."

Melvin looked at his shoes. "It's . . . a girl."

Serge slapped him on the back. "You *are* a sly dog."

A luxury motor coach blocked traffic in both directions on A1A as the driver negotiated a challenging turn radius.

Car honked. Not from annoyance. They recognized the company name and paint job. *Girls Gone Haywire* had come to town!

The driver finally cleared the road and pulled into the parking lot of a towering resort.

Rood and staff climbed down.

His chief assistant assessed the new shooting locale. "Sir, I don't think kids come to Fort Lauderdale for spring break anymore."

"Some still do," said Rood. "We'll just have to be patient."

"But what if those hags show up again with their signs?"

"Nobody can follow us forever."

The assistant looked up the strip. "I still haven't seen a single babe."

"Like I said, be patient."

The gang regrouped outside the convenience store.

"Where's Andy?" said Serge.

"Think he's in the bathroom."

Andy was torn. He sat on the toilet, staring forever at his new cell phone.

He'd started to dial and hung up three times already. Serge was clearly insane. But so had been his own life ever since that day in kindergarten. And Serge was smart. Andy figured it a 50-50 proposition he was right about a mole and the danger of going in.

Decision time.

He dialed again and let it ring through. Answering service.

"Dad, it's me, Andy. I think some people discovered our witness identities. I wanted to call the special number they gave us, but there might be an informant. Except the guy who told me that is— . . . I'm so confused. I don't know who to trust . . ."

Banging on the door. "Andy, it's me, Serge. You okay in there?"

"Fine. Just be a minute." He set the phone's ringer on vibrate and returned it to his head. "What am I supposed to do? I'm in Fort Lauderdale; call when you get this message . . ."

CHAPTER FORTY-ONE

THE CRADLE

*S*tudents assembled on the sidewalk in front of Serge, getting wasted but remembering his advice to keep drinks concealed because they were now "behind enemy lines."

He looked across sunburnt faces. "Anyone?"

A hand went up. "Didn't it start with the movie *Where the Boys Are?*"

"Excellent answer," said Serge. "And wrong. That's when it really exploded, except it actually began in 1935 just up the street. But since we're outside Tour Stop Number One, the infamous Elbo Room, let's talk about that movie . . ."

They went inside and ordered a round. ". . . This area here is where they filmed. Students had been flocking from northern universities for years until the migration reached twenty thousand in the late fifties, still extremely modest by today's standards. Then in 1960, after that movie came out, numbers exploded to more than three hundred thousand, making the required pilgrimage to this very bar. If you look closely at the carved-up wood, you might find your parents' initials. Or grandparents' . . ."

Andy was in the rear of the group, facing the other way, surreptitiously sliding a cell phone from his pocket.

". . . Until that movie, Middle America had been in the dark about what was going down in Florida . . . But their first hint came the year before when, on Monday, April 13, 1959, *Time* magazine exposed the secret world of booze, sex, throwing alligators in motel pools, driving twenty-seven hours from Pennsylvania's Dickinson College and rioting when a bar ran out of beer during an all-you-can-drink-for-a-dollar-fifty special."

"Dollar fifty!" said a student.

"Ain't heritage an ass kicker? And here's your free bonus: an ultra-cool history footnote that has come to be known as my signature, or obnoxiousness, depending on the reviewer. Remember, it was still 1959, the year before the movie. And that *Time* article ended with a girl being asked to explain the attraction of spring break. Her answer? It's 'where the boys are.'"

"Wow."

"Andy!" yelled Serge. "What are you doing back there?"

"Nothing!" The cell went back in his pocket.

"The Elbo was even slated for the wrecking ball a couple years back, but the condo market went bust and saved her, for the time being . . . Kill those drinks—we're on the prowl!"

Three minutes later, the convoy parked in metered slots a few blocks south. Serge led the gang on foot around a private gate.

"And this is Bahia Mar Marina, home of literature's Travis Mc-Gee and his houseboat, the *Busted Flush* . . ." He walked briskly through a dock entrance. ". . . His creator, John D. MacDonald, died in 1986, and the following February they erected a magnificent brass memorial plaque on a stately concrete pedestal at Travis's boat slip, F-18, which is . . ."—he turned the corner—". . . right here . . . What the fuck?"

"What is it?"

"The monument! It's gone!"

"It's a pretty big marina," said Spooge. "Sure you didn't get the wrong spot?"

"Not a chance," said Serge. "This shit I know inside out. Always have to stop and touch the plaque each time through town, ever since the '97 World Series when I came here with Sharon and nearly shot—Better stick with my official account."

A security guard in a golf cart zipped by.

"Excuse me!" yelled Serge. "Mr. Make-Believe Cop!"

The cart stopped.

Serge sprinted across the dock.

"Can I help you?" asked the guard.

A-GO-GO **259**

Serge pointed behind him. "The monument! . . . MacDonald! . . . Disappeared! . . . Was it Maoists? . . ."

"Oh, the *plaque*. About some books. Yeah, they moved it to the dockmaster's office."

"Why'd they do that?"

The guard shrugged.

"Which way?"

"Last building over there."

Serge looked back at the gang and made a big wave of his arm. "I found it! Hurry! . . . Andy, what's that behind your back?"

"Nothing."

Serge and the students ran down a seawall along the Intracoastal Waterway. Andy fell farther and farther behind. He began slipping a hand into his pocket again. Before he could reach the phone, it vibrated.

Andy almost fell in the water. He quickly flipped it open with a whisper: "Hello?"

"Andy? Is that you? Andy McKenna?"

"Who's this?"

"Agent Ramirez. Are you all right?"

"Thank heavens! You have to help . . ." He stopped and looked at the recently bought disposable phone. "Where'd you get my number? Nobody has it. You're . . . Guillermo, aren't you?"

"I can explain. Don't hang up!"

He hung up.

Serge cut across a lawn and burst through the doors of the dockmaster's office, lunging at the woman behind the nearest desk.

"Can I help you?"

Serge straightened his posture and collected himself. "Yes, the helpful security guard told me about the relocation of one of our state's holiest touchstones."

"Our what?"

The office was small. Students snaked behind Serge and out the open door. Andy was last. His phone vibrated again. He opened it slowly but didn't speak.

"Don't hang up! I got lucky and decided to give your father's answering service another shot. This number was attached to your message."

Silence.

"Andy? Still there?"

"You know my father?"

"I'm one of the agents who originally moved you fifteen years ago."

"I had a Dolphins poster in my room—"

"Larry Csonka."

More silence, this time from shock.

"Andy?"

"Thank God! You're telling the truth! You've got to get me out of here!"

"Where are you exactly?"

"With some lunatic . . ."

"Andy!" Serge yelled out the door. "What are you doing out there?"

"Nothing!"

"Don't hang up!"

Click.

Andy trotted toward the office.

"Feeling okay?" asked Serge, holding the door. "You've been acting kinda weird."

"I'm fine."

"Good, because these kind people just showed me where the plaque is. It's behind the door on that little stand unworthy of Travis." He turned to the rest of the group. "Listen up. This puts us behind schedule, so keep the line moving . . ."

The dockmaster's staff thought they'd signed up for marina administration. But the new placement of the plaque had drawn a stream of hard-core MacDonald buffs and their spectrum of behavior—so barely a blip registered on their radar as the column of young visitors marched past the stand and ritualistically touched the plaque. They finished and walked out the door. Except one.

"Andy, why aren't you touching the plaque? What's wrong with you?"

"What's wrong with *me*? How can you goof around at a time like this?"

"I'm not goofing around. It's all part of the Master Plan . . ." —he lowered his voice—". . . Remember what we talked about in the car?"

"What does touching plaques have to do with any of that?"

"The plan . . . has tangents."

"There is no plan! You're going to get me killed!"

"Touch the plaque. For me?"

Andy sighed and halfheartedly brushed it with the back of his hand.

"Now, how hard was that?"

"I am so dead." He walked out the door.

Serge turned back to the office staff. "Appreciate the hospitality. But the plaque really should be back on the dock."

"What?"

"I know it wasn't your doing." Serge winked. "We'll talk later."

CHAPTER FORTY-TWO

MIAMI

Another phone call.

"Hello?" said Juanita.

"Credit card's been used again."

"Where?"

"If I may say something, they've got agents all over this. Good ones. We could take a big fall, and for what?"

"The address."

"You hear what I said?"

Juanita went from ice to thermonuclear in a blink. "You never speak disrespectfully to me! I took you in! I stood by you!"

"Didn't mean it that way."

"Anyone else would have been killed for letting Randall Sheets slip away!"

"I made it up to you. Even with everyone looking at us, I still went back for those informant files. Jesus, they were your brothers!"

"You're the one who gave me their names."

"And I've regretted it every day since."

"Are we not paying you enough?"

"That isn't what I mean. This is a business, and this makes no business sense."

"Because of who you are to me, I will make an exception and ask you one more time, but only one more time. What is the address where the credit card was used?"

A pause. "Have something to write with?"

"That's a good boy."

The Challenger-led convoy sped south on A1A and turned right onto Harbor Drive.

A well-kept old Florida motel. Two floors, fresh yellow paint, blue trim. Configured at acute, retro angles protecting a courtyard with lush tropical plants and picnic tables.

Serge hopped out. "This is our place! The fabulous Bahia Cabana!"

Serge checked in at the office across the street. They gathered again in the middle of the courtyard. "Here are your room keys . . ."

Serge stopped and stared up the street at a much more expensive resort.

"What is it?" asked Coleman.

"The *Girls Gone Haywire* bus."

"*Girls Gone Haywire* is here?" said Coleman. "Cool!"

"Not cool," said Serge. "They exploit children."

"So why are you smiling?"

"Because I have an idea." He turned back to the students. "Okay, I'll need some help with the pickup truck."

"What kind of help?"

"Our next spring break history stop—this one's the best! Clear everything out of the back bed."

"You got it."

Students emptied trash and tools. Serge retrieved a duffel bag from the Challenger's trunk and flipped down the pickup's tailgate. He unzipped the bag and pulled out what looked like a giant plastic tarp covered with cartoon fish and octopuses.

"What's that?"

"The commemorative revival of where it all started." Serge laid it in the pickup's bed, uncapped a clear tube and began blowing.

Nothing happened for the first minute. Students watched curiously. Then the plastic began taking shape, slowly unfolding itself with each breath, until it flopped open in a circle.

Serge continued blowing furiously. The circle began to rise. Serge began to slide down the side of the pickup.

"Serge, you're hyperventilating! Take a break!"

Serge shook his head and clenched the tube in his side teeth. "Only way to inflate anything is all at once as fast as you can."

Blowing accelerated.

"Serge! Stop!"

"You're going to hurt yourself!"

Bam.

"Serge fainted!"

Coleman ran over as air wheezed out the inflation tube.

Serge sat up with giddiness. "I see sparkly things."

"Inflating stuff gets you high?" said Coleman. "I'm there!"

He took over where Serge had left off. Puffy cheeks turned scarlet. He fell on the ground next to Serge. "Sparkly things. Excellent."

Students peered over the side of the truck. "A kiddie pool?"

Andy hid in one of the motel's alcoves, dialing a cell phone. He put it to his head.

"Andy, what's happening?" asked Agent Ramirez.

"I think Serge is inflating a kiddie pool."

"Serge?"

"The lunatic I told you about."

"I know all about Serge," said Ramirez. "You have to get away from him immediately. He's extremely dangerous."

"I'm scared."

"You should be."

"What happened in Panama City?"

"Best to put it out of your head. The important thing is that you let me take you in. But we need to hurry."

"Because there's an informant."

No answer.

"Agent Ramirez?"

"I'm here."

"Serge said there's an informant. Is that true?"

"Yes. I'm so sorry. It wasn't supposed to happen like this."

"Serge said if there's an informant, then taking me in is the most dangerous time."

"That's why I'm personally going to escort you myself. I'll be the only one you'll meet."

"You won't have a giant SWAT team or something?"

"I shouldn't be telling you this, but when there's an informant, you never know," said Ramirez. "That's how they've been able to track you down the coast. I'm not sure who I can trust anymore."

"Oh my God."

"Andy, you have to keep it together just a little longer." Ramirez looked out his car window at surf and palms. "I'm almost to Fort Lauderdale. Tell me where you are and I can pick you up in no time."

Andy took a deep breath. "Okay, I can handle it."

"Where are you?" asked Ramirez.

"Andy!" yelled Serge. "Where are you?"

"Shit!"

"Don't hang up!"

Click.

Andy pocketed the phone as Serge came around the corner.

"There you are! What are you doing lurking back here?"

"Nothing."

"Come on! You're missing all the fun!" Serge looked left and right. "Just need to find a hose . . ."

Andy pointed behind the building.

"Glad to have you on the team." Serge unscrewed the fitting and carried green rubber loops over his shoulder.

The rest of the students were waiting. Serge attached the hose to another nearby faucet and unrolled it back to the truck.

"You're probably wondering, 'What the heck is crazy ol' Serge up to now?' We're at the finish line! All the way back to the beginning of our history quest! Or at least we will be when we get to the next stop." He pointed the hose, and water splashed down into the bed of the pickup. "Spring break is one of the very few social phenomena where you can actually pinpoint the exact geographical location of its origin, latitude 26-06-59 north, longitude 80-06-19 west, the tiny bowl of primordial soup from which it bubbled to life. Now symbolized by our kiddie pool . . ."

Water reached the top of the first inflatable ring, then the second.

". . . It all started just blocks north of here on the side of A1A when, in 1928, the city constructed the first Olympic-size pool in the state of Florida. It would have stopped there, except for the father of a student attending Colgate University in Hamilton, New York. Back then, they didn't have many indoor facilities, and swim teams couldn't practice in cold months." Water cascaded out the back of the pickup. "That dad was living in Fort Lauderdale and contacted legendary coach Sam Ingram, saying the team could gain an edge if they came down and worked out in Florida—"

"Serge, the pool's overflowing."

"And we're in a drought. Another sign of what's gone horribly wrong with society . . ." He ran and turned off the faucet, then quickly returned and pulled a Magic Marker from his pocket. "Where was I?"

"Colgate."

"Right. In 1935, the swim team came to practice in the Casino Pool, filled with comfortably warm saltwater from the Atlantic." Serge reached into the bed of the truck and wrote something on the plastic. "Besides splashing around, they also enjoyed pristine beaches and an incredible climate that stood in stark contrast to what they'd just left. The very first spring breakers! When they returned to school, word spread. The following year: Why hunker down in snow when paradise awaits? More and more teams descended, and the informal practices turned into the massive annual College Swim Coaches Association forum. Non-athletes started joining the party, their numbers swelling steadily over the next twenty-five years until *Where the Boys Are* blew the roof off." Serge pulled a plastic specimen jar from his pocket and set it next to the pool. "Let's rock!"

A Crown Vic with blackwall tires drove past the end of the street. Agent Ramirez opened his phone.

CHAPTER FORTY-THREE

FORT LAUDERDALE

𝓢erge's convoy peeled out on A1A. "Remember to take plenty of pictures . . ."

A Delta 88 passed them northbound. Guillermo pulled up to an independent convenience store and went inside. He casually collected sodas and granola bars.

The man behind the register was bald with gray on the sides.

Guillermo set his purchases on the counter. "You the owner?"

The man nodded and began ringing up.

"Noticed your security cameras . . ."—pointing fingers in different directions—". . . That's the business I'm in. Make you a great deal on a new system."

The owner scanned the bar code on a Sprite. "We like the one we got."

"I know those models," said Guillermo. "They never last. And when they go, you won't find another offer like mine."

"Thanks, but I'll pass. That'll be nine sixty-two."

"Understand." Guillermo pulled a ten-spot from his wallet. "But mind if I take a look at the monitors and recorder in the office anyway and see if I can work up a price? What do you have to lose?"

"I don't think so."

The '73 Challenger turned off A1A and parked under a sign.

FORT LAUDERDALE AQUATIC COMPLEX.

Serge led the gang through yet another gate.

"Damn!" said Joey. "Look at the size of this place!"

Competitors triple-twisted off high dives and breast-stroked down lap lanes.

"Is that the Casino Pool?"

"No," said Serge. "Fuckers demolished it in the mid-sixties." He dipped a hand in the new pool and rubbed it on his neck. "This is its spiritual replacement, so we'll have to make do. The cool part is that it's open to the public for swimming."

"We're going to swim here?"

"Got something far better in mind. Follow me."

They walked out the rear of the patio, across a lawn and past a giant abstract sculpture of someone doing the Australian crawl. Ahead: a nondescript building stashed in the rear of the property. Serge stopped at the entrance. "Andy, come here . . ."

Behind: A white Crown Vic with blackwall tires raced by the swim complex on A1A, Agent Ramirez frantically dialing and redialing his cell phone. "Come on! Why won't he answer?"

"Check it out, Andy." Serge looked down at the sidewalk and old inlaid blue-and-white ceramic tiles: INTERNATIONAL SWIMMING HALL OF FAME. "I'm getting tingles."

Andy stood next to Serge, staring down with a pained expression of desperation as his pocket silently vibrated.

"You need to loosen up." Serge slapped him hard on the back. "I know you're thinking something utterly horrible might happen any second, but I have the same feeling all the time and it doesn't stop me from being a happy chipmunk. Let's go inside!"

Serge signed the guest book with bold calligraphy. They had the place to themselves as he gave the group his whirlwind A-tour. ". . . Here are Buster Crabbe's medals and trophies . . . life-size mannequin with a creepy wig of Duke Kahanamoku, father of modern surfing . . . Mark Spitz . . . Rowdy Gaines . . . 1935 seashell plaque honoring Katherine Rawls, the greatest swimming sensation of her day, who trained here . . ." Students rushed to keep up with Serge's unbroken stride. ". . . Esther Williams's movie poster . . . 1958 photo of the Casino Pool with Mediterranean bathhouse . . . and finally the pièce de résistance—check out this glass case. Those are Johnny Weissmuller's five gold medals from the 1924 and '28 Olympics in

Paris and Amsterdam. Imagine that! Tarzan's coolest shit! And nobody knows it's just sitting here in this fabulous empty museum, which should be mobbed but isn't because they don't have any rides. Let's get the hell out of here!"

"But, Serge"—Joey held up his watch—"We've been here less than two minutes. And we only stopped running when we got to the gold-medal case."

"That's right. I like to turn it into a ride." Serge ran out the door.

Despite their age advantage, the kids had to hustle. They jumped back in vehicles as Serge left the parking lot. He raced fifty feet and parked in another.

The kids pulled into adjacent slots. "We drove ten seconds just to park across the street?"

"It isn't about parking. It's about hallowed earth." Serge dropped to his knees and placed a palm on the hot tar. "This is the exact birthplace of spring break, where they paved over that first pool. A moment of silence. That's too long." He flipped down the pickup's tailgate and hopped into the kiddie pool, reclining with arms hooked over the inflated edge. "Who wants to join me?"

Students stared at Magic Marker on the side: THE CASINO.

"Andy?" said Serge.

He jumped and swung the phone behind his back. "What?"

"Get in here! The water's great!"

"I don't really feel like—"

"Andy!"

"Okay." He hid his phone on top of the pickup's front left tire and climbed over the side of the pool in shorts.

Serge pumped his eyebrows. "How do you feel?"

"Stupid."

"All the best things in life feel stupid at first. I think Dahmer said that."

A police officer approached the pickup on foot. "Excuse me?"

Serge turned. "How may I help you, officer?"

"I'm not saying what you're doing is wrong. But what *are* you doing?"

"Resurrecting our state's lost heritage!"

"Why do you have a kiddie pool in the back of a pickup?"

"Because if I set it up on the ground, that would be unusual."

"Are you okay?"

"Excellent! You're standing on sacred ground," said Serge. "This was the original site of the Casino Pool, birthplace of spring break. So existentially any pool set up on this spot becomes the Casino, like this one. Under new management. Tarzan, Amsterdam, Colgate. I drank a lot of coffee today."

The officer had seen everything but this extended the list. "Well, you're not disturbing anyone and . . ."—he craned his neck to survey the pickup's bed—". . . I don't see any beer cans or drugs, which is a welcome change, so I guess there's nothing else here for— . . . Are you trying to signal me?"

"Me?" asked Serge.

"No." The officer pointed. "Him."

"I was just scratching," said Andy.

"The heartbreak of psoriasis," said Serge.

The officer tipped his cap. "Have a nice day."

A few blocks north, other students with beer on their minds ran across A1A toward a convenience store.

The first jerked the door handle.

Bolted.

"That's weird."

They cupped hands around their eyes and pressed them to the glass. "I don't see anybody."

"The lights are on."

"Damn."

In the back room, Guillermo sat at a surveillance monitor and rewound a tape. It was a split screen: the view from behind the register, and another outside toward the gas pumps, in case of drive-offs. On the desk in front of Guillermo lay a sheet of paper with the location and time of a cell phone purchased with a credit card.

Guillermo stopped the tape and pressed play. Customers buying cigarettes and scratch-off tickets. The digital time record in the top corner was two hours early. He hit fast-forward. People comically scurried around with coffee, hot dogs and Alka Seltzer. The white numbers at the top of the screen flipped rapidly until they approached the time on Guillermo's printed record. He hit play again.

A young man bought a cell phone with a credit card.

Guillermo froze the image. "So that's what Andy McKenna looks like now."

He unfroze the video and watched the other side of the screen. The youth climbed into a pickup with a Florida Gators bumper sticker.

Guillermo ejected the tape and took a wide step around a slick of blood spreading from the store's owner.

Serge slapped the water's surface in the kiddie pool. "Who's the next lucky winner?"

Cody climbed up.

"Are you digging it? I'm digging it!" Serge reached over the side of the pool for his plastic specimen jar and dipped it in the water. "I'm saving this sample forever! . . . Who's next?"

Students continued swapping places. Andy walked around the front of the pickup and grabbed his phone off the tire. He pressed buttons.

"Agent Ramirez?"

"Andy, where are you? I've been driving up and down A1A!"

"No. It isn't safe."

"You're less safe where you are."

"You don't understand Serge. There's no telling what he's capable of if you show up."

"Think he might be with Guillermo?"

"At first I wondered, but now I'm sure he's not. He thinks he's protecting me. Which I'm beginning to believe is even more dangerous."

"Why do you say that?"

Serge stood behind the pickup with a map of Florida rolled into a cone like an old-style megaphone. "Swim! Swim! Swim! . . ."

Two students in the water. "Serge, our bodies are longer than the pool."

"Swim! Damn it! . . ."

"I hear yelling," said Ramirez. "Is everything okay?"

"No. Listen, you coming to me is out."

"What do you suggest?"

"Think I can slip away later. Then we'll meet. It'll eliminate any unpredictable confrontation with Serge."

"Just tell me when and where."

"I saw this place yesterday . . ."

Serge raised the paper megaphone. "That's it! Keep swimming! Tonight we'll shave all your hair and come back to break every Casino record!" He refolded the map and walked around the front of the pickup.

"Andy, what on earth do you think you're doing?"

"I . . . What? . . . This?"

"Where'd you get the cell phone?"

"At a convenience store."

"You were trying to make *a call*, weren't you?"

"Me? No. I swear."

"Gimme that thing." Serge snatched it away. "Now get back in the pool."

"I don't think it's a good time."

"Why not?"

Andy stretched out an arm. "Look."

Students chanted: "Cole-*man*! . . . Cole-*man*! . . . Cole-*man*! . . ."

Coleman stood on top of the pickup's cab. "Wooooooooo!" He licked a finger and stuck it in the air.

". . . Cole-*man*! . . . Cole-*man*! . . ."

"Coleman!" yelled Serge. "No!"

Too late.

Serge and Andy defensively raised arms as they were soaked by the belly-flop splash. They ran around the back of the truck. Coleman lay facedown on a plastic mat.

Serge stood in horror. "You popped the Casino pool!"

CHAPTER FORTY-FOUR

BAHIA CABANA

Serge burst in the door.

"There you are," said City.

"When are we going to do something?" asked Country.

"Not now."

"But we've been cooped up in here all day."

"I offered to take you with us," said Serge.

"On one of your lame tours? No, thanks!"

"I want to go to dinner," said Country. "You promised."

"Someplace nice this time," said City.

Serge opened his cell phone. "But you already have plans for tonight."

"That's *tonight*?"

"We went over it several times. You agreed in exchange for the dinner I promised . . ." Serge walked to the far side of the room and dialed a number.

"Hello?"

"Hey, Guillermo. It's me, Serge."

"How'd you get this number?"

"Pedro. He's a real talker. Just yap, yap, yap."

"Got your greeting card."

"Like it? Always try to be thoughtful, but you can't be sure what to get some people."

"You're a dead man."

"I've been called worse."

"What do you want?"

"Remember De Niro and Pacino in *Heat*?"

"I saw it."

"Didn't you love that movie? I sure did! One of my favorites, especially the codes they lived by—"

"Is this going anywhere?"

"That scene when they took a time-out and met in that coffee shop."

"You want to meet?"

"This is getting out of hand. We should negotiate a truce."

"Sure, we can negotiate a truce. When would you like to chat?"

"I knew you were a reasonable person. How about this evening?"

"That works."

"Great," said Serge. "Here's the hotel and room number . . ."

A '68 Dodge Monaco raced south on A1A and screeched into the parking lot of a convenience store.

The address matched Agent Mahoney's credit card trace.

He ran to the front door.

Bolted.

"Don't tell me . . ."

Without hesitation, he grabbed a metal trash can, smashed out the door's bottom glass and crawled through.

First check: behind the counter. Nothing.

Then the back room.

Mahoney's feet went out from under him as he crashed in a pool of blood.

He made a quick 911 call and dashed over to the surveillance recorder. A finger pressed eject.

Empty.

A camera crew in matching red shirts and low spirits sulked back to their custom motor coach.

Rood leaned against the side of the bus and kicked sand off a shoe. "This sucks."

"All afternoon and no decent women who'd let us film," said his assistant. "Unless you want to count those four old ladies."

"The G-Unit, for God's sake." Rood kicked his other shoe against a tire. "Have I been reduced to this?"

"We should go back to Panama City. Those bitches can't still be there."

"I think you're right." He turned to the rest of the crew, unstrapping gear and collapsing tripods. "Everyone, back on the bus."

"Hold it," said the assistant. "What's this?"

"What?"

"Three o'clock. Can't miss 'em."

Rood turned. "Holy mother."

Coming toward them: a pair of women hotter than anything they'd netted the whole trip.

"Excuse me," said the blonde. "Aren't you Rood Lear?"

Rood glanced at his assistant. "Patience." He sucked in his gut. "Why, yes I am. What can I do for such exquisite creatures?"

"I can't believe it's really you," said the other. "You're famous!"

"Like a star!" said the blonde.

Rood licked his lips. "Would you like to be in one of my films?"

"Would we! . . ."

"You really mean it? . . ."

"That would be a dream come true . . ."

"Better not be playing with us . . ."

Rood smiled at his assistant. "This can't get any better." He held out a hand to shake. "What are your names?"

"City and Country."

Another sideways grin from Rood. "It just got better."

The assistant: "Why don't we all head up to our suite?"

"Can't right now," said City. "Have to be somewhere."

"But this evening?" said Country. "Will that mess it up?"

"We're booked pretty solid," lied Rood. "But I think we can fit you in."

The women huddled and whispered. They smiled and giggled in Rood's direction, then whispered some more.

"What are you ladies talking about?" asked Rood.

"Uh . . . could we . . ."—Country lowered her head and feigned bashfulness—". . . talk to you in private?"

Rood smirked at his assistant. "Be right back."

"Go get 'em, tiger."

He walked a few steps. "What is it?"

"We'd kind of like to ask a favor," said City.

Uh-oh, thought Rood. Here it comes. Money. "What kind of favor?"

"You're cute," said Country. "I'd like to get to know you better."

"Me?"

She blushed and looked down again. "I've never . . . *been* with a celebrity before."

Rood almost choked. "That's the favor? You want to spend some time?"

The women smiled at each other.

This time Rood did choke.

"Need a glass of water?"

Rood shook his head. "You mean *both* of you?"

They nodded eagerly.

He gulped and blinked hard. "Think I can clear the suite for a bit."

"No." Country pointed toward one of the resort's upper floors. "Our room."

"Why?"

"That's where we have all our . . . *toys*."

Rood became woozy. "What time are you free?"

"Say nine?"

"Nine's my favorite number."

The women waved as they sauntered away. "Don't be late."

Rood walked back to the bus and braced himself with an arm against the door.

"Jesus," said the assistant. "You look like you're about to have a stroke."

"They want a threesome."

"Them? Holy shit."

"And just when I started to think life wasn't fair."

THAT EVENING

Two men sat in an idling Delta 88 with the lights off. Into their second hour with little conversation. Watching the high-rise hotel a block away.

"Don't like the looks of this," said Miguel. "I think it's a trap."

"I *know* it's a trap," said Guillermo.

"Then what are we doing here?"

"Every trap is an opportunity to set your own trap."

"So that's why you're wearing a room service uniform?"

"Nothing gets by you."

"Who is this Serge guy anyway?"

"A nuisance we can no longer afford." He looked at the car's analog clock and grabbed his door handle. "It's time."

"He said an hour from now."

"That's why it's time."

"What are you going to do?"

"I'll be fine. Just make sure not to fuck up your end." He patted his jacket pocket. "Call me on the cell if it looks like I'm made on the way—or if anything else is out of place once I'm inside." He hopped out.

Miguel watched as Guillermo waited for traffic to clear before jogging across A1A, still moist and shining in the moonlight from an earlier rain. Miguel picked up binoculars, tracking his colleague. Guillermo avoided the main lobby entrance and circled to the pool deck. Binoculars slowly panned the main entrance. Tourists unsteadily getting out of a cab and laughing. Idiots. The magnified field of vision drifted southward over the parking lot. A family at an open trunk struggled with a stubborn baby stroller that wouldn't close. Miguel smiled. Farther, a bum on a park bench. Worth watching. Common stakeout disguise. A romantic couple strolled past the bench and suddenly high-stepped as the bum vomited explosively toward their feet. Well, there's undercover and then there's what can't be faked. The binoculars moved on, reaching the street straight out the windshield in front of him. Coast clear. Time to pan back the other way.

Suddenly, his entire view was filled with a crazy, smiling face.

"*Ahhhhh!*" Miguel jumped back in his seat and dropped the binoculars.

Serge waved manically, wearing his most tattered comfy T-shirt and sweat pants. He walked around and tapped the side glass.

Miguel hit an electric level, lowered the window a slit. "Get lost!"

"I'm not asking for money or to clean your windshield with spit."

"I said, get lost!"

"Just need a light. Mine got all wet when I was caught in the rain."

"Are you deaf?"

"It's only a stupid light."

The window rolled up.

Serge knocked on the glass. Miguel stared straight ahead. Serge knocked and knocked. His voice was muted through the closed window: "Be a neighbor."

"Goddamn it!" Miguel lowered it a slit again. "I'm warning you!"

"We're wasting time arguing, when I could already be long gone. Just a light. Come on."

"Fuck it." Miguel reached in a hip pocket for his Zippo, opened the window the rest of the way and held it outside. "Where's your cigarette?"

"I don't smoke."

"Then why'd you ask for a light?"

"To keep your hands busy and away from the gun. You're the lookout."

"Shit!" Miguel went for the piece in his jacket but stopped when he felt a cold barrel on his cheek.

CHAPTER FORTY-FIVE

NINE O'CLOCK

*R*ood had been waiting by the bus since eight, wearing his sexiest, tightest slacks and a silk shirt. He checked his watch again.

9:01.

Two women trotted across the street.

"There you are," said Rood.

"Worried we were going to be late?"

"Not for a second."

He took one on each arm. "Shall we?"

The trio strolled up the drive and through the resort's automatic lobby doors.

"My gosh," said Country. "Can't believe we forgot."

"Forgot what?" asked City.

"You know. The *drug*store."

"What's at the drugstore?" asked Rood.

The women tittered. "It's a surprise."

"Something we can't do without." City opened her purse. "Here's our room key and number. Why don't you go up and make yourself at home? This'll just take a few minutes."

"You both have to go?"

Giggles again.

"I get it," said Rood. "A chick deal, like restrooms."

They took a couple steps back toward the entrance. Country stopped and turned around. "Oh, one more thing. If anyone asks, your name is Serge."

"Serge?"

"That's my uncle."

"Why do I have to say I'm your uncle? For that matter, who's going to ask? Is someone else staying with you?"

"No," said City. "And it'll probably never come up."

"That's right," said Country. "Shouldn't have mentioned anything. Forget about it."

"Wait a minute," said Rood. "I don't want to get in the middle of a situation. Is this like a jealous boyfriend or something?"

"Or something."

Rood fished the magnetic room key from his pocket. "Maybe I ought to take a rain check."

Country went over and wrapped sultry arms around Rood's neck. "Look, it is my boyfriend. And he is jealous. Very jealous. But he's also totally harmless. I'm not worried about him doing something crazy; I'm worried about him breaking up with me."

"Guy's a pussycat," City said from behind. "Once he thought *my* boyfriend was flirting with Country, and it took us twenty minutes to stop his crying."

"He's got a good heart," said Country, tightening her arms around Rood's neck. "But sometimes I need a real man."

"I help where I can," said Rood. "My name's Sal."

"Serge."

"Right, Serge. How long you going to be?"

Automatic doors slid open. "Back before you know it."

A rabbit argued with a Martian.

Coleman giggled on the couch and popped a beer. "Serge, come quick! This is the one where Bugs goes to the moon and saves our planet. It's so realistic."

"I'm busy." He grabbed his cell and started to dial. He stopped and looked at it. "Battery's dead! Of all times—not now!" He ripped apart his suitcase. "Where's that damn charger? . . ."

"What about the room phone?"

"Might be traced . . ." He snatched car keys from the dresser.

"Where are you going?" asked Coleman.

"*. . . You have stolen the D-12 modulator . . .*"

"Find a pay phone." He ran for the door, unbolting locks. "But where are pay phones these days with all the cells? Now I'll be late and screw up the Master Plan. I'm so stupid!"

"Why don't you just use Andy's phone?"

Serge slowly walked back. "Just about to think of that." He reached the dresser and picked up the disposable phone he'd confiscated at the Casino kiddie pool.

"*. . . Earth to Bugs, come in . . .*"

Serge dialed. "Hello, is this the anonymous Crime-Stopper Tip Reward Hotline? . . . Oh, I've got a tip all right! Real doozy! Someone you been looking all over for, possibly committing a crime as we speak. Here's the address . . ."

Bugs clung to the tip of a crescent moon.

"*. . .* Thanks," said Serge. "And may I say your phone manners have been impeccable, not like those 911 operators who never take me seriously when they're tearing down a landmark. If that isn't an emergency, what is?"

"*. . . Get me out of here!!!!! . . .*"

Serge plopped on the sofa next to Coleman. "What did I miss?"

"The whole thing."

"Dang, and it was one of my favorites."

"Another's coming on."

"Righteous! I love this one!"

Coleman grabbed another beer. "What about that lookout guy you got in your trunk?"

"He'll keep," said Serge. "Pump up the volume."

Rood pressed an elevator button. His mind fluttered through porno reels of his deepest fantasies.

The appointed floor was empty except for room service trays. Rood whistled down the hall. He stopped in front of a door and checked the number against the magnetic key's sleeve.

Rood went inside the dark unit and closed the door behind him. He felt along the wall for a light switch. Before he could find one, a lamp came on across the room.

"Who are you?" asked Rood.

Guillermo sat in a cushy chair, gun resting on the arm. "You know who I am."

"Let me explain."

"Please do."

"I'm Serge."

"I know."

Back at Bahia Cabana.

Serge and Coleman cackled through another Looney Tunes.

The door opened.

City grabbed a wine cooler and plopped into a chair. "Better have reservations at the Four Seasons for what we went through."

"Serge, are you listening?" said Country.

No answer.

She stepped in front of the television. "I'm talking to you!"

Serge tilted to the side. "Could you please move? You're blocking—"

"After all we just did!" said Country. "And you're watching fuckin' cartoons?"

"But it's a classic," said Serge. "The one where the guy doing demolition finds a singing frog in the cornerstone. *Everybody's doin' the Michigan rag!* . . ."

"Un-freakin'-believable. Not even a thank-you."

Serge looked up. "When you're right, you're right." He stood. "Come with me."

"Where are we going?" asked Country.

"To show my gratitude."

He led her into the bedroom and closed the door.

Another typical round of female shrieking. "*. . . Oh, yes! . . . Harder! . . . Faster! . . . Didn't think it was possible, but you've gotten even better! . . . Dear God! . . . Is it because of what you've got around the base of your cock? . . .*"

Serge thrust again. "That would be my guess."

"*. . . Ohhhh! . . . Ohhhh! . . . Yes! . . . Yes! . . . What is that thing? . . .*"

Another thrust. "I enlarged the hole in the middle of my favorite View-Master reel of the Everglades."

"... *Don't stop!* ... *Oh, God!* ... *I'm coming!* ... *I'm coming!!!!!!!*"

The ecstatic yelling came through the wall into the living room. Coleman turned and grinned drunkenly at City.

An empty wine cooler glanced off his forehead.

"Ow!"

In the bedroom, Country tried catching her breath after going off like a string of black-cat firecrackers. She wiped sweat from the blond hair matted across her face. "That was beyond incredible . . ."—still panting hard—". . . The best I ever—"

"Just wait till round two."

"Round two? I don't think I can take any more."

"You'll take it and like it."

He jumped up and went across the room in the dark.

"Where are you going?"

"To get more inspiration."

Country strained to see in the blackness. "What are those sounds?"

"Shhhhhh!"

He returned to the bed, immediately picking up where they'd left off.

". . . *Oh, God!* . . . *Yes!* . . . *Yes!* . . . *Oh—* . . . Hold on. Time out! Time out! . . . What the hell's hitting me in the face?"

"Uh . . . nothing."

More thrusts.

"Shit! You got me in the eye!" Country rolled over and clicked on the bedside lamp. She stared at Serge's chest, then up at his face. "What in the fuck?"

"Is something the matter?"

"What's all that crap hanging from your neck?"

He looked down. "Oh, Tarzan's five gold medals."

"Gold medals?"

"From the Olympics."

She looked at his chest again. "They're just those chocolate coins wrapped in gold foil that you taped string to."

Serge looked down again. A pause. "No, they're not."

"Yes, they are!" Country snatched one off a string, peeled the foil and took a bite.

A gasp. "The hundred-meter freestyle!"

"Sorry . . ." She set the coin on the nightstand. "Didn't mean for you to have a cow."

"No . . . ," said Serge, breathing quickly. "Heritage . . ."

She looked him in the eyes and dropped her voice a sensual pitch. "That turns you on, eh?" She grabbed the coin and took another bite, this time running her tongue around the edge first.

Country almost choked on it as Serge lost control and harpooned her deeper than ever before.

Her chin snapped up toward the ceiling. ". . . *Yesssssssssssssss! . . .*" She snatched the rest of the coins from Serge's neck and swatted the lamp off the nightstand, shattering its bulb on the floor.

On the other side of the wall, Coleman pointed at the TV with the remote. "No, you see, that's why it's so funny: The frog only sings and dances for the construction worker."

"Frogs can't sing and dance," said City.

"This one can."

"Hold it," said City. "Turn down the volume."

Coleman did, and they both listened to new sounds from the wall.

"*. . . Yes! . . . Faster! . . . Harder! . . . Chocolate, mmmmm! . . . I'm unwrapping another one . . .*"

"*. . . Eat the history! . . .*"

LATER THAT NIGHT . . .

"Development, development, development!" said Serge. "Will they never stop with this state?"

"What are you going to do to me?" asked Miguel, a gun pressed to the middle of his back.

"Construction sites everywhere!" said Serge, carrying two large monkey wrenches over his left shoulder. "On the other hand, I *love* construction sites, especially at night. Ever since I was a kid, poking around with a flashlight to see how things are made and what's going on inside walls. I'm naturally curious that way."

"You're the one who whacked Pedro, aren't you?"

"No, that was gravity, the senseless killer."

"You're going to fire me into the air?"

"Negative." They walked past a pallet of bricks. "But you will be facing gravity, so I suggest you start thinking of a counterstrategy. I always am. Like a jet pack. You wouldn't know where I can get one?"

Miguel shook his head.

Serge began to smile as they stepped through the wire mesh of a concrete form. "There isn't much security at construction sites, because who's going to walk off with sheets of drywall and twelve-foot rebar except me? And that was just to take care of another jerk . . ."

Miguel began to weep.

". . . Plus this place is *totally* unguarded, lucky for us. Well, for me. There's luck for you, too, but it's not the right kind."

Weeping became racking sobs.

"Buck up," said Serge. "You weren't too misty when your gang was trying to kill Andy. He's just a kid, for heaven's sake."

"That wasn't my idea," said Miguel. "I was going to try and stop it. You have to believe me!"

"Really?"

Miguel nodded furiously.

"Then I guess the only fair thing is to show some mercy."

"You're going to let me go?"

"I said *some* mercy. Jesus, you give people an inch . . ." Serge tucked the gun in his pants. "Now lie on your stomach right there. And don't try anything. I'm a pretty quick draw."

Miguel flopped down. Serge clamped the monkey wrenches on a circular metal hatch and pulled in opposite directions.

Creak.

"Wow, that was easy. Probably didn't even need those things." He tossed the wrenches in the dirt and unscrewed the loosened hatch the rest of the way.

The gun came out again. "On your feet."

"I'll give you money."

"Get in."

Miguel stared through the opening, then back at Serge. "In *there*?"

"It's a two-foot hatch, but you should fit."

"Isn't it full of—"

Serge shook his head. "Completely empty. They don't fill until ready for use. Otherwise it destroys the works."

"But I'll suffocate."

"Not a chance. It's deceptive, but there's a ton of room once you're inside, more than enough air till morning." Serge pulled a flashlight off his belt and held it together with the gun, sweeping its beam through the hole. "Loads of space. The real trick is the blades."

"Oh my God! I'll be chopped to pieces!"

"Will you stop making everything worse than it is?" Serge aimed the flashlight through the hole again. "You must be a real treat on long trips . . . See? They're just generally called blades, but the edges are completely dull. And not too tall, about a foot, so you shouldn't have much difficulty stepping over them, at least for the first couple hours." A wave of the gun. "Now *in*."

Miguel trembled as he climbed headfirst through the hole. He got stuck halfway and hung by his stomach, kicking his legs.

Serge threw his hands toward the stars. "Everyone wants my help." He grabbed Miguel by the knees and boosted him the rest of the way inside. Miguel fell to the bottom with a heavy thud and an echo: *"Ouch!"*

Serge picked up the hatch cover.

Miguel's face appeared in the middle of the round opening. "You mentioned mercy?"

"That's right. I always like to give my students a way out of jams. Because I'm into optimism. What about you?"

A blank stare.

"Should try it sometime," said Serge. "No point going through life sweating the small stuff when shit like this can spring up. In your particular case, the mercy is gasoline capacity. Once I turn this baby on, it can't run forever. If you just keep hopping over those blades until the fuel runs out—which should be around dawn when work crews arrive—you get to live. But if the blades start tripping you up"—Serge winced—"well, let's just say things start going downhill pretty fast."

"You really think I have a chance?"

"Definitely." Serge fit the hatch cover over the hole and began screwing.

A knock from the other side.

Serge sighed. He unscrewed the cover and pulled it back. "What now?"

"I can't see in here. It's completely dark."

"Shoot, thanks for reminding me. If you don't see the blades, they'll start tripping you immediately, and then there's absolutely no way you can make it." Serge pulled the flashlight off his belt again and handed it through the hole. "You'll need this."

"Thanks."

He screwed the hatch back on.

Five minutes later, Serge finished stripping insulation from a pair of wires and flicked his pocketknife shut. He touched the metal ends together. Sparks. The sound of a heavy industrial mechanism coming to life. The copper tips were twisted into a permanent connection with rubber-handled pliers.

The noise grew louder as Serge walked back around to the hatch. He banged a fist on thick steel. "How are you doing in there?"

"Not too bad. I think I might be able to make it."

"That's the spirit!"

"So how long are these flashlight batteries supposed to last anyway?"

"Oops, I didn't think of that."

CHAPTER FORTY-SIX

THE LATE NEWS

*T*elevision satellite trucks filled the parking lot of a resort hotel. Correspondents were stacked on top of one another, using a custom motor coach for backdrop.

"... Authorities still have no leads on the gangland-style assassination of *Girls Gone Haywire* founder Rood Lear, whose bullet-riddled body was discovered ..."

"... Witnesses said two young women were seen earlier in the lobby ..."

"... Following a heated confrontation in Panama City Beach ..."

"... Described only as 'persons of interest' are leaders of the activist group MAGGH, Mothers Against ..."

"... Responding to an anonymous tip, police arrived at the motel room seconds after the shooting but were too late to apprehend the assailant ..."

"... Meanwhile, online sales of the controversial videos continue to shatter records ..."

Someone held a microphone in front of Rood's tearful chief assistant. "... He was always giving and giving ..."

Two people sat in front of a TV, convulsing with laughter.

"Whew!" Serge wiped tears from his face.

"That was a good one!" said Coleman.

Serge's laughter bled into an expression of concentration.

"What's the matter?" asked Coleman.

"Not sure," said Serge. "You know how you sometimes hear something and it doesn't seem important at the time? But days later, out of the blue, when you're doing a completely unrelated activity, the significance suddenly dawns on you?"

"No."

"Andy said his mother shot herself."

"Poor kid."

"Coleman, women take sleeping pills or jump. *Men* shoot themselves."

"Maybe she didn't have pills or bridges."

"Can't explain it, but I just have this feeling."

Coleman fidgeted on the couch.

"What are you doing?"

"I think I'm sitting on something." He clicked the TV remote and reached for a beer.

"Most other people would find out what it is," said Serge. "Maybe even get off it."

"Really?" Coleman rolled to his side and reached down.

"My phone charger!" said Serge.

"Why'd you put it under my butt?"

"Gimme that thing." He went to the wall and plugged it in. The display came up. "Coleman, you made me miss a call." He redialed. "Serge here. You rang?"

"Nice try."

"Hey, Guillermo. Thought you'd like that touch. Guess the cops didn't get there in time."

"You underestimate me."

"Likewise; I got Miguel," said Serge. "So I guess it's just you and me now. We're going to have so much fun!"

"Where's Andy?"

"Someplace safe where you'll never find him."

"You're not getting my meaning," said Guillermo. "I'm not asking you to tell me where he is. I'm asking if *you* know where he is."

"What's your point?"

Click.

Serge looked quizzically at the phone.

"What is it?" asked Coleman.

"Shit!" Serge jumped up and ran out of the room. He knocked hard on the next door.

Spooge answered.

"Andy with you guys?"

"No, thought he was with you."

He ran to the next room and knocked again. City and Country passed joints with the rest of the gang. "Andy in here?"

"Said he was going for a walk."

Serge's head fell back on his neck. "Andy, Andy, Andy, what have you done?" He looked at the students again. "How long ago?"

"Just missed him."

"Wonderful!" He turned to leave.

"Oh, Serge. You know when Melvin's coming back? He's got the keys to the truck and we need it."

"What do you mean, 'coming back'? Where did he go?"

"I don't know. Left with this guy in a car."

"Guy?"

"Really old dude. Your age."

"Wouldn't happen to remember what he was driving?"

"That's easy. Wicked excellent ride, Delta 88."

"You guys are supposed to be smart," said Serge. "None of this raised any flags?"

"Thought he was alumni or something."

"Why do you say that?"

"Because he was looking at the Gators bumper sticker on the pickup before Melvin went over and asked what he was doing."

"And then what happened?"

"I got more beer."

LAS OLAS BOULEVARD

The case dossier lay in a lap.

"Agent Mahoney's Monaco sat in a parallel space along the bistro district. Wine, sidewalk tables, palm trees wrapped year-round in strands of white Christmas lights—just down the street from the demolished Candy Store nightclub, national birthplace of the wet T-shirt contest in the bygone spring break era, making it a church of sorts. Mahoney had rescued his share of cops from that lounge, and now the chips were due. He stared at the folder of paperwork and faded photos resting on his legs."

Mahoney stopped talking to himself. He couldn't put his finger on it, but the answer was in there somewhere.

He started back at the beginning again, the whole strange saga of Randall Sheets. Wife's illness, the flights, Madre—that really took him back to the old days—grand jury testimony, son pulled from kindergarten, Battle Creek—

The agent paused on the page. He took off his fedora and ran a hand through his hair. "Women don't shoot themselves." He fished out the autopsy, looking for caliber. "Nine-millimeter? That's weird . . ."

His eyes widened. "Oh, no."

The agent flipped open his cell and dialed.

"Bugsy, I need travel records for a specific date."

"How long ago?"

"Fifteen years."

"That's almost impossible."

"Plus I need a sealed juvenile record."

"That *is* impossible."

"And I want both in a half hour."

"You're crazy. What's the big rush?"

"Someone's going to die."

MIDNIGHT

Rain started again.

A light drizzle, but with ocean gusts that promised a bigger show. Students in sports cars and Jeeps cruised the strip. Decent numbers, but not like the sixties, when it brought A1A to a standstill.

The rain came down harder, scattering people off sidewalks and into bars.

Or bushes.

Andy poked his head up from shrubs along the front of a seafood grill. A quick scan of the surroundings, then another hundred-yard dash south, hugging buildings, staying as far from the street as possible. Another dive into manicured hedges.

A '73 Challenger rolled down the strip. Serge cranked his windshield wipers from intermittent to full. "How far could they have gotten?"

"Finding one person in this rain is hard enough," said Coleman. "But two?"

"We have to find them!"

The Challenger blew through a yellow light at Sunrise Boulevard. The Crown Vic behind him ran the red. Agent Ramirez checked his watch and his gun.

Andy wiped rain from his eyes, surveying the street again from behind landscaping.

A Delta 88 crossed a drawbridge at the causeway and made the northern swing onto the strip.

"Maybe he went the other way," said Coleman.

"You might be right." Serge made a skidding U-turn where A1A forks at the Oasis Café.

Andy waited for the taillights to fade, then jumped out from behind a coconut palm at the Oasis and bolted across the street through honking traffic.

Guillermo drove past a marina just as Andy dove behind a closed ticket shack for fishing charters. But Guillermo wasn't looking for Andy. He turned to his passenger in the front seat. "Get both hands back on the dash."

"What are you going to do to me?" asked Melvin.

"Nothing," said Guillermo. "Just need you to straighten something out for me."

"Why do we keep driving back and forth?"

"Waiting for a phone call . . ."

Guillermo reached Oakland Park, passing a southbound Challenger in the intersection.

"I'll never forgive myself," said Serge.

Another U-turn. And another.

Coleman rode out the centrifugal force against the passenger door. "I have no idea which way we're going anymore."

The driver of an '07 Mustang tried to make the light at Sunrise, then changed his mind. Tires didn't hold the wet street, and he spun into a lamppost.

"Why are we slowing down?" asked Coleman.

"Must be some kind of accident." Serge strained to see through sweeping wipers that couldn't handle the volume. Flares in the road. "Can't even imagine Floridians driving on snow."

Police put out the cones, snarling traffic to a single lane.

"Dammit!" Serge punched the steering wheel. "What a time for this!"

They crept along, getting closer to the traffic cop in a rain poncho waving cars by with a lighted baton. Only twenty vehicles back now, which put them five behind a Delta 88, ten behind a Dodge Monaco and fifteen behind a Crown Vic with government plates.

The rain became a sheeting downpour, killing visibility. Hazard lights blinked. A glowing baton waved the Crown Vic by. Ramirez hit the gas and raced a block to the appointed street corner.

The Vic hadn't come to a complete stop yet when Ramirez saw Andy jump from behind the charter-boat shack and sprint down a knoll. The agent leaned across the front seat, opening the passenger door, and Andy dove in.

Ramirez took off.

A Delta 88 and a Challenger rolled through the intersection.

"Serge, what's the point . . ."

"I'm not giving up on Melvin and Andy!"

"I ain't saying give up, just that all this driving back and forth isn't working."

"I know, and time's running out! It might already be too late. If only there was some way to turn back the clock and give me time to think—" Serge cut himself off and snapped his fingers.

"Is this like what you were talking about before?" asked Coleman. "A thought pops into your head later?"

"Hang on to something." Serge cut the wheel hard for a vicious right turn.

Three blocks ahead, Andy crossed his arms tightly, soaked and shivering.

"Sorry," said Ramirez, turning off the car's AC. "How you holding up?"

Teeth chattered. "I'm not."

"That'll change," said the agent. "It's all over now. You made it in."

The Crown Vic passed Bahia Mar and disappeared south on A1A.

The rain let up. People emerged from restaurants and bars, resuming the nightly sidewalk stroll along the strip.

A Delta 88 drove south past Bahia Mar.

CHAPTER FORTY-SEVEN

TWENTY MINUTES LATER

*A*ndy sat on a couch in dry FBI clothes that were three sizes too big.

Ramirez peeked out the curtains again.

"What now?" asked Andy.

"Wait."

"Can I watch TV?"

"No. We might not be able to hear."

"Hear what?"

Ramirez laid out a collection on top of a bedspread. Glock, extra clips, pistol-grip twelve-gauge, Taser, .38 ankle backup with snap release.

"Agent Ramirez," said Andy. "Hear what? What are we listening for?"

"Anything. Just a precaution."

"Thought you said I was safe now."

"You are, as long as we follow procedure." He grabbed his phone. "Just have to make final arrangements."

Ramirez went in the bathroom and dialed.

A half mile away, Serge burst through the door at Bahia Cabana.

City and Country looked up from a bong at the clamor.

"Where the hell have you been?"

"Wal-Mart." Serge ran across the room.

"Wal-Mart?" said City.

"Time slows down," said Coleman.

Serge pawed through luggage. "Just the cushion I needed to retool the Master Plan and catch back up . . . Here it is!" He grabbed Andy's disposable cell and frantically pressed buttons.

"What are you doing?" asked Coleman.

"Trying to find his call log . . ." More menu buttons. "Here it is." Serge scanned the tiny screen, the same number repeating all the way to the bottom, both incoming and outgoing. "Just as I thought."

He hit redial.

"That's right," Ramirez said into his cell. "With me right now. Perfectly safe . . . Okay, we'll sit tight."

The agent hung up; the phone instantly rang again.

"Agent Ramirez."

"Where's Andy?"

"Who's this?"

"Serge. What have you done with him?"

"Done with who? I don't know any Andy . . ."

Andy sprang from the couch in alarm.

Ramirez held out an arm and shook his head: nothing to worry about.

The boy tentatively sat back down.

"You're not a good liar," said Serge. "This phone number's all over his cell. That's why we're talking right now."

"Why *are* we talking?"

"I want Andy."

"I just told you—"

"Knock off the act. I know about his mother."

"Why don't you come down to the local office and discuss it with us?"

"That's the last thing you want."

"This conversation's over."

"You killed her."

"Now it's really over."

"Hang up on me, and the next call I make *will* be to the local office."

Ramirez looked toward Andy, then faced the other way and lowered his voice.

"You still there?" asked Serge.

"I'm here," said Ramirez. "You need to calm down. I know you cared about Andy, but he's safe now. Your mind's playing tricks."

"My mind tells me women don't shoot themselves."

"Some do."

"You're the informant."

"You really do need to settle down."

"Seen *The Godfather*?"

"You're insane."

"When I figured out there was an informant, I knew that whoever eventually contacted Andy to take him in would be someone he trusted. And the traitor. But what sealed it was his mother."

"Quite an imagination."

"Let me tell you a story. A long time ago, Madre had an agent on the payroll. No biggie. Just a little intel now and again—tip-off to a raid or shipment about to be intercepted. Then it all changed with a witness for the prosecution. It wasn't what you bargained for, but too late. They had enough leverage for a life sentence. Now are you following?"

No answer.

"So you went to see Andy's dad in Battle Creek—one of the few people who knew where he lived. He wasn't home. But Andy's mother was. Except you didn't shoot her."

"I thought you said I did."

"You were responsible for her death, but no, you're not cut out to be the shooter."

"Who then?"

"My money? Guillermo was with you. Madre would have insisted, so you couldn't fake McKenna's death and have him pose for confirmation photos with ketchup on his chest. Guillermo was the right age back then and the wrong psychological makeup to find the house with no McKenna. I'm guessing you tried to stop him."

"Some story . . ."

A Delta 88 made a U-turn. A phone rang.

"Hello?"

"Guillermo?"

"Hi, Madre. I have great news. I got Andy. Was just waiting for the call from you where to meet Ramirez for the positive ID, so we don't go through another Panama City."

"What do you mean, you've got Andy?"

"Right here in the front seat with me. Matches the convenience store video."

"My name's Melvin."

"Shut up."

"Guillermo," said Juanita, "I did get the call from Ramirez. He says *he* has Andy."

"That can't be right."

"Somebody's wrong. I hope you can sort it out."

"Where's Ramirez?"

She gave him the hotel and room number. "How far are you?"

Guillermo looked in the distance at a giant lighted sign atop a high-rise hotel. "Almost there."

"I don't want you to disappoint me."

"I won't, Madre."

"I know you're a good man," Serge told Ramirez on the phone. "That's why I'm betting you lied that you couldn't gain access to the family's new address when they were relocated. They've just twisted you for so long you can't see up or down."

"How'd you know about his mother?"

"I didn't. It was guess," said Serge. "You told me just now."

"It wasn't supposed to happen like that."

"So her condition hadn't recurred at all," said Serge. "She was in perfect health?"

"She was fine."

"Hasn't this gone on long enough? There's still time to make it right."

"No, there isn't."

"It gets worse," said Serge. "You have a second problem."

"What do you mean?"

"They've got Melvin."

"Who's Melvin?"

"Another kid that Guillermo apparently got confused with Andy."

Ramirez fell down in a chair.

"I'm guessing Panama City didn't stomach well," said Serge. "You have a conscience, but Guillermo's out where the buses don't run. You couldn't stop Battle Creek, but you can stop this . . ."

Banging against the wall of Serge's room. Laughter, shouts, students getting restless and deeper into the alcohol supply.

Serge walked toward the window to hear better. "Listen to me. If I know anything about human nature, this is one you're not going to be able to live with. There's a defining point in every life where you have to do the right thing no matter what personal cost . . ."

Ramirez could no longer face Andy.

". . . Tell me where you are," said Serge. "We'll take out Guillermo together. And I won't say anything to Andy or anyone else about our conversation."

"It's too late."

"No, it's not! I can . . . hold on—" Serge pressed a hand over his other ear as more noise drowned out the call. A fire engine screamed by with all the sirens and bells, fading down the street. Serge uncovered his ear. "I'm begging: Tell me where you are!"

"I have to go . . ."

"Don't hang up!"

From Ramirez's end of the line, Serge heard a fire engine.

Click.

CHAPTER FORTY-EIGHT

A1A

A '68 Dodge Monaco raced south.

Mahoney punched buttons on a cell.

Agent Ramirez's phone rang. He stared at it for the longest time. Mahoney's name in the display. Then:

"Ramirez."

"Where are you?" said Mahoney.

"What's going on?"

"Please don't hurt Andy."

"Andy? Why would I do anything to him?"

"You're the informant."

"What are you talking about?" said Ramirez. "*I* was the one who told *you* there was an informant."

"Nice ruse. Like when you're playing Clue and hold the card for Mr. Mustard but ask other players if they have Mr. Mustard."

"You're insane."

"You're the one who told Madre about the class ring and the credit card trace."

"Madre?"

"I know about the convenience store."

"What convenience store?"

"The work of one of her boys."

"Her boys?"

"You should be familiar," said Mahoney. "You're one of them."

"What I am familiar with is your hospital stays."

"Got your juvenile record. Probation lists Juanita as your employer. Fits her MO, grooming young guys out of jail."

"How many times were you committed?"

"I also know about Andy's mom. You had a Detroit flight the same day."

Ramirez's brain reached overload.

"You still there?" asked Mahoney.

"What do you want?"

"Andy."

"I have to go."

"Where are you?"

Click.

The Challenger screamed out of the motel parking lot.

Coleman slammed into the door again. "He told you where they are?"

"No, the fire engine did."

"What fire engine?"

"Passed our hotel northbound. At that speed and the delay I heard on the phone, it's a half mile, give or take. Which can mean only one hotel . . ."—a skidding left up a driveway—". . . This one."

"But how do you know which room?"

"We'll just have to play that by ear."

They jumped from the car.

"Coleman! Watch out!" Serge grabbed his arm and pulled him from the path of a speeding Delta 88 that screeched to a stop in the fire lane.

"What a jerk," said Coleman.

"Guillermo!" said Serge.

"And there's Melvin!"

Guillermo entered the lobby. Melvin was two paces in front and one to the right, standard separation for someone at gunpoint, unless the gunman's left-handed.

Serge and Coleman ran for the entrance.

Behind in the street, squealing tires and rubber smoke. Even in darkness, there was no way Mahoney could mistake the distinct outlines of that odd couple running for the hotel.

The Monaco backed up and whipped into the lot.

Guillermo reached the elevators, holding a black leather briefcase in his left hand and staring up at descending numbers. Serge charged through the front doors and immediately saw the pair on the far side of the lobby. Couldn't risk an all-out assault with Guillermo's gun still pointed at Melvin. He broke stride and walked casually toward the elevators, mentally walking through the next few moments: standing next to Guillermo waiting for their lift. "Good evening . . ." Guillermo responding in kind. Then all three getting in the elevator, and only two would get off. Serge just prayed Melvin could hold it together and not give him away.

He was closing fast, walking as briskly as he could without drawing notice. Thirty feet to go. He didn't count on one thing.

Guillermo and Melvin stepped into an elevator.

"No!" Serge sprinted across the rest of the lobby. The doors closed just before he could stick a hand through the crack and pop them back open.

A thumb mashed the up button.

Coleman arrived. "What's happening?"

Serge muttered to himself, staring up at ascending numbers.

The next elevator dinged open. "Coleman! Hold that one!"

"I got it." Coleman stood on the second car's threshold, its doors repeatedly banging open and closed against his shoulders. "Aren't you getting in?"

Serge continued staring up. "Just a sec." The numbers went higher and higher.

Mahoney dashed into the lobby. "Serge!"

Serge watched the elevator numbers pause. "Eighteenth floor!"

He jumped in the second car with Coleman, and the doors closed.

Mahoney ran to the elevators, pressed a button and looked up at numbers.

Agent Ramirez sat on the edge of a bed with eyes closed.

Knock-knock.

Andy flinched. "Who's that?"

Ramirez didn't respond, just walked across the room and opened the door.

Guillermo came in with his briefcase and young guest.

"Melvin," said Andy. "What are you doing here?"

"Not my idea."

A poke in Melvin's back. "Over there with your friend."

He walked toward Andy, revealing the gun behind him.

Guillermo set his briefcase on the dresser. "What's this business about two Andys?"

"That's what I need to talk to you about," said Ramirez.

Guillermo flipped latches and raised the top. "It's all there, two fifty. You can count if you want."

Andy backed up against a wall. "Serge was right."

The agent closed the briefcase.

Guillermo cracked an unfriendly smile. "We always did work on trust."

"That's not it," said Ramirez. "I want to make a deal."

"Deal?"

"You keep the money. Nobody will ever find out, not even Madre."

"What do you get?"

"The kids."

Guillermo laughed.

Andy eyed Ramirez's weapons spread out on the bed.

"I'm serious," said the agent. "He was just five at the time, never had anything to do with our business."

Guillermo turned with his .380 automatic. "Little too late to grow a conscience."

"Serge was right," said Ramirez.

"Serge!" said Guillermo. "What is it with that guy?"

"Listen to me," said the agent. "This accomplishes nothing."

"Accomplishes revenge."

"You can't deposit that in a bank."

"I always do what Madre wants. You did too, until now."

Guillermo stepped forward.

Ramirez side-stepped to block his path.

"Have any idea what you're doing?" said Guillermo.

"This needs to end."

"You're making a big mistake. If Madre ever found out you—" Guillermo stopped and smiled again, placing a hand on Ramirez's shoulder. "I understand this isn't your territory. Like our trip to Battle Creek. Bothers most people . . ."

"Battle Creek?" said Andy. "What about Battle Creek?"

". . . So I'm going to forget about this, okay? Now move aside."

Ramirez didn't budge.

An elevator opened at the end of the hall. Serge and Coleman jumped out running.

"Which room is it?" asked Coleman.

"I don't know," said Serge. "Andy! Andy! Can you hear me? Just yell! . . ."

Guillermo stepped chest-to-chest with Ramirez. Half foot taller. He looked down into the agent's eyes. "This has become tiresome. Last chance to give you a pass."

In the next split second, events cascaded.

Ramirez's eyes briefly glanced toward the bed.

Guillermo caught the look and began raising his gun.

Before he could, Ramirez shoved him hard in the chest. Guillermo stumbled as the agent dove for his weapons.

Guillermo's automatic and Ramirez's ankle gun came up at the same time.

Standoff.

They stared without blinking. Ramirez carefully walked backward. "Andy and Melvin, get behind me."

"Put the gun down," said Guillermo. "Move away from them."

Serge reached the west end of the floor and turned down another corridor.

"This hotel's freakin' huge," said Coleman. "How many hallways are there?"

"Too many," said Serge. "Andy! . . . Andy! . . . Where are you?"

At the east end of the floor, someone in a fedora ran around a corner. "Serge! . . . Andy! . . . Where are you? . . ."

Andy peeked over Ramirez's shoulder.

"It doesn't have to end like this," said Guillermo.

"I might as well be dead," said Ramirez. "All those horrible things you got me into. This won't make up for it, but at least it won't add to it."

"There's more money," said Guillermo. "We should have talked

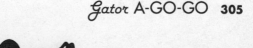

about that earlier. The kid took a lot of work on your part. It's only fair."

"Even if I give him up, you'll still kill me. Maybe not here, now. But you will."

Still aiming guns, trigger fingers twitching, getting sweaty.

"Nonsense," said Guillermo, waiting for the slightest distraction to get off the first shot and not take a slug in return. "Even if you don't trust me, think about it: We've got too much invested in you. How will we replace such a valuable asset?"

"My guess is you already have others," said Ramirez. "I never should have gotten mixed up with your fucking family."

Guillermo gritted his teeth. Nostrils flared.

Faintly, from outside: "... *Andy! Andy!* ..." The voice trailing off as it went by. "... *Call out if you can hear me!* ..."

"In here!" yelled Andy. "I'm in here!"

CHAPTER FORTY-NINE

*S*erge hit the brakes and ran back a few doors.

Coleman crashed into him. "Is this the room?"

"Don't know . . . Andy! You in there?"

"Serge! Quick!"

Serge threw his shoulder into the door.

Ramirez involuntarily glanced toward the sound.

It was a microsecond, but all the time Guillermo needed. He fired, hitting Ramirez in the stomach. The agent shot back, but he was off balance from the gut wound, and the bullet went wide, splintering through the door.

Serge grabbed his ear and looked at his hand. Blood.

Guillermo's second shot hit Ramirez's shooting hand. The gun ricocheted off a wall. Guillermo marched forward, continuing to fire at the defenseless agent.

Ramirez's mind attained clarity. This was why he was born. Anyone else would have gone down long ago, but with whatever strength the agent had left, he willed himself to remain an upright human shield for the two boys.

More shooting, now from two directions: Guillermo riddling Ramirez, and outside the room, where Serge blew the doorknob off.

Guillermo's next shot struck Ramirez in the forehead, dropping him like an anvil.

No place for Andy and Melvin to hide.

Guillermo pulled the trigger. *Click.*

"Shit." He replaced the clip.

Another shot from the hall blew the deadbolt halfway across the room.

Guillermo aimed between Andy's eyes.

Serge kicked the door open and fired.

The bullet struck Guillermo's arm from behind, spinning him. He returned fire as Serge ducked out of the doorway.

Serge hit the ground in the hall and poked his gun around the door frame, aiming at an upward angle so if he missed Guillermo, stray lead wouldn't hit the kids.

He didn't miss. The second shot hit Guillermo in the same arm. It pissed him off. He switched the gun to his left hand.

There are two distinct types of firefights: police and military.

Police take up defensive positions behind squad car doors and trees. Military strategy is to overrun the enemy. Guillermo favored the latter. He ran for the hall, firing on the way.

Serge retreated, shooting behind him without aim. He turned the corner and joined Coleman, who'd already ducked down another corridor. They pressed themselves hard against the wall. Plaster exploded past their heads.

Back in the room, Andy was paralyzed, staring at a side view of Guillermo in the hall, framed by the open door. Blasting away toward Serge and Coleman.

Andy surprised himself with what he did next. Almost like an out-of-body experience, looking down from the ceiling observing someone else. He dove for the bed, grabbed Ramirez's nine-millimeter Glock and pulled the trigger. Nothing happened.

He turned the gun over and back in confusion. TV cop shows ran through his head. "Don't they pull some kind of slide thing to load a bullet?"

Guillermo emptied his gun again. The ejected clip bounced on the carpet as another magazine slammed home.

Andy watched out the door as Guillermo pulled a slide thing. He looked down at his own gun and followed the example.

"He's changing out clips," Serge told Coleman. "Now's our chance!" Serge reached around the corner. A bullet whistled by before he could get off a round. He jumped back. "Faster than I thought."

Guillermo heard sirens coming up A1A. Then he heard something slam into the wall behind his neck. He looked at the bullet hole, then turned quickly to trace the line of fire to its source: an open-mouthed Andy, stunned that the gun in his hand had actually gone off.

He raised his pistol toward the boy. A bullet ripped into Guillermo's thigh from Serge's direction.

"Son of a bitch!"

"Is he still up?" asked Coleman.

"Guy's like a Frankenstein."

Andy fired again, but Guillermo had disappeared from the doorway, racing toward Serge's position.

Serge peeked around the corner. "Shit. Run!"

They took off down the second corridor, Serge again shooting wildly behind them.

Guillermo reached the corner in full psychopathic bloom. He fired over and over at the retreating pair, but handgun accuracy delivers rapidly diminishing returns over distance. A hail of bullets from both directions passed each other in the middle of the hall and hit nothing but walls and fire extinguishers.

At the other end of the hall a man in a fedora rounded the corner. One of Guillermo's last bullets found a target. Mahoney went down, grabbing his calf.

Serge heard the gunfire end. "Why's he stopping?"

Guillermo turned in the middle of the hall and reversed field.

"He's going back for the boys!" Serge crouched for a steady shot. *Click.*

"I'm out!"

"Serge!"

He turned.

"Mahoney, what are you doing down there?"

"Catch!"

Serge grabbed a .38 police special out of the air and sprinted back toward the room, where Andy was slapping the side of his gun. Jammed. Actually he'd just accidentally hit the safety. He heard something in the hall and looked up. Guillermo grinned wickedly and took aim. "Good night." He pulled the trigger.

A ceiling lamp shattered. Andy covered his head as glass rained.

Guillermo continued twirling in the hall from Serge's well-timed slug in his unwounded arm, which had sent Guillermo's last shot high into the lighting fixture.

"Motherfuck!"

Louder sirens. Then they stopped. Which meant they were here.

Guillermo had never taken such a beating before. He emptied his gun in Serge's direction and limped away for the fire escape.

"Coleman! He left!" Serge ran to the doorway. "Let's go, kids."

They all fled through the corridor where Mahoney had been hit.

"You going to be okay?" asked Serge.

"Don't move," said Mahoney.

"What are you doing?"

"Guillermo's gone now, and the kids are safe." Mahoney aimed his backup piece. "You're under arrest."

"That's fair. I know our rules, but . . ."—he gestured with an upturned palm at two peach-faced students—". . . They're *not* safe. Guillermo and Madre are still out there, and who knows who else they have inside. You know I'm their best bet. Another time?"

Mahoney kept steady aim, then lowered the gun. "Get the hell out of my sight."

The entire building had heard the gunfire. Nine-one-one operators and the hotel's front desk became swamped with freaked-out calls that placed the shooting on almost every floor. First officers at the scene were spread thin as they responded to a dozen false locations.

Guillermo grabbed a bath towel from a cleaning cart and wrapped it around his shoulders—one of the least noticeable people as he casually escaped out the pool deck in a multi-directional stampede of screaming sunbathers.

Serge's group caught a break with the service elevator. They ran into the kitchen.

Chefs had armed themselves with their largest carving knives. "What the hell are you guys doing in here?"

Serge, still running, pointed behind him. "Someone's shooting!"

The trio pushed open a steel door to the loading dock with a box compactor and crates of rotten lettuce.

"What now?" asked Andy.

Serge looked up the alley toward the front of the hotel and the back edge of a growing throng of onlookers.

"If we just can get into that crowd . . ."

More and more squad cars screamed into the parking lot.

The quartet watched from the rear of the mob, then slowly retreated across the street.

Back up in the blood-soaked room, two hands grabbed a briefcase.

BAHIA CABANA

City and Country were bored, starved and car-less.

They had clicked the remote through all TV channels ten times.

Serge ran into the room.

City jumped up. "Where the fuck have you been?"

"Someplace." He ran for the sink, stuck his face down and splashed water.

"Holy Jesus! What did you do to your ear?" said Country.

"What the hell happened to Andy and Melvin?" said City.

The pair collapsed on the couch, pale as they come.

"Give 'em space." Serge held paper towels to the side of his head. "They just had a close one."

Andy stared at nothing. Shock suddenly gave way to delayed emotion. Weeping and shaking.

Serge sat and put an arm around his shoulders. "It's okay."

"I'm so sorry. Should have listened to you. I almost got us all killed."

"That part wasn't good."

"Swear I won't screw up again."

"You can relax—you're safe now."

Andy sniffled and wiped his eyes. "But what about Guillermo? He's still out there."

"You leave that to me."

"What are you going to do?"

"Andy, I have to tell you something. This might not be the best time, considering what you just went through, but I'd want to know if I was in your shoes."

"What is it?"

"It can wait till later. Just let me know when you're ready."

"I'm good now."

"You sure? It's pretty heavy."

Andy nodded.

"Your mother."

"What about her?"

"Andy . . . I'm just going to say it. She didn't kill herself."

"Of course she killed herself. She shot—" He stopped and read Serge's face. "Are you saying she was murdered?"

"Afraid there's not much of a happy distinction between the two. But you've been under the impression all these years that she lingered through prolonged suffering and put herself out of misery."

"She wasn't sick?"

Serge shook his head. "Some of the happiest years of her life. And if it's any consolation"—Serge crossed his fingers behind his back—"Ramirez told me she never heard it coming. Almost like going in her sleep."

"Ramirez killed her?"

Serge shook his head again. "Like I said, you leave that to me."

"Guillermo?"

Serge pulled the pistol from under his shirt for a tear-down mechanism check.

Andy remembered something, feeling the bottom of his own shirt and Ramirez's Glock, which he'd concealed underneath in all the excitement. He decided not to bring it up. "What are you planning to do?"

Serge reassembled the gun. "I'm foreclosing on his karma."

CHAPTER FIFTY

THE NEXT MORNING

Six A.M.

Dawn on the way. But still half-dark.

Headlights from pickup trucks bounded onto the construction site of a new downtown Miami condo.

The trucks stopped and doors opened.

Work boots, lunch boxes, hard hats.

A foreman began unfurling blueprints, then heard a sound that wasn't supposed to be there. He looked back at his crew. "Someone leave that thing running?"

Seven A.M.

Crime scene tape, police, TV cameras.

The head of homicide arrived. "What have we got here?"

"One twisted bastard," said the case detective. "Nobody hot-wires these things."

They watched as paramedics passed what was left of Miguel out the hatch of a cement mixer.

"I've heard of death by a thousand cuts," said the detective. "This was death by ten thousand blunt traumas. All minor enough to let him last for hours."

"Wouldn't he just roll around and get dizzy?"

"Most people might think, but the foreman explained that these trucks have blunt stirring blades to mix the cement—much like laundry dryers—and once the victim kept tripping and couldn't get up, those blades continued lifting and tumbling him over and over.

"Who would do such a thing, let alone think it up?"

Eight A.M.

South of Miami. A Delta 88 sat in the driveway of a nicely kept hacienda with barrel tiles.

Only one person home.

The shower was running. A bottle of Jack Daniel's hung in the soap caddy. A diluted pink mixture of water and blood swirled down the drain.

The leg wound had been a pass-through in the meaty part of the thigh, and another bullet had just grazed the right shoulder. That left two in his favored arm.

Guillermo screamed.

A twisted piece of lead bounced on a rubber shower mat. Guillermo hung tweezers from the caddy and grabbed the bottle of sour mash. Some went in his mouth, the rest over an inelegantly gouged-out wound. Another scream.

He set the bottle back and grabbed the tweezers again.

Drain water turned darker red.

Nine A.M.

Ice cubes fell in a crystal rocks glass, followed by two fingers of Jack Daniel's. A first-aid kit lay open. Two pools of spilled whiskey on the dining room table and more dripping off Guillermo's fingertips from the limp arm hanging by his side.

He cringed and gently eased himself into a chair at the table, gauze bandages bleeding through. Guillermo unwrapped the worst and tossed the wad in a trash basket next to his seat.

He reached in the first-aid kit and took another slug of whiskey, then tore off a fresh stretch of white tape with his teeth.

A Mercedes pulled up the driveway. The front door opened. Juanita hummed merrily, a bakery sack in her arms. The foyer filled with the aroma of just-out-of-the-oven Cuban bread. Then she smelled liquor.

Juanita came around the corner to the dining room, only seeing his back and the bottle. Uncharacteristic.

"Guillermo?" She slowly set the bag on a counter. "Are you . . . drunk?"

"Not yet."

"Guillermo, I'm surprised . . ." She took a few more steps. "Oh my God! What happened to you?"

The bottle poured. "Ramirez double-crossed us."

"He's a dead man."

"Right."

"You're in no condition." She picked up the phone. "I'll take care of this Ramirez. Almost makes me cry what he did to you."

"No, I mean, 'right,' as in he's already dead."

She put down the phone. "You handled Ramirez?"

A boozy nod.

She patted him on the head. "Good boy . . . What about Andy?"

He shook his head. "There were like a million of 'em. I was ambushed."

"You didn't take care of Andy?"

"No, but I'll find him."

Another pat. "You rest." She grabbed the phone again. "I'll send someone else."

"Who?"

She opened her mouth to say "Pedro," then stopped. She thought of Raul. Stopped again. Miguel. A longer pause. "Is anyone left at all?"

"Just me."

Juanita took a seat at the table and stared down in thought.

SIMULTANEOUSLY

A '73 Challenger cruised south on Biscayne Boulevard.

Just Serge and Andy.

They crossed the intersection for the causeway to Bal Harbor. A skyline came into view.

"Holy smokes," said Serge. "There's more every time I come here, and that's usually only months apart."

Andy was in a funk.

"Andy"—shaking his arm—"are you looking?"

"Yeah, I'm looking. More what?"

"Condos under construction." Serge stopped at a red light next to the Miami Shores Country Club. "They're all over the dang place, blotting out the sun."

"I thought those were office buildings." Andy stared out the window at towering high-rises, most with unfinished upper floors. "They're putting condos downtown?"

"Now they are. Almost outnumbering businesses." His eyes moved north to south. ". . . Nine, ten, eleven . . ."

"What are you doing?"

"Counting construction cranes. I do it every time I'm here . . . thirteen, fourteen, now fifteen! Amazing. I still remember one of the local TV anchors joking that the city's official bird should be the crane."

"Fifteen are getting built at the same time?"

"Probably a couple less," said Serge. "They glutted the market in the housing crisis. I'm betting work's stalled on a few from lack of presales. That's how the Elbo Room was saved." He aimed his camcorder out the windshield at the skyline.

"Serge, what are you doing?"

"I'm always in awe at the scale of those things."

"How can you be so flip at a time like this? Talking about buildings and cranes when Guillermo is still loose."

"You were just talking about them, too."

"I was distracted."

"Promised I'd take care of this." Serge turned on the radio, Randy Newman. "That's where we're going now."

Andy bolted up straight. "We're driving to Guillermo?"

"Heck no."

"Then where are we going?"

"Research. Putting an end to something requires thorough preparation and a killer sound track."

"Why do I have to come?"

". . . *Gee, I love Miami* . . ."

"After what you pulled yesterday, we're joined at the hip." Serge clicked off his video camera. "In the meantime, no sense fretting between stops. Enjoy the beautiful day!"

Andy pounded the dashboard in whining desperation. "Please . . ."

"It's almost over," said Serge. "Just a little longer."

"It *is* over. Ramirez was the traitor. So now you can take me in."

"Sometimes there's more than one. We have to cut the snake off at the head. Then it doesn't matter how many they got inside . . . Look! One of the cranes is starting to move!"

"*. . . every building's so pretty and white . . .*"

"Serge!"

"Shhhhhh!" He grabbed his camcorder again. "It's incredible how those things work. Ever watch *Modern Marvels*?"

"No!"

"Check out that tiny guy fifty stories up in the glassed-in control cab. He's just moving little levers . . ."—Serge panned down to a massive steel beam leaving the ground—". . . yet able to lift tons of metal hundreds of feet into the air and place it precisely where he wants . . ."

The Challenger continued south along the waterfront, past the American Airlines Arena, Freedom Tower, Bayside Market. Serge made a right on Flagler and drove through a district of small shops with Spanish signs.

"Where are we now?" asked Andy.

"Here." Serge parked on the street.

"The library?"

"Not just *any* library. The main Miami-Dade." Serge ran up steps. "Hurry! Crime-fighting's loads of fun!"

"Wait up!" Andy chased Serge across a vast, elevated brick courtyard, where people in business suits ate takeout lunch on shaded benches.

Serge knew right where to go. In minutes, he was sitting at a projector, reading negative images of a fifteen-year-old *Herald*. It was a Wednesday, final street edition.

Andy dragged over a chair. "Why are we reading newspapers?"

"You're too young to remember . . ."—Serge turned the advance knob; Thursday, Friday—". . . but back then, Madre was legendary, like the bogeyman. Everyone knew what she was up to, but five levels of law enforcement could never touch her. Witnesses were petrified, and those who did talk ended up in the Miami River, not all in one place."

"How does that help us?"

"There was a big raid with her brothers. And when arrests make the paper, there's an address." Serge turned the knob again. Front-page story with four-column photo: Two men and a woman being led handcuffed from a south county hacienda. "Here we go. And I lucked out. Not only the address, but a photo of the house . . . Man, she looks young there."

"But what are the odds she's still living at the same place after all these years?"

"You'd be surprised." Serge dropped coins in a slot and pressed a button. A copy spit from a printer. "These old families don't move."

Serge slid the folded page into a pocket and left the microfilm room. They waited at the elevators.

"Hold on a second," said Andy.

"What is it?"

He ran back toward the microfilm room. "I forgot something."

"I'll be here."

Andy went inside, stuck a spool back on the machine and fed coins in a slot.

CHAPTER FIFTY-ONE

I-95

A '73 Challenger drove back toward Fort Lauderdale.

Serge avoided interstates in most situations, except when time was critical.

"Time's critical!"

"What are you planning?" asked Andy.

"Can't tell you," said Serge. "Sorry, but it's for your own good. You'd become an accessory."

"They killed my mom."

"I know."

"I should be the one."

"Andy, don't throw your life away." Serge took the Broward Boulevard exit as an Amtrak pulled into a station by the overpass. "Outcome will be the same."

"But I want revenge myself."

"It pains me to see this change." They crossed the bridge to the beach. "You're one of the good guys. Leave this to me and forget about it before these assholes turn you into something you're not."

"Can I at least be there? For closure?"

"*Closure?*" said Serge. "Don't bullshit a bullshitter. But yes, you can come along. Only if you agree to remain way back."

"Will I be able to see from there?"

"I have a funny feeling everyone will be able to see."

The Challenger reached A1A and turned south.

Serge ran back in the room with a bucket of ice and jammed two water bottles inside.

City and Country passed a joint and watched more tube.

Serge pulled a map from his suitcase and laid it down next to the microfilm printout from the library.

"We're going to dinner now?" asked Country.

"What?" Serge combed streets.

"You swore to take us to this great place," said City.

"When?"

"Fifty times. Pick one," said Country. "And after your last lie, you gave your word it would be today."

"I'm working."

"You always say that."

"This time I really am working." Serge circled a spot on the map in ballpoint. "Something big's come up."

"We're tired of being stuck in this room."

"Why aren't you taking advantage of the pool?" asked Serge.

"Because we were waiting to go to dinner!" said Country.

"We fucked up and believed you," said City. "This is just like when you ditched us on the side of the road."

"Except worse," said Country. "It's a perpetual ditch. Popping in and out. Stringing us along with promises."

"I promise." Serge rummaged through his hanging toiletry bag. "Just let me wrap this up."

"You're doing it again," said City. "At least last time we could get on with our lives."

Serge dug through all the pockets, then started again with the first.

"Are you listening to me?"

"Where are my car keys?"

"Andy took 'em."

Serge's head swung. "Andy's not in the room?"

"Duh!"

"But I told him to stay put," said Serge. "Where'd he go?"

"He took your keys, so I guess somewhere else."

"Why didn't you tell me?"

City took a hit. "What's the big deal?"

"Oh, Andy, Andy, not again!"

"Again what?"

"When did he leave?"

"Just before you came back from getting ice," said Country. "Surprised you didn't bump into him in the hall."

Serge grabbed his map off the dresser and ran out.

"When are we going to dinner?"

Students in the next room flipped quarters into shot glasses.

Serge charged through the door. "Need to borrow your car."

"Here . . ."

Keys flew across the room and broke a mirror.

Serge jumped in a station wagon and raced south.

SOUTH OF MIAMI

A '73 Challenger rolled down a quiet residential street with burglar bars and neglected lawns.

Andy slowed, reading mailbox numbers. He reached what he was looking for and stopped at the curb. A microfilm printout in his lap, the old *Herald* photo of the arrest. Andy looked up at the hacienda. New roof and trees, but not much else had changed. A Delta 88 and a late-model Mercedes sat out front.

He drove off.

The Challenger parked seven blocks away at a baseball field with a rusted Pepsi scoreboard. Standard getaway vehicle placement from the movies. Andy set out on foot. The Glock slipped from his waistband into his underwear. He stopped to pull it up.

The front door of a hacienda opened. Juanita strolled to the driveway. A Mercedes backed out.

There'd been better days.

Guillermo had disappointed her again. Not only that, but Serge had depleted her crew. To recruit reinforcements, she now was compelled to do what she hadn't in years. But Juanita could still drive to the jail in her sleep.

 *Gator* A-GO-GO **321**

Five blocks down the road: "What's this?"

She drove past a young man trotting up the sidewalk the other way, glancing around suspiciously.

Juanita looked in the rearview. A gun suddenly fell from Andy's belt. He quickly grabbed it off a lawn.

Juanita smiled. Obviously green, but already into the life. The day's fortune had just changed. She made a wide U-turn in a vacant intersection.

Andy jogged through another cross street, holding his stomach. Three blocks to go.

A Mercedes pulled alongside. The passenger window went down. "Need a lift?"

Andy almost came out of his skin.

"No!"

"You sure? It's awfully hot out today. Your shirt's soaked through."

From nerves.

"I'm fine."

"You look hungry."

Andy and the car simultaneously slowed until they both stopped.

Juanita leaned over the passenger seat and opened the door. "Why don't you get in?"

Andy stared at the car and it fell into place. From the hacienda's driveway. Either incredibly good luck or terribly bad. The perfect opportunity for him to get the drop. Or, if he'd been recognized, then they had the drop. He didn't give a shit anymore.

"Okay, thanks."

Andy climbed in. Air-conditioning chilled his sweat. He recognized the way the car was going.

"I'm Juanita, but all my boys call me Madre. What's your name?"

"Bill. Billy."

"Which is it?"

"Billy."

Juanita smiled. "How old are you?"

"Nineteen." Andy's heart pounded so hard now he was sure she could hear it. His hand slowly fell toward his belt, in case . . .

Juanita stared straight ahead. "What's the gun for?"

His heart almost blew. "What gun?"

Another smile. "Don't worry, I won't tell anyone."

"Tell who?"

"You were running." She laughed. "And looking more than guilty. Where'd you just come from?"

"Nothing . . . I mean nowhere."

"Have you been a bad boy today?"

"I didn't do anything."

"Relax, I don't like the police either."

"Why do you think I don't like the police?"

She patted his knee. "I've raised a lot of boys."

Andy, thinking what might await him at the house: "How many boys do you have?"

"Why don't I make you lunch?"

The Mercedes pulled up a driveway.

"Nice place," said Andy.

Juanita turned and looked into his eyes with decades of maternal manipulation. "Would you like a job?"

"What kind of job?"

"Pretty much the same as you're doing now. Except better pay. And less sloppy. You won't get caught."

"What do I have to do?"

"Whatever I say." She opened her door. "Are you obedient?"

"Yes, ma'am."

"Call me Madre."

Serge barreled down South Dixie Highway, timing green lights. Ignoring red.

"God, just this one favor . . ."

Juanita led Andy through the front door.

"Guillermo," she called from the foyer, hanging her purse on a hook. "There's someone here I'd like you to meet."

They came around the corner into the dining room.

Guillermo's back was to them, head sagging. The clear part of the Jack Daniel's bottle now much bigger than the brown.

Juanita turned to Andy. "Don't get the wrong idea. He just had an accident, in a lot of pain."

"Not anymore," said Guillermo, reaching for the sour mash.

They walked around the table into his view.

"Guillermo," said Juanita. "I'd like you to meet Billy . . . Billy, Guillermo."

"Yo." Guillermo was now pulling straight from the bottle.

"Billy," said Juanita. "Let me see your gun."

Moment of truth. The pistol was his only ace. Unarmed, he'd be helpless. A calculation.

He pulled it from his shirt. "Here you go."

Juanita popped the clip and racked the slide. A bullet ejected into the air and bounced across the wooden floor. She replaced the clip and racked again.

"Glock. Nice one." She handed it back. "You said you were obedient?"

Andy nodded.

Juanita looked toward Guillermo. "Shoot him."

CHAPTER FIFTY-TWO

Serge got stacked up behind five cars at a traffic light.

"Screw it!"

He cut the corner through a gas station, briefly leaving the ground as he sailed over a curb where there was no exit.

"Shoot him?" asked Andy.

"That's what I said."

"Ha!" blurted Guillermo. "The test!"

"What test?"

"Don't worry," said Guillermo. "Just to see if you're loyal."

"Shoot him," Juanita repeated.

Andy raised his arm, lowered it, raised it again.

"Go on, shoot me," said Guillermo, knowing he was her favorite and remembering how she'd rigged his own test in the beginning. "What are you waiting for?"

Juanita stepped up to his side. "What *are* you waiting for?"

Andy raised his arm again. This is what he'd come for. Why couldn't he close the deal?

"I'll make it easy," said Guillermo, pushing himself up from the table to create a larger, swaying target.

Andy aimed the gun at his face, hand shaking heavily.

"Look," said Guillermo. "It's not loaded. So make her happy and pull the trigger."

Andy pulled the trigger.

Bang.

Guillermo's eyes went wide. He grabbed his neck, blood running between his fingers.

"Son of a bitch!"

He looked at Juanita. "Madre, you left a round in the chamber. Have to be more careful."

"I know."

"Well, it's just another flesh wound, like I don't have enough." He grabbed paper towels. "But this is getting ridiculous."

"Guillermo," said Juanita, "when I said 'I know,' I meant I know I left a round in the chamber."

"What? Why?"

"You used to be magnificent. What's happened to you?"

"But I've always done everything you asked."

She turned to Andy. "Shoot him. This time steady it with two hands."

Andy stretched out both arms. Guillermo backed up and crashed into a china hutch. Adrenaline. Liquor haze parted.

"Madre," shouted Guillermo, lighting up with recognition, "that's Andy! Andy McKenna!"

"Andy?"

"I recognize him from the hotel room with Ramirez."

Juanita shook her head. "You're just saying that now to save your hide. If it really was Andy, you would have mentioned it when we first came in."

"That was because of the whiskey, but now I'm sure!"

"You disappoint me."

"Just listen," said Guillermo.

Juanita smiled at her new recruit. "You're not Andy, are you?"

He shook his head.

She looked back at Guillermo. Out the side of her mouth: "Shoot him."

Instead, she felt the barrel of a Glock against her temple.

"I'm not Andy. But I *am* Billy. Billy Sheets, son of the mother you killed. And the father you tried to." He raised the gun and cracked her in the side of the head. "Now go around the table and stand next to him."

● ● ●

A woody station wagon skidded up the driveway of a hacienda south of Miami.

Serge ran through the front door with gun drawn. "Andy? Are you here? . . ."

He turned the corner into the dining room. "Andy, don't shoot!"

"Fuck it." He steadied the gun in two hands like Juanita had instructed.

"Easy with that trigger," said Serge. "You're shaking."

"Good! . . . You two ready to die?"

"Let's calm down and talk," said Serge. "This isn't the Andy I know. You haven't shot yet, which means something."

"Yes, I have."

Guillermo pointed at his neck.

Serge raised his eyebrows. "Okay, but you haven't shot twice."

"Shut up!" Andy stretched his arms to the fullest.

"Don't make any sudden moves," said Serge. "I'm coming up behind you."

"What do you care? I thought you wanted 'em dead almost as much as me."

"Not by your hand. Mine are already dirty."

"He's crazy!" said Guillermo.

"You ain't seen nothing yet," said Serge. He stepped beside the boy and slowly reached. "Carefully let go of the trigger and I'm going to take the gun, okay?"

Andy stood rigid. As Serge's hand grabbed the top of the barrel, an index finger uncurled.

The youth let go the rest of the way and fell crying into one of the dining table's chairs. "I let my family down."

"Just the opposite." Serge took aim. "Where'd you leave the Challenger?"

"Up the street."

"Get in it, go back to the motel and forget everything."

"But—"

"I've got it from here. This isn't your turf. Now go."

Andy stood up and went out the front door.

Serge motioned with the gun. "Have a seat." The pair slid forward and pulled out chairs.

Serge grabbed his own on the other side of the table. They sat facing each other.

"What are you doing?" asked Juanita.

"Waiting for dark." Serge leaned back, bracing the gun against his stomach. "Now no more talking."

FOUR A.M.

"Where are we?"

Serge poked the gun into Guillermo's back. "Keep walking."

The air atop the Miami skyline was electric with decorative floodlights bathing the sides of banks and offices. A bridge over the bay glowed blue underneath like a car pimped with neon tubes.

A different story down in the dark streets south of the MacArthur Causeway.

Underpass world. Shopping carts, malt liquor bottles. The lobster shift of bums begged at red lights.

Serge kept the pistol aimed as he approached yet another construction site and pushed down a loose stretch of chain-link fence that had previously been vandalized by graffiti artists. He waved them through, then picked up the gym bag at his feet and followed.

"What's in the bag?" asked Guillermo.

"You'll find out soon enough."

CHAPTER FIFTY-THREE

MONDAY

*E*ight A.M.

Morning rush, downtown Miami.

Traffic crawled. Honking. People on phones, shaving, applying makeup.

Movement began at one of the high-rise condos under construction.

Sixty stories above Biscayne Boulevard, a worker sat in a small control booth with green-tinted windows. The booth slid along grooved tracks in the arm of a massive crane.

When the operator was in position, the booth stopped. A lever went forward.

Down on street level, a temporary fence with No Trespassing signs surrounding the work site. A steel girder began rising from the ground.

Tied beneath the beam were two long stretches of thick rope that weren't supposed to be there. The other ends trailed behind large piles of construction material and debris concealing the view to the road.

When the ascending beam reached the second floor, the rope pulled two people to their feet.

The feet left the ground.

Madre and Guillermo were three stories up before anyone noticed. Then *everyone* noticed. They screamed and waved at the crane

operator, who smiled and waved back. People called police on cells; others ran along the fence, trying to find someone in a hard hat on the other side. The rest simply looked up in horrified shock.

Madre and Guillermo passed the fourth floor, hands tied behind their backs, kicking and wiggling at the ends of their nooses.

By the fifth floor, wiggling became spasmodic twitches. Madre went limp by the seventh, but Guillermo held on for two more.

The girder kept going up, higher than most of the neighboring buildings, which no longer blocked a stiff onshore wind at that height.

Word finally reached the crane operator. A level yanked back. The girder shuddered to a stop. Fifty stories above the boulevard—with magnificent views of Key Biscayne and South Beach, all the way to distant Fort Lauderdale—Madre and Guillermo swung side by side in the breeze.

EPILOGUE

GULF COAST OF FLORIDA

*T*he Final Four.

Serge, Coleman, City and Country.

Not much had changed.

"Dammit, Serge! You said you were taking us to a fantastic resort!"

"Yeah," added Country. "With an incredible pool."

Serge innocently held out his hands. "What? You don't like it?"

"*This* place?" said City.

"But it's a historic mom-and-pop!" Serge looked up with a glow in his eyes. "The motel is one of the last shining examples of 1950s parasol architecture."

"It's in the middle of nowhere!"

"Actually between Fort Myers and Sarasota."

"Same thing."

"That's why heritage survives! Developers haven't had a chance to strip-mine this section of the Tamiami yet. Don't you like the pool?"

"It's hot," said City, wading up to her stomach.

"I'm going back to the room!" said Country.

The door opened to number 31. Coleman was already there, after getting tossed from the pool for doing cannonballs.

"Make you a deal," said Serge. "Watch the world-premiere screening of my spring break documentary, and I'll take you to one of the best dinners of your life."

The women looked at each other, then warily back at Serge.

"Swear?"

Serge held up two fingers like a Boy Scout.

"City," said Country, pointing at a counter. "Grab the vodka. We're going to need it."

Everyone settled in with booze, snacks and joints as Serge hooked up the DVD player. He inserted a disc that had been edited and burned from a laptop. A thumb pressed the remote.

PLAY MOVIE

The show began. Students streaming into Panama City Beach, yelling out car windows, dragging coolers . . .

Two hours later, the TV showed a long-range shot of a giant crane hoisting a steel beam up into the downtown Miami sky.

Fade to black.

Serge hit pause.

He slapped his hands together. "What'd you think?"

"Have to admit," said Country, "not as painful as I'd envisioned."

"Still two hours of my life I'll never get back," said City.

"But it's not over," said Serge.

"You've got to be kidding."

Serge aimed the remote.

PLAY

Large, white block letters filled the black screen.

EPILOGUE

Black dissolved to a sunny shore and a rolling montage narrated by Serge. The Eagles played in the background. The kids from Bahia Cabana waved good-bye and took off up A1A.

". . . It's another tequila sunrise . . ."

"Spring break finally ended, and the students returned north with a lifetime of stories to tell . . . Except one . . ."

A telephoto shot of a young man entering the lobby of the local FBI office, where Serge had dropped him.

"*. . . Andy McKenna was reunited with his father at an undisclosed location and assumed a new identity.*"

Four elderly women in leather leaned against the bar in the Iron Rhino Saloon.

"*. . . The G-Unit established themselves as regular fixtures in the Florida biker scene, took up baking with an Internet brownie recipe, and were last spotted at a local planetarium for the midnight Sergeant Pepper's laser show . . .*"

A kiddie pool sat in a parking lot near Las Olas with a fully clothed man in the water.

"*. . . Agent Mahoney recovered from his wounded leg and continued an indefinite leave for 'needed rest' . . .*"

Next: pandemonium in front of the shootout hotel, where Mahoney flashed a badge and limped away with a handle in his hand.

"*. . . The department didn't know it yet, but Mahoney would never return to active duty, instead opting for a well-funded fishing retirement, thanks to the contents of the briefcase Guillermo left in a hotel room . . .*"

A dozen police cars screeched up to a downtown Miami construction site. A sixty-story crane slowly lowered a girder.

"*. . . To this day, the double murder of Guillermo and Madre remains unsolved . . .*"

As the girder came down, a growing crowd of onlookers watched from the street, including a homecoming queen from Indiana who ran crying up the sidewalk, followed by Johnny Vegas, pointing up in the air behind him. "But, baby, we don't even know those people."

The scene switched to a pair of incredibly sexy but angry women in the backseat of a '73 Challenger.

"*. . . City and Country became less annoying, learned to appreciate Florida's history and enthusiastically accompanied Serge across the state on his never-ending fact-finding mission . . .*"

The TV zoomed in on the vintage sign of their current motel.

THE END.

"You made that last part up," said City.

"Audiences have to like the characters," said Serge.

"What about dinner?"

"You promised!"

"And I keep my word," said Serge. "Let's go."

"Where?"

He spread his arms and smiled almost as wide. "Church!"

"You lied again!" said City. "I knew we couldn't trust you!"

"This is bullshit," said Country. "You're crazy if you think I'm eating free pancakes."

"Have faith." Serge grabbed his keys.

A quick drive up the coast to Tampa, and the foursome was soon seated in a magnificent dining room.

"Now *this* is a restaurant," said City. "I've never been in Shula's Steak House before."

"You really had us going with that church business," said Country, reading the menu on the side of a football. "I can't believe you actually came through."

"But this *is* church," said Serge.

A waiter wheeled over a cart with exquisitely marbled slabs of meat for them to select.

Serge made an S with his fingers and whispered, *"Shula."*

"What?" said the waiter.

Serge winked.

An hour later, dinner came to a spectacular conclusion. Country set a napkin in her plate. "I'm stuffed."

"Me, too," said City.

"But there's more!" said Serge. "I got you a present!"

"You did?"

He placed a gift-wrapped box on the table.

Country looked up at him. "This is so . . . unlike you."

"That's the problem," said Serge. "You judge by my work mode."

"What can it be?" asked City.

"Let me get the bow off."

Country opened the box. "Portable DVD player?"

Serge grinned. "Already has a copy of my documentary inside so you can watch it over and over!"

"Not exactly diamonds," said Country. "But it's sweet." She leaned across the table and gave him a peck, then placed the player back in the box.

"Aren't you going to watch it?" said Serge.

"We just did."

"Not the bonus material."

"Maybe some other time."

"For me?" said Serge. "I did keep my promise on the dinner."

"I guess we could watch it a little," said City, smiling coyly. "Give us time to make room for dessert."

"That's the spirit," said Serge. He took the player back out of the box, clicked through the menu and turned the screen around to face them.

"What's this?" asked City.

"The 'making of' documentary," said Serge. "I gave Coleman a second camera to capture my groundbreaking directorial technique."

"It's just a sidewalk and some sneakers. Does it change?"

"No. Coleman left the camera running from his shoulder."

"I think I'm ready for dessert," said Country.

"Me and Coleman are going to the bathroom," said Serge. "I'll have the waiter send over a menu."

The women sat alone at the table, sipping what was left of their wine.

On the DVD player, Coleman's feet began weaving—"*Whoops, having a little trouble here*"—then the view quickly accelerated toward the sidewalk, until lens cracks spread across the tiny screen and went black. The player returned to the previous menu.

Country leaned toward the screen. "What's this other bonus thing here?"

"What?"

"It says 'Alternate Ending.'"

"Play it."

She pressed a button.

"Look," said City. "It's the inside of Shula's Steak House . . ."

". . . Now it's the outside," said Country.

The waiter came over. "Hope you'll come back and see us again."

"*Again?* We were going to have dessert."

"But . . . ," the waiter said haltingly. "The gentleman just paid."

"He did what?"

They looked back at the small screen. A muscle car drove away from the restaurant.

"Don't tell me—"

The women ran through the dining room and out onto the sidewalk, just in time to see Serge and Coleman speeding toward a bridge over Tampa Bay in the '73 Challenger.